City of Ghosts

*

Also by Kelli Stanley

✳

MIRANDA CORBIE SERIES
City of Secrets
City of Dragons

OTHER TITLES
The Curse-Maker
Nox Dormienda

City of Ghosts

✳

Kelli Stanley

Minotaur Books
New York

76776498

This is a work of fiction. All of the characters, organizations, and events portrayed in this novel are either products of the author's imagination or are used fictitiously.

CITY OF GHOSTS. Copyright © 2014 by Kelli Stanley. All rights reserved. Printed in the United States of America. For information, address St. Martin's Press, 175 Fifth Avenue, New York, N.Y. 10010.

www.minotaurbooks.com

LIBRARY OF CONGRESS CATALOGING-IN-PUBLICATION DATA

Stanley, Kelli.
   City of Ghosts / Kelli Stanley.
       pages cm. — (A Miranda Corbie Mystery ; 3)
   ISBN 978-1-250-00674-5 (hardcover)
   ISBN 978-1-250-01805-2 (e-book)
   1. Women private investigators—California—Fiction.   2. Nineteen forties—Fiction.   3. San Francisco (Calif.)—History—20th century—Fiction.   4. Mystery fiction.   5. Historical fiction.   I. Title.
   PS3619.T3657C584 2014
   813'.6—dc23

                                                              2014010641

Minotaur books may be purchased for educational, business, or promotional use. For information on bulk purchases, please contact Macmillan Corporate and Premium Sales Department at 1-800-221-7945, extension 5442, or write specialmarkets@macmillan.com.

First Edition: August 2014

10 9 8 7 6 5 4 3 2 1

For Tana, who makes the sun rise.
And for the memory of my parents,
Van and Patricia Stanley,
whose unconditional love and support
made everything possible.

Acknowledgments

*

City of Ghosts was a difficult book to write and would never have been completed without the support, understanding, and help of friends and colleagues.

I was in the middle of the first draft when I lost both of my parents to cancer within a month of each other. I'm an only child with no close extended family and my parents were my best friends. Learning to live with the grief, despair, and health complications generated by their loss necessitated that I set the book aside for a while.

Fortunately, my publisher—Andy Martin at Minotaur Books—is a very understanding man. I thank him and the rest of the team at St. Martin's—Sally Richardson, Sarah Melnyk, Hector DeJean, Talia Sherer, indefatigable production editor Elizabeth Curione, and my esteemed editor, Matt Martz—for their patience and support while I learned how to write and live all over again. A special thanks as well to Marcia Markland and Kat Brzozowkski.

My agents are incredibly supportive and a writer's dream team; I am blessed to call them friends. Kimberley Cameron of Kimberley Cameron and Associates and film agents Mary Alice Kier and Anna Cottle at Cine/Lit encouraged me, nurtured me, and helped guide me over difficult terrain. They are not only great agents; they are truly great people.

The mystery community in general is a bit spoiled when it comes to wonderful people—we have more than our share—and I owe far too many thanks to too many friends to thank them all here. But I'd like to give a shout to a few friends who helped see me through some of the darkest days: Rebecca Cantrell,

Joshua Corin, Tasha Alexander, Andrew Grant, Heather Graham, Margery and Steve Flax, Rhys Bowen, Sheldon Siegel, Tom and Marie O'Day, Cornelia Read, Jon and Ruth Jordan, Carla Buckley, Kate Stine and Brian Skupin, Jordan Foster, Julie Rivett, Hallie Ephron, Laura Benedict, Naomi Hirahara, Tim Hallinan, Bill Cameron, Judy Bobalik, Janet Rudolph, Bill and Toby Gottfried, Chantelle Osman, Lesa Holstine, Deborah Ledford, Roni Olsen, Judith Starkston, Jen Forbus, Peter Maravelis at City Lights Bookstore, Julie Lindow, and Pam Stirling, Jen Owen, and all the former crew at the much-missed M is for Mystery. And as always, a special thanks to the real Bente Gallagher for the use of her glorious name.

City of Ghosts, like its predecessors, was a research-heavy project, and I owe thanks to the following people and places that helped me: the San Francisco Public Library History Room, the Doe Library and the Bancroft Library at UC Berkeley, and UC Berkeley librarians Randal Brandt and Cody Hennesy. EBay dealer Tim Baganz very generously and kindly sent me helpful letters from the era, and reader and retired SFPD officer James C. Fraser-Paige shared invaluable firearms details.

I'd also like to thank some personal friends: Pam and Stuart Vaughn, Sherry Hazelton, Shirley and Mike Foster, Gregg Foster, Jeremy and Kris Toscanini and family, and Sam Siew. A very special and ineffable thank-you to Pamela Bellah and Pamela Cassidy, who are angels on earth.

At the end of the day, of course, I thank you, the reader. You complete the book; it would not be possible without you. I hope you enjoy it, whether you're new to the Miranda Corbie series or have been waiting eagerly for *City of Ghosts.* I think you'll find that it marks a transition for Miranda, and my hope is that we will walk down many more streets together.

And, as always, I thank my partner, Tana Hall, for all the love, support, and care. This book—and indeed, my every breath—would not be possible without her.

City of Ghosts

✳

Act One

*

Bait

God hath given you one face and you make yourselves another.
—William Shakespeare, *Hamlet,* Act II, scene 1

One

*

Miranda watched as the thin arm, pocked and dotted with needle points, snaked under the dirt-gummed bars of the pawnshop.

Swan dance, like a prima ballerina. Except the fingernails were chipped and filthy, the muscle wasted from too much hop. She nodded to the pawnbroker, his chubby stomach still quaking, eyes darting from her to the arm. The Chinese was as rapid as his breath.

Hand froze, jade necklace still dancing in its grip.

She prodded the proprietor with her shoe and his eyes came back to her, wide and scared. He bit his lip, tucking small feet behind the dented stool he perched on, while she threaded her way past a scarred wooden counter loaded with cameras and musical instruments, the sleeve of a moth-eaten beaver jacket thrown carelessly over a half-eaten plate of chow mein.

Hoped she'd remember how the hell to get out of Yick Lung, Chinatown pawnshop, hoped she wind up somewhere near the small, almost invisible side door used by the embarrassed customers. The Chinese didn't like to show their faces to a pawnbroker. Too much shame.

No shame for Mr. Kwok. Just a fat bank account he could spend in Quentin if he didn't play along.

Dark, uneven warrens, sound of her footsteps lonely, with occasional shrill laughter from an upper story and the smell of damp kitchen slop and cooking rice drifting up from below.

Right then left, up a small incline, walls crooked and peeling, right again . . . light coming faster, past the green door, whatever lurked behind it, and back to the shiny brass knob and wide-mouth lion guarding the home of Mr. Leon Kwok, pawnshop owner and fence.

Air. Sunlight. Chinese violin ached a rendition of "Red River Valley," the smell of spent firecrackers blending with sandalwood and incense. Her stomach growled at the thought of a fried sesame ball, and she could use a goddamn Chesterfield.

Miranda took a deep breath. No time.

She walked quickly around the corner to Spofford Alley and the side entrance to Yick Lung. Men with dead eyes threw dice against a joss house, rubbing hands on worn pants, threadbare shirts. They looked away from the entrance and back again, drawn like moths, their fingers rattling the change in their pockets, dice to determine who would pawn what to keep throwing, keep alive the chance to win.

A black Buick hurtled down Washington, riding the brakes, radio cranked high with Glenn Miller and Ray Eberle, punctuated by the tinny horn.

Fools rush in . . .

Miranda leaned against the brick wall, out of sight of the door, next to a poster advertising Southern Pacific Weekend at the Fair.

Come out, come out to Treasure Island, celebrate the City's one hundred and sixty-fourth birthday, grand old lady, dirty old dame, naughty and bawdy, still flirts like jail bait. You want the real thing, mister, try Pickles O'Dell down on Pacific. Don't know 'bout virgins, mister, ain't got many left in San Francisco . . .

She shook her head. Meant to find out why Pickles was pushing babies, not the dried-up B-girls she was known for. Too busy since May. Too busy trying to make money. Too busy trying to find her mother.

Miranda's gloved hand crept up to the left side of her cheek. Scar still there, small, under the makeup. Little souvenir from the Musketeers, one for all and all for one. Heil Hitler.

Just a month ago. She knew all about fools rushing in, almost rushed in to a lobotomy.

Her breath was coming out quicker, shorter, and she stared at the door, shutting out memory. Couldn't shut it down at night, couldn't push the images out of her mind, Technicolor, nude girls and dead gangsters, brain splattered on a bathroom wall. Spain and Johnny and red-orange sunset, violin strings up and out, no *Gone with the Wind*, no Tara, no tomorrow was another fucking day.

Miranda shook herself and reached into her handbag. Drew out a Chesterfield and lit it with the Ronson Majorette, one click. Thought of the woman who hired her, cool and immaculate, husband in the Bohemian Club, eyes like dry ice.

Jade parure. Missing from her home. Houseguests? Three friends up for the weekend, for the Fair. Family? Daughter and a son. Husband? Absentee. Lover?

She remembered how the woman's eyes flickered, the thin white parchment skin on her lids veined blue, eyelashes black and bristled.

Everything insured, of course, no scandal, nothing public, but she'd like them back, whether the daughter sold them out of spite and jealousy or the friend needed a temporary loan to pay expenses. Whether her friends weren't her friends, and her lover wasn't her lover. She wanted the jade back. For sentimental reasons, of course. That, and the fact that it was worth fifty thousand dollars.

The rich don't like to part with their money, especially if it's old and has been in the family a long time. Jeeves the Butler and the bank account. Both deserved a little loyalty. The lady was new money, studied elocution at a Los Angeles soda fountain by way of Schenectady. But her husband was as old as sin in San Francisco, and he might start asking questions.

St. Mary's chimed her bell. *Son, observe the time and fly from evil . . .*

Goddamn it, something was wrong.

Miranda pinched out the cigarette with her fingers. Carefully turned the tarnished brass of the doorknob.

A too-skinny man in traditional garb, loose-fitting brown silk and smock, held a knife to fat Kwok's throat, his back to Miranda. The pawnbroker's arm was already bleeding from one cut, dripping on the wooden floor, held out stiffly to his right. His pudgy body pressed against an antique cherrywood wardrobe, his face contorted in a silent scream.

The skinny man didn't hear the click behind him, so Miranda stuck the .22 in his back.

"Drop the knife, Randolph. Your mother wants her jade back."

*

Took her half an hour to calm down Kwok and pry Randolph off the floor. He lay in the corner, drool drying at the corner of his mouth, mouth open and mewling, looking for a pipe to smoke or a tit to suck. Scion of the rich and powerful, progeny of old money and a new shipment of heroin.

The fence wanted reparations, to his arm, his person, his shop. His reputation.

Miranda handed him three crisp one-hundred-dollar bills, pale scent of Narcisse Noir still clinging to the fibers. Not much hope for his reputation, she told him, but if he wanted it repaired, she could take it up with the bulls . . .

She finally left with a miniature red granite dragon the suddenly eager-to-please Kwok pressed into her hands, toothy smile, bits of bok choy still clinging to his teeth. Jade necklace—and the matching bracelet and earrings Randolph had already pawned—were in her jacket pocket. Her fingers gripped Randolph's arm. He wiped his mouth and grinned vacuously, eyes empty.

She walked him past the herbalist and the grocery shops, down Washington Street and Waverly and the Twin Dragons nightclub, "Make-Believe Island" floating from a radio, Mary Ann Mercer and the Mitchell Ayres Orchestra sounding faraway and blue.

Wonderful island . . . where broken dreams come true . . .

Miranda walked faster down the hill toward Kearny and the Hall of Justice, pushing and pulling the tall, thin man beside her.

Make-believe island, Treasure Island, where broken dreams lay dead and bloodied, an ice pick through the breast . . .

Randolph yelped, stopping in front of the Chinese Telephone Exchange. "You're hurting me!"

She needed a cigarette or even a Life Saver but knew better than to let go of his arm.

"March, Randolph. Mommy's waiting."

He made a strangled noise in his throat and she almost felt sorry for him. He dragged his feet, Chinese sandals scuffing the dirty cement.

"How much are you getting?"

"Not enough."

"I-I've got my own allowance, I can—"

Miranda threw up the arm that held her purse, flagging a Yellow Taxi dropping a middle-aged woman off at Puccinelli's Bail Bonds on Washington.

"You can't take a piss by yourself, Randolph, and your allowance is all gone. Do yourself a favor. Ask your father to spring for a doctor, and get off the juice." The taxi pulled up, dark-skinned man about fifty with black and gray stubble and a smile that was missing some teeth.

Miranda opened the door, shoved Randolph inside. Leaned in through the open window, her voice low. He was curling again, shaking in the corner.

"Hit up the old man. And stay away from the hop . . . and your mother."

She opened her purse and gave the driver a five-dollar bill and an address in the Burlingame hills. Watched him speed up Washington Street while she shook out a Chesterfield.

*

Lunch at the Palace's Rose Room felt like a shower. She splurged on *Poulet au Vin* with a Tomato Surprise salad, sipped an iced tea, and tried to ignore the up-and-down stares of a businessman at the bar, chin mapped with five o'clock shadow, smile full of false teeth. A traveler left a *Los Angeles Times* on the chair next to her, partial to his hometown paper despite the *Examiner* building across the street.

HITLER ENDS WAR IN FRANCE, it broadcast. Count on Hollywoodland to write a war headline that sounded like a fucking happy ending. Below the thick black letters, BOMBERS RAID ENGLAND.

She swirled the iced tea with a green glass stick, stared into the brown liquid. Vague images of a dark-haired woman, voice low and melodic, singing, warm hands, large hands.

Her hands.

The figures were melting, ice cubes drifting apart. A deep voice cleared its throat.

Miranda looked up. Businessman from the bar. He pulled out a chair and sat, tongue flicking at his thick, wet lips.

"I couldn't help but notice you were alone . . . hope you don't mind."

She sat back in the chair, eyes on the watery blue ones of the middle-aged Lothario. His blue suit was pinstriped and double-breasted, gapped in the chest and hugged his hips like a grass skirt. Display handkerchief, dirty white.

Flash of false teeth again.

She said evenly: "As a matter of fact, I do mind."

He chuckled, as if she'd made a joke. "Haven't always been so, er, particular, have you?"

Miranda's eyes narrowed and flashed green inside the brown. She leaned forward, her hands curled into fists on the table.

"What do you want?"

He reached into the inside of his jacket and took out a chromium-plated cigarette case. Lit a Camel, smirked at her.

"You're a looker, all right. They said you looked like that actress, what's-her-name, Rita Hayworth. The black and whites in the paper don't do you justice."

He pushed some smoke out the side of his mouth, then pulled out his billfold, imitation alligator, and shoved it toward her with a hairy finger.

"How much, baby? I know you're supposed to be a peeper now, but I figure you might turn one or two on the side."

Miranda froze for a moment. Then she adjusted the black velvet beret on her head, while the businessman leaned back, grinning at the movement of her breasts underneath the white blouse and snug velvet jacket. Her left hand fell into the pocket, and she touched the jade, cold and implacable.

She forced a smile and put on her gloves like a striptease. Stood up. He grinned more broadly, repocketing his wallet, pushing his chair in. The young blond waiter was walking over to the table to ask about dessert, and she caught his eye, shaking her head. He stopped in the middle of the floor, puzzled.

Miranda kept the smile glued on, shifted her weight, and sauntered over slowly. Stood in front of the leering man with the blue suit and shadow on his chin. She looked up at him, waiting until his grin was big enough to show off the whole set of his false teeth.

A flash of thigh, while her knee came up. He bent over, his mouth an O, eyebrows in his hairline. She threw all 124 pounds behind a right to his jaw.

The set of false teeth flew out in a spray of spittle, skidded across the floor and landed in front of a shocked dowager in sequined gray.

He toppled and fell backward, landing on his ass. The blond waiter sprinted for the maître d'. A couple of male customers were standing, sleeves tugged on by their dates.

Sit back down, Roger. Don't you dare interfere. Shouldn't let her kind in here. Harlot. Slut.

Whore.

Miranda knelt by her adversary's face, his cheeks and jaw still bright red with shock and pain.

"Who did you talk to? Who, goddamn it?"

The shrunken mouth caved in on itself, breath coming in gasps, and he shook his head.

"Bianne Mwaroche."

Dianne and her venom, southern spider, sitting in the middle of a web. Twitch it and they'll come running back, you never escape, you'll never be through, Miranda, unless you're dead and buried like Betty Chow . . .

The maître d's hand was on her shoulder. "Is there a problem, Miss?"

"Not anymore."

She stood up, rubbing her gloved right hand. They didn't want to hear it, didn't want to know why, just wanted her out and gone. No thorns in the goddamn Rose Room.

Miranda reached for her purse and threw a dollar on the table. Turned briefly to the short, bald maître d', his eyes pleading like a spaniel's. She stared down at the businessman. He was still on the ground, hand in front of his shrunken mouth.

"Remember me to Dianne."

She walked out of the Palace Hotel, left hand fingering the jade in her pocket.

✳

The Old Taylor swirled in the Castagnola glass, pain in her swollen knuckles subsiding. Miranda pushed aside the receipts and papers, cracked the office window.

Artie Shaw's "Traffic Jam" blew wild from Tascone's jukebox, and two pigeons were mating on Lotta's Fountain.

Happy 164th Birthday, San Francisco, celebrate your heritage, your phoenix wings, your life. Throw a party on a treasure island, toast the steel monsters that spanned your Golden Gate. Masque of the red-orange death for the ferryboats, but hell . . . let's dance.

She sank into the overstuffed leather chair, hands trembling. Not whole, not yet, too soon after too many cracks, too soon after the Musketeers and Pandora Blake and Ozzie Mandelbaum. Too soon after the postcard from Westminster Abbey, from a mother she thought was long dead.

Bombs were dropping on England, last target for the steel-toed jackboots, last island for the Blitzkrieg. And somewhere in London, amid the bomb shelters and cool, ancient churches, somewhere between the chip shops and pubs and Piccadilly Circus . . . was her mother. Somewhere.

And she had to find her, help her, save her. Get her out, get her away, before the Nazis killed the only family she had.

Her father didn't count.

She threw back another gulp of the bourbon, finished filling in the report. She knew better than to give up the jade before she was paid, and the out-of-pocket expenses—including the three hundred dollars to Kwok—bit hard.

She took the job to make money. No choices, not now, she needed a ticket to Liverpool or Ireland, preferably on a ship that the U-boats wouldn't sink.

The office door rattled and Miranda looked up, eyes wide.

Not Allen, the Pinkerton was off on a case today, the Monadnock quiet, most of the city at the Fair.

Jade was in the safe. She opened the right-hand drawer. The .22 gleamed dully at her.

Her voice came out clear. "Come in."

The handle turned and Miranda held her breath. A tall man in his late thirties, dressed in a light wool blazer of conservative cut, his tie maroon, his dark brown hair oiled and immaculate, crisp brown fedora from Dobbs Brothers in one hand, a large brown envelope in the other.

He smiled at her. Walked toward her desk.

"Hello Miranda. It's been a while."

James MacLeod. From the State Department.

Two

*

MacLeod flicked his eyes over the Castagnola glass and the half-empty bottle of Old Taylor, still sitting on the top of the desk. Threw himself in one of the chairs, easy grin.

As if it hadn't been a year since the Incubator Babies case. As if he'd stayed in touch and written her letters and just flown out to San Francisco for a goddamn fourth at bridge.

She shook a Chesterfield out of a crumpled packet. He jumped up, holding a monogrammed lighter flickering bright against the "J. M." etched in silver plate. She held his hand and lit the cigarette. Wished her fingers weren't trembling.

"I thought you'd have laid off those by now. Confidentially, they'll kill you."

She pressed her back against the leather, massive weight of the chair giving her strength.

"You didn't cross the country to discuss my personal habits, James. Don't you have enough to do in Washington? Or are you just here to check on the 'experiment'?"

The government man reached into his jacket pocket with a smile and pulled out a matching silver cigarette case.

"As a matter of fact, I just started up again. Susan—my wife, you may remember—calls it 'war nerves.'" He stuck a Kool between his lips, smell of menthol blending with the tobacco. "Menthol helps me keep the number down. You should try it."

Miranda took a deep drag, blew a smoke ring over his head.

"I prefer to meet the enemy head-on."

He chuckled, tossing the thick brown envelope and the Dobbs fedora on the chair next to him, eyes darting over the file cabinet, the dusty radio, the safe.

"One reason why I made sure you got your license. You, the so-called experiment—and a successful one, too. Your last two cases made some noise. It reached all the way to the capital."

She raised an eyebrow. "Did it wake anyone up?"

He blew smoke through his nose and laughed. Stretched his arm across the back of the small chair, wool jacket revealing the black butt of a .45 in a shoulder holster. Eyes on her face, her hands, her hair.

James MacLeod, the man who believed her when no one else would. The man who listened to her, trusted her.

The man she owed her license to.

Collection time.

"You're a swell girl, Miranda. You don't look a day older. I'm sure Susan would love to know how you keep your glamour girl looks."

"What are you here for, James? It's not that I'm not grateful to you for pushing my license through last year—but the State Department doesn't walk into my office every day. When it does, it wants something."

"If I weren't married, I'd want you. But you already know that."

Same fucking story, every fucking time. It didn't matter that she'd worked for a year, made a name, a career.

Maybe even a goddamn life.

Half a stick left. She twisted it out in the ashtray.

"I said I'm grateful, but you don't own me. Nobody does."

He ran a hand through his hair, separating the curls, dulling the shine of the oil and pomade.

"We knew that wasn't an option a year ago, Miranda, no need to get defensive. I've come to collect other dividends. We've got a problem. We want it to go away."

Her eyes fell to the thick brown envelope next to him. "I'm not your best bet for an exterminator."

"No. But what you do is get to the heart of things. It's a particular gift, and not every good detective has it. Look at what you've done already: crime syndicate crippled, international smuggling ring smashed—that made a stink with the Jap ambassador, believe me—bombing thwarted, another group of fifth columnists uncovered . . . speaking of which, the Christian Front boys got off, whole case dismissed."

"I read about it this morning, buried in the back of the *Chronicle*. Buried in Hoover's back, too, I imagine."

"You've done more than a whole squad of Hoover's agents. Don't think he's not pissed about it."

Blue eyes crinkling at the corners, like Rick's when he wanted a story. Miranda thought about the license in her purse, carefully creased and folded, more precious than the jade in her safe.

Only thing she had. Only thing she owned. Only thing she was.

And now . . . she had to pay for it.

"You're not here to offer me a role on *Gang Busters*. We like each other. I owe you something. That's all."

He stood up from the chair and ambled to the window.

"Do you know what it is I do?"

"No. You never told me. And I never tried to find out."

"I was a field agent. Right now I'm responsible for certain Intelligence matters relating to the Nazis."

"I didn't figure you for a diplomatic job." Her fingers were trembling again. She yanked open the top drawer, found half a roll of Life Savers Pep-O-Mint.

"Want some?"

He took the candy and unrolled two. "New addiction?"

"They're better than fucking Kools."

He laughed aloud for a few seconds, genuine this time. Hesitated in front of her desk, then leaned in suddenly, hands pressed flat against the surface.

"Miranda . . . you've met the Fifth Column. How'd you like to tackle the war head-on? Help your country and earn five thousand dollars?"

Scent of mentholated tobacco and Dunhill for Men, and somewhere south of Market a church bell. Toll four times, *ding dong ding dong*, but don't ask for whom the bell tolls, lady, because no man is an island, and no woman, either. Favors don't come free.

She chewed the candy and swallowed.

"That's a lot of money. What is it, a suicide mission?"

Silky voice, persuasive. "Nothing of the kind. But we can't risk government involvement. No Bureau, no Dies Committee, no Army and Navy investigators, no State or War or even Treasury Department. Nobody traceable to us."

Miranda reached for the discarded cigarette half. Flicked the Ronson, deep inhale.

"I see. I'm expendable, and my reputation isn't exactly Lady Astor. So if I'm caught—I'm caught. What am I supposed to be caught doing?"

"As I said, service to your country at a time of crisis and uncertainty . . ."

"Christ, you sound like a politician. Which crisis, James? Which country? The miners in Kentucky? The Negroes in Georgia? Or the middle-aged bankers who think FDR's a Red and want to leave England to Oswald Mosley and Unity Mitford?"

He retreated to the edge of the chair, hands held out as if trying to push her back.

"We both know the war's coming, Miranda. We don't have a choice."

"Bullshit. You had a choice in '39, when they blitzkrieged Poland, tanks against horses. You had a choice in '38, when Hitler swallowed Czechoslovakia, and Chamberlain waved a piece of paper in the air. You even had a choice three years ago, when the Spanish Republic was begging for guns and the Germans bombed Guernica, and most of the world sat by and watched from a front-row seat."

Miranda shook her head. "The war's already here, James. It's been here for a long time."

He ran his fingers through his hair again, fidgeted with his hat brim. She kept her eyes fixed on the red coal of the Chesterfield and the fine line of gray at the tip, voice low and terse and careful.

"Go ahead and talk. Lay it all out, nice and neat, and maybe I'll take you up on your offer. But don't for a fucking second try to sell me a story about the grand old flag and the boys in Congress. If I work, I work for myself—not you or Uncle Sam."

He looked up and cocked his head, mouth stretched in a conciliatory line.

"Look, ducks, politics is an ugly business. And I know you love your Uncle, or I wouldn't be here. Be thankful you can still make speeches like that. The French can't."

Miranda crushed the stub in the ashtray.

"My terms, James. Talk."

He sighed, hands pressed together between his knees.

"We have reason to believe a local university professor is a spy. Possibly for the Nazis, possibly for the Reds, though the German connection is most likely. He's been in and out of the Nazi consulate here several times a year, social oc-

casions, parties. He's on friendly terms with Hitler's old commander Fritz Weidemann, your burly consul general—both members of the Olympic Club. He
travels, too . . . took a few trips down to Mexico, visits Chicago and New York
regularly."

Miranda reached for the Old Taylor bottle, pouring another shot in the Castagnola glass. Held it up to MacLeod. "Want some? Or will this kill me, too?"

He shook his head, smiling. She tossed back the bourbon, shuddering a little.
Wiped her mouth with the back of her hand.

"So you don't know who he's spying for. Any idea about whom or what he's
spying on?"

The lines around his mouth deepened. "We're afraid he could be smuggling
information related to weapons and armament development. He's a professor
of chemistry, has access to certain research going on at Berkeley. He's written
papers on how gas was used in the last war. We think he may be passing what
he knows to the Germans."

"So why not sic the FBI boys on him—or even hire Pinkerton? Why come
to me?"

"Hoover can't be everywhere, no matter what his PR men claim. Our department would like to handle this ourselves, but we can't risk one of our own
agents. And Pinkerton's too big, too political, too well known—and too
risky. We need someone outside the establishment, someone they'd overlook.
Someone unim . . ."

He caught himself. Half a smile played across her lips.

" 'Unimportant'? Go ahead and say it, James. I've heard it all my life. Don't
forget to add 'expendable' . . . just in case."

"I didn't mean—"

She waved a hand dismissively. "Yes, you did. That's why you're here. You're
slumming with the ex-escort you helped set up in business, a female private
investigator you figure nobody would miss if she wound up floating in the Bay.
Tell me something: Is this supposed information he has access to really that
important? Would it make a difference, a real difference?"

MacLeod picked up the fedora in the seat next to him and ran his little
finger under the hatband. Said slowly: "He's supposed to be a science whiz,
Miranda. Teaches chemistry but spends his money on art. We're not sure what
the connection is . . . or if there's a connection. All we know is that he has access to sensitive information we'd rather not have him near. Plus his background shows an interest in weapons, particularly gas."

He looked up at her. "We're worried. Yeah, it could make a difference."

Church bells south of Market and a fire siren up Battery, clang of the White Front, smell of the trawler's catch and homemade wine drifting on the wind from North Beach.

Miranda nodded. "What do you want me to do?"

He let out a breath and spun the fedora on his index finger, back and forth, back and forth.

"Hitler's agents paved the way for him in Holland and France, and we've already uncovered a large spy ring out of New York—that's been dealt with. But we don't know what this bird is doing, what he's selling, what he's buying. He travels too much and makes too much money. We want to know what his business is with the Krauts and the Reds."

"I'm not a scientist—how would I know what to look for?"

"You don't need to recognize a formula, Miranda. We just want you to follow him, report on where he goes and who he meets, times, places, faces. If you could get a look at his luggage, so much the better."

He stretched a hand across the desk for the Old Taylor bottle and poured another shot in the Castagnola glass.

"You mind?"

"Be my guest."

MacLeod swallowed, setting the glass down with a clank. Rubbed the back of his neck uneasily.

"I shouldn't have come. I don't have a right to get you involved, but Jesus, Miranda, nobody knows what the hell to do. Hoover wants control over South America and everyone else is fighting over what's left. Bill Donovan's canvassing England on some kind of hush-hush mission for FDR. No one expected France to fall so hard and so easy. Pétain officially surrenders today, you know. The collaborators are already in line. Goddamn Germans seem invincible."

He stared past her toward the window.

"Everything we do had better make a difference, because that fat old man in Downing Street is the only hope Europe's got left."

Churchill and a little island of green. Plenty of Blackshirts there, too, Lords and Ladies, Old Order welcoming New, Duke and Duchess of Windsor claiming Hitler as a pal and the Honorable Mitford girls giving the Fascist salute. The sun may never set on the British Empire, but the swastika might, jackboots crushing the toy planes and teenage boys of the RAF.

England. Last hope for the world, for Europe, for two women named Corbie who may or may not be mother and daughter.

She passed a shaking hand over her forehead and opened the top drawer of the desk. Slid a Martell's Liquors calendar out from between two accounting books and set it in front of her, flipping the pages to June.

"How long is the assignment?"

"As long as it takes to confirm or deny our suspicions."

She raised her eyebrows. "That's pretty open-ended."

"The pay's good. Half up front, plus all expenses. You'd travel. In style, too. The target likes the *City of San Francisco* streamliner."

He cleared his throat and looked away, flush creeping up from his collar. "I can also sweeten the pot, Miranda. We had word from the British consulate that you'd like to get to England. Mind telling me why?"

No secrets. Not from Uncle Sam. Final trick played, goddamn blue eyes making her forget he held the cards.

"You don't own me, MacLeod. I thought we established that."

"There's a war on, Miranda."

She grasped the edge of the desk, knuckles white. "And I don't need you to remind me of the fact. Either you trust me or you don't. And if you don't, then why the fuck are you wasting my time?"

He grunted. Match point.

"I can get you booked on the *Cameronia* provided a U-boat doesn't sink it first. August or September. I'll pay for the train ticket to New York and a round-trip passage to Liverpool."

"You expect I'd be finished in time to collect?"

He hesitated. "I don't know. I wish I did."

They sat across from one another in silence, Market Street horns and the guttural roar of White Fronts and Municipals filling the room, blending and dancing with the blue-gray smoke.

She said: "I'd be completely on my own?"

"You'd report to me. But if something happened—I couldn't do a goddamn thing. No friends, no family involved . . . though that wouldn't be a problem for you."

Her voice was heavy. "No. No, it wouldn't."

"Your father teaches at the University of California. Same place as the target. It's a perfect cover."

Her eyes fell back to the cracks and scratches in the dark, shining wood. A tremor ran through her left arm.

"When do I have to decide?"

Apologetic smile. "Right away, unfortunately." He gestured toward the brown envelope. "I brought the briefing papers in the hope you'd say yes."

"I'm already working on something else."

"As long as you're prepared to travel whenever the professor does, you can keep up your normal casework, Miranda. In fact, we want you to—it'll help shield you from suspicion."

Another church bell, slow and sonorous, and she could almost smell the olive trees, taste the thick red wine.

Johnny, who wanted to cover the war in Spain.

Who wanted to make a difference.

You're a good soldier, Randy. A good soldier . . .

Her eyes stung, unexpected moisture. Her voice was steady.

"I'll do it."

No grin of triumph from MacLeod.

"I won't lie to you, Miranda. You'll be taking your life in your hands."

A warm breeze blew through the window, disturbing the dried-up wings of dead moths from the sill. It smelled of salt and beaches and Ivory soap, of coeds in bathing suits and young men building sand castles on the shore.

"It's been there for a long time."

He jumped up, impulsively grabbing her hands across the desk and holding them in his. They were warm and strong, palms dry, skin rough and reassuring.

"Welcome aboard, Miranda."

She poured another shot of bourbon and raised the glass. Gave him half a smile. "To making a difference."

Three

＊

The money lay on the rusted shelf, crisp, dry, and green, two bundles still wrapped in bank paper.

$2,500. A hell of a lot of cash. Now she'd have to earn it.

Miranda started to close the door of the old Wells Fargo safe, the thick doors and dark, quiet interior remembering earlier days, when gold dust was the currency and Lotta Crabtree danced in the mining camps, ankles flashing amid gold nuggets thrown on the ground at her feet.

James held a hand out. "Wait."

She watched him, curious, as he reached inside and picked up the Baby Browning on the shelf below. He held it in his palm, grinning.

"This isn't legal, you know."

"So I've been told."

"I'd advise you to carry it from now on. Excellent gun for undercover work."

Her mouth twisted up at one corner. "So I've been told."

He laughed and replaced the pistol, letting her shut the safe. The heavy door squeaked until it finally latched with a clack.

"Was that a .38 next to it?"

"Astra. Spanish. Takes .38 ACP or 9mm Largo. I prefer loading it with the former."

"Ah." He was silent for a moment, watching her twist the dial. "Pick it up when you were there?"

She flicked a glance at him. "Why the hell are you so interested in my guns, MacLeod? I've got a license to carry and I know how to use them. End of story."

The grin spread across his face, making him look younger, more like the man she remembered. "Wanted to make sure you're taken care of, is all. We normally issue a .45 pistol, the M1911. I can get you one, if you'd like."

Miranda shrugged. "I don't need it, but go ahead if it'll make you feel better."

He laughed, put a hand on her shoulder. "I want you armed and dangerous, ducks."

She handed him his fedora. "I can shoot."

"Yeah, so you've told me."

MacLeod pulled the hat brim low and gestured to the brown envelope on her desk.

"Check-in instructions are there, along with the long distance and local telephone numbers. I plan to be in San Francisco for a few more days, unless they call me back to Washington for something else. If Jasper leaves the area, phone me immediately. I probably don't have to tell you to memorize what you need and destroy the papers when you're done."

"I've already seen *Confessions of a Nazi Spy.*"

He clapped her on the back, laughed again. "Miranda, you're giving me my heart back. But then again . . . you've always had it."

He winked at her, bent over her hand and kissed it. She pulled it away and spun him around to face the door.

"Don't get giddy. I plan to collect on that *Cameronia* ticket."

He angled his head back to look at her, hand on the doorknob. Blue eyes warm, voice almost tender.

"I hope you do, ducks. I hope you do."

✳

Miranda flung herself in the desk chair, pulling out a new Big Chief pad from the bottom drawer. Flipped the cover, scent of the blue-lined paper and ink from the Esterbrook reminding her of grade school, wooden desks and ink wells and stern-faced women with jam on their aprons, scratching out arithmetic on a grimy chalkboard.

School was a refuge, a place of safety most of the time, even down on Harrison and 8th, and she'd learned to fight down there, to protect her own. No mother to help her, no big-hatted, big-bustled ladies on Pacific Avenue to feed her mutton and beer.

No one to watch over her.

She looked down at the ruled paper. Wrote: *Berkeley, Old Man, Chemistry Department.*

Frowned, tapping the end of the fountain pen on her lips. Glanced at the brown envelope next to her.

She'd put off a visit to her father, and she needed to question him, about all he knew, if he knew anything, and all he'd done, if he'd done anything other than drive her mother away.

Away from her.

And now there was a possible spy in the hallowed halls, University of Cal-i-for-ni-a, the Golden State, hard to get in, but once you were in you were made. Hymn to learning for the right or at least the rich, where tenure and a paper in the *Classical Review* could buy a case of the finest gin, but no family, no, only a mistake, an error in computation, one last animal response to the smell of death on April 18th, nineteen hundred and aught six.

Miranda closed her eyes, took a breath. Mrs. Hart first, finish the job, collect her fee, and get the jade out of the office. She pushed the tablet and envelope aside and reached for the phone.

Tired operator, middle-aged monotone. "Who're you dialing?"

"Mrs. William Hart the Third, please, in Burlingame."

The woman on the other end woke up, electricity in the wire and now in her voice. Something to tell the girls on break, hey Marge, guess who got a call today on my exchange?

"Hold the line, please."

Five rings.

The butler.

"Mrs. Hart, please. Miranda Corbie."

Three beats.

The maid.

"Yes, Miranda Corbie. A confidential matter."

Four and a half minutes.

The bitch.

"I'd like to return something to you, Mrs. Hart."

Flicker in the voice, drifting like an iceberg. "I'll send someone."

Miranda pressed her back against the leather, a smile at the corner of her lips.

"Will you send him with eight hundred fifty-six dollars and seventy-five cents?"

"You said five—"

"I said five hundred dollars, a quick job and no publicity, plus expenses. You owe me the balance of two hundred dollars for my fee. Expenses totaled six hundred six dollars and seventy-five cents, three hundred of which I had to outlay today to one particular gentleman—to ensure the no publicity clause, Mrs. Hart."

Sigh on the other end, chill winter wind in her ear. She moved the phone to her shoulder, opened the desk drawer, and rummaged for the remnants of the Pep-O-Mints.

Last two. She popped them in her mouth, waiting for the woman with seven million dollars to make up her mind.

"Very well, Miss Corbie. I shan't be able to get away this evening, but—"

"Uh-uh. You wanted speed and results and you paid for it. We make the exchange tonight. I don't want a green rope around my neck. You can meet me here or I'll meet you there."

Panic thawed a few icicles before they froze over again. "I'll meet you there. At your—office." She managed to make the word sound like "bordello"

Miranda shook her head, smiled dangerously. "If you can manage to get away this evening, come by at eleven. Just a little interlude in between dropping the rest of your mad money on roulette. Oh, and bring cash, Mrs. Hart. Checks bounce."

She let the phone fall abruptly on the cradle, the loud clang startling two pigeons cooing on the sill.

✳

Miranda looked down at the thin sheets of government-issued paper, SECRET stamped in red ink across every page.

Dr. Huntington Jasper.

Chemist, professor, and possible Nazi spy. A tall, thin man of fifty-three with a perpetual stoop and a severely burned left hand from one too many late-night sessions with the Bunsen burner. A man with no wife and no children, whose only loves seemed to be research on poison gas and mortuary compounds and buying modern art.

A man who visited the Nazi consulate twelve times last year.

She riffled through the typed pages, plucking out one near the bottom. In late '39, he paid one visit to the Russian consulate. This year, he showed up twice.

She frowned. Didn't need a degree in chemistry to figure out whom Dr. Jasper was spying for.

She rubbed out the Chesterfield, brow furrowed. Jumped when the phone clanged. "Miranda?"

Half-Irish lilt, buzz and clack of the *San Francisco News* going to press. Rick Sanders, news hawk, member of the New York gang.

Another man she owed something to.

She sat back in the chair, smile on her lips. "I finished the Hart case."

Low whistle on the other end. She could see him shove his always-battered fedora above his forehead, blue eyes crinkling at the corners.

"That was quick. Where'd you find the jade?"

"Chinatown."

"Anything printable?"

"She's paying me for hush-hush, Sanders, not to give you tips."

"How about me giving you a tip over dinner?"

Goddamn it.

She yanked open the top drawer violently, flinging the accounting books on the desk. Pulled out the Martell's calendar. June 25th was circled in blue ink. Her eyes jumped to the clock above the safe. Almost five-thirty.

She'd forgotten about Gonzales.

"What's all that noise? You out of Chesterfields again? I figured we'd go to Number 9, grab a Blue Fog and a shrimp cocktail, maybe hit up the Mark for dancing . . ."

Miranda shoved the accounting books back in the drawer, shuffled the scattered papers together.

"Sorry, Rick. I'm meeting Inspector Gonzales at the Moderne tonight."

Pause on the other end, *rat-tat-tat* of typewriters gunning for a deadline. Rick said slowly: "You're going out with him again?"

Miranda tucked the phone receiver under her chin and held it with her shoulder, banging the papers on the desk to get them stacked and even.

"He's a friend of mine, Sanders. Like you."

His voice was heavy. "Not like me, Miranda."

Reproach, regrets, recriminations. Because he couldn't not be with her and he couldn't not want her. He wanted her in New York, wanted her and Johnny laughed at him, laughed at his brother in ink, fourth estate friend closer than a brother, a friend to them both, but always wanting more.

She picked up the pack of Chesterfields on the desk and shook one out on the desktop. Watched the smoke form a hazy question mark above the chairs in front of her desk.

"I don't know what the hell you're talking about, Sanders. I'm meeting Gonzales at the Moderne. You can drop by if you want. Any news for me?"

Click, clack, rat-tat-tat. Click, clack, rat-tat-tat.

His voice was under control again. "No news, but I've got an idea. You want me to meet you at the Moderne and fill you in?"

Rick and Bente, her friends, part of who she was, who she was going to be. The only ones who could help her find the woman who called herself Catherine Corbie. The only ones who knew.

She tapped ash into the tray. "Can't, not over dinner. I never told Gonzales and don't intend to."

More *click clacks* in the background and a muffled reply to someone else. "Sorry, Miranda. Just found out I've got to cover a new Picasso show opening at Civic Center tonight."

She sat up. "Picasso? Any chance of meeting me at the Moderne and taking me with you?"

Slow, surprised. "Sure . . . if you want. Never knew you liked that kind of thing."

"I'm full of surprises. What time?"

"Show runs from nine to midnight. I can pick you up at the Moderne at eight."

"I'll buy you a steak if you want to eat before."

Pause, confusion, warmth back in his voice.

"Hart the Third must be paying off with some scratch. All right, Miri, as long as I'm not rolling along as a third wheel. I'll see you at eight."

"See you, Sanders."

Miranda dropped the heavy receiver on the cradle. Twisted the cigarette out in the tray.

She slid the papers on Jasper into the brown manila envelope and walked to the safe, combination sticky, creak of the dependable Wells Fargo door solid and reassuring.

Set picked up the Baby Browning, along with the trick cigarette case that had saved her life more than once.

Balanced the small pistol in her palm, checked the magazine. Fit the Browning back in the cigarette case. Dropped it in her jacket pocket.

A thick gust of fog was pulsing down Market Street, brushing against the fourth-floor window, dotting it with streaks and specks, a San Francisco rain.

Miranda threw open the window.

The fog enveloped her, caressed her face, cold embrace but still living, still breathing.

Still her City.

Still home.

*

Last bottle of Vol de Nuit.

She'd come by it dearly, bribing the blonde at the City of Paris cosmetic counter with an extra five dollars.

No more French perfume, ladies, at least not free French. Oh, Chanel will design and the houses will stay open, never fear, never let war and occupation stand in the way of fashion, but the Baccarat bottles and je ne sais quoi, the flowers and the fragrance, the spirit and the sensuality, no longer all French, pure French, the embodiment of night flight and freedom.

We just surrendered, Mademoiselle, signed an armistice today in the same train car the Germans did twenty-two years ago . . . Monsieur Hitler and his droll sense of humor. So much for *liberté, égalité, fraternité.*

No more France, no more French perfume.

Miranda dabbed it carefully behind her ears, in the soft curve of her elbow, between her breasts. She closed her eyes, inhaling the oakmoss and narcissus, the deep vanilla creme and the acrid scent of wood bark, straight from the Ardennes.

Vol de Nuit, replacement for Je Reviens and the happy time, the other Miranda, the girl in New York who liked carnations and violets, the scent of freshly cut oranges and coffee, the sound of the Elevated pounding above her tiny apartment, shouts of kids running to buy candy and a *Shadow* magazine at the corner store.

The girl who went to Spain and never came back.

She studied herself in the vanity mirror.

The Helena Rubinstein Town and Country foundation promised that "fresh face" look, but thirty-four was creeping up and she wasn't going to look twenty-five forever. She lifted a finger to the small scar on her cheek, partially concealed by the makeup.

Especially if she accepted cases like Pandora Blake and Eddie Takahashi.

Miranda twisted the Bakelite knob of the small portable radio, tubes warming up while she rummaged through the jewelry box. KSAN and the sweet, sultry tones of Artie Shaw's Orchestra, Helen Forrest singing "Day In, Day Out."

That same old pounding in my heart, whenever I think of you . . .

She drew the terry cloth robe close and reached for the pack of Chesterfields. Shook out a cigarette, lighting it with a White House matchbook propped near the jewelry box.

She'd pushed tonight out of her mind, bent on the Hart case and finding her mother. Pushed responsibility away, too. She shouldn't have let him kiss her, touch her, but the Pandora Blake murder had left her weak.

Left her shaking, frightened, and wanting to remember.

Arousal and life and work and death, and sex somewhere in the middle, "the little death" the French called it, and for a time she had died over and over, but not enough to kill her, no, not enough to send her back to Spain. Back to the churches, the vineyards, back to the red dirt where Johnny was.

Little death, but not enough.

Miranda inhaled, blowing smoke past her own reflection.

She'd gone out with him last week, first time since he'd kissed her on his way to Mexico, thank you so fucking much, Inspector Gonzales, leave your goddamn fedora and join the Dies Committee, just when she thought she might start to like him.

She did like him.

She liked the way his body felt against hers, liked the smell of his cigarettes and cologne. Liked his hands on her skin.

Miranda arched her back, rubbing her neck with her left hand. Artie Shaw was through and the KSAN house band was taking requests. She turned the knob again, interrupting the slick-voiced announcer in the middle of an ad for Johnson Floor Wax. Stubbed out the cigarette in the glass ashtray, "1939 World's Fair" in gold letters wearing out and turning gray.

Sure, she liked Gonzales. But he was too rich and too good-looking, too easy at changing jobs, too easy at life. He'd suffered and she respected him for it. But he'd never been trapped, didn't realize the danger, didn't recognize how lucky he really was.

Didn't understand what it meant to rebuild your life, to make a life.

Didn't understand her.

She stood up, checked her legs critically. Snapped the garters.

It would be a long night at the Moderne.

Four

*

Raphael left his post at the Club Moderne doors and took Miranda by the arm, leading her behind the red velveteen rope. Loud murmur from the congregation, a peroxide blonde in a blue fox stole making indignant noises to the fat businessman who owned her. Raphael gave a low whistle between his teeth, high cheekbones burnished in bronze and raised high in a smile.

"*Che bella!* You look like a Botticelli come to life, Signorina Corbie. You working tonight?"

She smiled and shook her head. "Not tonight, Raphael."

The Italian held her off at arm's length, looking her up and down with a critical eye. Her long cream-colored velveteen coat hung open, revealing a spring green silk evening gown with a plunging neckline and fabric gathered delicately at the shoulders, not quite the same model as the one she'd been shot in on the Gayway. Matching green gloves reached almost to her elbows. She wore a pearl necklace with matching earrings purchased last year and her hair in a chignon. A small orchid clung to her left temple.

"You, how do you say it, make me not breathe. I think I never see you look so beautiful, even when you work. Will you be visiting Vicenzo tonight?"

"*Grazie*, Raphael. No wheel, just dinner. I'm meeting some friends."

He held his hand up to his heart and gave a small bow. "You favor us, *mia cara*. Joe will be happy he is here to see you tonight."

He pushed open the chromium double doors for her. Marie wasn't working hat check. The redhead in her place smiled sprightly.

"Coat to check, Miss?"

Miranda was slipping out of the long velveteen wrap when she heard the redhead titter and felt a hand on her bare back. She spun around to find Gonzales holding the coat.

He looked down at her, brown eyes warm, teeth white and perfect.

"Miranda—you look lovely. Allow me."

He passed the coat to the redhead, who was staring at him, jaw slack and eyes misty. Gonzales handed Miranda the ticket, his fingers brushing hers.

"Thanks. You're a little early, Gonzales."

He bent over her hand, tuxedo jacket stretched tight against his wide shoulders, scent of leather and lime from his skin.

"We have much to discuss."

Well-bred cough behind her. Clark clicked his heels together and bowed, blond comb-over stiff and in place.

"Miss Corbie. The usual table?"

Gonzales's voice was pleasantly firm. "Not tonight, if you don't mind, Miranda. I would like to start someplace new. Please give us a table near the orchestra."

Miranda shrugged, nodded to Clark. The maître d' clicked his heels again, ignoring Gonzales entirely.

"Very well, Miss Corbie. Follow me, please."

Gonzales took her elbow, leading her between the giant faux-marble columns of the grand entrance and down the steps to the main floor, golden light dripping from the giant seashell sconces, smell of Fleurs de Rocaille rising from tables carefully positioned between large potted palms.

The band tonight was sweet swing, a slight, balding man leading a feeble rendition of "That Old Feeling," while a few of the older couples moved stiffly around the dance floor. Gonzales, smiling, held out the chair for Miranda.

She shrugged again, sat down. Clark looked from one to the other and handed them menus, frown line between his eyes. He leaned in toward Miranda, voice low.

"Should I tell Joe you are here, Miss Corbie?"

She looked up, surprised. "Of course. I don't need a menu, Clark. Just make it the usual."

Gonzales bent forward attentively, black hair thick and lightly oiled, shining where the light caught it.

"Miranda . . . if you permit me, I'd like to make a recommendation. The *Lobster Fra Diavolo* with ravioli, *antipasti misti* to begin."

She looked up at Clark. He pursed his lips and nodded.

"The lobster is very delicious."

Miranda frowned, locking eyes with the tall brown-skinned cop in the custom tuxedo.

"I said I'd have dinner with you, Gonzales. That doesn't mean I check my decisions with the coat." She tilted her head up to meet Clark's wide smile. "The usual, Clark."

Gonzales laughed, showing his teeth. "Lobster for one, then, please. And perhaps you will at least allow me to order some wine. A dry red wine, I think. Château Margaux '29 would go very well with your steak."

"I will see what we have, sir." Clark spun on his heels and marched to the bar, throwing them a backward glance.

She took out her cigarette case. He held out a gold-plated lighter and clicked it on. Her eyes flickered up to meet his, while she held his hand and lit the stick.

"Is wine part of police training now? Or just a little something you picked up along the way?"

He laughed again. "I hope that cigarette case doesn't contain your Baby Browning."

"I don't need a gun with you. You learned your lesson the first time."

His grin grew wider, the white of his teeth contrasting with the firm tanned skin.

"Perhaps, perhaps not. Thank you for agreeing to meet me tonight, Miranda. Though I still don't know why you would not let me escort you here."

"I was busy. I work for a living. You did too, once."

He waved a hand. Perfectly shaped nails with a faint polish.

"I still work, Miranda, you know that. We've met once already since I returned from Mexico, and still you do not allow me to take you anywhere. Am I such a bad driver?"

He laughed again lightly as she watched his throat muscles tighten, the play of the tux against his arms and shoulders. More lime and leather, mixed with mint and French cigarettes. He reached across the table with an easy motion and picked up her hand. His fingers were warm and strong.

"But I am glad you are here tonight. With me."

She pulled her hand away. "Don't get carried away."

Jorge and another waiter she didn't recognize appeared with a large plate of prosciutto, peppers, mozzarella, and sourdough bread, along with a bottle of wine.

Jorge bowed to Miranda. "The *antipasti misti* are compliments of the house, Miss." He turned to Gonzales, lithe body shifting into a stiffer posture. His lip curled slightly.

"We do not carry Château Margaux, sir. We can offer you a Burgundy from the Sonoma Mission Winery, or a wide variety of the most excellent cocktails."

Miranda said: "I'd like a Blue Fog. What about you, Gonzales?"

He stroked his thin mustache. "Open the Burgundy, please."

Jorge uncorked the bottle with an extra flourish, pouring a small amount into a glass. Gonzales sipped it. The waiter shot a glance at Miranda, eyebrows raised, smirk on his lips. She shook her head very slightly.

Gonzales said: "The wine is all right."

The waiters left, Jorge, like Clark before him, casting a backward glance at Miranda.

A fatherly hand fell on her bare shoulder. "*Carissima, come vai?* I understand you are here with a friend tonight."

Joe Merello gave a slow wink and broad grin under his white derby, red carnation in his boutonniere nodding in response. He looked down at her, beaming like a proud uncle.

"Raphael tells me you are most beautiful *stasera, e si, è vero. Sei una dea. Una dea d'amore, forse?*"

He laughed like a cherub, clapped another hand on Gonzales's shoulder. "You take good care of *mia bella, capito?* You want to play tonight, Signore, you are most welcome. You have already found *la bella fortuna.*"

Joe nodded toward Miranda, squeezed her shoulder, and ambled toward another table. She watched as he bent over the hand of an old lady in gold lamé who giggled like a schoolgirl and made Betty Boop eyes, eyelashes fluttering madly.

Gonzales leaned forward, voice low. "I don't understand why you will not let me take you to the Mark Hopkins or Bal Tabarin. They have far better food and music, and no gambling."

Her eyes flashed green. "These are my friends."

He reached out for her hand again. "I am also your friend, Miranda. Don't worry, I won't report Joe."

She pulled her hand out of his grasp. A short brunette was warbling "It's Only a Paper Moon," and a few more couples got up to fox-trot. Gonzales cocked his head.

"Are you all right? Would you like to dance?"

"No. I want to hear more about Mexico and the Fifth Column situation."

Gonzales smiled and poured the wine. "I shall, Miranda, but please join me in a glass first. This is not the best vintage or the best vintner, but it isn't too bad. Red wine is healthful—much better for you than gin."

Jorge danced up to the table, still grinning. He set the Blue Fog down in front of her, and bowed.

"Anything else, Miss Corbie?"

"Not right now, Jorge. But I'm expecting another friend soon, and he'll want a drink." She watched Gonzales, voice slow and deliberate. "Mr. Sanders."

Jorge backed away, smile broader, extra bounce as he glided off. Gonzales set the wineglass down slowly, red flush highlighting his cheekbones. His tone held a hint of reproach.

"Sanders is joining us? When did this develop, Miranda? I thought . . ."

She crushed her cigarette stub in the glass ashtray. "I said I'd eat dinner with you, Gonzales, not go on some kind of moon-and-spoon date. I warned you the first time. I even gave you a nosebleed."

She sipped the Blue Fog and held his eyes until he looked away, anger and hurt tightening the line of his jaw.

"You already played your dramatic scene, gave your best Rhett Butler imitation before you left for Mexico. We picked it up again last week, and I let you. I shouldn't have."

"Miranda, I—"

"Let me finish. So you've kissed me a couple of times. So what? You saved my life, you're a good cop, and yes, I like you. I consider you a friend. That's why I've met you twice, why I want to hear about your work. But I'm not Scarlett O'Hara or Eliza fucking Doolittle, and I don't need to be told what to eat or what to drink, and incidentally, where to sit, and yes, I have a college degree, and yes, I've heard all about the so-called finer things in life. I'm not impressed."

"I only mean that I want you to have the best, and—"

"You don't understand, Gonzales. The Club Moderne is part of who I am. Joe took me in when no one else would. And I'm comfortable here. I work here."

He looked down at the wineglass, red drops dripping down the inside slope. His lightly accented voice was low and hoarse.

"You don't have to work, Miranda. You have a choice."

She set the highball glass down with a clink.

"If you're saying what I think you're saying, you're either drunk or stupid. I'm going to forget you said it and move on."

His large hands balled into fists. More red flushed his cheeks.

"I will not forget it, Miranda. I know you feel something for me, as I do for you. Your touch . . . your body does not lie."

Julius's Castle, last week, last time they'd met. First time after Mexico.

He'd told her about intercepted cables and shadowy men in corner *tabernas*, of swastikas and Spanish dancers. It was the stuff of Hollywood, a John Buchan novel, and she remembered how his eyes shone, how he'd held her.

Clear night on Telegraph Hill, colored lights of San Francisco winking back at them while he kissed her, hand on her breast, tongue in her mouth, his hips pressed to hers. Heart in her chest, in her ears, making her shake, roaring like distant bombs, pulse artillery-fast, and she pulled away gasping, not yet, not yet . . .

It's only a paper moon . . .

Rip down the curtain, charade over, no nights in Madrid, no olive grove, no Johnny, no, just a rich, good-looking cop who saved her life and felt oh so good against her skin, but that wasn't enough.

It was never enough.

Her voice was even, lips a red gash against white skin, auburn hair burning under golden light.

"I like you, Gonzales. But you live in a different world, and it's not mine. Never will be."

He pulled a gold-plated cigarette case out of his tuxedo pocket. Lit one of the brown-tipped French cigarettes. His hand shook a little. He avoided her eyes.

"I spoke to my mother about you when I visited home. She advised me against a formal relationship, but I stand by what I said. You do not have to work, Miranda. I want to marry you. I am in love with you."

The room spun, seashells and warm beaches, palm fronds and Palm Beach, golf on the coast, skiing at Sun Valley, newest dress by Hattie Carnegie, fresh from the twice-yearly trip to Manhattan. Bloomingdale's and I. Magnin, the May Company and Bullock's, Marshall Field's and a special jaunt to Chicago just to buy a goddamn hat.

Tall, dark, and handsome, looks just like a movie star, whispered conversation and schemes from the blonde in the country club bridge tournament, that Mark Gonzales is a Mexican, but one of the good ones. Wife's history, though . . . why, Nancy said she was actually a *whore*! Can you believe it? And he seems so nice, and good-looking, too . . .

She looked up at the earnest, somber man in front of her.

Searched his eyes, but Miranda Corbie was nowhere to be found.

She drained the Blue Fog and the room spun again, the band starting to play "Someone to Watch Over Me," and it was Paul Whiteman at the band-stand and Sherman Billingsley at the next table, Walter Winchell scribbling on a napkin for his next column, 1936 and marcelled hair and silk gowns with sheer, silk stockings. The music ached, oh it ached and throbbed and filled her with such joy, such ineffable joy, an echo of the man who held her in his arms, tall dark and handsome, Irish grin, white teeth, hard muscles on his arms from working at the docks, from growing up in New York and fighting his way out.

To the *Times*. To the Stork Club.

To her.

Johnny.

She said: "I'm sorry. I shouldn't have let you kiss me. I like you, Mark, but I don't love you, and I never will. I don't think you love me, either, not really. You don't know me."

His shoulders sank. He reached for her hand. She let him.

"I could try to, Miranda. May we remain friends?"

She withdrew her hand, gave him a sad smile.

"I hope so."

✳

Gonzales left most of the lobster untasted, drank three more glasses of wine, spoke little and about trivial things, the department, when he was going back to work, about the possibility of a transfer to Los Angeles when he was through with the Dies Committee. Miranda ate the steak, green beans, and scalloped potatoes methodically, trying not to listen to the voice of reproach, of guilt, reciting a memory of his hands on her skin, and how her pulse had raced against his long, lean body.

Rick arrived fifteen minutes late, breathless, hat and tie askew, mustard on his display handkerchief. Starch in his back when he walked up to the table, jaw squared and stoic, handshake stiff and abrupt.

"Inspector. Good to see you again."

Gonzales wiped his mustache with the dinner napkin, eyes glistening. "You too, Mr. Sanders."

Rick pulled a chair out and sat down, and Jorge appeared like a genie in a bottle, smiling as if he knew a secret.

"Drink, sir?"

"Bourbon and water. And the usual, Jorge . . . Miss Corbie and I will have to leave soon."

The waiter nodded, eyes flickering over Gonzales, who flushed, looking back and forth between Miranda and Rick.

"You did not tell me you had an appointment, Miranda."

She glanced at Rick, whose jaw muscles popped in and out while he studied his nails.

"I told you I'm working, Mark, and this is work. Rick's taking me to the Picasso exhibit at the San Francisco Museum of Art."

The Inspector raised his eyebrows, swallowed another portion of wine.

"I know something of Picasso. My family purchased several of his drawings at a Mexico City gallery."

She asked quickly: "Which one?"

"I believe it was the Count Lestang Gallery. It was several years ago."

He turned to Rick, glancing down at the mustard stain.

"I did not take you for a fan of modern art, Mr. Sanders."

Rick's blue eyes bored into Gonzales's brown ones. "There's a lot you don't know about me."

Jorge and the new waiter arrived with a highball glass and steak and spinach for Rick. The reporter tucked his napkin in his collar and draped it over his tie. Picked up the knife and fork, and said, aiming at Gonzales: "You mind my digging in? Missed lunch today, and I'm as hungry as a mama wolf with a litter of pups."

Miranda plucked a Chesterfield out of the cigarette case.

"I'd like another Blue Fog. We have time, Rick?"

The reporter nodded, mouth full. Gonzales stretched across the table with his gold lighter, flame flickering. She lightly held his hand and took a deep drag on the cigarette.

Gonzales looked around the room and raised a hand. The waiter Miranda didn't know threaded his way past tables and palms and a middle-aged woman drowning in mink and black crepe.

"The lady would like another cocktail. Or would you like to try my wine, Miranda?"

She looked from Rick, bent over his plate and furiously eating, to Gonzales and his unfocused eyes. Gulped the cigarette until she could feel her lungs warm up with smoke.

She told the waiter: "Go ahead and bring another wineglass."

The inspector smiled, leaned back, arm draped behind his chair. Rick looked up and swallowed.

"You look swell, Randy. Sorry I didn't mention it before."

She winced at the old nickname. "Thanks, Rick."

The waiter brought another wineglass, and Gonzales poured, pushing it toward her with a smile.

"Drink, Miranda. You will like it. It is not as good as what the Mark Hopkins serves, of course."

Rick raised his fork. "Not as expensive, either, Inspector. Personally, I think Joe runs a pretty classy joint."

Miranda held the wineglass in her hand and raised it to her lips. Gonzales turned to Rick, a slight sneer stretching his perfectly proportioned face.

"I do not think you would recognize a well-cooked steak, let alone the right wine, Mr. Sanders."

The Burgundy hit Gonzales and dripped from his chin, mouth hung open, eyes shocked and stinging, red tears on his cheek. Gasps at nearby tables, several middle-aged women trying to peer through thick glasses for a more focused view.

Rick set the fork and knife down, looking back and forth between Miranda and the Inspector. Gonzales fumbled for a napkin, started to wipe his eyes and mouth. Red drops clung to the white of his ruffled tuxedo and dripped down the black satin lapel.

"You're drunk or I'd have thrown the glass. Don't kid yourself, Gonzales. You don't want to get to know me. You want to change me. You don't like my license, don't like that I eat at the Club Moderne, don't like my friends. You think you can control and own me, change me to what you want me to be. Not want me for who I am."

She stood up, face white. Clark and Jorge hurried from the back of the room.

"Put everything on my tab, Jorge. I'll settle up tomorrow."

The waiter looked around the table, eyes big, and disappeared quietly.

Rick was out of his chair, body tense, posture unsure. Gonzales calmly wiped wine from his tuxedo.

Her voice was low and cutting. "I was hoping we could be friends. But you're just another client, Gonzales. Just another fucking client."

Miranda shoved her chair in hard, the empty wineglass on the table shaking. She strode across the dance floor and climbed the short stairway between the false marble columns, not once looking back.

Five

*

Rick found her on the corner of Sutter and Mason, braced against the brick wall of an apartment building, looking up the hill toward her apartment. Her left arm hugged her stomach. She was finishing off the Chesterfield Gonzales had lit for her.

The crowd waiting at the Moderne pushed against the red velvet ropes, still gawking at the woman in green who'd run through the chromium doors.

Rick's broken-down fedora was in his hands, along with Miranda's velveteen coat. He slapped the hat on his head and pulled her away from the wall, draping the coat around her shoulders.

"It's foggy as hell out here. You're goddamn well going to catch pneumonia if you're not more careful."

College boys in a depot hack drove by, necks craning out between the pillars of the wooden framework. One let out a wolf whistle. Rick left a hand on her shoulder, walked around to face her.

"Gonzales was obviously tight. I wouldn't have slugged him. Probably not, anyway. Miranda . . . Miranda, look at me."

She tilted her head up, blew a stream of smoke from the corner of her mouth.

"You ready to go to the Picasso show?"

He took off his hat and ran fingers through his dark brown hair, thick strands separating, a few falling in his face. Frustration made his voice scratchy.

"Jesus Christ, Miranda, you can't just pick up and leave and not talk about this. What the hell happened in there? I mean, I appreciate you defending my honor and ability to choose a good Porterhouse and all that, but I thought—I thought you liked the guy. What happened?"

She dropped the cigarette stub, stamped it out three times. Looked down at her feet and the new open-toed pumps she'd had dyed to match the gown.

"I wasn't just defending you. He asked me to marry him."

Rick's eyebrows climbed into his hairline.

"He what?"

"You heard me."

He stood staring down at her, breathing hard, then grabbed her by both shoulders, hands rough and voice sharp.

"And you said what?"

Miranda shook him off angrily. "What the fuck do you think I said, Sanders? He's not in love with me. He doesn't even know me. It's ten to nine, let's get to the Picasso show. And tell me your idea about my mother."

His eyes roamed hers, blue against brown, and he took her by the shoulders again in a tight grip.

"Goddamn it, Miranda . . ."

He kissed her. Hard and deep and angry, and she caught her breath at the fury in it, surprised, relenting, until she realized what was happening and brought up her arms as hard as she could, shoving him away. The sound of applause rippled through the waiting crowd at the Moderne, along with shouts and a few jeers.

His lips were smeared with Red Dice lipstick, eyes burning, jaw set.

She wiped her mouth with her hand, out of breath, voice shaking. Legs shaking.

"I'll forgive you for that, Sanders, as long as you forget it. But if you ever try to treat me like a piece of meat again, I'll break your fucking arm."

Rick swallowed a few times, eyes on her face.

"Guess I was overcome by your perfume. They ought to put a warning label on that stuff."

She straightened her coat and buttoned it. Tried to sound casual.

"Bought the last bottle of Vol de Nuit at the City of Paris. No more French perfume until it's really French again."

He gave her a crooked smile, wiping his mouth with his dirty display handkerchief.

"Maybe that's a good thing."

She held his eyes for a few seconds, then turned and nodded toward Market Street.

"Let's catch a cab to the Picasso exhibit."

*

Academics and socialites trickled in by the score, fashionably late to the fashionable show, cabs and chauffeurs pulling up to the Veterans Building, twin to the War Memorial Opera House across the landscaped Memorial Court.

San Francisco, the city that rose from the dead to shimmer like a pearl at the Panama-Pacific Exposition, just nine short years after the Quake and Fire nearly killed her. Rebuild her for the opera lovers and aging Russian ballerinas, rebuild her for the symphony creaking by with Mendelssohn, rebuild her for the arts. Make her look like Paris, the Paris of the West.

Then the Great War, inconvenient interlude for the fund-raising class. But once it was over, the War to End All Wars, they named one of the buildings for veterans, Green Room lounge on the second floor, boys who were no longer boys but only half men able to meet, to congregate, to talk, a temple to memory.

A temple to sacrifice.

Miranda craned her neck, looking up at lights on the top of the roof, shining gold on the stout fluted columns.

Rick took her by the arm. "Let's go inside."

The large formal and dimly lit gallery was crowded with the well-to-do and curious, intellectuals and Sausalito painters of ocean scenes, with a sprinkling of the anemic breed of lunch club ladies who thought all art began and ended with Raphael. Chatter and clatter of heels on marble, Blue Book hostesses and quiet art students, gimlet-eyed dealers frantically estimating, and once in a while a hush amid the glittering conversations before they renewed themselves, words upon words, rushing to fill the vacuum.

"Blue Period, clearly" and "Can you really see a mandolin?" "I prefer Rivera, myself, and you can see him paint in person at the Fair . . . ," fragmentary conversation floating past, as Rick headed toward *The Red Guitar* to scribble notes and find a curator, and Miranda scanned the walls. She was hunting a man and a painting. Neither one was there.

Her gloved hands unclenched. The painting she'd been afraid to see wasn't part of the new retrospective. No need to brace herself, to try to pull away from *Guernica*.

She'd waited in line patiently last year, August 27th, 1939, a foggy Sunday, day off from Sally's and in between the divorce cases that were coming her way. She'd eaten at the St. Francis in the morning, wanting good coffee in her stomach, a full breakfast of hotcakes, eggs, and ham. She remembered the old lady with crinkled white hair on the number 5 White Front that morning, the *click-clack-click* of knitting needles, pink woolen blanket for a grandchild.

Funny thing to remember.

Picasso intended the painting to raise money for Spanish refugees, homeless, like the canvas itself, and so it too traveled America on rails of steel, hobo, vagabond, celebrated protest of a new kind of war.

DAR dowagers in old beaver coats and young earnest bluestockings from art history seminars stood on the Veterans Building steps and hawked pamphlets for the "Sanity in Art" organization, pressing them eagerly into receptive hands, protesting Communist propaganda and the degradation of good taste.

"Fight Foreign Influence and Modern Art" the pamphlets exhorted, DAR lady nodding a feathered hat vociferously at the message, why I know good art when I see it, Mildred, my dear father painted ships at the Golden Gate. This Picasso fellow can't even draw. Keep American art American I say, these so-called artists are just degenerates, them and their ugly, foreign propaganda . . .

While Franco and the Fascists marched through what was left of Spain, the painting wandered through San Francisco and Boston, Chicago and Los Angeles. It played the sad song of the *alboka* and told the story of a small Basque village, about what happened to the women and children, the cows and horses, what happened to life on April 26th, 1937.

Broad brushstrokes. Oil and canvas, mind and deft fingers, passion and prayer and eyes of a Spanish artist. Bold, savage lines, black with the shadows of Junkers, gray with painted screams.

Town and canvas, herald and victim.

More real than Hemingway's dispatches. More real than film.

Guernica.

The dowager-critics sniffed, thinking of Grandpapa's *Et in Arcadia ego* landscape in the attic, while Stanford art professors stroked their beards and mumbled, wondering if Picasso had lost his way. A veteran from the Green Room hobbled down the marble steps, clawed hand clutching the ornate wrought iron of the staircase. He stood rooted before the painting, staring, before stumbling away, back to the light of the Memorial Court.

Miranda didn't know how long she'd been there or when she arrived. All she could hear were the planes. Low, throbbing buzz and whine and deep, deep rumble and thunder, primal bass rising up from her feet to her gut, shaking her, shaking the earth.

A little girl in shock, blood on the dirty dress between her legs. Eyes vacant, half-empty bag of beans clutched in her arms.

Woman in black and white, smeared with yellow and red, rosary clutched in rough, soiled hands, she touches the girl on the shoulder, ushers her in the dark, ancient cathedral, gaping hole in the roof, candelabras long gone.

Shattered wine bottle. Bloated, dead bull, flies buzzing.

Johnny's face.

The guard on duty that day touched her arm. Her hands were as wet as her cheeks. He looked at her and tried to understand. She never went back.

Five days later, the Nazis invaded Poland.

The current retrospective included a few of the preliminary drawings for *Guernica* along one section of a wall, and Miranda resolutely stood with her back to them, focusing on her search for Jasper. Anyone in San Francisco who professed a knowledge of contemporary art was already here or due to arrive, and given his predilections, she expected him to make a showing.

She felt something crawl down her back and glanced to her right, catching eyes with a slick-haired man in a tuxedo standing underneath a small colorful panel of two women racing down a beach. He looked about forty and showed a lot of teeth. His companion, a much younger brunette in summer white with a white fox stole, gave her the flickering up-and-down dismissal society girls learn in the cradle, then hone and sharpen with the bones of uglier, poorer classmates.

Miranda stared at her until the brunette flounced off to another painting, pulling the toothy beau in her wake. She smoothed the green silk of her dress, glad she'd kept on the velveteen wrap instead of checking it. Her evening clothes weren't exactly inconspicuous.

Society column habitués jockeyed for position against the most flattering painted backdrop, searching continually for a photographer from the *Chronicle* or *Call-Bulletin*, Picasso as set designer for the Sun Valley set. Rick stood off to one side, interviewing a middle-aged woman with a frightening overbite and a sapphire-and-ruby necklace rope around a chicken-wattle neck. Miranda grinned until she remembered Mrs. Hart and the jade in her safe. She half expected the Bitch of Burlingame to show up, if only for a few minutes. Appearances are so important, especially when your son's a thief and a hophead, and you're fucking a state senator on the side.

Miranda moved toward the opposite end of the long wall, where the high-toned, high-class patrons of the Museum of Art were dressed in top hat and tails and floor-length mink coats, congratulating each other on their taste, on bringing Art to the Common Man, accepting homage and genuflections from the curators before finding better amusement in a Chinatown gambling den or an offshore ship with a deluxe wheel and a free hand of keno.

Art was always a fashionable cause, even if the artist is a Communist, makes philanthropy more exciting, more like the Derby or the latest Louis fight. Rice Bowl Parties come and go, but art lingers, neither marble nor the gilded monuments of princes, boasted Shakespeare, but he never met Mrs. Hart and the Junior League.

Art historians rubbed elbow patches in a far corner, debating artistic merits and the ism of the day. Surrealism, Cubism, Fauvism, Impressionism, so much more important than Communism and Fascism, though most of them agreed that Hitler and the Nazis defined kitsch, and trembled at the thought of jack-boots in the Louvre, swastikas hanging next to Leonardo da Vinci.

Too fucking little, too fucking late, thought Miranda. She unrolled two Butter Rum Life Savers, looked to her right, and almost choked. "Fingers" Molloy was standing in front of *Woman with a Mandolin.* Two security guards stood against the walls and tried to look tough, but they were private cops from the museum, not the boys in blue.

He was a short, pudgy little man with wrinkled ears and skin and a smooth way of picking pockets.

She walked up next to him. Spoke softly. "Never knew you liked Picasso, Fingers."

The little man jumped. He spun around and his face relaxed a little when he saw Miranda. Hoisted his gray flannel trousers a little higher. Licked his lips.

"I got a right to see art, ain't I? I ain't doin' nothing."

She nodded, studying the painting. "Don't worry, I'm not trying to get you copped. I appreciated the information about the jade."

He preened a little, stuck out his belly, coarse face a leer. " 'Preciate it enough to lay some more dough on me, sister?"

She stared at him until his red-rimmed eyes finally fell. "I'll let you know when I've got a job for you. If you're flat again, lay off the juice." She nodded toward the painting. "What's your play?"

His eyebrows climbed into his oiled, curly hair. "Whaddya mean? I told ya, I like art. Though I can't see no titties. Big Joe over at Pago Pago told me this guy Picasso paints a lot of titties."

Miranda's lips twitched. Big Joe was a lumbering six-foot-five mountain of flesh that ran a clip joint in the Settlement, the kind of place where the B-girls lasted maybe six months before they were too bruised or broken to be of any use.

"Pay two bits and go to Sally's. You should be on the Gayway, Fingers, plenty more action at the Fair."

The small watery eyes met hers again stubbornly before he shoved a crumpled derby on his head and grunted.

"Yeah, maybe you're right. I ain't doin' myself no favors standin' here jawin' with you."

He looked around nervously, seemed to catch eyes with a stout man dressed in black. She couldn't make out his face. Fingers gave a faint nod, glanced sideways at Miranda, and melted into the crowd, the laughter of a large woman in gold velvet and a stone marten scarf chasing him toward the stairway. The stout man waited ten seconds and followed. While Miranda watched, her skin prickled again, and she turned her head to the left.

Her eyes met cold gray ones, wreathed in a matching hood and cape of filmy gray gauze. The gray eyes looked away quickly, and the woman slid toward the exit, a tall, well-built man with a dark mustache trailing behind her.

So Mrs. Hart had shown up, and with a paid escort. Miranda checked her watch. Nearly ten. She'd meet the woman in an hour, return the jade, collect the money, and close the case. Not much time left to wait for Jasper.

She looked around the room again. Rick was speaking to a tuxedoed man with silver hair and a well-groomed mustache. Her view toward the entrance cleared, and she spotted the registration table, what she'd been looking for and what she'd missed on arrival. Best to make sure Jasper hadn't come and gone.

She threaded her way through the crowd and stood in line behind a youngish couple in gaudy evening clothes. The thirtyish blond was tight, and the girl's eyes were bright and feverish. They finally finished, the girl signing with a flourish and then loudly demanding to be taken to the Mark or the Peacock Room, dark hair arranged like Brenda Frazier, boyfriend nodding like Charlie McCarthy.

Miranda threw a bright smile at the severe-looking woman in black behind the counter and picked up the pen.

"Such a marvelous exhibit! I just adore Picasso. You know, I thought I saw a friend of mine earlier, but I'd hate to embarrass myself if it's not really he . . . would you mind terribly if I just check to see if he's signed?"

The woman raised a long single eyebrow, then nodded brusquely before turning to answer a question from a thin man stroking a sandy-colored goatee.

Miranda bent over the book, flipping back to the beginning, her finger running down the names. She'd almost finished when a voice behind her cleared its throat in disapproval. Miranda looked up, smiled again at the counter woman and her eyebrow.

No professor.

She scrawled her name in the book. It could have been Miranda or Mary, Corbie or Carp.

"Thank you again."

Miranda shut the book with a thump, brushing roughly by and almost knocking over the brunette in white, who'd been waiting in line behind her, making disapproving noises. Miranda posed for a moment, shifted her weight and turned on the electricity. The brunette's slick-haired date opened his mouth and kept it open, while a few other men stared, lips parted and eyes wet. Her lips curved upward in a smile, and she stared into the pale blue, furious eyes of the brunette.

"So sorry, my dear—I didn't see you. White fades so, doesn't it?"

Miranda glided through the crowd toward Rick, green dress shimmering in the muted light.

*

"So why exactly did you want to come tonight, Miri? I've never heard you mention art, much less the modern stuff."

Miranda popped two more Life Savers in her mouth, keeping her eyes on the door.

"You get a good education at Mills."

He pushed the fedora back off his forehead and grinned down at her. "Yeah. And I studied ballet. C'mon, Miranda . . . maybe you know your way around an art gallery, but that's not why you're here. You're looking for somebody. Who is it?"

She threw him an irritated glance and refocused on the entrance. They were standing in a corner with a few of Picasso's earlier drawings and studies. The crowd congregated toward the better-known paintings, and the view gave her an angle on the entire gallery.

"Ever hear of client confidentiality, Sanders? I can't tell you anything even if I wanted to. So drop it."

He covered a yawn with his fist. "OK, so maybe I'll go home. I got my story, such as it is, we've been here over an hour, and Mrs. Sanders's little boy needs his sleep. But while you're waiting for your mark—whoever he is—I figure I'd better spill my idea. About"—he dropped his voice—"your mother."

Miranda's voice was sharp. "You got something? What is it?"

He threw a hand up. "Wait, Miri. I don't have anything, but I need your permission before I go forward."

She glanced at her watch: 10:18. Mrs. Hart, she of the gray eyes and gray snood and green bills and jade would be punctual and arrive at eleven, the pitter-patter of handmade Corsican leather pumps echoing down the hallway of the Monadnock, sound as hollow as the woman's soul. Miranda wanted the goddamn jade out of her safe and her life. She looked up at Rick expectantly. His voice was soft.

"I know—at least I think I know—what this is doing to you inside, Miranda. But I'm worried you're not catching all the angles. We don't know if the postcard is from your mother—it could be someone posing as your mother. It could be some kind of trap, a grift, even revenge."

Her eyes swung back to the entrance. A large florid man in tails was panting up the stairs.

"Nothing new. I realize the risks. What's your idea?"

He sighed. "OK. I've looked at ship arrivals and departures, morgue and hospital records. All for 1910 and '11, since you figure you don't remember her after you were three or four years old. I checked for Corbie with an *ie* or *y*, Katherine with a *K*, Katy, and everything else. Nothing. So here's my idea: I want to search the criminal records."

Catherine Corbie.

Mother and fugitive, mother and criminal, lost woman, giving birth to a bastard and then abandoned by one. Pantomime memories, early and faded, like old photographs and scratchy Victrolas, and after three or four years . . . nothing.

Miranda spoke slowly. "I should have thought of that myself."

He gazed down at her, wide mouth twisted. "Just make sure you're ready for whatever we find, Miranda."

She shook her shoulders. Gave him half a smile and placed a gloved hand against his cheek.

"You're a good friend. Thank you, Rick."

He covered her hand with his for a moment, then turned to pick his way through a group of five or six giggling art students. Miranda's eyes followed him before they caught at an older man, tall and thin with sloping shoulders in a rounded hunch. He wore a white glove on his left hand.

Dr. Jasper.

Six

*

He was dressed in a brown worsted vest and coat and buttoned trousers, buff-colored shirt and pale gold paisley tie, all a few years out of date. A watch chain hung from a vest pocket.

Quintessential costume for the conservative academic.

She wove her way between patrons. The crowds were thinning; her watch read 10:27. Not much time.

Jasper quickly positioned himself in front of two of Picasso's most recent works, the *Girl with Dark Hair* and the *Girl with Light Hair*. He stood at a distance, tilting his head and gazing back and forth between the paintings.

She moved in close, stooping to read the information cards. Oil on wood, they'd been painted a day apart, on March 28th and 29th of last year. The blond version was lent by Rosenberg and Helft, Ltd., the companion piece from an unspecified private collection. Jasper focused on the latter, walking to within a few inches of the painting, peering over thick glasses at the brushstrokes, then backing up again.

The man with the sandy goatee she'd noticed at the registration desk made a noise of recognition, clapped his hands, and glided toward Jasper. Miranda turned her back, pretending to study a larger oil, *Portrait of a Lady* from 1937.

The light glinted off the bearded man's spectacles. He clapped his hands again before grabbing Jasper's right and pumping it up and down.

"Dr. Jasper, I'm delighted to see you again! It's been far too long since you've honored my . . . little shop. Tell me, are you still in the market for"—he dropped his voice to a playfully conspiratorial stage whisper, eyes dancing with the excitement of a sales pitch—"'*Entartete Kunst*'? As you can see, Rosenberg has managed to weather the storm quite well. You know what Jews are. But he is far from the only source, my dear Doctor, and—"

Jasper interrupted him brusquely. Miranda froze, not daring to turn around.

"Not here, Wardon, and certainly not tonight. As you know, I am in the market, but only for very specific pieces . . ."

The voices were receding. She glanced to her left. The two men were bunched together near a large canvas she didn't recognize and whose title she couldn't make out. The bearded dealer was stiff, clearly uncomfortable. Jasper's hand was on his wrist. Jasper was bent over the smaller man, and the dealer, growing more uncomfortable, withdrew his display handkerchief and mopped his face. Miranda thought she heard "Kirchner" and "Warsaw," words rising high from Jasper's throat before he subdued his voice again.

The dealer finally smoothed his thin sandy hair against his bony skull and bowed briefly, trying to smile. Jasper's white-gloved hand was still clutching the other man's arm as if he'd forgotten it was there. He nodded dismissively, dropped his hand to his waist. The dealer backed away, smile still plastered, and beat a path to the exit.

The gallery was finally quiet and almost deserted. She circled Jasper in a wide arc and headed for the exit, passing the registration desk and the heavyset woman in black, who raised her one thick eyebrow in farewell.

Miranda peered once more through the wrought-iron railings of the staircase. Jasper was staring at *The Acrobat,* narrow head moving back and forth as if he were listening to a symphony.

*

Miranda strode through the lobby, waving hurriedly to Gladys who was helping a distinguished-looking party in a bowler and tweed vest with a selection of pipe tobacco. The Monadnock crowd was thinning out. Even the Tascone's jukebox was quiet.

Entartete Kunst. She'd heard it before, couldn't remember where. Her gloved finger pressed the button and she checked her watch and the clock above the crate. 10:58. No time to think about art or Jasper or the goateed art dealer. Her Hamilton watch was running a little slow, and she wound it until the automatic elevator dinged and the doors parted.

A well-preserved woman in her mid-forties stood in front of her, draped in iron gray and looking like rain over the Pacific. The heavy odor of Narcisse Noir steamed through the doors.

Mrs. Hart.

Miranda hesitated for a brief moment before stepping inside. Her stomach tightened, and she nodded to the woman in gray.

"Good evening."

The socialite tilted her head back, opened her purse, and withdrew a silver cigarette case with a monogram. She plucked out a Marlborough and lit it with a matching silver lighter she materialized from the gauze of her cape.

The door clanged and opened on four and Mrs. Hart inhaled, stick elegantly cradled between two long gloved fingers. She stepped out, waving what was left of the Marlborough in a graceful arc, large steel eyes stuck to Miranda like frostbite.

"You're late."

"Not by my watch."

They walked side by side down the fourth floor of the Monadnock, shoe taps echoing down the deserted hallway. Miranda paused in front of her office and extracted the key.

Mrs. Hart's voice was low and drawling, gray like her cape, gray like the fog creeping through the Golden Gate.

"I'd advise you to invest in a decent Swiss timepiece. If you plan to stay in business, of course."

She drew out "business" in three syllables of sin, blue veins under her translucent, barely wrinkled skin drawn and defined like a road map, her white face immobile . . . except for the eyes.

Miranda flung open the door, flicked on the light, and tossed her evening bag on the desk. She turned sharply, back pressed against the edge of the desk, cream-colored outer wrap hanging open. The green of her dress glowed against her skin in the blinking pink light from the Top Hat Club across Market.

"Maybe you should save your worries for your son."

Eyes like dirty snow moved over Miranda's body. "My son. He's cost me enough as it is. Where's the jade?"

"In the safe. Where's my fee?"

The woman in gray shot a glance at the ancient Wells Fargo safe against the wall, one penciled eyebrow arched.

"The whisper of my name is good enough for every shop of significance in this city."

Miranda shook her head.

"I said cash, Mrs. Hart, and I meant it. Two hundred for me, and the rest for the payoff in Chinatown. Unless you want the morning papers to be full of the story."

The socialite glided soundlessly toward Miranda's desk. She crushed the remains of her cigarette in the Tower of the Sun ashtray, twisting the stub until the paper splintered and the tobacco made a small brown pile. A smile stretched her carefully lined lips. She opened her evening bag, withdrawing a smaller black wallet.

"Seven million dollars can buy things other than jewelry, Miss Corbie. Yes, I brought you your cash, but only because it amuses me and because you were, after all, successful. But please don't make the mistake of thinking I can be bled."

Miranda nodded at the desk. "Lay it out there. I'm not a blackmailer, Mrs. Hart. I merely want to finish the job I started and collect my fee. Your whispered name won't pay my rent, no matter how many necklaces it buys you . . . or Picassos."

The woman's hand froze in mid-air for a moment while she counted out eight C-notes, two twenties, a ten, a five and finally, a single dollar bill.

"Eight hundred fifty-six, you said. I want my necklace."

Miranda stared at her for a long second. "Eight hundred fifty-six dollars and seventy-five cents. I'm sure you didn't lose that much at roulette."

Car horn outside. A girl's high-pitched laughter. Miranda walked toward the safe and rotated the creaky dial, door swinging opening with a moan. She turned around, holding the heavy green jade in her hand.

There were three quarters on the desk next to the bills.

Miranda held the necklace, bracelet, and earrings out to the woman in gray, staring into liquid metal eyes. Mrs. Hart glanced away, finding refuge at the window.

"You'll want a receipt."

The socialite nodded, still examining various corners of the room, mouth in a well-bred curl. Miranda slid behind the desk and sank into the overlarge leather chair, twisting the Bakelite knob on the lamp. She found another key and opened the middle drawer, pulling out a receipt book with a crumpled piece of carbon paper sandwiched in between the leaves. She riffled through it, folded the cover back, and reached for an Esterbrook.

Miranda carefully recorded the amount received, divided into expenses and fee, and glanced at her watch before noting the date and hour. She looked up and held out the receipt.

"I'm returning your jade to you at 11:17 P.M., Mrs. Hart. I don't know what time it is in Switzerland."

The woman pinched the edge of the paper with the gloved fingertips, folded the paper carefully and returned it to her purse. Her voice was slightly higher in pitch.

"May I ask—what were you doing at the Picasso exhibit? Were you following me?"

Miranda stood up, eyebrows raised. "You read too many magazine stories. Private investigators don't usually shadow their own clients. I was there on my own time. I happen to like Picasso."

It was Mrs. Hart's turn to look surprised. "I wouldn't have thought a woman of your background . . ."

The first syllable was emphasized, with a long, drawn-out Lady Esther radio voice, Boston by way of Bakersfield. Miranda's lips curved dangerously.

"I'm a college graduate. I assume that's the *bahk*ground you mean."

The woman in gray murmured: "Yes, of course . . . I merely thought . . ."

Miranda stepped sideways out from behind the desk and faced the socialite directly.

"Since you offered me advice, I'll return the favor. Number one, get Randolph off the juice before it's too late. It may already be too late, but seven million pieces of sugar can buy a lot of doctors. Number two, lay off the senator. Maybe you think you're being discreet, but two stoolies offered me the information for a fiver and a pint of rye. You're cheap news, Mrs. Hart."

The ice was cracking, a sharp high *tang* as the liquid steel eyes melted in panic and the blue map on her face suddenly led back to boardinghouses and boiled potatoes. The eyes darted around the room, searching the office, looking for her husband, looking for the flashbulbs and the inevitable fatal trip to Reno. Miranda almost felt sorry for her.

"Number three. You need a new escort. Edmund Whittaker's a washout. I saw him with you tonight, and it's no good, he's too well known to act as a front for you. Where's the husband—New York?"

The woman took a few seconds to resolidify. She placed a gloved hand on the edge of Miranda's desk, then curled her fingers into a fist and straightened her spine. Her eyes were back to the color of coal and coke.

"How—how dare you? What do you know of Edmund? He's a fine man, an architect, and a good friend. He'd never—*never*—stoop to . . ." Her head made a sweeping, circular motion, encompassing all of Miranda and the office. She held her hand up to her neck as if she were choking.

Miranda opened her purse and plucked a cigarette out of her gold case, lighting it quickly with the Ronson One-Touch on the desk. Her eyes lingered on the older woman's red-and-white face, the diamonds at her ears and throat. She blew a stream of smoke over Mrs. Hart's right shoulder.

"You're right for once. Whittaker prefers men to women. The problem, Mrs. Hart, is that your friends will eventually discover the charade. So will your husband. And sooner or later—and my guess is sooner—someone's going to tell him about the senator."

She pointed her Chesterfield at the woman in gray. "You can take my advice or leave it . . . I don't give a damn either way. Consider it a bonus, Mrs. Hart. Noblesse oblige."

The socialite gathered her purse and raised the hood of the cape over her head, gray reaper in fabric by Irene. She glided quickly to Miranda's office door, staring at the black and gold letters:

MIRANDA CORBIE. PRIVATE INVESTIGATOR. CONFIDENTIAL-DISCREET.

Mrs. Hart swung her neck to the side, spoke to the air. "Thank you."

The pneumatic door swung slowly shut, as the taps on her gray French leather pumps rang like iron spikes against the marble floor. Miranda stood and smoked, watching the door click into place. Her hands were still shaking.

Seven

✳

The red and pink neon from the Top Hat stained the dark, closed office like a bloodstain.

Miranda sat at her desk and smoked, listening to the juke from downstairs, music floating up from Tascone's, "Love for Sale" and "Time on My Hands," and "Only Forever," fucking forever . . .

Reached for the Old Taylor, thought better of it. Flipped through the Chief tablet until she found a blank page, then grabbed the Esterbrook, fingers clutching it savagely, pen nib pressing down too hard.

She swore, slammed the tablet shut.

Mrs. Hart. James. Gonzales . . .

Her eyes closed, music transporting her, different time, different place, somewhere else.

Do I want to be with you as the years come and go . . .

Someone else.

✳

Early 1936.

"Mmmm . . . I like that. You smell like spring. Maybe you'll melt the snow outside . . . On second thought, I like it better here . . ."

Laughter, free and easy like the fluffy white flakes falling on Manhattan. "Don't you have a job, Mr. Hayes? Someone to question, some politician to grill?" She pushed him away, not hard, hands still on his chest.

He cupped her face in his hands, brushed her lips with his, let them drift to her neck, voice muffled by her skin.

"What is this stuff? Don't take it off. Everything else, sure, but leave the perfume."

This time she pushed him hard and he fell back over on the small bed, white shirt askew and not really white, top two buttons of his trousers undone, necktie flung on the well-worn fedora at the foot. He was grinning. He always seemed to be grinning.

Miranda caught her breath at the heat in his eyes, the white of his teeth, the strength of his lean body. The energy that wrapped around him, wrapped around them both, crackling like electricity. Her stomach was knotted and there was sweat in her palms. She took a deep breath to steady herself.

"Je Reviens." She nodded toward the minuscule vanity dresser in the corner. "The blue bottle that looks like a skyscraper. You were with me when I bought it, don't you remember? Macy's, day before yesterday."

John Hayes looked at her meditatively for a moment, then pulled himself up from the bed, stretched and yawned.

"Honey, I only remember what they smell like. They could be spritzed from a spittoon for all I know. ''Cause I only have eyes for you, dear . . .'"

He reached out a hand to pull her in again, giving the song his best Dick Powell impression. Miranda shuddered as his hand ran down her side, fingers brushing her breast. He bent over her, eyes dancing again, grin still in place, face only a few inches away from hers. She kept her eyes open while he kissed her, tongues probing each other, hands and fingers in hollows and curves, wanting to remember the scent of his skin and the way the warm yellow light hit his hair.

He pulled up and looked down at her, eyebrows knotted. "What's wrong, Randy?"

Randy. He'd announced it as her new name when they met, just four weeks ago. It was her name now, and she couldn't imagine any other. Couldn't imagine any other man.

Miranda reached a finger up to trace his face, from the mole on his temple to the small scar on his cheek to the blond-brown whiskers on his chin. She let her fingernail rest in the cleft.

Her voice came out as a whisper. "I love you, John Robert Hayes."

His face crinkled at the corners, grew somber. He held her off by the shoulders, stared down into the brown eyes. He'd called them "truth tellers" that first time, a deep brown flecked with green, eyes that never lied.

He spoke slowly. "Well, now, Miss Miranda Corbie. That's convenient. Because whether you smell like violets and orange blossoms or Ma Drexel's potato soup, I think I love you, too."

They stared at one another for a few seconds. Johnny looked away, uncharacteristically awkward. When he met her eyes again, business was in his face. The reporter was back.

He hurriedly tucked his shirt in and buttoned up his brown trousers.

"I've gotta go cover a political rally or the boss'll have my hide. How 'bout a late-night spaghetti dinner at Maggio's?"

"I'll wait up."

"Don't. I'll buzz you. You're still pounding the pavement for dutiful employment, honey, and you need to stay fresh."

John knotted his tie quickly and finished before Miranda could help him. He grinned at her and shoved the fedora on his head, slipped into a jacket and a thick wool coat.

"Now I'm ready to tackle Tammany and the weather. You I'll tackle later."

He bent forward and brushed her cheek with his lips. "What does Je Reviens mean, anyhow?"

Her eyes searched his. "It means 'I'll return.'"

The white teeth flashed again, cleft in his chin deepening. "You bet I will. *Je reviens*, baby!"

He laughed as he pulled open the thin wooden door and stepped into the boardinghouse hallway, the low, mellow rumble of his laughter filling the decaying Victorian house with light. Miranda stepped across the threshold and watched him bound down the stairway, his hand sliding on the worn, smooth wood of the banister. He threw up a hand, blew a kiss, and she held up hers as she watched him slide around the entrance door and head for 29th Street.

She stood at the top of the stairway for a few moments.

"*Je reviens e revenez à moi,*" she whispered.

*

Early August 1937. Spain.

Two large flies were mating in the small puddle of tobacco juice and Tempranillo. The tired official, sallow faced with purple bags under his eyes, raised a rolled-up Fascist poster of a lion, vivid yellow and reds faded to pastel, paper crushed and smeared with the guts and blood of previous insects.

He swung it heavily on the desk. The tobacco and Tempranillo sprayed tiny red dots on Miranda's skin.

His Spanish was slow and measured, and she nodded. He stamped her passport three times, desk trembling. More flies settled in a three-inch-wide crack of wood, chromatic prism wings covering dead comrades.

Miranda rose from the wooden stool. The official lifted the paper, brought it down again.

"*¡No pasarán!*"

He looked up at her, dead eyes searching hers, and tried to smile.

"Gracias." Miranda shook his hand, palm cold, and limped through the door. Her hand brushed the broken marble around the door frame.

She stood on the cratered street, watching a woman holding two children by the hand, a skinny dog scavenging for food. Distant roaring shook the aged stone.

Her eyes were dry, voice thick. "*Vaya con Dios, España.*"

*

October 1937. Paris.

The soldier was young and smelled like bay rum, hair gelled and slicked back like Tyrone Power in *Love Is News*. Skin impossibly white, eyes a pale blue, face a mixture of old school ties and proper scones and English breakfast tea.

His omelet was cold. He was staring at Miranda.

Morning moisture rose from the Seine, wafting across Metro railings and arrondissements, soupçon of danger, while the smell of strong coffee steamed from thick white cups perched on wrought-iron tables, waiters flying in and out, orders shouted to the back.

Businessmen ate alone, reading *Le Figaro* and the *International Herald Tribune*. Couples with clothes askew and covered in cigarette ash ordered brioche and *deux cafés*, eyes on nothing but each other. Inside, the sound of breaking dishes and French oaths accompanied Maurice Chevalier singing "Toi et Moi" on a scratchy Victrola.

The soldier cleared his throat. "I wanted you to have something to remember me by, Miranda. The last few weeks . . . you've been grand, really grand."

Être deux, c'est peu, pourtant, mon Dieu, ça suffit quand on s'aime . . .

Nuns led a group of noisy schoolchildren out of the church across the street. Two old women locked arms, blockading the sidewalk, stout black boots clodding against pavement stone.

Miranda sipped the coffee. "That wasn't necessary, Albert."

War of the Roses in his cheeks. "It is for me. To do for a chap—you're such a fine girl—and to, to . . . well, you've given me back my courage. Let the Nazis come—we'll send them packing in time for cricket!"

A balding organ grinder with bright blue eyes ambled toward them, mountain scene on the organ box faded, alpine promise of paradise half peeled away. He started to sing "Les Amants de Paris," his voice a likable croak, drowning out the radio.

Mon couplet s'est perdu sur les bords d'un jardin. On ne me l'a jamais rendu . . .

Miranda closed her eyes and opened them again to look at Albert. Face still round with baby fat, body hard from handling guns and planes.

"You're an officer and a gentleman, Albert. You've got plenty of courage. You're going to need it. We all need it."

She drained the rest of the coffee and set the cup down with a clatter. Opened her purse, searching for a pack of Gitanes.

Albert plucked a few of the coins off the table and turned toward the organ grinder.

"Here you are, old man. *Merci* for the *chansons*."

The musician's face showed confusion, staring at the naïve young soldier in love and the implacable, beautiful young woman, so cold, so frozen. Miranda avoided his eyes and lit the brown cigarette before Albert could extend a lighter. The organ grinder spoke softly, still staring at Miranda.

"*Merci, Monsieur. Et vous rappelez, mes enfants. 'Il n'y a qu'un bonheur dans la vie, c'est d'aimer et d'être aimé.'*" He nodded several times in emphasis, then shrugged with both shoulders and turned his mouth downward, drifting to the next café.

Albert looked eagerly across the table to Miranda. "What did he say? I'm afraid my French is rather limited, and they speak so fast, don't they?"

She inhaled the Gitane, sending a stream of blue smoke to drift through the wide street and the chestnut trees. Her voice was even.

"'The only joy in life is to love and be loved.'"

Albert tried to find her eyes. Then he awkwardly bent down to pick up the package and placed it in front of her. The wrapping was green with pale tan stripes, tied with a green silk ribbon.

"I hope this will help you remember me when you get to New York."

"I won't be in New York for long."

"Then where will you go? I feel responsible for you, Miranda, and I—"

"Don't." The word exploded, her voice rising. "Don't you goddamn ever feel responsible for me."

She crushed out the cigarette and reached for another. Her hands were shaking.

Albert slowly withdrew a military-issue lighter, his face whiter than usual. He lit the Gitane and Miranda inhaled, watching the red tip burn through the tobacco.

"I don't know where I'll end up. Maybe Chicago or Baltimore. Maybe back to San Francisco. Le Havre tomorrow, New York by the 24th, if the *Georgic*'s on schedule, and then who knows?"

She raised her eyes to his. "Forget about me. Go home and complete your assignment and enjoy what's left of the world, drink your goddamn tea and ride your goddamn polo ponies and play your fucking cricket. Do it while you can, take your furlough, take your time. Meet some nice English girl in lace and lavender, the kind with white skin and pink in her cheeks and a bun at the nape of her neck who knows all the right words and the right way to say them. Who you can bring home to meet your grandmother in Lambeth. Who's not me."

She glanced at her wristwatch. "I've got to go."

Albert reached for her wrist and held it. "At least open the package."

They looked at each other, Miranda's face unchanged, the young soldier's red and white with new lines around his lips. She slowly slipped out of his grip and used a fingernail to pry open the top of the wrapping, careful to keep it intact.

He watched her, voice hoarse. "You never told me about what happened. In Spain, I mean. And, I'm ashamed to say, I never pursued it. I knew you weren't—I mean, I knew you were a lady. And it was enough for me that you were willing to—well—I mean, I mean a fellow can be damned selfish, and I have been, Miranda, and now—now I'm not sure I'll ever know. About Spain. About what happened. About—you."

Miranda slid off the last of the wrapping paper to reveal a box with the Guerlain perfume logo and address on the Rue St. Honor. She opened the lid and removed a squat crystal bottle with radiating lines and a gold, circular center inscribing "Vol de Nuit."

Albert spoke softly. "It reminded me of you. 'Night Flight.' For the last week, I've been afraid you'd leave me in the middle of the night and I'd never see you again."

She replaced the bottle in the box and gathered the wrapping paper around it. Tied it carefully with the ribbon. She craned her neck backward, staring briefly at the blue and white and pink sky, watching the blue smoke of her cigarette dance and blend with the rooftop chimneys and yellow stone.

She crushed the Gitane in the glass ashtray. Her eyes came back to meet his. They lingered for a moment before she stood up to go, clutching her purse with one hand and the box in the other.

"Thanks, Albert. You're a swell guy. Most soldiers would have figured the steak dinners were enough, but you Brits are real gentlemen, through and through. Now do me a favor and take your broken English china heart somewhere else. Don't try to wait outside my hotel room, don't follow me to the train station, don't camp out in Le Havre. You're a soldier, goddamn it, and you need to grow up and grow up fast."

His face remained stoic and withstood the assault. He rose slowly from the table, stood at attention. Wouldn't let go of her eyes.

"I'll never forget you, Miranda Corbie. No matter what you say. No matter where you go. I'll never forget you."

She turned abruptly and stumbled through the black iron gate, heading for the hotel, not looking back.

The scent of oakmoss and vanilla rose from the Guerlain box.

*

The clock read 12:37 A.M. Boswell Sisters on the Tascone jukebox, singing "My Future Just Passed."

Life can't be that way, to wake me then break me . . .

She rubbed the stick out in the ashtray over Mrs. Hart's little pile of ashes and tobacco. Smell of vanilla, iris, and sweat rose from the green dress, mingled with nicotine and a lingering odor of bourbon.

The cab ride home was short and unmemorable, elevator at the Drake-Hopkins out of order yet again. She trudged upstairs and dragged herself across the threshold, shedding clothes, apartment smelling of lemon oil and cigarette smoke and stale milk.

Miranda felt in the closet for her red silk wrap, carefully peeled off the silk stockings. Unhooked her bra and pulled the wrap around her, shivering. Sat on the low vanity seat, facing the mirror, wallpaper dancing and singing in the background, all about "Cheek to Cheek" and "Thanks for the Memory" and "You Grow Sweeter as the Years Go By."

She shut her eyes, tried to shut the memory box, but the blue flowers kept nodding, voices rising in crescendo to a scream, forget me not, forget me not, forget me not . . .

Miranda opened a bottom drawer. Took out a blue glass bottle shaped like a skyscraper.

The tears came down, droplets on her cheeks timed to the forget-me-nots, night, always the night, no defense, no place to hide.

No place to forget.

Splash of perfume on her neck and breasts and behind her left ear, where he liked it.

Violet and bergamot, clove and hyacinth. Orange blossom sweet.

She looked in the mirror.

"*Je reviens,*" she whispered.

✳

The phone rang, interrupting a dream about bombs dropping on Chinatown. She woke up out of breath.

6:03 A.M.

She reached for the receiver, almost dropping it, and swore.

"Miranda Corbie."

"Miranda—it's Rick." His voice was somber.

Her stomach knotted. "What is it?"

"Call Meyer and get down to the Hall. A janitor found Mrs. Hart's body in the basement of the Monadnock an hour ago. She was murdered—strangled."

Miranda slowly placed the handle back on the phone cradle. She twisted the switch on the alabaster bed lamp and stared at the blue flowers, nodding against the pale pink.

Act Two

✳

Trail

Thou art thy mother's glass, and she in thee
Calls back the lovely April of her prime.
—William Shakespeare, Sonnet 3

Eight

*

The phone rang again. Miranda jumped, reached for the receiver.

"Darling girl, I hope I haven't awakened you . . ."

She let out a breath, leaning back on the padded blue satin comforter.

"When your attorney calls you at six o'clock in the morning, Meyer, it doesn't really matter if you're asleep. Rick just phoned. It's Mrs. Hart, right?"

He sounded surprised. "Mr. Sanders must be working the night beat. Either that or he has an internal alarm where you're concerned."

She sat up and reached for the nightstand drawer, hoping she wasn't out of Chesterfields. Life Savers were all well and good, Dr. Nielsen, but sometimes a lady just needs a fucking smoke.

"They find my business card and receipt copy?"

"Yes, my darling. That's why they want to talk to you posthaste."

She shook out a stick from the crumpled pack by her bed, found a match-book from the Moderne. "Let me guess. The jade wasn't on her."

His voice deepened. "No. There was no jewelry, no necklace on the poor lady. Just the cruel, ugly mark of a garrote."

Miranda stared at the smoke curling from the end of the cigarette, blue and gray. Gray lady, gray dress, now a gray-and-blue face, framed by a red-and-yellow smear.

Colors of death.

"Not a pleasant way to die."

"No, indeed. A brutal, barbaric murder." Her attorney sighed. "I understand she was the type of woman who attracted enemies—that she wasn't a particularly pleasant woman."

"Trust funds make their own enemies. She was my client, Meyer."

He spoke patiently. "I know that, my dear. There are a number of potential motives for the crime. A theme I will be playing ad infinitum for the police."

"You sound worried."

"Not worried, Miranda. Merely prepared."

She rubbed out the stick in the glass ashtray, "1939 World's Fair" still legibly gold through the pile of ash.

"Let me guess. They think I secured my fee and then had one of my 'underworld associates' murder Mrs. Hart and steal the jade."

He smoothed it out, voice like the silk against her skin. "Not 'they,' my darling. You have friends in the department, especially since you so successfully proved Mr. Duggan's innocence. That is why I am calling you and you were not awakened to the sound of boots at the door. I merely react to the possibility of hostilities from certain quarters."

"Collins doesn't have much power, but I suppose Johnson still hates my guts for not letting him play with the G-men. And God knows I'm not exactly a favorite with the D.A."

Miranda yawned, fist to her mouth. "All right. I'll answer a few questions, but only what's legally necessary. The case was confidential, Meyer, and the lady wanted it that way. She's still my goddamn client. I've still got to protect her interests."

"And I will be there to protect *your* interests, as always. Shall we meet, say, at seven-thirty? In front of the Hall of Justice?"

"Yeah. Thanks, Meyer."

She rang off and shuddered, thinking of the cold weight of Lois Hart's jade and how heavy it had felt in her hands.

✳

Quick, greasy breakfast at the Universal Café, sunny-side-up eggs and rye toast, coffee black, film on top swirling like a kaleidoscope.

Miranda's thick fingers wandered to her neck.

The pearl necklace was cold, but not as cold as Mrs. Hart.

A shrill stream of Chinese erupted from the short-order cook. He was gesticulating from behind the grill at a hobo who'd wandered in through the back alley door.

Tall, slim, unshaven, with a dented gray fedora, the bum took a step backward, still clutching an orange in his hand. The cook held up his egg flipper like a club, stomped with his left foot. The hobo stumbled again, braced against the inside of the door, and blended into the sun and shadows of Chinatown.

A woman with thick gray hair pulled back in a severe bun emerged from a backroom curtain and spoke sharply to the cook. She was dressed in black, skin like parchment, ancient aristocracy etched in her cheeks.

Miranda recognized one phrase, spoken with derision. One phrase, over and over.

Gweilo. Sei gweilo.

She'd heard it before, usually aimed at the men who were buying twelve-year-old girls around the corner on Ross, or sometimes at beat cops like Doyle, on the make and on the take, silk scarves and silken thighs, wife in a Sears and Roebuck calico dress with six kids screaming for supper.

Ghost. Damned ghost.

Cantonese for the bad white man, the kind the Cantonese in Chinatown knew best.

The older woman touched the arm of the cook, soothing him with a murmur, until he shrugged and turned toward the bacon smoking on the flat-top grill. Her eyes caught Miranda's, and she arched her thin, penciled brows before nodding back, then disappeared behind the faded orange curtain.

Miranda drained the coffee, opened her purse, and pushed thirty-five cents toward the napkin holder. Meyer was meeting her in five minutes. She didn't have time to figure out why the bum was wearing new Florsheim shoes and a bulge under his left arm.

Too many debts.

Too many ghosts.

*

Meyer was gazing up at the Romanesque window arches of the Hall of Justice, while young women strolled along the green with baby carriages and a group of sharpies idled near the damp grass, passing a cigarette back and forth. A yellow '32 Lincoln screamed down Washington Street, Glenn Miller and Ray Eberle blaring from the radio.

Are you just careless, as you seem to be . . .

He smiled when he saw Miranda, tapping his ebony cane on the cement.

"You look as lovely as ever, my dear. Perhaps a trifle undernourished. Shall I buy you breakfast after the meeting?"

She flicked the Chesterfield onto the sidewalk and rubbed it out with a navy pump. The morning sun was bright, glinting off the dirt of Kearny Street. Miranda held up her hand to shade her eyes.

"It's kind of you to offer, Meyer, but I've eaten."

"Something quick and cooked in bacon grease, no doubt. I was planning on a tête-à-tête at the St. Francis, Eggs Florentine, perhaps. I worry about your health, my dear, I truly do."

Her lips turned up in a wry smile. "Then you shouldn't have hired me last month."

His soft, fleshy face dimpled and he clapped her shoulder. "You are very brave. Brave and brilliant, and you helped save more than an innocent man. You and Mr. Sanders. How is he, by the way?"

Miranda raised an eyebrow. "Rick? He's fine. And by the way, the green dress and tennis suit fit perfectly. But don't hire me again, Meyer—it's too hard on the wardrobe."

Two uniforms were coming off duty and clunking down the Hall of Justice steps, one spitting tobacco on the sidewalk. She nodded toward the stairway across the street. "So who are we meeting with?"

"We're in luck. Our friend Inspector Fisher is handling the case."

"Then why the hell are you so worried? And don't tell me you aren't. Who is it? Johnson?"

Meyer drew a curve on the sidewalk with the tip of his cane. "Johnson is not a concern. He's a sycophant but harmless. I've been led to understand, however, that Captain O'Meara—"

"The pompous ass on the Fair squad?"

"The same. He is, of course, embarrassed and humiliated that you not only solved Pandora Blake's murder—which you were specifically asked not to investigate—"

"I wasn't asked. The bastards fired me."

He held up a hand. "I know, my dear. Let me finish. You also prevented a bomb from destroying the Federal Building and quite possibly killing several dignitaries in the process. Your success has made him feel foolish and has threatened his upcoming bid for assistant district attorney."

"That arrogant sonofabitch is even worse than Brady. Thinks he's king of Treasure Island."

Meyer continued patiently, "District Attorney Brady doesn't trust you, Miranda, and he can't control you, and therefore he would like you to disappear. O'Meara bears a grudge. What you may not know is that O'Meara was in charge of the Anti-Radical and Crime Prevention Bureau six years ago."

"The year of the Strike. So he was Brady's Gestapo chief."

Her attorney nodded. "They smashed the so-called Communist and Workers Schools. O'Meara was a hated figure on the docks. Brady desperately wanted Harry Bridges to hang from the yardarm."

"Bridges isn't the hero some people make him out to be. He's been railing against FDR and the New Deal since Stalin made goo-goo eyes at Hitler. So what the hell does all this have to do with me and Mrs. Hart?"

Meyer sighed. "My dear, you are a feminine gadfly, and they think they've found your Achilles' heel. O'Meara still has Brady's ear and is whispering—loudly—that you are a Communist. Your relationship with Miss Gallagher—"

"Is none of their fucking business! So what do they think? That I killed Mrs. Hart because she's a rich capitalist? I'd be out of clients without rich capitalists. Stupid, stupid bastards."

Miranda breathed in deeply, blinking her eyes at the sun and blue, cloudless sky, smell of seagulls and crab cocktails and sourdough bread floating in from the piers. She started to laugh.

"Darling girl, this is no laughing matter, I assure you—"

She shook her head. "No, Meyer. I assure *you*. Gonzales works for the Dies Committee and he'll vouch for me. Not only that, I've got—well, let's just say I've got an in with Uncle Sam at the moment." Her eyes glinted green as they met his. "This is penny-ante stuff. Don't worry about it. Let's go talk to Inspector Fisher."

Meyer's thick brows furrowed while he laid a hand on her arm. "I will worry, my dear. Especially if you don't tell me about these dangerous new waters into which you are dipping your charming toes. You know as well as I do that politics are never petty."

She gazed across the street at the Hall of Justice, pigeons cooing on the warm stone, two more uniforms clomping down the stairs and headed for the Last Chance Saloon.

"Where angels fear to tread, Meyer. Let's go."

*

The wooden chair was soft and worn from years of sitting, pleading, crying, tears flowing like wine and gin and sin the night before. Men and women, drunk and stumbling, some staring at the wall, watching the clock, eyes vacant, others memorizing the details of the detective's face, figuring the lay for the mouthpiece, looking for the pressure point, the soft spot, getting ready for the day in court. Other men, in black and gray fedoras with cigarette ash on cheap checkered lapels, sat with fear in their eyes, cue chalk on their fingers, wondering about a bump-off . . . whether the boys would believe them, or whether they should squeal like a rat and catch the next freight out to Philly.

Miranda traced a finger along the desk, wooden mate to the ancient chair. Old and scarred, the deep grooves still smelling like Prohibition hooch, burn marks from one too many Fatimas and one too many crooks.

"I've told you what I can, Inspector. Mrs. Hart didn't call the police, didn't call her insurance company. She wanted it kept quiet and handled fast, and she came to me and I delivered. Her reasons were her own. Though a man of your resources should be able to figure them out."

Miranda crossed her legs, grinning at the short well-built cop. He ran a squat hand through curly salt-and-pepper hair.

"I admire your principles as a private op, but if you at least let us know where you recovered the necklace . . ."

She shook her head. "Confidentiality was built into the terms of the hire." She glanced at Meyer, who was perched on the edge of his seat, looking fat and uncomfortable. "I didn't have time to pick up the contract, but it's at the office."

Fisher sighed, rocking back in his chair until it squeaked. "Look, Miranda. Maybe this is a snatch-and-grab. If it is, it would make all of our lives a hell of a lot easier. But Old Man Hart is putting pressure on us from the top down . . . and there's already enough there to blow the whole department sky-high. Listen to your lawyer. Give us something, anything I can take upstairs. Help me out here."

Miranda tapped her cigarette in the chipped milk-glass tray on his desk. Took a breath and raised her face to his.

"You delivered for me on the Pandora Blake case. And you're a good cop. Where would you expect to buy a jade necklace in San Francisco?"

He opened his eyes wide. "OK. That helps. And look—in the meantime, I'm sorry, but I'm supposed to officially tell you not to leave town, as we may have more questions and we'll want a copy of your contract with Mrs. Hart." He shifted his gaze to Meyer before the lawyer could interrupt. "She's not being charged with anything."

Her attorney's voice was smooth. "I'd have her out in five minutes. You have nothing and you know it."

Meyer braced himself on his cane and stood up from the chair. "If you are, indeed, looking for a motive outside of robbery, read the society column, Inspector. There is a world of motives awaiting you." He gestured with his head toward Miranda. "Come, my dear."

She rose, looking down at the burly cop.

"I'm telling you right now, Inspector—and you can tell Brady and anybody else who wants to know—I'm on a case that may require me to go out of town. So don't get in my way."

Fisher studied her solemnly. The last month had aged him, but he still smelled like Ivory soap. A grin spread across his face and he started to chuckle.

"You are a pip, Miranda. One hell of a pip."

Nine

*

The Key train started to move, orange and silver livery still new, smell of fresh-roasted coffee on the wind from Hills Bros. Miranda blew a stream of smoke against the window, watching it form eddies and whorls like the choppy gray water across the Bay.

She'd have to transfer at Adeline, but better that than a ten-minute wait on an Interurban to take her straight to Shattuck.

Straight to her father. Straight to hell.

Miranda fidgeted with the large flat-sheened navy buttons on her jacket. Steel piers of the Bay Bridge clicked by, *tick tock, tick tock, tick tock . . .*

Treasure Island flashed into view, gleaming in a spotlight of sun. Parking lot nearly full, good attendance for a Wednesday. Magic City, four hundred acres of sand to bury your head in. Forget France, forget Germany, forget Japan, just watch Stella breathe, brothers, she'll give you a real rise . . .

The island disappeared, swallowed by the green of Yerba Buena.

Truth is, she missed it.

Missed Shorty and the Singer Midgets from last year, missed the magic lights and magic carpet, the high school bands and the quick-sketch artists and the Maxwell House Coffee Tower and the ridiculous Elephant Trains. Missed the shouts of barkers and the smell of Threlkeld's Scones and early morning steam from a scorching cup of coffee. Missed Sally. Missed the girls.

She thought of Lucinda, still recovering in Dante's Sanitarium, private hospital, where Phyllis Winters roamed the halls, shrinking in corners from men with brutal hands, while her mother the socialite threw a garden party in Alameda.

She'd paid for a week at Dante's, what she could afford to help Lucinda. Money couldn't help Phyllis.

Like the girls in Spain, the ones with dried blood on their thighs and buttocks, crouching in fields plowed with shells. Afterward, cleaned up by a nun or a Red Cross nurse, by a village woman who recognized the pain and had daughters of her own.

Dead eyes, dead girls, lungs in and out, heart still beating.

Alive in name only.

Miranda blinked, brown-green eyes focused on the blurred outline of Angel Island and Alcatraz.

No time to think about Spain, about Phyllis Winters. It was a little over four months since Eddie Takahashi's murder, four months since she'd killed Martini, and only a few weeks since she'd run in the Napa woods, dogs baying, breath coming out in stabs, waiting for the men in white suits.

Waiting to kill herself.

She arched her neck, rubbing it with her right hand, and sat up against the seat, straightening her hat.

Twenty-five hundred dollars lay crisp and cool in her rusty Wells Fargo safe, payment for chasing a Nazi spy. Mrs. Hart lay colder on a slab in the morgue, dead client, dead victim, the priceless jade, funereal green, missing once again and presumably the motive.

And somewhere in England, last bulwark against the Dark Ages, was Catherine Corbie . . . or at least a woman who knew enough about her to send a message.

Miranda carefully took the photo postcard of Westminster Abbey out of her purse and read it again:

Would like to meet you. Your loving mother.

The office was in a dark corner of Wheeler, down a long hall and tucked under a stairway. A small black hole, just like the ones Hatchett threw her in, attic or basement, cupboard or closet. Now he had one of his very own.

She raised her hand to knock at the door. Faded blue ink, handwriting precise:

DR. JOSEPH HENRY HARPER, ASSOCIATE PROFESSOR OF ENGLISH LITERATURE.

Still not full professor. Nights too full of something else, liquid gold, magic elixir, making mediocre teachers into poets and cowards into men.

She knocked.

A voice. Still melodious, though not as mellifluous as when it was primed with Scotch.

"Come in."

Miranda slid through the door and quickly shut it behind her. The thin, narrow-shouldered man with stretched and freckled skin sat behind an antique desk, mahogany polished from jackets with elbow patches and reams of student papers. He stared up at her, mouth slightly open, freckles fading into white, poised to scratch a comment on a page.

Greasy hair, parted on the left. Oiled, as always, to hide the flakes of dandruff. He blinked large brown eyes, as if sensory testimony were untrustworthy and indiscriminate, and carefully placed the fountain pen in a holder.

"What—what are you doing here? I told you years ago—"

"Ad infinitum et nauseam. Don't worry, Pops. I won't stay long."

She threw herself in a chair, dark wood smelling of lemon oil. Opened her purse and pulled out a hundred-dollar bill. Sat back and crossed her legs, holding his eyes, and rubbed the C-note between her thumb and forefinger.

"This should get you three days and a shot of B from Nielsen."

His eyes darted back and forth between the bill and her face. "You dare come here—"

"I dared. I'm here. I called ahead and spoke to the department secretary to make sure I'd find you. I don't have the time to hit every clip joint on Telegraph Avenue."

They stared at each other a for a few minutes, her father's breath uneven, light carpet of black and white stubbling his chin. Miranda's hand started to tremble. She set the money on the desk, smoothing it out flat with her palm.

"What do you want?"

She nodded. "That's more like it. 'If it were done, when 'tis done, then 'twere well it were done quickly.'"

"I see you remember your Shakespeare."

"Surprisingly, yes. Shakespeare, Tennyson, Coleridge, Blake, Keats . . . I even majored in English. Not that I expect you to recall that sad little fact."

He drummed his fingers on the desk and closed his eyes. "'How sharper than a serpent's tooth . . .'"

"Christ, don't you know anything but Lear? No wonder they haven't made you full professor."

He moved a stack of papers to his left, making sure the edges were neat and aligned. Sat back in the desk chair, eyes pink around the rims, thin lips pinched tight.

"You are the reason I haven't received my promotion. You—and your life, such as it is—have cost me dearly. Such was my sacrifice, such was my shame, such was—"

She recited it singsong. "'O, I have lost my reputation! I have lost the immortal part of myself, and what remains is bestial.'"

Miranda shook her head. "Don't talk to me about shame, old man. You'll lose the battle. Not when you cross the Bay once or twice a year and hit me up to pay for your bar tab and a few days of dry living at Nielsen's country clinic. Or maybe you really believe it. Maybe you need a real doctor, the kind that'll give you a private room and a barred window. I've met a few. I'd be happy to introduce you."

He opened his mouth, shut it again. Pulled a yellowed handkerchief from his pocket, wiped his forehead. Veins mapped his nose, spit was starting to fleck his lips. Retreat, withdrawal, and the stench of fear.

Round one, thought Miranda.

She stroked the bill on the desk.

"I don't give a damn if you use it to pay for a bender and an armful from Nielsen or buy a new *Oxford Classical Dictionary*. I just want information."

He picked up the fountain pen. "What sort of information?"

"Answers. You used up your annual tithe back in February, so I figured a C-note would make us even. I always pay my way, remember?"

He sat up in the chair, eyes aimed at the wall of books, English, Greek, and Latin, lining the tiny office, warm smell of decaying leaves as thick as the dust on the shelves. Voice dripped with acid, last attempt to rally.

"What knowledge, pray, might I possess? Surely, I cannot have any information in common with the sordid habitués of your office, the pool room hustlers and the jaded faded women of no virtue, your sisters in sin. In fact, I fail to see the purpose of your presence here . . . unless it was to flaunt your filthy lucre and taunt me with my own greatest mistake. That you have achieved, certainly."

Miranda slowly clapped her hands, not taking her eyes from his face.

"Bravo, Pops. John Barrymore by way of Henry Irving. Your eloquence is still impressive, especially for a lush. But we're not playing Lear or Macbeth or Othello, so save it for your class, for the freshmen who don't know the difference between a don and a drunkard. You want a hundred dollars or not?"

His eyes kept drifting to the C-note and finally rested there.

Round two.

His voice was thick, heavier, and his body seemed to shrink. "What do you want to know?"

Miranda placed both palms flat on the bill and searched his face.

"Why did my mother leave and where did she go?"

He twisted like a newborn rodent in a torn-paper nest, the starched, old-fashioned collars of his shirt beginning to wilt with perspiration.

"I told you a long time ago. She died."

"You're a fucking liar. She's alive."

He blinked at her. "I've answered your question. Your mother, such as she was, is dead." He made a gesture with his hand. "*'Dry up in her the organs of increase . . .'*"

She stood up and strode around the desk, standing over him until she was close enough to smell stale rye and the sickeningly sweet odor of unwashed skin.

"Listen, old man. I've taken all I'm ever taking from you. I've bought you your bottles and I've paid for Nielsen to keep blood in your fucking veins. I even buried Hatchett, my oh so devoted nurse. And guess what, Pops? I'm what stands between you and the goddamn gutter, another bum drowning in piss and shit and rye in front of a two-bit hooch house, mourned by no one, including the hallowed halls of hell you've made out of this place. Don't lie to me. Catherine Corbie may be dead to you but she's alive, goddamn it, and you're going to tell me what you know."

Panic filled his eyes, large and brown, flat with no depth. She unclenched her fists and took a few steps backward, unsteady, sinking into the wooden seat, breath hard and uneven. He lay propped in his chair, shrunken and old and so much smaller than she remembered. His eyes were unfocused, still aimed at the desk and the hundred-dollar bill.

She said it slowly. "I received a postcard from England. From a woman who says she's my mother."

He groped for a key in the small desk drawer and unlocked the drawer below. Lifted out a bottle of Mount Vernon straight rye whiskey, three-fifths gone. Took a long swig from the bottle, then wiped his mouth with the back of his hand and raised his face to hers.

"I did what I could. How do you think it felt, to be stained with illegitimacy? The Harpers are an old family, distinguished, and in a moment of fear I yielded to—to your mother—and you were the price I paid. She wouldn't—so no choice—though, yes, I did have a choice, Daughter."

He spat the word suddenly, spray flying across the desk. "I honored you, gave you a name you've since rejected, gave you a home. No orphanage, not even for the bastard girl, no, you were fed and clothed and sheltered, not left on an Attic slope like the Greeks would have done. I taught you, showed you the immortality of words, the light of poetry, the only God I've ever known, and still you turned, as worms always will, reverting to your natural state of indecency. Her indecency."

He finished up the bottle in one long pull. Cradled it in his right hand, close to his chest.

"Your mother left me. Became an 'actress,' they said. Just another name for whore. She was dead to me then, dead and buried. Sins of the mother, sins of the daughter." He shook his head. "'*To keep thee from the evil woman*' . . . would that I had heeded that proverb. But I was young."

Miranda leaned forward, voice sharp. "Where did she go?"

He nodded in a rhythm, still cradling the bottle. "She took you with her. Then a note came. She had to leave the country, suddenly, quietly. Would I take you in? And you were a wee child, like the mouse Burns turned over in his plow, big dark brown eyes, more like mine than hers, and I thought—foolishly, of course—that I could mold you, save you. Make you into someone to be proud of. I tried, God knows I tried, teaching you poetry, even taking you to New York, but it did no good. You're a crooked woman, Miranda. You are your mother's daughter."

She stared at him, controlling her breathing, while he rocked his chair back and forth, his face turned toward the small, dusty window.

"You never married her." Statement, not question.

He raised an eyebrow. "There could never be a question of marriage. I wouldn't sully the names of my ancestors by marrying an Irish whore. But I would have helped her. We could have grown a better life together."

"'*And I watered it in fears, night and morning with my tears.*' I know what kind of life you grow, old man."

"You owe me yours, inconsequential and debased as it is."

Her voice was a rasp. "Any debt I've paid and repaid and I've got the scars to prove it. Tell me where she went and why she left!"

He straightened up in the chair and for the first time his lips turned upward in a ghost of a smile.

"I imagine she returned to Ireland. As for reasons why, they were vague, but I remember holding the distinct impression that she had killed a man."

Ten

*

Miranda froze in position, weight thrust forward on her hands, tense and rigid on his desk.

Rick had been right. Her mother the killer, fleeing from justice, fleeing San Francisco.

Abandoning Miranda.

She fell back in the chair and fumbled with her purse. Took out a Chesterfield, lit it with a shaking hand.

Round three went to her father.

She inhaled deeply, pushed a stream of smoke out the side of her mouth. A small, prim smile, more a grimace, caught at the edges of his lips as he watched her.

"There are reasons to kill a man. Was it self-defense?"

He folded his arms against his chest and around the empty bottle of rye. Shrugged. "I have no idea. She was frightened of the law, as the ignorant often are. Not possessing an understanding or appreciation of legality or justice, I assume her people felt the animal urge to run and smuggled her out of the country."

"Ever hear from her?"

"She had some sort of relations in San Francisco to whom she owed her escape, as I said, but I was never contacted by anyone, before or afterward."

"Why didn't you tell me this before?"

He raised both eyebrows. "I've always sought to protect you, Miranda. To better you. Knowing your mother was a murderess would have diminished any small chance you had at a decent life. As it was, I needn't have been so particular."

Protection. No fucking protection from his friends, the stoolies and the drinkers, the respectable teachers from the primary schools, bare legs too long for the thin dress, little girl too old to be bounced on a lap, men with funny shudders and wet spots on their trousers, fingers exploring places they didn't belong . . .

She inhaled the Chesterfield, watching the ember burn. Counted one Mississippi, two Mississippi, like she had when she was eight or nine, and he'd take off his belt after a long night at Clancey's, Hatchett holding the strap in reserve.

She stood up suddenly and shoved the bill forward on the desk with two fingers. "Here. If you kept anything in writing from my mother—or anything at all—send it to me. Postage due or COD. Not that I expect you to have saved any records of your 'greatest failure.'"

Miranda crossed to the door, hand on the doorknob, and hesitated. Turned around for a moment. He'd picked up the C-note and was holding it in one hand, face lost in alcoholic dreams.

"One more thing, '*poor, infirm, weak, and despised old man. Striving to better, oft we mar what's well.*' Remember that the next time you teach *Lear*."

She shut the door behind her softly and lay against the wall in the hallway, breath shallow, eyes closed.

*

Classes were letting out, and Miranda sandwiched herself between a glass case with woodcut illustrations from *Leaves of Grass* and the door of another office. She propped herself up with the wall, fighting to keep her stomach from heaving.

O Captain! My Captain, our fearful trip is done . . .

The old man still knew how to defend his thesis. Hyperbole-cloak, metaphor-mask, armed with irony, teeth and fang, teeth and fang, step right up, ladies and gents, it's the academic arena . . . thumbs up or thumbs down, the gladiator won't fall on her sword . . .

The ship has weather'd every rack, the prize we sought is won . . .

But what he'd told her sounded like truth, a faded memory, sepia-toned, photograph edges ragged and worn. Her mother, Catherine Corbie, the woman whose name she borrowed for her own, a dim figure backlit with the aureole of childhood and the song of an Irish harp, dark eyes, dark hair, swallowed up by dark deeds . . . Catherine Corbie had killed a man.

Out of the cradle endlessly rocking . . .

And left. Left Miranda.

Left Miranda to the ministrations of Professor Harper and his Hatchett woman, old before her time, old before time itself. Old woman wreathed in cruelty, wrinkled by indifference, her only life spark ignited by punishing the little girl who looked at her with eyes too old and too young . . .

I see the sleeping babe, nestling the breast of its mother . . .

Goddamn Whitman, I Sing the Body Electric but no Song of Myself.

Miranda took a deep breath, hands on knees, and pushed herself upright.

Pimply-faced kids rushed by in a hurry, clutching armfuls of books, while tall blond boys in letter sweaters flirted with girls in full skirts and smooth hair, voices low and modulated. Conversation about varsity and junior varsity, what Professor Englehart would assign for tonight, and whether Delta Sigma Phi was really going to hold a dance with Kappa Kappa Gamma.

She moved away from the light yellow wall, blending in with the sea of blue and gold. Pinched the end of the Chesterfield and dropped it in a trash can placed crookedly in front of an office three doors down. Pushed her way through the large door, breathing fresh-mown grass and redwood trees.

Miranda opened her purse and took out two Butter Rum Life Savers with shaking hands. Studied the map she'd bought at the station.

The College of Chemistry held faculty offices in the ten-year-old Life Sciences Building, west of the library and between Boalt and California Hall.

She watched a white, puffy morning cloud soar over blue sky and Sather Tower, the chattering of college students and the worn, soft clod of professors rising from the Faculty Glade, university noises carried by the wind.

Blowing away pain, blowing away memory.

*

The Campanile was chiming ten-thirty when she found the department office. She smoothed on a pair of white gloves and deftly removed the hat, attaching a veil she'd tucked inside the crown. Knocked on the door, *rat-tat-tat-TAT.*

Muffled "Come in" response from a wheezy tenor with a cough.

The voice belonged to a red-haired man of slight build and slighter demeanor, thin hands poised above a Remington typewriter, a black telephone at his left. He was dwarfed by black Bakelite trays filled with letters and forms on an adjoining desk to his left, and the threat of large, looming bookcases falling on him from the front. Everything about him read academic department secretary, bullied, harassed, and underpaid.

Miranda gave him a smile, shifted her weight. His freckles paled.

"May I help you, Miss?"

"I'm Jean Rogers. Did you get my phone message?"

His mouth opened several times before he scrambled through a pile of yellow phone slips, his fingers slipping through the pad next to the phone, his chair threatening to topple over from the violent spins back and forth. She took a step closer.

"I'm terribly sorry to put you to this trouble—you see, I phoned yesterday—I'm writing an article for the *American Scholar*—the Phi Beta Kappa magazine—and I was hoping you'd . . . oh, dear, I am so very sorry."

One of the Bakelite trays fell on top of the Remington and dislodged the carriage, bell ringing like a fire alarm. Miranda turned her back tactfully and looked around.

The room was dark, heavy, and rectangular. Eight-foot oak bookcases and the secretary's desk set choked off any air and space. Another door with gold painted letters read DR. RICHARD HEINSICKER, DEAN, COLLEGE OF CHEMISTRY.

The outer door opened with a loud thump. She turned to face a beefy middle-aged man in a gray suit and bowler, eyes small, bright, and close together. He smiled, teeth unnaturally white.

The secretary's voice warbled. "Dr. Heinsicker, this is—this is Jean Rogers from Phi Beta Kappa. She's writing an article for the *American Scholar*."

Miranda held out her hand, wide smile, glad she'd remembered the gloves. "I left a message yesterday. I'm hoping to write an article about some of your college's exciting research—and the exciting men behind it."

Heinsicker's eyes glowed, jovial grin. Perfect model of a Tammany Hall politician, minus the cigar.

"Welcome to the University of California, Miss Rogers. First time here?"

She shook her head. "No, not at all. But about that article, Dr. Heinsicker—"

He placed a large, fatherly hand on her arm. "It would be a tremendous honor, of course, but you understand that many of our research experiments are classified. Government secrets, just like you see in the pictures. But come into my office—we'll discuss it there."

He twisted the knob and pushed open the heavy door, calling over his back to the secretary: "Hold all calls for fifteen minutes, Wilbur."

Miranda settled in a large wooden chair with a black leather seat. An oil landscape—eighteenth-century French, from the style—sat on the wall above, and a Belgian tapestry hung next to an antique bookcase.

Opulent, surprisingly so.

The door swung shut, and Heinsicker slid behind his imposing desk with unexpected agility.

She crossed her legs. He noticed.

"Now, then, Miss Rogers—"

"Call me Jean."

He dimpled. "Jean. What is the scope of your article, and when will it see print?"

She sat back, her ankle slightly bouncing. "Well, Dr. Heinsicker—"

"Please. Call me Richard."

"A pleasure, I'm sure. As I was saying—Richard—our editor has been reading so much about Berkeley—the 'neutron ray' and how it might help conquer cancer, the successful treatment of leprosy, of course the famous cyclotron—and your local chapter of Phi Beta Kappa is highly active—so he suggested a story about the departments and scientists behind these tremendous achievements. Nothing top secret is necessary, I assure you."

She gave her laugh a merry tinkle, hands folded in her lap. Watched him through the veil and fought the urge for a cigarette.

Heinsicker withdrew a wooden box from his desk and removed a cigar, gesticulating with it toward Miranda. "Do you mind?"

"Not at all."

He lit it with a Strikalite in the shape of a Scottish terrier, puffed once or twice, and sat back with another smile. Clouds of smoke rose in an arabesque. Smelled like chocolate and Spanish cedar. Quality tobacco.

"I'm curious, Jean. The achievements you mention—the cyclotron is the physics department, and so is the neutron ray. Evans in Experimental Biology is responsible for many of the medical advances . . . leprosy, vitamin E. Even sex hormones."

His grin grew broader, and Miranda summoned a blush.

"Why chemistry? Not that we're not flattered, of course, but I'm wondering how you stumbled on us."

She uncrossed her legs and leaned forward, all bluestocking earnest in an I. Magnin skirt.

"Dr. Heinsicker—Richard—everyone knows that chemistry is the mother of all other science . . . advances in biology and physics are, in a broad sense, yours as well. But what we were hoping for, really, is the story of the men who toil and teach, who contribute so much to our current way of life and still find the time to instill the love of learning and research in the next generation of scholar. What personal sacrifices have they endured? What are their dreams, their interests, their hobbies?"

She pointed to the landscape above his head. "Take this beautiful painting, for example. So many members of the public—even members of Phi Beta Kappa—share the mistaken notion that a scientist is humorless and inhuman. What we're looking for is human drama, the story of the man behind the lab coat."

The man behind the desk was obviously enjoying the view. He puffed the cigar again and finally rubbed it out in a black-and-white marble tray. Cleared his throat.

"Well, I thank you, young lady. This has the making of a truly worthwhile article, and I wouldn't stand in your way. I can't give you clearance on any government projects, you understand, but you can ask all the human interest questions you'd like. I do think it would be best to focus on just three or four faculty—but there, I'm lecturing again." He leaned forward, eyes drifting down to her legs. "How and when would you like to start?"

"May I see a list of your faculty? I know there were a few professors our editor was particularly keen on me interviewing. I'd like to save you, Richard, for last."

She chased it with one of her kilowatt smiles. Heinsicker's teeth gleamed.

"That would be lovely, my dear. I've a meeting to attend, but Wilbur will give you a list. Three or four should be sufficient, don't you think? As for my painting, I'm sure you recognize the scene: Mercury slaying Argus, Hera's watchman. Early eighteenth century, Nicolas Bertin."

The grin was ferocious as he led her by the elbow out of the office, gray derby in his other hand. He nodded at Wilbur. "Give Miss Rogers the list of our faculty and any assistance you can, Wilbur. Good-bye, my dear."

"Good-bye, Dr. Heinsicker. And thank you." She watched as the door closed behind him.

"Here you are, Miss Rogers." The words came in a rush as the secretary handed her a sheet of mimeographed paper. "Sorry for not remembering your call earlier, and thank you for not telling Dr. Heinsicker—"

"Our secret, Wilbur." She looked up, holding his watery blue eyes.

"I think an office tells you so much about a person—and I'd prefer to see their surroundings before I actually meet the professors. I'll call you later to set up the interviews." She pointed a gloved finger at "Jasper, Huntington."

"May I see Dr. Jasper's office? I see he's not teaching today, and I understand he's an art connoisseur . . . though that doesn't seem quite as unusual after meeting Dr. Heinsicker."

Wilbur snorted. "Dr. Heinsicker enjoys the finer things in life, Miss Rogers, but Dr. Jasper is the real expert." His eyes grew big and he stared up at her in panic, Adam's apple bobbing. "Please don't think I intend any disrespect by that remark. Dr. Heinsicker is a great man." He scrambled nervously for keys in a drawer and stood up, still twitching. "I'll take you to Dr. Jasper's office now, Miss."

*

Light admitted from a window on the side, like her father's office, but blinds were shut tight. Wilbur flicked the wall switch.

Chrome-and-glass desk, room sleek and streamlined. No oak. Spare, rectangular metal lamp, red Bakelite letter opener and the latest in fountain pens waiting for Jasper to sit in the wide Buck Rogers–looking aluminum chair and write a formula or an art review on the shimmering surface. No photo frames, no ashtrays.

Paintings lined the dun-colored walls in copper frames and mirrored metal. Books and journals filled spare blond wood shelves interspersed with small abstract sculptures in bronze and marble. A couple of hand-blown beakers, red and orange like Venetian glass, the only visual ode to his profession . . . and the money that paid for the room.

Miranda lifted up her veil and quickly removed a notepad and pencil from her purse. Wilbur cleared his throat.

"See what I mean, Miss Rogers? Dr. Jasper could be one of those modern art critics for the newspapers if he wanted to. You won't see much of the old-fashioned around his office, no sirree. And a real art connoisseur. As a matter of fact, he's the one who sold Dr. Heinsicker that painting above his desk."

Miranda flung back sharply. "I didn't know Dr. Jasper was an art dealer."

The clerk made a gesture of panic. "No—no, Miss Rogers, I didn't mean to imply that Dr. Jasper sells anything professionally. Once in a while he—well, he just knows people who know people, if you know what I mean." Wilbur was turning red, so Miranda gave him a smile.

"Of course, Wilbur—I'm just trying to flesh him out for our readers. I think—I *know*—you could be of tremendous help, since you get to work with him so closely, day by day."

The clerk blushed again, staring at the floor. "Thank you, Miss. Whatever I can do."

She was walking around the office now, examining the art. A Léger and a study for Picasso's *Red Tablecloth,* and on the wall of honor behind the stark desk, a painting of an emaciated man in yellows and reds. It was hung next to the only traditional art in the room: a small portrait of a handsome young man, probably seventeenth century.

"So when did Dr. Jasper help Dr. Heinsicker acquire his painting?"

"Last year. He came back on a trip from Mexico—he usually takes a vacation there during winter break—and I think he arranged for Dr. Heinsicker to buy it as kind of a thank-you."

She scribbled a few notes. "What makes you say that? Did Dr. Heinsicker do him a favor?"

Wilbur tugged at his shirt collar. "I don't really know, Miss, and it's not my place to speculate. I just mentioned it because I thought you wanted human interest, and Dr. Jasper's a very generous man. He brought me back a print once."

Miranda arched her eyebrows. "How very kind of Dr. Jasper. I'd like to see that print sometime, Wilbur. Perhaps use it as an illustration for the article."

His face glowed. "I'd be happy to show you, Miss Rogers. It's a copy of that painting." He pointed to the modernist work above the desk, voice proud. "That's the *Ravens Feeding Elijah* by Christian Rohlfs." He pronounced the German name carefully.

She could make out the black figures now, one in the foreground with a piece of bread in his beak, the starving prophet all angular lines of red and orange, face a mask of misery, body blended into the rocks.

Prophet of God, black birds of mercy, unclean and wild.

Ravens. Corbies.

Symbols of truth.

She played a hunch.

"Does Dr. Jasper usually come back from Mexico with an artwork or two?"

Wilbur looked surprised. "I guess so, Miss Rogers, though I never thought of it that way. Terms blend into terms, you know, and he takes trips down there once and sometimes twice a year. But now that you mention it, I guess he does.

Dr. Jasper likes to travel whenever he can. Even now, in summer session, he'll sometimes visit Chicago or New York. Of course, he's always in demand as a speaker, and you'll see why when you meet him."

Wilbur looked at his watch nervously. "Miss Rogers, I really should be getting back to the desk . . ."

"I can't thank you enough, Wilbur. You've been a tremendous help. Just one more question for the article . . ." She held the pencil poised above the notebook. "Dr. Jasper is such an interesting man, of such diverse interests. Given his taste in art and design, I would have thought he'd travel to Europe, not Mexico . . . I mean, before the war, of course."

Wilbur nodded. "That's so, Miss. He was in Germany and Switzerland for a brief time just last summer, and before that . . . let me see, I've been here for five years, and the last time I remember Dr. Jasper going to Europe was . . . I think it was three years ago. 1937."

Miranda plastered a smile back on her face. "Thank you. Now, I know you have to keep the office running—after all, the men I'm writing about couldn't accomplish what they do without your help—"

The clerk stood up straighter, red skin shining through red hair.

"—and I don't want to keep you, but I'd really like a quick look at Dr. Jasper's library. Would it be terribly inconvenient for you to let me stay here a few minutes?"

Watery blue eyes held hers while she smiled.

Hesitant nod from Wilbur. "I—I guess so, Miss Rogers. It's not like you're a student or anything."

She reached out and squeezed his hand. "Thanks. I promise I won't be long and it'll be our little secret. Like the phone call."

The reminder of his earlier failure to record "Jean Rogers's" appointment sent him toward the office door in a hurry. He was halfway through when he looked back at her and whispered, "Not too long, OK, Miss Rogers? Dr. Jasper really doesn't like people in here when he's not here."

She held up a gloved hand. "Not to worry, Wilbur."

Miranda waited until she heard the door clatter in place, fully shut by the pneumatic mechanism. She quickly ran behind the desk and threw open the slim drawer on the right.

Pencils, pens, and a stack of graph paper with equations.

The Campanile bells chimed mournfully. Footsteps in the hallway outside, a dropped book on the tile floor. She jumped. Not much time left, had to make it count.

She felt for a drawer underneath the sleek desktop and located something with her fingers. She depressed a button, carefully sliding out a thin tray.

Inside it was a date book.

The noise in the hallway outside was getting louder. Voices rose and fell, talking about the weather, about the Fair, about France.

Goddamn it. Not enough time.

She hurriedly paged through, times and dates and names in careful, precise blue ink. She reached the current week.

There was one entry, June 26th, today's date, same blue ink.

"Weidemann. Consulate, 8 P.M."

Fuck.

Fritz Weidemann, playboy, Olympic Club member, and Nazi consul general of San Francisco. Hitler's old lieutenant, the most powerful member of the party in the United States.

Jasper had an appointment with him tonight.

Miranda stared down at the entry.

And . . . so did she.

Eleven

*

More voices outside. Miranda shut the black leather book and shoved it back in the drawer, sliding it noiselessly into the slot.

She pulled down her veil, plucked the notebook and pencil off the shiny desk surface, and walked quickly toward a bookcase.

She was halfway there when the door opened.

Wilbur poked his head around, grinning sheepishly. Miranda breathed out, glad the veil was in place.

"Thought I'd come back and check on you, Miss Rogers. See if you needed anything else."

"Thank you, Wilbur. As a matter of fact, I was about to look for you. Do you know any German?"

"Enough to get by, Miss Rogers. German is a requirement for the degree in Chemistry."

Miranda nodded, gesturing toward a tattered and well-read program facing a small cubist bronze of a dancer.

The word *Entartete* was at the top of the cover, overlaid on a photo of a large stone head. In large, red, crayonlike lettering, *Kunst* was printed at the bottom.

She looked up, watching him carefully. "I'm hopeless with it. Do you know what this means?"

"That? It means 'degenerate art.' The Nazis made a big stink about it a few years ago, you probably remember hearing about it. They've labeled all kinds of things degenerate, including most modern art." He shook his head. "And now they're in charge of France. I just try to mind my own business and not think about it."

"What does Dr. Jasper think about it?"

Wilbur raised his eyebrows. "Dr. Jasper thinks the Nazis are stupid. I've heard him say so. They buy art no one else wants because it's so terrible and burn the kind of art he collects. And he says we'll beat them in science. He says we'll be in the war in a matter of months."

Miranda nodded her head while she made notes. Looked up to meet Wilbur's eyes and smiled.

"Thank you, Wilbur. I've got enough for today. I'll schedule the interview with Dr. Jasper later."

"He's only here Tuesdays and Thursdays, Miss, and his appointments fill up quickly, so call as soon as you can."

The secretary held open the door for her and she walked quickly down the now quiet hallway, heading toward an exit. The back of her neck tingled, and she turned around quickly. Wilbur was still standing outside the main office, staring at her.

She found a telephone booth inside the Owl Drug Store on Telegraph and Bancroft. Waited impatiently for Jack Armstrong, All-American Boy to get off the phone with one of his string of sorority girls, blue and gold on his letter sweater clean and pressed, smile Pepsodent white.

Miranda dropped the Chesterfield stub and crushed it with the toe of her pump. Then she kicked at the door of the phone booth. The soda jerk glanced over, little white cap dotted with chocolate syrup. He pushed it higher on his wide, sweaty forehead.

No sign of waning conversation from Jack. Two campus couples bounced up to the counter, book bags in hand, bobby socks and hairpins and Brylcreem, girls giggling and boys trying to act like Clark Gable. They ordered brown cows and banana splits, soda jerk too busy to pay attention to the phone.

Miranda counted to three and kicked again. The kid in the booth craned his neck, caught eyes with her, mouth still glued to the receiver. She tapped her wristwatch, jerked her thumb. He grinned, nodded, and spoke for another five or six seconds before ringing off. Shoved the door aside, shaking his head.

"Sorry, Miss. Gee, I don't know what's wrong with girls these days. A fella just can't make any hay, and for a real ring-a-ding, too!" He looked down at her and grinned. "Bet you wouldn't give a fella the high hat just for saying hello. Got a clambake tonight—wanna come?"

Miranda squeezed past him and into the booth. Turned to close the glass doors, gave him a smile.

"Sorry to throw you a curve, Bright Eyes. I've got my own clams to dig."

She shut the partition with a clang. Operator, brisk and professional.

"Number, please."

"MArket 3741."

"Deposit ten cents, please."

She plucked out two dimes and two nickels, hoping it would be enough.

"State Department."

"Mr. James MacLeod, please."

"I'm sorry, Miss, but there's no one here by that—"

"Look, I know he's there, he told me so yesterday. Tell him it's the Ugly Duckling."

She'd rolled her eyes at the code name when James suggested it, grinning, adding no one would ever guess it from looking at her. But the operator's voice lowered and he spoke even faster.

"Hold, please."

Two clicks, and James. He sounded delighted.

"Something already, ducks?"

"Jas—I mean, the subject—is meeting a Consul General tonight. Three guesses as to which consulate."

MacLeod sighed. "We've known about that for a while. It's a party . . . the consul throws them rather frequently. Anything else?"

Exasperation made her voice sharp. "I don't know what you already know and what you don't already know. But from what I can see thus far, the only thing the subject seems to be buying and selling is art. Buying modern art and selling older works. Every time he comes back from Mexico, he brings back more. If he *is* selling anything else, the art may be how he's transferring it."

James spoke patiently. "Yes, honey, we realize that. That's why I told you we're not sure if his—activities—are connected. What we need is proof—an indisputable yes or no. Can you get it?"

A gravel voice broke through the connection, making Miranda jump.

"Please deposit five cents."

She dropped a nickel in the slot, waited until she heard the click of the operator going off-line.

"You still there?"

"I'm here. Can you get proof?"

"It's why you hired me. But I'm working in the dark and I need to see his face. How he reacts, what he thinks, what makes him uncomfortable. I want to go in. To the party. I need help with the cover."

Three beats. James finally spoke, voice sober. "You're right. It is why we hired you. This goes against all training and collected wisdom, but it is your show . . . ducks."

"OK. I'll need some protection from you and the French consulate. Marion Gouchard—G-o-u-c-h-a-r-d. Born in Montreal, grew up in Chicago. You remember—same identity I used for the Incubator Baby case."

"Oh, yes, dear Marion. Give her my regards. I can't remember, did she work at the consulate? Your French isn't good enough to pass for a native."

Miranda frowned. "I'm aware of that. She works there, unspecified capacity, but privy to sensitive information. A mystery woman."

"I warned you that we couldn't officially step in, ducks. I'll try to arrange something with the French consul, but it'll be difficult, especially now. No guarantees."

"There never are."

Bumps, thuds, and a long squeal came over the receiver, and Miranda held it out from her ear. "Hello? Hello? James, are you—"

"I'm here. Just wanted to examine the phone." He lowered his voice. "Please be careful. Not only do you not officially exist, but you're dealing with diplomatic immunity."

Her finger traced one of the carvings on the wooden ledge, "Bobby Loves Cathy."

"Immunity comes in all varieties. Anything else I should know?"

"The consul will be in a temper. A young man named Dr. Herbert Hoehne—a German spy—was arrested by the FBI in Los Angeles just five days ago. He calls himself a pharmacist, but he's a courier—delivering messages to Mexico, Venezuela, and Argentina. Before his arrest, he brought information to Fritz we'd love to get our hands on. Of course, Weidemann denies ever hearing the name Hoehne, won't front for bail, and is pleading ignorance of the registration law. The U.S. attorney in L.A. wants to press charges, but Washington will never agree."

Miranda was furiously writing in her notebook. James cleared his throat.

"I wanted you to see what you're up against, ducks. This is the way the game is played. We may be able to help you with the cover, but if you're caught, you're on your own. I don't officially know a 'Miranda Corbie.' Don't compromise the mission, of course, but try to take someone with you . . . someone you trust.

Even if he waits outside. When you walk into that consulate, you're out of our reach . . . and in Hitler's Germany."

Her stomach twisted. "Understood."

"One more thing—I'm leaving for Washington tomorrow, so call the other num—"

Crackle and two dings. A whiny voice interrupted the line.

"Your time is up. Please deposit five cents to continue this call."

"Goddamn it—"

"There is no need to use profanity, Madame."

Miranda shoved a nickel in the slot. "Your money's in the machine. Now fade."

The operator clicked off the line aghast, her "Why, I never—" making Miranda grin.

"James? James?"

No luck. She hit the switch hook twice more, turned to look through the glass.

A line of three Berkeley kids, two bored, one in a panic. Maybe three minutes before a revolt at the soda fountain.

"EXbrook 6700."

"Deposit ten cents, please."

Miranda slid the dime into the slot and heard the click as the coin was deposited, static on the line while the woman connected the number. Another female voice, smooth, unruffled, with overtones of Kay Francis.

"*San Francisco News.*"

"Newsroom, please—Rick Sanders. It's important."

The mirror cracked a little, as the woman sighed. "It always is, sister."

Tapped her foot while counting the seconds of dead airspace. Sudden clatter, male voice a deep bark.

"Sanders here."

"It's Miranda, Rick."

She could hear the Irish lilt smooth over the sandpaper, picture the wide-mouth grin and the crinkly blue eyes, two fingers pushing the crumpled fedora off his forehead.

"About time—I've left you two messages. You were mentioned as a person of interest in your client's murder last night."

"Goddamn it. All the papers?"

"Yep. No photo, though, except for *The Examiner*—they just put out the afternoon edition and ran a small shot of you from February, the Eddie Takahashi case. I convinced Tony to go with a splash on the Hart dame instead."

"Thanks. It's that bastard O'Meara. Listen, we can talk later—"

"You want to go to dinner?"

"I don't know, I'll call you when I'm in the office, I've only got about a minute or two left—"

"Where the hell are you?"

"Quit interrupting me, Sanders—"

A click and a cough signaled the operator. "Please deposit five cents."

Miranda swore, scavenged the bottom of the bag with her fingers, and pulled out another nickel.

"Rick—Rick, you still there?"

Mournful sigh. "Aren't I always, Miranda?"

"Can it. I need to know something pronto. Fritz Weidemann's hosting a party at the German consulate tonight—got any details?"

"Since when do you follow the West Coast Nazi social calendar?"

"Damn it, Sanders, either give me the information or—"

The phone dropped. Cacophony of typewriters and men's voices in loud discussion, punctuated with guffaws. She tucked the receiver between her ear and her shoulder and quickly looked through her change purse, found one last nickel, and deposited it before the operator could make another tired demand.

A Butter Rum Life Saver churned up from the depths of her purse. She popped it into her mouth. Studied the graffiti carved with pen knives and thick pencils: "Andy Loves Sally" and "Professor Engstrom's all wet" and "Effie Richardson's an easy lay."

Another loud clatter signaled Rick's return.

"Fritz and his Nazi Princess Stephanie von Hohenlohe are apparently throwing a costume ball for the diplomatic and Fascist elite of the Bay Area tonight at eight . . . SS uniform optional. Maybe they misplaced your invitation. What the hell are you up to now, Miranda?"

"Thanks, Rick, I've gotta go. I'll phone in an hour."

"I might be at lunch or even, as hard as it may be for you to believe, on an assignment. How about if I meet you at your office?"

She glanced at her wristwatch: 12:10. Half an hour to get back to the Monadnock and calls to make.

"OK. Make it two-thirty. I owe you something. Maybe some background on the Hart case. And I've got another favor to ask."

"Mind telling me why you're interested in Weidemann?"

Half a smile curved Miranda's lips upward. "See you later, Rick."

Twelve

*

Miranda remembered the Lee Wiley recording she'd bought in '34, height of the Depression. Played it over and over again on a ten-year-old gramophone.

Sometimes I feel like a motherless child . . .

She puffed the Chesterfield, slow inhale, watching the train approach the Bay Bridge.

Maybe not anymore.

She opened her purse. *Chadwick's Street Guide* had finally run out of margins, so she'd bought a small reporter's notebook at Schwabacher-Frey on Market. Picked up some monogrammed stationery, too, in case she really had someone to write to.

Miranda flipped open the small cardboard-bound book and stared down at what she'd scrawled in Jasper's office.

Entartete Kunst. Degenerate art. She should have remembered.

The Nazis' infamous exhibit of banned, defaced, and defiled modern masterworks was still touring somewhere in Germany or Austria or the Greater Reich, as most of Europe would soon be renamed. Along with burning books by John Dos Passos and Thomas Mann and Ernest Hemingway, Hitler was systematically exterminating modern film, modern music, modern artists.

Never mind that much of the art was already thirty or forty years old and acknowledged as genius, from Kandinsky's Compositions to Dalí's surrealist nightmares. Never mind that Nazi-approved art, its "tasteful" nudes and heroic landscapes, was full of *Kitsch* and *Kriegsspiel,* extolled only by bootlickers, bigots, and the earnest ladies who handed out flyers for the National Christian Patriots.

Never mind that Adolf Hitler was a failed art student. His revenge on Vienna's Academy of Fine Arts was global.

No modern artist of note was spared, not the impressionists, not Picasso, not even Emil Nolde, whose party membership couldn't save him.

Many of those still living fled, some to Amsterdam or Paris, forgetting how easily lines are erased, Maginot or otherwise. Ernst Kirchner, poet of Berlin street scenes, committed suicide in '38. Miranda remembered reading about it in the paper, surrounded by the warm, suffocating scent of magnolia blossoms and peppermint tea, while she waited for a customer at Dianne's.

She shook herself. Read the words again.

Degenerate art.

Jasper liked "degenerate" art, whether or not his friend Fritz Weidemann knew the difference between Klee and a comic book. He kept a copy of the program in his office. Maybe he saw the actual exhibit . . . the secretary said he'd gone to Europe in '37.

The leaves of brown came tumbling down . . .

Goddamn it. Not on an F car, not now, not nineteen-fucking-thirty-seven. She gulped the stick again, then stabbed it in the ashtray on the seat arm.

1937. Year she should have died.

Fuck, most of her did.

Miranda passed a trembling hand over her forehead.

If I must die, I will encounter darkness as a bride and hug it in mine arms . . .

But now it's three years later, and surprise, little girl, surprise, surprise. You've got a mother. Sure, she's never contacted you in thirty years, sure, she wasn't there for you when you fought off your father's bridge partner and hid by Lake Merced for three days, or when you graduated from high school and a Stanford track star taught you what a diaphragm was. She wasn't there when you tried to feed Mexican kids in Santa Clara, heads too large for shrunken stomachs, or when you won a black bottom contest and got sick for a week on homemade gin. Not there when you saved your money and took a train to New York. Not there when you met John Hayes.

She held herself tight around the waist with an arm. Memory, dim and nagging, footlights and music and a dress sparkling like a starry night . . .

Catherine Corbie had killed a man, or thought she did, and maybe that was enough to keep her away. Enough of a reason to leave her child.

Miranda looked through the dusty window, brown-green eyes focused on the Ferry Building, spire tall and alone, slowly abandoned by the boats and ships that had nourished her for decades.

Maybe . . . maybe if you take away the reason, her mother could come back.

*

Miranda picked out ten rolls of Life Savers, five Butter Rum and the rest Pep-O-Mint, Gladys busy with another customer but shooting Miranda meaningful looks. She shoved a few *Examiners* forward.

Miranda picked up a paper. Mrs. Hart was front-page news, right under the World War. At least money could buy you that.

She flung the pages back. There it was—page five. Photo of her from February. "According to some sources, Mrs. Hart had just left the offices of Miranda Corbie, the notorious female private investigator who earlier this year . . ."

"Miri—did you see? You're 'notorious'—I bet that brings in the customers. Say, sugar . . . you're looking awfully white. You want some candy or something? Here, have a Baby Ruth."

Gladys unwrapped a candy bar and thrust it at Miranda, blue eyes warm with concern, blond curls bouncing in an upswept hairdo.

Miranda took a bite, chewy caramel and chocolate delicious.

"Thanks, Gladdy. I'd better get lunch. I'll be down when I can—we'll catch up later. Thanks for saving the newspapers."

Her friend's practiced fingers played the register. Gladys looked up, said: "Any Chesterfields?"

"Two packs."

The blonde smiled, shook her head. "You're really cutting down, Miri. And still not gaining weight! Just don't starve yourself, sugar. Besides, that Inspector Gonzales likes you just the way you are."

She gave a broad wink to Miranda along with the package and change, then turned to help a young man in a gray pin-striped suit with freshly combed hair and a wilted boutonniere.

"What'll it be, mister? Lucky Strike or Camels?"

Miranda walked away, remembering how Gladys had saved her life in February. The counter girl would jump and squeal if she knew Gonzales had proposed.

Goddamn Gonzales, poster boy for the nice guy, the good cop, the tall, dark, and handsome type, the rich boy from Mexico who thought a quick pulse and a French kiss meant fucking matrimony . . .

The juke at Tascone's was creaking out "This Is No Dream" when she walked up to the register, red counter stools crowded with various degrees of businessmen, newsmen from the Hearst Building and bored phone operators slumped and quiet at a large table.

This must be love the way I feel . . .

"Miss Corbie? You want something to go?"

"Yeah. Hamburger medium rare, sliced tomatoes, French fries, and an iced tea. How's Sam?"

Jerry gave her a big grin, freckles on his nose spreading to his cheeks. "Can't complain, Miss Corbie. He brought in a winner at Bay Meadows the other day, bought us all expensive cee-gars."

"Good for him. Listen, I'm in a hurry—can you bring up the food? Number four twenty-one?"

"Sure thing, Miss Corbie. I know where your office is." He stuttered a little getting it out. "You were in the newspaper today."

"Don't believe everything you read, kid."

Miranda strode quickly to the elevators. Goddamn it.

Examiner coverage on Mrs. Hart would make being "Jean Rogers" or "Marion Gouchard" or anyone else that much harder. She'd need a wig, maybe some special makeup, in addition to a costume.

She reached her door, gold and black letters, slightly faded.

Automatically reached into her purse and pulled out a pack of Chesterfields and the Ronson Majorette. Lit the stick, first spark.

Inhaled gratefully. Life Savers didn't come in tobacco flavor.

Miranda walked to the window and fought open the sash. Shouts of newspaper sellers, men with five o'clock shadow and flat blue caps with patched knees on their dungarees, boys with dirt on their cheeks and fingers. Flower vendors pushing dahlias, buy one for your girl, mister, you won't be sorry, she'll make it worth your money . . .

June sunlight, pale rays, bounced off brownstone on the de Young Building across the street, resting on Lotta's Fountain, gathering strength to assault the coming fog. Church bells tolled on Mission, percussion for the trains, squeal of breaks and clash of the metal, symphony of *rumble clang, rumble clang, dong, dong dong* . . .

Foghorns began to bellow beyond the orange bridge on the northwestern side and mixed with the sellers' calls and the chant of the bells, the workaday machinery of hardened metal and harder men, while songs tinkled from the pool hall on Kearny, and Tascone's juke, fed a steady diet of nickels, played "Maybe," Dolores O'Neill mourning forgotten love.

She closed her eyes, letting the music carry her, memory flashing like the faded sunshine, receding, drifting, hold them, hold them tight, all she had, all she was, pain only bearable because it was the record, the record of her life. Maybe her mother wasn't her mother, maybe she was risking her life for a con, a grift, and it hurt, God it hurt, no Johnny, no Johnny, no Johnny.

The wind bit her face and she opened her eyes again.

Maybe you'll sit and sigh, wishing that I were near . . .

Her left hand balled into a fist, and her knees were trembling. Walking into Nazi Germany, he said, no protection, no rescue. Spies and jail time, worse than death, she'd chew her goddamn leg off before being shackled.

She leaned out the window, looking down Market toward the Ferry Building, shining like Sodom, as holy as the Promised Land.

Still there. Her city.

Mother and father and lover, always changing, always constant.

Never untrue.

San Francisco, built and rebuilt, wicked and always willing, forever old, forever young, smelling of sex and sin and newly minted money, guardian, lover, mentor, the cobbled streets and dim lights and salt-stained tears and wave-lapped piers, the smell of fresh-baked sourdough and *jook* from Sam Wo's, grappa in front of the Italian saints, quiet Victorians nodding on quiet streets, ice shaking in cocktails at the Top of the Mark.

Lying city, dying city, Lazarus and the phoenix. Wide open and proud of it, a city built on stolen sand and abandoned ships, reclaimed by the ones that stayed and built for the ones that left. A city made by dreamers who died paupers and paupers who lived like kings, dream keeping them alive in the only way that mattered.

City of Dreams, broken or not, it didn't matter.

No need for a City of Angels when there's gold in the mountains and cars that climb hills and bridges that span seas.

Miranda watched the smoke from her Chesterfield float across the DO NOT

WALK sign and curl around a lamppost, caressing the dark metal before gently falling apart, falling to earth.

She closed her eyes and said a prayer to San Francisco.

*

Miranda frowned at the copies of *The Examiner* on her desk.

Five messages since yesterday. Three potential clients—two divorce cases and more missing jewelry—a salesman selling mimeograph machines and a solicitation for the Mills College alumni fund. Nothing like a little publicity, good, bad, or indifferent.

She dragged the phone book toward her, flipping to car rental agencies. She'd need something new, something expensive and chic. Something that suggested Marion Gouchard made more money out of the consulate than she did in it.

Her finger ran down the list until she found the place she'd used for the trip to Calistoga . . . Berry-U-Drive, TUxedo 2323.

Five rings, and the same growl on the other end of the phone, fat cigar clenched between teeth.

"Berry-U-Drive, we deliver, latest models our specialty."

"I'd like your newest model coupe—Packard, preferably—something with speed and smart looks."

She heard him swallow, move the cigar around to the other side of his mouth. "Little lady, all Berry-U-Drive cars got smart looks. I've got a Plymouth four door on special, ready to go anywhere, mountain cabin, river in the Redwoods—"

Miranda glanced at her watch. "I want a Packard, two-door coupe, eight cylinder, bright color, all the trimmings, and I need it by three o'clock today in San Francisco."

Silence. She was about to hit the receiver when he came back on, voice slow and devoid of conviviality. "Lady . . . I think you've rented from us before."

Her lips twitched in half a grin. "And I paid you in advance—and in cash. What've you got?"

His cigar ground between his teeth, and the sigh came out like a whistle. "Got a 1940 Packard One-Twenty convertible coupe, eight cylinder, hydraulic brakes all the way around, three-speed Synchromesh with independent front suspension, heater and dee-frost, radio, and them fancy leather seats. The top's power operated and the car's cherry red. I can let you have it for seventy-five dollars down, nine cents a mile, ten dollars a day, insurance included. You want it or not?"

"I'll take it. Three o'clock sharp, Monadnock Building, 681 Market Street, number four twenty-one. Cash in advance for three days. Name's Miranda Corbie."

"It's your money, lady. Show your license to the driver. And say . . . ain't I seen your name in the papers?"

"Only the funny ones, mister."

Miranda hung up, hand still on the receiver. Even if no one at the Nazi consulate read *The Examiner,* she'd need a wig. The costume she could supply herself . . . an old dress from her college days, short enough to distract. Besides, dressing in Weimar Republic clothes would make her feel a little better about walking into the Third Reich.

She opened the yellow pages again, found the number.

"Goldstein and Company, costumes for all occasions, may I help you?"

Young girl, fresh out of school. Probably thrilled to be working in the "theatrical world."

"I'd like to rent a flapper wig—you know, from the 1920s, something like Clara Bow's hair in *Wings.*"

The girl's voice rose. "Oh, we have just the perfect thing, Miss. We've got a whole section on the Roaring Twenties. That's what my mom calls them, anyway . . . I don't really remember much except Lucky Lindy and Babe Ruth, I'm only eighteen, but my mom says—"

"Your mom's right. Can you put one aside for me? I take a seven and a half hat size."

"Of course, Miss, I'm happy to do it! I'll put one away for you right now—when will you be by to pick it up?"

Miranda hesitated. "Probably between four and four-thirty. Will that be all right?"

The salesgirl squealed and Miranda winced, holding the phone away from her ear. "Oh, I'm so glad—I'll be here to rent it to you. Just ask for Peg, Miss. Oh, I'm sorry—I almost forgot. What's your name?"

"Miranda Corbie."

An awestruck pause. "Not—not the lady detective? The one in all the papers?"

Goddamn it.

Miranda reached for the pack of cigarettes on the desk. "Look, Peg. You've got to keep this between us, OK? It's very important. And very—secret."

Peg breathed heavily into the phone. "Oh, you can count on me, Miss Corbie. I won't tell a soul. And—and—there's just one thing . . ."

"Yes?"

"Can I have your autograph?"

Miranda grinned. "Sure, Peg. See you later."

Miranda's stomach growled again. She ignored it, puffing furiously on the Chesterfield. Turned to the mimeographed type of Jasper's file.

Ran through it, looking for dates of travel.

Bingo. Page three.

Jasper was in Germany in '37. Just in time for the "Degenerate Art" exhibit. That jibed with the program in his office.

His latest trip overseas had been just last June, for only a week.

She picked up a pencil and pulled out the Big Chief tablet. Wrote *art dealer, Mexico,* and *degenerate art show?* when the pencil tip broke. Slammed the pencil down and grabbed the fountain pen.

Whisper of movement in the hallway, soft tread. She looked up, listening, saw a shadow behind the glass. Not Jerry or any of the other boys from Tascone's. Her heart was beating too hard, and she cursed herself for leaving the .22 at home, for not opening the safe and taking out the Baby Browning or the Spanish pistol.

The door slowly swung open.

Thirteen

*

A tall, well-dressed man in his late thirties stood in the doorway, hat in his hands. Dark brown hair, small mustache, smaller than Gable's but not as wispy as Mischa Auer's. Good-looking enough to play the lead in B pictures, with a high forehead and frightened blue eyes. They were fixed on hers.

Miranda let out a breath, unclenched her hands on the desk. Stubbed out the Chesterfield in the Tower of the Sun ashtray.

"It's been a long time, Edmund." Her voice was even, measured, as if she didn't know why Dianne's escort for frigid or straying upper-crust socialites and the occasional underground queer trade had suddenly appeared at her door.

"Come in. Have a seat." She gestured toward one of the wooden chairs haphazardly arranged in front of her desk. "Want a drink?"

He was blurry around the edges, desperation and fear welling like the little beads of sweat dotting his skin. He hesitated, nodded. Miranda busied herself with finding a semi-clean glass by the file cabinet. Made sure the safe was locked.

The cops must have gotten to Edmund, and knowing the bulls, they rode him hard. Any whiff of his Saturday nights and they'd make his life hell—probably even throw him in jail. Doyle could sniff around fourteen-year-old Chinese girls all he wanted, Phil could spend his Wednesday afternoons at Dianne's, no questions asked—but if you fucked the wrong gender, brother, you were ridden out of town on a goddamn rail, held up in the papers as an example of immorality run amok, never mind Finocchio's and all the drag money it brought into the City of Sin.

Miranda took out the bottle of Old Taylor and poured a shot. He'd finished it by the time she sat down.

Expensive fedora, tailored clothes. He'd come up in the world.

"How often did Mrs. Hart call you for an escort job?"

He opened his mouth, shut it again, passed a hand over his sweaty forehead. Leaned forward and set the glass on her desk.

"I noticed you at the Picasso show. I hardly thought I'd need your services the next day."

Miranda unraveled a tube of Butter Rum Life Savers, held out the candy to Edmund.

"Want one?"

He shook his head, and she popped two in her mouth, watching him.

"Mrs. Hart was my client. Did you know that?"

His hands folded and wound together, thumb rubbing the palm. His right cheek looked powdered, faint blue and yellow showing through.

Souvenir from the SFPD.

"Certainly I knew it. Lois told me she'd hired you to find the jade and that you'd been successful. She was gloating over how little she had to pay you."

Miranda bit down hard, cracking the Life Savers. "Your Lois was quite a prize. All the same—the way it works, Edmund, at least for me—is that she is still my client. That means I protect her interests. That means I can't represent you."

Skin bleach white, then red, gradually pink again. Voice the slow, syrup tone before panic.

"Miranda—I need—you're the only one who is safe for me, the only one I trust. You worked for Dianne. You—understand—the situation. And from what I could determine from the police and saw in the papers . . . you are under suspicion, too."

Eyes large, blue, thick lashes, tears behind them like the bruises and scars behind the powder.

Like the man behind the mask.

Edmund Whittaker, small-time architect, cultured, good-looking and debonair, perfect decoy for blind husbands. Knew his Bach from his Beethoven, an escort only for the very rich and very exclusive, but his personal tastes ran to older men, a habit that brought him to Dianne's and later kept him there.

Dianne's Escort Service and Tea Room, 41 Grant Avenue.

They all met there, the dying and the already dead, trapped by the fat southern spider, another fly on her web, soft curls coiffed like an extra in *Gone with the Wind,* scent of magnolias and Cuban tobacco, while poison dripped from small white teeth splattered red with tea and burgundy.

No one escaped from Dianne Laroche.

Miranda lit another Chesterfield with the One-Touch on the desk. Someone put another nickel in the Tascone jukebox, Tommy Dorsey again.

If it's the very last thing I do . . .

She leaned forward, hands on the desk. "I said I couldn't represent you. That doesn't mean I won't help you." She glanced at the clock above the file cabinet. "I don't have much time. Listen, Edmund, let me ask some questions and then we can meet tomorrow or the next day. All right?"

The promise calmed him down a little. "All right. You know I had nothing to do with her death or the theft of the jade and other jewelry, nothing. The police . . . one of them hit me, he'd heard about—heard about me somewhere. I'm scared, Miranda. Scared to death."

She frowned. "Hit the sonofabitch back next time. They'll throw you in the cooler anyway, may as well hang for a sheep. Was it Collins? Red face, beady eyes. Number 598. All-American Fascist."

Edmund shrugged, eyes drifting to the bottle still on the desk. "I don't know. Could have been, I guess. Probably was. I wasn't paying much attention . . . all I could see were the guns and the sticks and all I could think about was that it was the end. The end of everything."

Miranda reached for his empty glass and poured another shot of the Old Taylor. "Tell me what you were doing at the Picasso show."

He threw the whiskey back in a long toss, wiped his mouth, and sighed. Set the glass down on the desk again, gazing at the pale brown drops clinging to the side.

"All right. Here it goes. Lois calls me out of the blue the day before, tells me about the Picasso show. She knew I like art and that I know something about it, just a little knowledge here and there I've picked up along the way. Anyway, her husband was in Sacramento on business and her lover won't—wouldn't—go out in public with her at all."

Miranda wrote a few notes in the Chief tablet. Murmured: "That would be State Senator Bodwin, yes?"

The architect smiled for the first time. "I've got to protect Lois, too, Miranda. If you heard it, I won't deny it. But you won't get it directly from me."

She looked up at the man in front of her. "You've always been an honorable sort. Too honorable to work for Dianne."

"I don't work for her anymore—at least, not unless she threatens me with exposure, which she has done on occasion. No, I've been on my own for a while."

"For decoy dates or the real thing?"

Discreet smile. "Both. I've developed a few connections."

Miranda gulped the stick once more and rubbed it out. "Don't let her pull you back. Whatever happens. She won't go through with the blackmail. Dianne just likes to toy with her prey before she eats it."

"I hardly think she'd call me now."

Miranda shook her head. "Let's hope so. So you took Mrs. Hart to the Picasso show, and she told you about the jade. What happened afterward?"

Panic started up again, and his eyes wandered around the room, coming to rest on the window, two or three inches left open. He spoke apologetically. "Mind if I close it?"

The door rattled under a loud knock. Edmund froze, face drained of color. The odor of grilled beef filtered through the room . . . Tascone order.

She stood up, patted him on the arm. "Go ahead and shut the window and keep your back to the kid. It's my lunch."

Miranda opened the door halfway, holding it in place with her foot. Jerry was carrying her hamburger and fries on a tray, skin blushing red to the roots of his hair.

"Sorry it took so long, Miss Corbie. The cook lost your order, but I checked up on it, and found it again."

"Thanks. Just set it down over there."

She pointed to the front end of the desk. The kid was looking around the office as if he expected Sam Spade to climb out of the file cabinet, followed by Casper Gutman and Brigid O'Shaughnessy. His eyes wandered over Edmund's back. The architect faced Market Street, hands gripping the window-frame tight on both sides. Miranda dug into her purse and pulled out a dollar.

"Here. Keep the change."

The kid's eyes protruded and he stared at the money. "Gee . . . thanks, Miss Corbie. Sorry to bother you."

She ushered him out the door. "Never be sorry when you're bringing lunch, Jerry."

*

Miranda concentrated on the food. Edmund declined her halfhearted offer of sharing the sandwich and weathered the interruption well, lighting a Dunhill cigarette and walking around the office, pausing to notice the Wells Fargo safe and the dusty Martell's calendar on the wall.

Bun crusts and a few French fries littered the Buffalo China when she shoved the tray aside. Held the napkin to her mouth and stifled a burp. Pulled the Chief tablet over and picked up the Esterbrook.

"Sit down. I've only got a few more minutes. What happened after the Picasso show?"

He stiffened again, rubbed the cigarette out in the ashtray. His voice rose. "We were followed, Miranda. That's what I came here to tell you."

"Someone shadowed you when you left the Veterans Building? How, on foot, in a car? Did you get a look at him?"

He picked up the Borsalino fedora from the next chair and held it with both hands.

"No, not really. A man in a dark hat and suit, mid-thirties, maybe, from his posture. First on foot, when we walked to the parking lot . . . that's when I got the feeling, you know, when someone is staring at you. Then in the car behind us, until I dropped Lois off on Kearny, corner of the de Young Building. She said her chauffeur was picking her up promptly at Lotta's Fountain on Market. She didn't want anyone to see her enter the Monadnock."

Miranda nodded. "Too many detectives. Cops question the chauffeur?"

"Three times, from what I've heard."

She made a note. "Go on."

"I caught a glimpse of him in the mirror when the light hit us right—just an impression, really. Medium height, medium build . . . light skin, no facial hair, probably a blond, but I couldn't say for sure because of the hat. It looked like a wide-brimmed, dark gray fedora, the kind that was popular about five years ago. There was nothing exceptional looking about him at all."

"What make of car was it?"

He shook his head. "I'm not sure. Nothing large, a two-door coupe of some kind, newer than the fedora."

"Did you tell this to the police?"

"Of course—and I assured them that I'd be able to spot the man again, if they could come up with a suspect. They didn't believe me, of course, but it's true—I've got a photographic memory. I always recognize something if I've seen it before."

She stared at him thoughtfully. "Handy talent to have. You ever see this man before last night?"

He hesitated. "I—I can't really say, Miranda. As I said, it was a brief impression. He reminded me of someone, a photograph, perhaps, but I couldn't be sure. I'd know him if I saw him again, but I couldn't make out his features exactly—"

"Would be better for you if you had seen him. The bulls don't trust photographic memories. They barely trust photographs. They'll be dying to nail you on a moral turpitude charge, anyway, and any chance of linking sodomy to murder is a chance the D.A. might take. They'll think you either knew this guy or made him up. Anything else to tell me?"

His eyes held hers, large, sorrowful, light welling in the corners where the small red lines made a map in the white.

"It's the truth, Miranda. I don't lie. I've never lied."

She sighed and bit her lip. "I believe you, Edmund. Though that doesn't do you a whole hell of a lot of good right now, considering I'm persona non grata. But I don't think they'll expose you. Exposing you would mean exposing Mrs. Hart—and that would embarrass Mr. Hart. Embarrassing Mr. Hart is a criminal offense . . . even more than sleeping with the wrong gender."

His shoulders relaxed. "I hope you're right. I don't have much of an alibi. I stayed up and listened to some music on the radio—Beethoven—had a drink and went to bed."

"Anybody see you come in?"

"I don't think so. I live in a smallish apartment house in North Beach, and we don't have a lobby man after midnight."

"Try the neighbors—one of them may have heard your radio. The cops can check the radio listings, too, so try to remember exactly what you were listening to, though unless the program wasn't originally scheduled it's not much of an alibi—listings are in the papers or *Radio Guide*. Why didn't Mrs. Hart's chauffeur drive both of you last night? Because of the jade?"

He nodded. "She didn't want any of her employees gossiping about her comings and goings. Or to find out about the parure." He ran a finger along his mustache thoughtfully, sadly. "Poor Lois. She was terrified of that necklace. She should have let Raymond sell the damn thing."

Miranda raised her eyebrows in surprise. "She told you her son was responsible?"

His hands folded like a prayer, voice urgent and earnest. "You have to understand, Miranda. We were friends, Lois and I. We had a lot in common. It's one reason she felt safe with me, she knew I'd never hurt her—or use her."

She held his eyes for a moment, then stared down at her notes, tapping the pen against the desk. "There was a pickpocket at the show last night. I braced him—Fingers Molloy. A man I've never seen before left almost at the same time he did, maybe his partner. I'm wondering if he could be your shadow. Could you tell whether he split off after Mrs. Hart or followed you back home?"

"I kept an eye behind me for a few blocks, and thought I saw him on a side street—Post or Sutter. By the time I got home there was no one."

Miranda scribbled in the Big Chief pad for a few minutes, then slapped down the Esterbrook and looked up to find Edmund anxiously watching her. She stood up.

"OK. We can strategize tomorrow. Just ring me first—I might be out. I don't have any time to check into this right now, but I can't turn down a friend. And there's my own neck, too."

He picked up the Borsalino and walked toward her smiling, hand outstretched.

"Thank you so much for coming to the aid of an old colleague, Miranda. I feel much better now, about both of our chances."

She placed her hands on his shoulders. "We served on Devil's Island together. And I'm glad to know you got out. See you tomorrow."

They walked to the door, the architect standing straighter than before.

"By the way—you seeing anyone on a regular basis?"

He reddened, hand on the doorknob. "Just ended a relationship not too long ago. It's so awkward when you run into old lovers, especially at social functions. I was glad to get out of that exhibit."

She patted him on the back. "We'll get through it. Be seeing you."

He leaned over and kissed her cheek. "Be seeing you, Miranda."

Checked her wristwatch when the St. Patrick's church bells starting ringing. Took her a minute to realize the phone was ringing, too, shrill insistence blending with the sonorous warning to gather, confess, and repent. Miranda picked up the phone, still thinking about Edmund.

"How are you, Miranda?"

Goddamn it. Not Gonzales, not now.

"Busy. You should know that, Inspector. I spent an hour at the Hall this morning, getting grilled by Fisher, who doesn't like grilling people, and for that I'm thankful. He's a good man in a hard position, since O'Meara and Brady, the Bobbsey Twins, think I'm a Red and apparently garroted my own client."

He made a noise in the back of his throat. "I will speak to them, Miranda, perhaps a word from me will help. I have some small standing I did not have before, thanks to my work with the Dies Committee. I'm sorry."

"Don't worry about it. Comes with the territory."

She lit the cigarette with the One-Touch Ronson, heart beating hard through the silence on the other end of the phone.

"I—I am sorry about last night. I do not normally drink so much or act so poorly. I've also sent a note of apology to Mr. Sanders. My behavior was . . . not myself."

Miranda dragged on the Chesterfield and fell into the chair. "Apology accepted. I've got to go."

Slight hesitation, then smooth again, rough spots swallowed like a poison pill. "Shall I see you again, Miranda?"

"In the funny papers. I've got to go, Gonzales."

His voice was soft. "I will be here if you need me."

She dropped the phone in the cradle, loud clang, and leaned back in the chair, watching the smoke curling from the end of her cigarette, watched it form a dragon before the currents from the window and the hallway slid under the door and dismembered it.

Goddamn it.

Fourteen

*

Miranda opened the Big Chief tablet and turned the pages back to her list. *Art dealer, Mexico.*

She tapped the Esterbrook against her lips, trying to remember the name of the dealer at the Picasso show, the man with the sandy goatee . . . what did he say? "*You know what Jews are . . .*" and "*far from the only source.*" And then Jasper humiliated him, hurt him physically. She remembered his expression of pain and how forcefully the professor had shut his mouth.

Warden? Wearden? W-something. Shit.

He'd done business with Jasper before, fit the anti-Semitic dogma. And they'd huddled together, murmuring something about Kirchner and Warsaw and *entartete Kunst . . .*

She reached for the directory, thumbed through and dialed the number.

"Museum of Art."

Gruff voice. Possibly the Cyclopean woman from the registration desk.

Miranda cleared her throat. Time to play Social Register.

"Good afternoon. I attended your current Picasso exhibit last night."

Pause, with the implication that the museum should contemplate how very fortunate it had been.

"And what is the reason for your call, Madame?"

Tough customer. Miranda turned up the frost, let it bite through the phone, equal parts impatience and iceberg.

"I have been contemplating a significant bequest. Before I consult with your director, however, I would like to have my collection appraised. There was an art dealer at the exhibit whom I found very congenial, and I unfortunately have misplaced his calling card. Would you be so *kind*"—she punched the last word like a boxing bag—"as to look up Mr. Warden's information for me? I'm sure you'll find it in your registration book."

Quiet choke, vocal constipation.

"Cert-tain-ly, Madame."

And the hell with you, too, sister.

"There are a number of names that sound like Warden, Ma-dame. I will read out the names and cities. Perhaps one will sound familiar."

Barely concealed sneer, resentment of the rich, their taste, their tempers, their unfortunate and unfair ownership of what is known as Art, largesse upon which museums depended. Miranda almost felt sorry for her, remembering the debutantes and society matrons lining up to get their pictures taken with *The Acrobat*.

"Thank you. I shall commend you to the director."

The woman cleared her throat, above flattery. "Mr. and Mrs. Frank Warden, Burlingame. That is W-a-r-d-e-n. Mrs. Connelly Warden, San Francisco, same spelling. Mr. and Mrs. Taylor Wardin, Hillsborough, W-a-r-d-i-n. Mr. Hugo Wardon, San Francisco, W-a-r-d-o-n. Mr. Anthony Weardon, Berkeley, W-e-a-r-d-o-n. That is all, Madame. May I inform the director and curator of your interest in a bequest?"

Miranda gave it her haughtiest. "Thank you. My estate attorney will contact them."

She dropped the phone in the cradle quickly, took a deep breath, then laughed. Looked around the office at the Martell's calendar and the tattered, dusty page of the *Chronicle* on the wall by the radio, rotogravure from the opening day of the Fair.

Murmured: "Some bequest."

She opened the directory again, eyes squinting at the faded black ink. Only seven art galleries. Most centered in Union Square, most just branches of large houses in New York.

She couldn't remember a companion for the slight, precise man with the sandy goatee. He was probably one of the single men on the list, either Hugo Wardon or Anthony Weardon, if he even bothered to sign the register. Since there was no phone listing for a Wardon or Weardon gallery, she'd just have to play society dame again and call them all.

Miranda lit another cigarette. Ran her finger ran over the raised letters of the State Department report—heavy typewriter keys—finally pausing in the middle of a paragraph.

> *Jasper received a grant of five hundred dollars from the Pioneer*
> *Fund.*

He eyes widened. She reached for the phone, dialed the memorized number. Three rings and an answer.

"State Department."

"Mr. MacLeod, please. It's Ugly Duckling."

She smoked furiously, hunched forward over the phone.

Rattle and the sound of papers shuffling, a click. James.

"You caught me just when I was leaving the office. Something else?"

"I know you're heading back to Washington tomorrow, but I need more information. Anything and everything about art dealers or galleries Jasper patronizes, if anyone's bothered to check. This report is too general . . . I'd like specifics."

"We'd like them, too, ducks, that's why I hired you. That report is what we have . . . and all we have."

"What about the agent who made the report? It reads like a synopsis with a few details, and maybe he . . ."

His voice was sharp. "Like I said—that's all we have. And it's all the agent had time to write before someone put a knife to his throat."

"I see." Miranda sat back in the chair, Chesterfield between her fingers, gray ash slowly eating the thin white paper. "That's something you might have mentioned earlier, James."

"I warned you. I've been warning you. And it's not too late. I can cover the expenses you've incurred, you can keep a hundred dollars for a retainer, and we'll call it even. I'm not going to be able to sleep nights as it is."

"You can't get rid of me that easily. But thanks for the offer. I've got one more question: the Pioneer Fund."

"Off-limits, ducks. Focus on the subject."

Her face darkened. "What do you mean 'off-limits'? It's in the goddamn report, James. Jasper received money from them for research—don't you want to know what kind of research?"

He lowered his voice. "Just let it be. Certain—certain people will attempt to label any exposé of the Pioneer Fund as a Communist plot. It's the reality we're working with, ducks. I'm sorry."

"Sorry? Jesus Christ, James, I read a report on them—a Pinkerton report, in fact, and we all know how Red Pinkerton is. They're no better than the Silver Shirts and the Ku Klux Klan, just richer. The bastard who founded it visited Hitler and friends in '35, came back all aglow with 'better living through selective breeding' . . ."

"No. N-O, no. Either continue on with the subject or quit, ducks, but don't drag this into it. The Dies Committee—"

"I don't give a damn about the Dies Committee, the Pinkerton report said—"

Two sharp raps on her office door.

Rick never knocked.

Miranda half-covered the receiver with her palm, whispered "Tomorrow," and set it down in the cradle as quietly as she could.

"Come in." Her eyes and voice were steady.

Allen craned his head around the front of the door, scalp shiny and pink, red tie askew and sporting a mustard stain.

"Did I hear you take the Old Man's name in vain?"

She scattered ash from the forgotten Chesterfield, bent forward and rubbed it out in the tray.

"Since when do you wait for an invitation?"

"I always knock, sweetheart. I never know what I might be interrupting." He winked, ambling toward the most comfortable of the wooden chairs. Sat down and crossed his thick legs. The brown wool trousers rode up too high, revealing gray socks.

Miranda pointed to his ankles. "Your wife throw you out?"

He grinned. "An astute observation, Miss Sherlock. She's staying with her mother for two weeks. Did I or did I not just hear you mention Pinkerton?"

Allen Jennings, bald, mid-forties, with a potbelly and muscle that had run to fat. Not Hollywood's idea of the best damn op she knew.

"What are you, Pavlov's dog? This part of the training?"

He reached into his vest pocket and pulled out a half-smoked Old Gold. Smoothed the stick between his fingers, struck a match on his shoe, and inhaled, shaking his head.

"Haven't seen you much, kid. Thought I'd drop in and say hello, and being the good shamus that I am, I overhear 'Pinkerton' and 'Dies Committee' and my natural curiosity is aroused. Don't quote me, but that's a goddamn unholy combination. What are you up to?"

She rubbed the back of her neck. "Nothing I can talk about."

The detective raised his eyebrows. Took a long drag on the stick and scratched his cheek.

"I've pulled a few of those myself. Got too old and the wife got too scared. It's why I'm here, man Friday for lost dogs and divorce cases."

She lifted her face to his. He shook his head.

"Just watch yourself and your back, because you can't win. You think maybe you can, at first, you come in with ideals and believe the recruiting posters and the man who gives you the orders. But you can't win. If you're real damn lucky, you'll break even. They change the rules on you, kid . . . sometimes in the middle of the game."

Miranda plucked out two Butter Rum Life Savers from the roll on the desk and offered the tube to Allen. He waved at it dismissively.

"Been eatin' lemon drops all damn day."

She picked up the pencil and rolled it between her fingers.

"I appreciate the advice. Nothing I hadn't figured on. What I could really use your help with doesn't affect anybody else but me."

He bent forward, tapping ash into the tray. "You're the reason I'm here, kiddo."

Miranda glanced at the wall clock. Ten minutes to three. Wondered what the hell had happened to Rick.

"I've got a car outside waiting for me. I'd like to tell you the story later."

The Pinkerton stood up, grinning. "As good a brush-off as I've heard."

"Wait."

She walked to the safe and struggled with the sticky combination, while Allen turned his back obligingly. Slid out five one-hundred-dollar bills from the stack James had given her. Her hand fell to the lower shelf, touching the Baby Browning and the gold cigarette case. She grabbed them both and shut the door.

"You can turn around now." Miranda threw the Browning, the bills, three rolls of Life Savers, and a new pack of Chesterfields in her purse, grabbed her coat off the rack in the corner, and shoved her hat back on.

"I'm trying to trace someone. A woman, late forties or early fifties. Irish or Scots-Irish, lived in San Francisco. Black hair, dark eyes, pretty enough to be on stage when she was young."

The detective looked at her thoughtfully. "She kidnapped or something?"

"No . . . she disappeared, was apparently smuggled back to Ireland."

Miranda turned her face to Allen's.

"She may have been wanted for murder, and apparently killed a man. All this happened around thirty years ago."

He whistled as they stepped out of the office and Miranda shut and locked the door. A middle-aged couple walked down the hall toward them, and they said nothing until the couple's footsteps could be heard rounding the corner.

Miranda lowered the hat's veil across her face, voice low.

"Any help, any leads, would mean a great deal to me, Allen."

The Pinkerton op stuck out his lower lip and nodded. "I'll take a look-see, sweetheart, but I'll need a name for your mystery woman."

Miranda's eyes searched his for a moment.

She whispered, "Catherine Corbie. My mother."

She turned her back to the Pinkerton, walking quickly down the long corridor to the stairs and her waiting car.

Fifteen

*

Long, low wooden tables, books, ladders, and crowded shelves, only sound an occasional cough or whisper and the low hum and rumble of nearby Market Street trains.

Cool, quiet brownness of the Mechanics' Institute Library, soothing, private, an oasis in downtown San Francisco—and across the street from the Monadnock.

Miranda tapped her fingers on the desk, frowning.

The secretary at the Berkeley art department mentioned that Jasper traveled to Europe the previous summer, and the State Department report narrowed it down to Germany and Switzerland in late June. Crossing the Atlantic took time, planning, and money, and Jasper had spent only four days in Germany and three in Switzerland.

Secrets or art? Or was art—particularly *entartete Kunst*—the secret itself?

She dislodged the May 1939 issue of the *Burlington Magazine for Connoisseurs* from between *Art News* and *Art in America,* turning quickly to the section on "Forthcoming Sales."

Christie's, Chippendales, "A portion of Mr. William Randolph Hearst's collection," Sotheby's with German and Bohemian glass . . .

Her finger stopped, nail tracing the raised print.

Galerie Fischer, Lucerne. "Paintings and Sculptures by Modern Masters" from German museums. Purged by the Nazis from their own cultural heritage, enemy to the state religion of Fatherland, Fuehrer, and fear.

Names on sale included Klee and Kokoschka, Franz Marc, and Emil Nolde.

Non-German art, too, was offered at the sacrificial block, bought by German museums when the country led the world forward, Weimar Germany, spirit of modernism, spirit of freedom . . . Picasso's *The Soler Family,* a self-portrait by Van Gogh, works by Gauguin and Matisse.

Burlington alerted its connoisseurs that bargains were to be had: "Revolutions have often in the past led to the dispersal of art collections, and thus aroused interest in particular schools of art in new quarters."

Bid now, Mr. Hearst, who gives a damn if the money buys more coffins for France and England? Germany doesn't want modern art anymore, debased currency, just like the Mark in 1923. Buy it up, buy it up, buy it up . . .

"There is little doubt that in the present case new admirers will be found for these rejected works in an atmosphere free from political prejudice."

Political prejudice.

Such a well-bred euphemism for purges and murder and cultural patricide. And how noble of *Burlington,* how brave and optimistic, to envision the circling vultures as saviors and titular connoisseurs of fine art. Van Gogh might be staring again, hollowed-eyed and mad, from a recess on a panel wall at San Clemente or the Hamptons or a nineteenth-century castle in Boston. Maybe even an American museum in Cincinnati . . . or the office of a Berkeley chemistry professor.

Miranda reached for a cigarette and frowned, her fist closing around the purse.

Far from the only source . . . you know what Jews are . . .

Maybe the Galerie Fischer is where Jasper last saw Wardon or Weardon, the sandy-haired sycophant from the Picasso exhibit. If she could find a list of the dealers at the Fischer Gallery . . .

A large male hand, nails ragged, slapped the page in front of her.

She looked up into blue eyes crinkling at the corners, lopsided grin spreading across his face.

"Sorry I'm late. Gladys told me you were holed up across the street."

"Where the hell were you, Sanders? Hot news story?"

He shook his head. "Turkey just declared its neutrality—a Norwegian and a Greek ship were sunk by U-boats—and Russia wants to swallow part of Romania. Same old war."

He threw himself into the chair across from her, legs outstretched, face falling into serious lines.

"What's wrong, Randy—worried about me?" His tone was light, the upturned tick of an Irish lilt caressing the syllables. She met his eyes stubbornly.

"Can the Irish, Sanders. You're about as Irish as Mrs. O'Leary's cow. Maybe I was worried. Maybe I don't have enough goddamn time to be worried. And don't call me Randy."

"I'm half Irish."

"And all bullshit."

"Shhh." He grabbed her hand and looked around in mock fear at the only other occupant of the reading room, a middle-aged woman in black sitting four tables away and reading a *Saturday Evening Post*. "You want us to get kicked out of here?"

His grip was warm and reassuring, skin unexpectedly comforting against her own. Miranda pulled her hand away and shut the magazine and her notebook.

"I'm leaving anyway. You coming along?"

"Where are we going?"

"Goldstein and Company."

"Costume for the Nazi ball?"

She nodded, whispered "Keep your voice down," and stood up, shoving her chair back under the table. Rick stood up and stretched, yawning.

"OK, Mata Hari. Lead on."

She threw him a baleful look, and together they headed for the central staircase and exit to Post Street.

Rick whistled when he saw the car, hand gliding over the red curves. "Christ, you're coming up in the world. Why the fancy wheels?"

She slid in on the driver's side and slammed the door shut.

"Get in. We can talk on the way."

He climbed into the Packard, mouth turned upside down, blue eyes on her hat, her dress, her legs.

"You make it awfully hard on a man to be chivalrous, Miranda. Mama Sanders didn't raise her boys to be neglectful of the niceties."

She shoved the car into gear and eased out into traffic behind a Yellow Cab, accelerating before a sharp, quick right on Montgomery. The cab stayed in front, silhouetted couple in back kissing in a long embrace.

"You never told me why you were late."

Rick's eyes flicked over the dashboard, and he ran a long finger over the Cordoba brown leather on the seat. Tried to make his voice nonchalant.

"We'll need someplace to talk other than this beauty. I was late for two reasons. One, the new typist in the steno pool downstairs . . ."

Miranda hit the gas pedal as she made the right turn on Market, still behind the cab. A contractor's truck, five- or six-year-old Ford, crossed lanes to pull up behind her, riding the bumper. She glanced into the rearview mirror.

"You've always had a weakness for dishwater blondes. The second reason?"

Rick shifted sideways to face her. He hesitantly reached out a finger to trace her cheek, and she flinched.

"What the hell—is there a bug on me or something?"

Someone on O'Farrell was sitting on a horn, matched by a siren down Grant. Miranda inched the Packard forward, waiting for the light to turn green, avoiding his eyes.

Rick sighed, turned back to the windshield. Voice somber. "It'll keep till later."

She glanced at the tall man in the battered brown fedora sitting beside her, broad shoulders slumped.

"We can talk after Goldstein's. And Rick . . . thank you."

She took a gloved hand off the steering wheel for a moment and found his left, squeezing it. Rick opened his eyes, sat up taller in the seat.

She parked on Taylor across from the Golden Gate Theatre, red Packard drawing looks from the line of men and women waiting for the new "Crazy Show" stage show, playing with the programmer *Pop Always Pays* and a short film called *United States Navy, 1940.*

Crazy show. Just like a Nazi costume party . . .

They crossed the street in silence, Rick's arm brushing hers.

Miranda stopped on the corner to dig out a Chesterfield, hand shaking, and lit it with a Ronson before Rick could strike a match in the Bay wind, sheets from the morning *Chronicle* wadded and blowing up the sidewalk, pretzel crumbs, cigarette butts and a Necco Wafer wrapper skidding toward the Market Street curb.

She took a deep inhale, then looked up at him. He shook his head, lips pursed, and took off his hat, wind mussing his hair like Gene Krupa's.

"Just once, Miranda . . . let me light the goddamn cigarette."

She stared at his comically sad face and gave him half a smile.

"C'mon, Lochinvar. Let's go in."

They got lost in the medieval section, Rick waving a wooden sword and pretending to duel with Basil Rathbone until Miranda stalked off toward an antebellum display straight out of *Jezebel* or *Gone with the Wind,* turned around in confusion and made a left into *David Copperfield.* She puffed furiously on the rest of the Chesterfield and pinched the remainder with her fingers, tucking it back in her purse, surrounded by Oliver Twist in the poorhouse and Victorian widow's weeds on a long rack of black. Rick held up the arm of a starched formal suit, complete with side whiskers and a walrus mustache.

"Costumes for all occasions is an understatement."

"Goddamn it, I need a wig, not the fucking *March of Time* . . ."

She was headed for the French Revolution when a thin, flustered floorwalker scurried up from nowhere.

"Would you help me, please? I'm looking for a flapper wig. A young woman named Peg is holding one for me."

He bowed, long hands folded Uriah Heep–style, stuttering against his high-collar dress shirt.

"Very sorry, Madame, and r-right this way. I'm sure she has found exactly what you're looking for."

Rick sprinted away from the guillotine on display to catch up with Miranda, nodded at the clerk.

"You should hand out maps to this place. It's like Madame Tussaud's without the wax."

The floorwalker glanced at him and turned right, gesturing complacently toward a diorama of the *Mayflower* and mannequins dressed as John Alden and Priscilla Mullins.

"Yes, we are a rather large firm. The largest in the San Francisco Bay area, in fact. I'll let my superiors know—a map is an excellent suggestion. One doesn't want to get lost, does one?"

He followed the question with a honking laugh. Rick grinned at Miranda, who was checking her watch again, mouth a thin line of impatience.

The floorwalker finally halted in a more open area, amid recognizable bustles and parasols from Miranda's childhood, and a large hanging photograph of Market Street after the Quake and Fire.

"Ah, here we are. Recent history. Can't really be called history at all, I suppose, but we do have customers who want to relive their youth, black bottom and so forth. Peg? Peg!"

The floorwalker frowned, fingers clutching his lapel. A young blonde emerged from a rack of Gibson girl dresses and bloomers.

"Yes, Mr. Phipps? Oh, it's—I beg your pardon, Miss Corbie, I have your wig right here."

She crossed to a small counter next to a cluster of short dresses and straight-hemmed gowns that hung, all sequins and satin, yellows and reds shimmering like an Erté, Pola Negri and Gloria Swanson and Mae Marsh, the Roaring Twenties, in with a bang and out with a whimper. Only fifteen years ago . . .

Phipps raised his eyebrows and peered at Miranda through thick lenses.

"Corbie? That name sounds familiar . . . have you rented from us before?"

She turned the full force of a smile on him. "I'm afraid not, Mr. Phipps, but I surely expect to do business with you again."

Phipps took a step backward, stuttering again. Rick stepped in front of his line of sight, while Miranda walked up to where Peg waited at the cash register.

Rick's lip twitched. He said: "Good-bye, Mr. Phipps."

The floorwalker bowed again, patchy gray and brown eyebrows knitted together as if trying to remember something.

Peg was seventeen, attended Sacred Heart, and was aglow with the chance to meet a real-life celebrity. Miranda and Rick were treated to a nonstop monologue of where she lived, what her parents did (father was a bookkeeper, mother involved in 4-H), and how her friends Edna and Nancy were never going to believe it.

The shopgirl had chosen two wigs: one was red and reminiscent of Clara Bow, short and teased upward in a halo effect. The other was black and stark, inspired by Louise Brooks in *Pandora's Box* and every other picture she made. Miranda felt the hair on both and chose the latter, adding a small black domino mask, two small tins of Pan-Cake makeup, and lip rouge.

"Thank you for your help, Peg. I'd like to buy the wig, not rent it, just ring me up and I'll pay cash."

Peg's blue eyes grew enormous. "I just had a hunch, Miss Corbie, you know, a real hunch, that the black wig would be better for you. Oh, I do hope you let me know how it turns out! I mean, I'm sure I'll read about it all in the papers and everything, but it sure would be swell if you let me know."

Miranda nodded solemnly. "I'll do my best. I'm in a bit of a hurry, Peg, so if you could ring me—"

"Oh, of course, Miss Corbie! Right away!"

Miranda glanced over at Rick and grinned. She opened her purse and plucked out a five-dollar bill and a business card. Picked up a pencil from the counter and signed her name, handing the card to Peg, who squealed with delight.

"Wait'll Edna sees this! She'll be pea green!" She counted the change carefully back to Miranda, chattering again.

"I just can't believe it, a real lady private eye, just like Myrna Loy in the *Thin Man* pictures . . . 'cept I think you're prettier. Nancy loves Myrna Loy. Wait'll I tell her I know the real thing!"

Change counted, wig wrapped and bagged, Miranda smiled.

"Thanks again, Peg. You've been a big help."

Rick pushed the fedora off his forehead and leaned his arm across the counter.

"Young lady . . . can you show us the way out?"

"Sure thing, just follow me."

They heard more about bookkeeping for Standard Oil, the quiet West Portal area her family lived, what 4-H clubs her mother ran, how her little sister was an insufferable menace, and how her older brother was working at a garage and saving up for Berkeley. Her saddle shoes skipped along the concrete floor, blue-and-white gingham dress as bouncy as her talk.

They finally reached the double glass doors after another whirlwind trip through Western history.

Rick opened the door for Miranda and she walked quickly through, turning to smile and wave at Peg.

"Bye, Miss Corbie! And thank you and Mr. Corbie for coming in!"

Rick let the door close, face crestfallen, while Miranda coughed, shoving two Butter Rum Life Savers in the side of her cheek.

Sixteen

*

Old Leo was snoring behind the front desk when they walked into the Drake-Hopkins. Miranda stepped toward the staircase, hand grasping the round white knob on the balustrade. Rick plucked her sleeve, nodding toward the elevator.

"What about the crate?"

"Broken."

He shrugged, silent climb to the fourth-floor landing. Bent down and picked up the bottle of Borden milk from the recess next to the door.

"Anything to go with this?"

"Not unless you brought it with you."

The key stuck in the lock for a few seconds and she wrestled with it, finally shoving the door open, odor of cigarettes and coffee and Vol de Nuit rushing out, hint of Pine-Sol and lemon oil wood polish rising from the parquet floor.

Miranda dropped her purse on the gold cloth armchair and pulled open the living room window, cool air blowing the curtains back. Picked up a pack of Chesterfields lying on an end table, shook one out.

Rick set the Grade A milkbottle on the dining table. Pulled a Pig n' Whistle matchbook out of his trouser pocket and struck a match, flame licking the cigarette between her lips.

She inhaled, looking up at him, and blew a stream of smoke from the side of her mouth.

"Feel better?"

He gave her a sideways grin and flopped down on the couch. "I will once

I've had a steak and you tell me what you're doing with a Packard convertible and a date with the Nazi consul general." He patted the brown-and-white checked fabric next to him. "Sit down. I've got a lot to tell you."

Miranda picked up the milk bottle and walked into the kitchen. "We don't have a lot of time. It's twenty after four."

"And fashionable Nazis always arrive late. Just bring me a Scotch and I'll tie my stomach up in knots."

Rick flipped his fedora on the couch and was reading a two-day-old copy of the *Chronicle* when Miranda came back from the kitchen, carrying a tray with two highball glasses.

She set the tray on the coffee table, sank into the armchair, and crossed her legs. Tossed her hat on the couch next to Rick's and ruffled her hair.

"I'll go first. You remember Marion Gouchard?"

Rick swallowed the whiskey, eyebrows raised. "One of your covers, right?"

"For the Incubator Babies last year. I'm going to Weidemann's tonight as Marion. That's the reason for the red Packard."

He ran a thumb along the side of his chin, murmured, "Not like you want to attract attention or anything . . ."

She shook her head, deep puff on the stick. "Oh, but I do. That's the plan."

"The plan for what? You know how dangerous this is? And you haven't told me why the hell you of all people need to walk into the German consulate."

Her eyes met his, stubborn blue, anxious, protective. Possessive.

"And you won't know, Rick, because I can't tell you. But my client suggested I enlist the help of a friend tonight, so I'm asking you. You'll need to keep an eye on the entrance and watch for me. Follow me if I drive somewhere."

She opened her purse, wedged beside her in the chair, and handed him a fifty-dollar bill.

"Hire a taxi—have it waiting near the entrance, somewhere where you can see who comes and goes. I'll be in a red dress from my Mills College days, and don't forget: hair like Louise Brooks."

Rick held the bill with both hands and stared at it uncomprehendingly for a few seconds, lines down the sides of his mouth.

"First the car and then the wig, and now all this cash. Sounds like you're up to something for the FBI or the Dies Committee, and that's dangerous work. What about Gonzales? This is right up his alley—unless he's already involved. You working for him now, Miranda? Is that where the money came from?"

Miranda ground out the Chesterfield in the ashtray. "Look—I asked you.

If you can't or won't help me, forget about it. I gave you the rules, and that's all I can give you. My cover's fine. Marion Gouchard works for the French consulate—"

"Which is now part of the Third Reich. This is nuts. You can't play a Nazi to save your life—"

"I do whatever the hell I need to do, Sanders. I'm a professional—and don't forget it."

He stared at the highball glass in his hands, eyes unfocused, voice stretched too taut.

"How can I? Gangsters, fifth columnists, killers . . . and now some hush-hush assignment for your boyfriend on the Dies Committee."

Rick shook his head, highball glass hitting the stoneware tray with a loud clink.

"I say let Gonzales hire his own goddamn help. I may open doors and light cigarettes, Miranda, but I'm not watching you walk into the lion's den again, especially not for the sake of that rich sonofabitch. You've almost gotten killed twice in the last few months—third time's a charm. At least before I knew why, I understood, didn't like it, but understood. Now you tell me nothing, not a goddamn thing, and what the hell—expect me to help you put yourself behind the eight ball for Gonzales's sake?"

"Don't be an idiot—I don't work for Gonzales—he doesn't have anything to do with this. I can't tell you more than I've told you, and I wish I could, it's . . . it's important, Rick. There are certain people at the party I need to get close to."

Rick drained his glass and stood in one fluid motion, face red, unsteady on his feet.

"Just how close, Miranda? How fucking close? Or is that my answer?"

White and red.

Like the bathroom walls when she blew Martini's brains out.

Too late for Rick, too late to swallow the words, too much Scotch and not enough food, too much jealousy, too much Gonzales, too much resentment and fear.

Too much Miranda.

Pain like little razors, cutting, bleeding, cutting again, and she gasped, armor off and no scars, not with Rick, no cover, no protection, no poultice.

Her arm flew out in an open-faced slap, and it landed on his cheek as hard as she could make it.

He bent backward, stumbling, arm flung behind him, couch holding him up, other hand wiping his cheek. Pulled himself up, tears on his cheeks, blue swimming in red, red trickle from his mouth, and he put two hands on her shoulders and crushed her to his chest, head bent beneath his, bloodied lips bruising hers, savage and sorry, apology and attack, hungry, always hungry, lean body hard and on fire.

Her arms hung stiffly by her side. Unbent, unmoving. She licked her lips, tasting salt.

He held her face in his hands, desperate to find something, then cradled her head against his chest. Stroked her hair.

"Goddamn it, Miranda, I love you, I've always loved you, and I'm going away. I've been thinking about joining the army, and I will, I'll leave this week, goddamn it, but I won't hurt you again."

He held her at arm's length. Spoke softly.

"I'll—I'll leave now. I'm sorry."

She looked into his eyes, the man who wanted to be John Hayes, the man who wanted John Hayes's girl.

But he was more than that. He was Richard Sanders. His own man.

Her best friend.

Miranda drew a shuddering breath and wiped her mouth with the back of her hand.

"I've got to get ready. You coming tonight or not?"

He cupped her face with his left hand again, eyes searching hers, mouth still drawn impossibly tight, skin stretched and pale over the sharp edges of his cheeks.

"You—you still want my help?"

She shrugged out of his grasp, picked up the packet of Chesterfields with trembling fingers.

"I wouldn't have asked you if I didn't."

His forehead knotted as he watched her light her own cigarette with a Club Moderne matchbook, watched as she inhaled in a long pull, the ash slowly devouring the stick, tiny ring of fire creeping upward.

"Miranda, I—"

"Save it, Sanders. You in or out?"

He swallowed, rubbed his mouth with his thumb. "In. I'm in, Miranda."

"OK. Use your best judgment. No need to approach or even talk to me."

She sat back down in the armchair, eyes expressionless, watching the smoke spiral upward.

"Now tell me why you were late. Though I can guess—did you find something out? Something about my mother?"

Rick nodded, hat in hand, staring at the floor. "I'll give you the story, Miranda. I think—I think you'll start to remember—and fill in the details."

*

Once upon a time there was a little girl from Ulster who sailed on a ship. The ship landed in a sooty city with tall brick buildings, and she worked in a factory and sewed clothes, until she left on a train with several brothers and rode for days, watching prairie winds and dust storms, passing small clapboard houses with wasps' nests tucked in corners, old men rocking in older wooden chairs.

The family arrived in another city, this one cleaner and more to her liking, and there they stayed, while the girl grew into a comely young woman and found ways of contributing to the family coffers that her parents would not have approved, but which her brothers appreciated.

She was sixteen and worked in an Irish pub on O'Farrell, serving cabbage and corned beef, pasties and porter, to men working the night shift on the printing presses. She kept the tips, saving them for a new dress, dreaming of hats and furs like the ladies wore to the theater and opera, longing for something other than the worn muslin with the small blue flowers and dark stains of beer and gravy.

She was happy, in her way, happy to help her brothers, saving money for their own pub and the cost of a train ticket for her parents in New York, happy to smile at the customers and pretend not to hear the rough language and feel the coarse hands on her legs.

April 18th, 1906, early Wednesday morning. Restless, she woke up and washed her face with the water in the basin, still in her thin cotton camisole, and then the earth opened up, roaring, angry, and God rained punishment on San Francisco.

The boarder who lived a few doors down and who would give her stony looks, Mr. Harper with the books and the neatly pressed and oiled hair, ran out in a nightshirt screaming, and together they fled down the back stairwell, passing Old Mrs. Hutchinson calling for her cat, and Mr. and Mrs. Dobbie, the landlords, knocking on all the doors. The ceiling fell in at the rear of the building, and they had to step around what remained of Mr. Shaughnessy.

Two of her brothers were married and all three were living on Guerrero

Street. She didn't want to think about them or the girls at the bar, or the fancy ladies in hats or Mr. Caruso at the Palace. Didn't want to think about San Francisco, the city she'd come to love as her own.

She held hands with the boarder and limped through the broken streets, Mr. Harper clutching his trousers, nightcap still on his head. They passed the dying and almost dead, trembling in the middle of Van Ness when the aftershock hit, horses and carts buried together under brick, babies screaming for mothers who would never come.

Feet bleeding from broken glass and brick, thirsty and covered in yellow and red dust, black soot from the fires, they finally reached Golden Gate Park, makeshift tents and way stations already set up. He told her he was a poet and a professor, and she clung to him like ivy.

They held each other's hands when the soldiers separated them, and she cried, not knowing if she'd see her brothers again on earth.

That night he entered her tent when the other women were out and she was surprised and glad. He called her Juliet and Roxanne and other names, and led her outside to a patch of green grass and juniper, well hidden. He held her and he was warm, and she liked the music he made with words.

A daughter was born nine months later.

The young girl, dark haired, pretty and less plump that she'd been before, was now a woman and a mother. All three of her brothers still lived, a sister-in-law dying of a heart attack in the aftermath, older brother in grief.

She guarded her baby like a lioness, not letting them own her, not letting them raise her.

Mr. Harper, poet and professor, thrust money in her hands, lifted his hat and bid her adieu, agreeing to call the child Miranda. She'd picked it from a book. He looked so surprised.

She was alone.

But Catherine Corbie was used to that.

After a few months when the money was exhausted, she relented, returned to her family and her work with her child in tow. Her brothers opened a bar, sorely needed as San Francisco rebuilt itself, and the ladies who sat in big hats and fancy dresses, feathers on their shoulders, doted on the little girl while the mother worked, making food, waiting tables, sunrise to sunset and beyond.

Always dreaming of something better.

One day when Miranda was about two years old, a man walked in with an ebony cane and a large roll of bills, some of which he left Catherine as a tip. He sat back, teeth showing underneath a luxurious mustache, and told her she should be on stage.

He handed her a card with flowers and gold leaf, told her to see him at the Empress on Market Street. Lifted his eyebrows, eyes folded in a wink.

And Catherine looked at her little girl, playing on the wooden floor behind the bar with milk caps and empty rum bottles. And she walked three blocks down Mason Street to the Empress, where the man with the mustache took her into a room and lifted her dress, feeling her breasts and thighs, and made her spread her legs while he pressed her to a wall.

She played a matinee the next day, with one of the "8 Big Acts 8."

Her brothers objected at first, but when they saw the money she made, the flowers and the tips, saw her progress from act to act until she was featured in skits, even singing an old Irish lullaby and headlining her own act . . . they stopped objecting. Her parents were coming out soon, thanks to Catherine, though she hadn't told them how she'd made the money. She'd changed her name for the stage, called herself Maggie O'Meara.

There was Miranda to think of. She wanted her beautiful young daughter to have the things she never had, and she'd sing to her when she could, voice worn from the laughter and the smoke, sounding old at twenty.

She sang to Miranda, always.

Until February 17th, 1911.

A gentleman caller, that's what he called himself, a Mr. A. O. Proctor, and he knocked at the backstage door of the Empress, Miranda sitting on a stool and crying for more oatmeal, Catherine hurriedly patting her face with rouge, spraying perfume on her décolletage.

He shoved the door in, holding a bouquet of wilted flowers, rye whiskey and garlic on his breath.

He claimed to know Catherine from her younger days, back when she was waiting tables and serving in her brother's bar. He held a thick, pulpy hand up to her side and pulled her to him, his other hand groping under her dress.

Catherine was a professional. She kneed him in the groin and dumped face powder on his head, opened the door and called in one of the hands.

Proctor woke up and shook a fist, said he'd be back. She ignored him.

Curtain in five minutes.

That night, after the show, she stayed to clean up the dressing room she shared with the girl in the seltzer sketch. Miranda was quiet, eyes big, until she fell asleep, legs long for a four-year-old.

Catherine left the theater and headed down Sixth Street to the boarding-house on Jessie. She was halfway home when Proctor lurched out of the dark-ness and seized her, his hand over her mouth. She kicked and bit, finally succeeding in freeing herself. He was drunker than he'd been in the afternoon, and his dim eyes lit on Miranda, crouched by a stoop, silent and still.

Catherine saw what he was staring at and flew at him, screaming, but he backhanded her and she fell, striking the pavement next to a construction site for a new house.

Proctor muttered words she couldn't hear, and she watched as he lurched toward the little girl, hand on the buttons of his pants. Miranda froze, eyes big and fathomless, chest rising and falling in short gasps, auburn hair long and wavy like her mother's.

Catherine felt the blood trickling from her lip, felt her hands, large, Scotch-Irish peat-picking hands, grasp a brick by the pile next to the fence.

Proctor was bent over Miranda, little girl in his shadow. Catherine tottered toward them, holding the brick high above her head with two hands. She crashed it into his skull as hard as she could.

They collapsed and huddled together, mother and daughter, until one of the neighbors, hearing no more screaming, ventured out of the house and found them.

They made it home to the boardinghouse, and she sent a messenger to her older brother, who lived above the tavern on Guerrero.

Police came in the morning. Newspapermen followed, and they made much of beautiful "Maggie O'Meara," half calling her a murderess (actress-whore, slut, and harlot), the other half claiming she was justified in saving her daugh-ter's life.

Miranda, who'd been a voluble talker, would not speak. She clung to her mother or sat by herself in a corner, large brown eyes flecked with green, un-fathomable and alone, legs drawn up underneath her.

Catherine blamed herself. Others followed, the School Board (why is your child not enrolled, Madame?), Matrons and Mothers Leagues. No mother, that Maggie O'Meara, or whatever she calls herself. Just another slut with a bastard, actress-whore.

Irish slut.

She stopped singing the lullaby, almost as silent as her daughter.

A sympathetic reporter from *The San Francisco Call* wrote about the actress Maggie O'Meara, not using her real name, about her brief life and upcoming trial, about how her brothers had mortgaged the business to get her out on bail, about the little girl who wouldn't speak.

The oldest brother thought hard and sent the article to Professor Harper. The child needed someone, and Catherine was falling apart. Only twenty years old, and she looked forty. No names had been mentioned in the story, and if he could see his way to helping them out of the predicament, no names would ever need to be mentioned . . .

The parents exchanged their train tickets for a third-class berth on a freighter traveling to Limerick. The brothers explained to Catherine what she must do. The courts of their adopted country wouldn't understand. Proctor had owned a grocery store, had a common-law wife who was riding the publicity for all it was worth. Catherine was Irish, and beautiful, and an unwed mother. Above all, she was an actress.

Actress-whore. Irish slut.

They vowed to follow their sister, to move out of San Francisco, to go back to Ireland with money and their name restored. And they promised her they'd look after Miranda.

Catherine wept, holding her knees, her long auburn hair flowing like a river down her back.

They smuggled her out at night into San Francisco Bay, and Miranda held tight to the edge of the boat, still silent, eyes still blank and empty. Catherine had insisted the little girl go with them, wanted one last look at the Earth-Shaker, as she called her, the child conceived during God's anger at the city of San Francisco.

She held her close, as the brothers and the Irish captain held a lantern, rocking, light dancing on the dark, turbulent water.

"Be strong, little one," she whispered, salt water stinging her skin and eyes. "Strong and brave. Your last name is Corbie, no matter what he tells you. I named you. I'll never forget you. I love you, Daughter."

I'd rock my own sweet child to rest . . .

She stepped out of the rocking boat, the men from the freighter in thick sweaters and dark caps, holding out hands to catch her and pull her up the ladder.

Sleep, baby dear, sleep without fear . . .

She was singing the song. Miranda could hear it, could follow the movement of her lips, even in the dark and the fog and with the lantern yellow and dim, the men cursing the Bay waters that she loved to smell and watch and play in.

Her mother was singing.

I'd put my own sweet child to sleep . . .

The men lifted Catherine Corbie into the freighter for the final few feet, and she turned around, gasping, hair blowing the cape from her face, searching for the tiny figure in the small boat huddled under a blanket.

She held up a hand. Miranda could still hear her voice.

Sleep, baby dear, sleep without fear . . .

Mother is here with you forever

"Good-bye, Mama," the little girl whispered.

Seventeen

*

S he was silent for a few minutes, Baby Ben alarm clock ticking from the bedroom. A foghorn bellowed from below the Golden Gate, signal for the mass of gray clouds to move eastward, swallowing orange bridge and blue and yellow cars, wrapped like a manacle around Alcatraz.

She was rubbing her right hand with her thumb, over and over. Her legs were shaking.

She asked slowly: "How much of this is guesswork?"

Rick inhaled the Camel, nostrils blowing smoke. "Some. Not a lot. The *Call* article was detailed enough. That's what linked Maggie O'Meara to Catherine Corbie . . . a daughter named Miranda, same age, same circumstances. Your mother fled before she could stand trial, and her real name never got in the papers. After she disappeared, she was yesterday's news."

"What about her brothers? Are they still alive?"

He shrugged. "I don't know, Miranda. Maybe. I put this much together by making a trunk call to New York and asking a pal to poke around some immigration records. That's the Ulster connection. I've got names, the name of the bar they owned—which is still there but has long since changed hands, especially during Prohibition—and that's about all. There will be more in the police records."

He bent forward on the couch, tapping the stick in the tray, and glanced upward, still finding it difficult to meet her eyes.

"I was hoping the little I told you would spark your own memory. I figured you knew more than you thought, remembered more. Did it help?"

She nodded, eyes faraway. A church bell tolled the hour, and Miranda started, eyes wider, green coming back to the brown. She stood up from the chair.

"Thanks. I need to get ready now."

He pushed himself up from his knees like an old man. Reached for the bent brim of his fedora and shoved it on his head.

"Don't worry about tonight. I'll be watching over you."

There's a somebody I'm longing to see . . .

"You—you're a good friend, Rick."

His voice was curt. "No, I'm not. I'm a poor bastard in love and useless to himself and most everyone else. And I'd rather take a bullet in the gut than hurt you. I was serious about the army, Miranda. I don't know how much longer I can stand this—whatever it is we have."

"Rick, I—"

"Don't say anything." He rubbed a hand down the side of his unshaven jaw, mouth lined and weary. "I'll be there tonight. But afterward . . . I don't know. I just don't know." He looked up at her sharply. "Go on, get ready. My masquerade is over . . . yours is just beginning."

Blue eyes, naked, in pain. No crinkles at the corner. No half-Irish bullshit lilt.

She placed a hand on his arm. "Be careful. I . . . I couldn't stand to lose both of you." Miranda reached up and kissed him gently on the lips, shutting the door on Rick's surprised face.

*

The foyer closet smelled of old wood shavings and clothes, lingering scent of Je Reviens and L'Heure Bleu. She brushed a cobweb from a wardrobe trunk and dragged it halfway out of the closet until it landed with a loud *thunk* on the floor.

Dusted off the latch. Opened the trunk.

Dresses, shoes, a menu. A handwritten note on a cocktail napkin.

Souvenirs.

Je Reviens and a flask on her leg, Mills College and boys from Berkeley, hair slicked with grease, feet moving faster than hands. Black bottom days, new and fresh and possible, smoky jazz played on wind-up Victrolas, long cigarette holders and high back kicks to the Texas Tommy, Joan Crawford in *Our Modern Maidens,* breathless sex behind the steamed-up windows of a LaSalle.

Taped-down breasts and long strands of pearls, whispered password for speakeasy-smuggled Scotch.

Three years, maybe four, close to happiness then, running, always running, either to someone or away from someone else, forward and back to the movement of the Charleston, gay, shrill laughter at the Cafe du Nord, sleeping through economics class, working at Joe's place, hatcheck girl, cigarette girl.

Newfound power. Newfound freedom.

Before she learned that nothing came free.

Miranda riffled through three dresses before finding the one she wanted.

Shining red beads over a cotton sheath, plunging back line, short with the waist at her hips, attached silver lamé bow. She fingered the label.

Yvonne of Paris, handmade in France.

She'd eaten liver and onions for three months to save up for it.

She held up the dress, heavy with beads. She'd taken care of it all these years, first in storage at Bekins, then finally here, once she had her own apartment.

Only fourteen years ago. Fourteen years, and already a fucking costume.

She sank on the couch holding the dress, legs trembling.

Too much to think about, Jasper and Hart and her mother and Rick, Great Flood of Memory, drowning everything in its path, and no ark to save her, no two by two, not for Miranda Corbie, forty days and forty years, no man, no child, no family, I ain't got nobody, the song said, nobody and nothing.

Except memory.

Memory, good or bad, the only goddamn thing left, and it hurts, Mama, it hurts, searing, burning, hold it until we die, best friend and enemy, and we grapple it to our souls with hoops of steel, never parting, never ending, afraid to let it go.

Ashes to ashes, dust to dust.

She raised her face to the ceiling, finding faces in the plaster patterns.

Catherine Corbie.

Johnny.

Rick.

Miranda reached for the Chesterfield pack and stood up awkwardly.

I'm afraid the masquerade is over . . .

✳

She checked her lipstick in the mirror, grabbed the small opera bag with the gold cigarette case and its hidden Baby Browning, and looked at her watch.

8:20. Fashionably late.

She climbed out of the Packard, long, silk-clad legs drawing eye-popping looks from a fat-bellied businessman walking out of a cigar shop on Stockton, disapproving head shakes and a few derisive squawks from a gaggle of matrons flocking back from Union Square. She posed, hand on her hip, bare head held high, bobbed black hair shining, red sequins glittering in the waning sun. A car horn honked loudly at a man gawking in the street.

No sign of Rick.

Stepped quickly, deliberately down O'Farrell, beading on the dress heavier than she remembered. Practiced the walk, up and back, hips swaying, intoxicatingly feminine under the boyish illusion of fourteen years and a lifetime ago. She pursed her lips, ignored the eyes. Breathed in the carnation and iris of L'Heure Bleue.

Marion Gouchard, not Miranda Corbie.

Hoped like hell she could pull it off.

She sashayed toward the burly doorman, who'd been watching her. He grinned, raised two thick callused fingers to his cap, and opened the door. The short, thin man at the elevator held a stiff sheet of paper in his hands and asked in a voice as clipped as his mustache: "Your name, Madame?"

Small, precise, just like Goebbels, the small precise man who labeled Matisse and Renoir "degenerate."

She flicked her eyes up and down over his navy blue double-breasted suit, languorous puff on the cigarette. Blew smoke over his right shoulder, watched the pale skin under his mustache turn red.

She lowered her voice, soft roll to the *r*'s.

"Marion Gouchard. French consulate."

One Mississippi, two Mississippi, while he scanned the list, and she prayed James had come through for her.

The short man frowned. She held her breath.

"Your name appears on the list in pencil, Madame. You perhaps did not respond to the invitation in time, yes?"

She shrugged. "I was away on business. You know how it is."

He nodded, adding a check to her name with a mechanical pencil. "Please— the elevator. Tenth-floor ballroom."

She nodded back, not bothering to add a wiggle when she walked into the elevator.

Inhuman Nazi bureaucrats.

A noise at the entrance signaled the arrival of a woman in a mink stole and a balding shipping tycoon, and the man with the list turned toward them with an ingratiating smile.

She pushed the button with a manicured finger, wishing her nails were longer, wishing the elevator door would hurry the fuck up. It slowly closed while the West Coast Fascist brigade chattered about the Fair and how hot Panama is in the summer. The gold doors finally locked together, and the elevator began to rise.

Miranda breathed out, heart pounding in her temples.

Next floor, Nazi Germany.

The elevator opened in an ornate foyer, gilded Ionic columns and a huge glass vase of calla lilies. Miranda opened her purse and pulled out the small black domino mask, securing it around her ears.

Double doors were thrown open to the right, din of conversation and on-the-beat swing. A booming bass guffaw punctuated the music, along with shrill, well-bred tittering.

Miranda kept to the shadows and angled for a view. The ballroom was sunken, a few steps down from the formal entranceway, littered with gold candelabra and crystal chandeliers. Oil paintings—Miranda spotted what looked like a Cranach—hung in niches between Corinthian pilasters. An unobtrusive portrait of Hitler glared at the crowd from the stairway on the far left. The small orchestra clung to the grand piano in the corner, playing a lackluster version of "Little Brown Jug."

The room stank of socialites and businessmen from the Chamber of Commerce, industrialists who frothed at the mouth whenever FDR or the New Deal was mentioned. Most were dressed in French court costume, the women with sagging breasts pushed up and powdered, faces masked, men in wigs and itchy leggings. Paul Dietrich, vice president of Bank of America, stood around nervously watching the crowd, sipping a highball every few seconds and surreptitiously scratching his ass.

Fritz Wiedemann and his mistress-Princess Stephanie von Hohenlohe-Waldenburg-Schillingsfürst, held court in the center, Hitler's favorite adjutant and former commanding officer and the Jewish woman the Fuehrer called "dear princess." Hard to believe the ugly, middle-aged hostess in pink was considered one of the most dangerous women in the country.

Weidemann stood like the Colossus of Rhodes, laugh booming across the room. Tall, athletic, with a heavy brow and pugilistic chin, he looked just like the photos in the *Life* magazine spread from the year before, a better-bred and more polished Max Schmeling. He laughed constantly, bending over shriveled hands draped in diamonds, bending farther when the cleavage belonged to a woman under forty. White teeth, strong hands, charisma of a klieg light. He was wearing a Bavarian folk costume, showing off thick, muscled legs in lederhosen.

A small man with a goatee and small, shifty eyes hovered over his left elbow. Vice Consul Rudolf G. Hübner, appropriately dressed as a medieval squire, ready to prompt his superior's memory by a whisper in the ear.

Princess Stephanie floated at the consul's right, wrapped in pink pastel gauzes and an embroidered floral dress out of Grimm's Fairy Tales. It came complete with a pointed hat and veil, weak weapons against the dragons of age. She was pushing fifty, according to reports, same age as her Prince Charming, but he looked ten years younger and she knew it.

The elevator made a lurching noise and started to move down, Miranda quickly scanning the rest of the room. A tall, thin man leaned against the balustrade, studying a landscape. He was dressed in a robe covered in chemical symbols, hands gloved, with a domino mask and a fake gray beard.

Dr. Jasper.

Time to charge the battlefield.

*

Miranda strode to the entranceway and struck a pose, arm up and hand on the door frame, leaning into her hips. Half-closed her eyelids, dark smoky shadow enhancing the mask.

She stood for a few seconds, heart beating loud enough to drown out the music.

And turned on the wattage.

Wiedemann was already staring; the princess flung her head around, whispering something to an overweight matron stuffed into a Heidi costume.

A cough, a few misplaced laughs. No music from the orchestra.

She gave a tilt to her chin, held her head up high, and shifted again, heavy beads making a swooshing sound, refracting the brittle light from the crystal chandeliers.

Stutters . . . then silence.

Wiedemann gracefully parted the crowd.

The consul climbed the five steps up from the main floor, oozing a sexual appetite rank enough to smell. She'd heard on the circuit at Dianne's about Wiedemann's prodigious appetites and equally prodigious appendage—supposedly the real reason why Der Führer idolized him. Her stomach tightened, and she tried not to flinch.

His eyes glinted as he took in her legs. Clicked his heels as she held out her hand and he bent over it, murmuring, accent thick: "I do not think we meet yet."

Vice Consul Hübner scurried forward, hands rubbing together, English impeccable.

"What Consul Wiedemann means is that we have not seen you before at one of our social events, Mademoiselle. May we inquire as to your name?"

Miranda smiled, pulling her hand away from Wiedemann's paw, letting her fingers drag against his coarse skin.

"Marion Gouchard. I am with the French embassy. Or perhaps we should rename it now, *oui*?"

Some of the surrounding crowd grew quiet, faux pas to mention the war at a social occasion. Wiedemann blinked, then roared with laughter, rough hand clapped against Miranda's bare back, heavy arm resting casually on her shoulder. She smiled up at him.

She was in.

Eighteen

*

Muted laughter and the tinkle of Austrian crystal goblets, middle-aged matrons dressed as Marie Antoinette comparing stories of Magnin minks, whispering the latest Eleanor Roosevelt joke. Men in powdered wigs relaxed with a whiskey and talk about the market, lips wrapped around thick cigars, swearing the usual exhortations to God to save America from the Communist in the White House. Husbands and wives craned necks to get a better look at the woman in the red flapper dress, silver lamé bow outlining her hips.

A younger man, tall and costumed like a Prussian officer, bowed over her hand and murmured something in German while Wiedemann grinned, teeth showing.

"This is Hans. My assistant."

Miranda nodded, making pleasantries, surreptitiously looking for Jasper. He'd moved on from the landscape to one of the Cranachs on the opposite wall.

Stephanie floated toward the forgotten shipping couple standing in the doorway looking lost, the balding, white-haired businessman red faced and irritated. Wiedemann trained his full attention on "Marion." Hübner, ever watchful, signaled to the orchestra. They launched into a spiritless version of "Smoke Gets in Your Eyes."

The consul grinned down at Miranda again, fatuous, transparent. He guided her toward the corner, arm exerting pressure against her back.

"Please. You call me Fritz, *ja?*"

She let her eyelids drop provocatively. "And you must call me Marion. Though I confess I prefer to think of you as 'Captain Fritz.'"

Wiedemann opened his eyes wide, surprised, guffawed again.

The room stank of mothballs and Ambre Antique, Havana cigars and Shalimar. Miranda wrinkled her nose and fought off a sneeze. Most eyes were still trained on her, whispers behind fans. Wiedemann continued to lead her forward, and she glanced toward the ornate stairway.

No Jasper.

Goddamn it—she'd lost him.

Stephanie, signaled by the ever helpful Hübner, glided like a Ziegfeld Girl down the steps toward her Fritzie, pink tulle flowing, arms outstretched, ferocious smile.

Wiedemann stiffened, dropped his arm from Miranda's back.

"May I present Fraulein—Mademoiselle—Marion Gouchard, my dear Steffie."

Miranda's lips curved at the corners as she extended her hand to the hostess. "An honor to meet you, Madame."

Miranda caught at the intelligence in the ugly face and knew the woman in pink was more than a cut-rate Wallis Simpson. Hard and coarse looking like her Windsor twin, the princess had actually arranged the meeting with Hitler and the Duke and Duchess three years before. Small black eyes, shrewd, merciless—and perceptive. They darted back and forth, taking in the minutiae of Miranda's makeup and wig. Miranda fought the rising color in her cheeks, feeling more clothed with Wiedemann.

"And you, Miss Gouchard. I must reprimand Consul General Gaucheron for keeping you to himself . . . I have not seen you at any of the parties this season."

Miranda opened her eyes ingenuously. "Oh, but Madame, I have been so very busy. And we must be honest . . . our consulate has not been so eager to attend your consulate's parties. We do not dance on the grave of the Maginot Line."

A few titters, sudden quiet again, room frosty and shocked. Stephanie glared at her, mouth quivering, while Wiedemann looked on helplessly, face florid and embarrassed. The band was struggling with "It Had to Be You," trying to play louder to cover the silence.

Miranda's smile stayed in place, while she removed a cigarette from the gold case, trembling hands hidden. No one stepped forward to light it, so she clicked the Ronson, inhaled deeply.

Spoke casually. "But, as they say, in love and war all is fair. And now we must all learn to speak German . . . *ja*?"

The room sighed with relief, Wiedemann roared again, and the princess narrowed her eyes and widened her lips. Resumption of cocktail conversation.

Well, of all the nerve—

She's honest, though . . . I give her that.

All the Frenchies know is wine and cheese and women. The Germans will teach them a thing or two.

I've heard Stephanie's fifty-five if she's a day . . . and Fritzie's got a wandering eye . . .

Wiedemann's eye wandered back to Miranda. Hans, his Prussian officer's uniform as stiff as a nutcracker, stood at attention, close to her right. A tired waiter appeared, summoned by Hübner.

"Drink, Mademoiselle?"

Miranda smiled pointedly at the princess. "I'll have whatever the princess is having."

The waiter bowed, retreated. Stephanie laughed lightly.

"Be careful, Mademoiselle Gouchard. It may be too strong for you."

Miranda shrugged. "I am young and resilient, Madame. I am willing to try . . . anything."

Stephanie studied Miranda's face. The fat woman dressed as Heidi plucked her sleeve, and the princess turned to greet another party of latecomers at the doorway, firing a parting shot over her shoulder.

"We have a saying in Germany, my dear: Ambition and fleas both jump high."

Miranda blew a smoke ring high in the air toward the chandelier and nodded, smiling.

"There is a French proverb, too, Madame. *On n'apprend pas aux vieux singes à faire des grimaces.* You cannot teach old monkeys to make new faces."

The pink tulle flounced, train dancing in the air, pointed hat making its way through the crowd, as Princess Stephanie retreated from the field of battle, smile glued ferociously in place.

*

Wiedemann stationed himself at her right hand, animatedly discussing his car (a Mercedes), his favorite restaurant in San Francisco (Schroeder's Café), his fondness for English suits ("easier to acquire when we win the war!"), his patriotic yearning for Augsburg and wistful nostalgia for the farm he left behind. No mention of Mexico, Los Angeles, or Herbert Hoehne.

He took out his pocket handkerchief and blew his nose, tearing up over farm equipment and Bavarian milkmaids. She patted his hand and smiled, smoked more Chesterfields than she could count, drank two Scotch and sodas.

No sign of the man in the alchemist robe.

Miranda glanced up the stairway from her vantage point in the corner. Only place Jasper could have gone. The landing at the top was dark, maybe three doors, maybe four. Only Hübner and Loeper, the consulate chancellor, used the stairway freely.

She'd need a reason.

The crowd was starting to break up, and Paul Dietrich gave her a distant nod as he left, eyes grave. Some local businessmen, not in costume, paid their respects to the consul, more cool than warm, maintaining a Swiss neutrality. A burly man in his thirties, dressed in a Union Civil War uniform, positioned himself in the corner, watching the departing guests. She wondered who he was.

Her eyes drifted toward a tall, well-built man costumed as Robin Hood lounging against the banquet table. She hadn't noticed him before. He caught her eye, stood up, and walked in the opposite direction toward the Civil War soldier, out of her line of sight.

Miranda frowned. Too goddamn familiar, but she still couldn't place him . . .

She was still staring after him when Hans bent forward attentively, accent thick.

"Looking for someone, Mademoiselle?"

Beckoned by Stephanie, Wiedemann was now deep in conversation with an older woman named Olga Kraemer, some kind of nanny to the Nazis. She studied the young man, his eyes blue and clear, chin covered with the faintest blond stubble.

"Yes. A tall, thin man in an alchemist's robe—I admired his costume. I was wondering who he was."

Young Siegfried raised his left hand to adjust his mask, and nodded. "*Ja.* Dr. Jas-per. He advises the consul on art." He gestured proudly toward the wall. "You see? Cranach. Dürer. Holbein. Great German art."

The back of Miranda's neck tingled, and she turned toward the banquet table. Ulysses S. Grant was watching her from the shadows. She placed a light hand on Hans's brocaded sleeve.

"I am very interested in art. Show me, please?"

Hans smiled broadly and stood taller, face red with pleasure. "*Jawohl.* We begin with Cranach."

He held out two hands to pull her out of the Empire-style chair, and they walked toward the back wall by the staircase. Wiedemann was talking with the others, voice too low to be overheard. The young man gestured to a yellowed oil painting on the wall.

"This painting is new. Study for a Nude. Cranach the Elder."

Miranda brightened her smile and turned toward Hans.

"Did Dr. Jasper help you find this?"

Wiedemann's heavy steps, followed by the coarse weight of hands on her shoulders.

"You like Cranach, *liebchen*? You not tell me before." He growled, faintly accusatory. "Hans, help Frau Kraemer home. She is not so young."

Goddamn it, just lost her best goddamn source so far . . .

Miranda held out her hand to Hans, who bit his lip and blushed scarlet at Wiedemann's reproach.

"*Danke,* Hans. I hope to see you again."

The consul barked "*Schnell,*" and the young blond marched hurriedly away. Wiedemann's right hand moved across her back to her left shoulder. He smiled down at her benevolently.

"You like art? We have more upstairs in the library. I show you."

Fritz and his fucking etchings. One way—maybe the only way—to get upstairs.

She opened her gold case, took out the second to last Chesterfield. The flames of Wiedemann's silver-plated lighter licked the stick. She inhaled, while he showed it to her.

"You see? From Der Führer."

The lighter sported an inscription she couldn't read except for "A. Hitler." She blew a stream of smoke from the side of her mouth. The orchestra launched into "Where or When."

"You must hold on to that, Fritz. It's quite a souvenir."

He squeezed her shoulder and stared into her eyes with meaning. "I keep everything precious, *liebchen.*"

She forced a laugh. Gestured to the stairway with the cigarette in her hand. "Hans tells me a Dr. Jasper helps you with your art collection. I believe I saw him . . . a tall gentleman in a funny robe, *oui*?"

"*Ja,* Jasper is an art expert. He is probably upstairs, studying my Dürer prints. Let us go see."

Wiedemann grinned, teeth showing, animal smell growing in intensity. He'd had too much to drink.

She was propelled forward by the huge, hairy paw on her back.

Miranda squirmed out from under his hand and climbed the stairs quickly. She glanced to her right, where the princess was following her movements, eyes venomous.

"Wait, *liebchen*. You are too quick for me."

She waited on the dark landing and took a gulp on the burning cigarette, facing three solid oak doors, while Wiedemann strode up the stairs, heavy feet thumping through the brown-and-gold carpet.

He arrived slightly out of breath, extending his hand to her back and rubbing her skin. She repressed a shudder. He moved closer, staring down at her, arm making another barrier. She could smell the Scotch.

"Which door is the library?"

His voice was thick. "You want to see art? I will show you art."

She playfully—but forcibly—pushed his chest with both hands, and he took a step backward.

"I want to see the art and meet Dr. Jasper, Captain. I have heard of him."

Wiedemann raised his eyebrows, blinked his eyes. "Jasper? *Ja*, I remember seeing him. He never stays long at parties. We will go in—here."

He grasped the brass doorknob of the farthest door on the left and twisted it open. The room was dark, full of dusty volumes of Goethe and Schopenhauer and military exploits of the kaisers, collection predating the Third Reich and reflecting German history in San Francisco.

The tall man in the purple robe with chemical symbols was seated at a large wooden table, studying a book of engravings. The mask was off his face. He looked up when they walked in.

Jasper.

Wiedemann clicked his heels together and bowed.

"Dr. Jasper. Marion Gouchard—from the French consulate. She wants to meet you."

Jasper raised his arched, matted eyebrows, skin mealy and with a yellow pallor. He looked older than fifty-three.

"You are interested in chemistry, Mademoiselle?"

She smiled and perched on the edge of a wooden chair, rubbing out the cigarette in a metal ashtray.

"Art, Dr. Jasper. I understand you help Fritz find treasures—like the Cranach downstairs. Our own poor consulate is in need of such help."

Jasper looked from one to the other and shut the oversized book, dust flying out from between the pages.

"I am nothing but a small-time collector, Mademoiselle. I offer amateur advice, that is all."

Wiedemann chortled. "You are too modest, Herr Doktor. We will soon be in need of more of your 'advice.'" He turned toward Miranda. "Herr Doktor helps keep us close to Berlin. We here in America work at a—a disadvantage, *ja*?"

Jasper stood up from the chair, clearly uncomfortable. "A pleasure to meet you, Mademoiselle. Enjoy the Dürers."

He stepped toward the door, Wiedemann all too eager to see him leave. Miranda flung the words at his back, desperate chance.

"I do love art, Dr. Jasper. Particularly 'degenerate art.'"

He froze under the heavy purple robe.

"Speak with someone at the San Francisco Museum of Art. There is a very fine Picasso exhibit showing."

"But I hear that you are an expert—"

Ferocity, sudden and feral. "Who told you that? I am a professor of chemistry, not an art critic."

Miranda's hands were shaking. Wiedemann was too tight and too much anticipating a long night with Marion to take offense at Jasper's distemper. He laughed, the guttural, deep-from-the-belly laugh of a man secure in his own castle.

"You are an expert, Herr Doktor, and we all know it to be true. Especially in what Goebbels has called 'degenerate.' How else do you make your bargains? Talk to the girl. She will not bite you." He winked at Miranda.

Jasper slowly turned to face her, hands hanging stiffly at his sides.

"I am sorry, Miss Gouchard. Art is far too serious a subject to discuss so lightly, at a frivolous party given by the frivolous Fritz." He gestured with his head toward Wiedemann. "If you are a serious student, you may call on me at the University of California."

"*Merci*, Doctor. May I say I admire your costume? You are an alchemist, yes?"

Jasper was terse. "I am Faust, Miss Gouchard. Faust."

The robe billowed behind him as he strode through the door, pulling it quietly shut. Wiedemann looked after him, shrugged, and turned back to Miranda, all teeth.

She stood up. He maneuvered gracefully toward her and leaned across the table, hands flat and splayed on the wood.

"And now, my *liebchen* . . . now we will finally learn art."

He stood up straight, arching his back. His hands moved to rest on his stomach. Keeping his brown eyes fixed on Miranda's, he slowly lowered them to the the crotch flap of his costume.

Nineteen

*

Miranda took out her last cigarette, lighting it with the Ronson. Held on to the gold case, feeling the weight of the Baby Browning within.

Blown cover, career over. Not much of a detective, no, not when she talked herself into a Nazi party with the fucking Nazi party and shoots the fucking Nazi consul general . . .

She looked up at him, brown-green eyes cool and appraising.

"Fritz, *chéri*, it is not appropriate now for us to—to get to know each other better. Your Stephanie is one flight away."

His neck was thick and red, Adam's apple bulged and prominent. She'd heard about his kicks at Dianne's, first a rape-and-pillage scenario followed by punishment for bad behavior. A girl named Lily wound up in a hospital bed for two weeks, Dianne graciously docking her future salary to pay for expenses.

"You like Fritz, *ja*?" The side of his hand drifted lower and rested alongside his prick, growing larger by the second under the lederhosen. He took a step closer, eyes unfocused.

"You like Fritz more."

She backed away and picked up the cigarette case, eyes steady.

Sudden knock. High-pitched voice outside the door.

Thank God. Stephanie.

Fritz wilted.

Hübner and the princess stood in the doorway, Stephanie's small black eyes taking in the scene with barely diluted fury. A few feet behind them stood the Robin Hood figure in green.

"Here you are. I've been looking for you, Fritz. Frieda wanted to know if we've heard from Putzi lately, wasting away in that horrid English prison—as if England weren't prison enough—and I said I knew you'd had a letter from him. Come down this instant and read it to her."

She turned on her heel, glancing back at Miranda as if in afterthought.

"And you, my dear, I had no idea you were interested in paintings. Hans told me you were asking after the Cranach." Her eyes raked over Miranda's dress critically. "I would have expected something more . . . contemporary." She managed to give her voice a sneer.

Miranda's lips curved upward. "I am interested in everything, Madame Princess. Modern, contemporary . . . even 'degenerate.'"

Stephanie's eyes narrowed. She grasped Wiedemann's arm, pulling him toward the door. He stumbled toward her docilely.

"Come, Fritz."

Hübner kept his eyes on the corner, started to say something that came out in a stutter, bowed toward Miranda, and left quietly.

She sank into a wooden chair. Puffed at the cigarette, forgotten between her fingers, and rubbed it out on the chair arm. Tossed the case back in her purse. Her eyes met the man in green still standing by the half-open door.

"You can come in now."

"Thanks." He bowed from the waist.

She stood up slowly, stretching her legs.

"Where did you pick up the costume? Goldstein?"

"It's a family heirloom—"

"Can the act. I asked you to help—from the outside."

His posture relaxed and the well-built man in green pulled off his mask.

Rick, complete with a fake mustache and beard. Blue eyes, familiar crinkle at the corners.

"I told you I'd watch over you, Miranda."

"And you meant it literally."

"My swan song. Thought I'd go out with a bang. Couldn't find a knight costume . . . all the krauts got there first."

"Did you send Hübner and the princess up here?"

He nodded. "I saw you go upstairs with Fritz. He's got a certain reputation."

"For good reason. Ever hear of Lily Cartwright? She worked for Dianne a couple of years ago. Wiedemann put her in the hospital. Split her open like a walnut."

Rick turned red, ran a hand over his forehead. Muttered: "I've heard something along those lines."

Miranda perched on the end of one of the tables, looking him up and down appraisingly.

"You look pretty good in tights. Don't worry, I won't tell the steno pool. So what's the story? How did you sneak in here?"

He grinned. "Society column for an Atascadero paper, known to be pro-Nazi, and a half-faked press pass. When you didn't come down with the creep in the weird robe, I figured I'd go ask Stephanie where you were. She noticed Fritzie was gone, too, and that was all she wrote."

She sighed, hopped off the table. "Speaking of Stephanie, we'd better get back. I don't want to make Wiedemann too jealous."

Rick scratched an ear, forehead wrinkled. "You're not angry."

Miranda took his arm. "No. No, I'm not. You helped save me from, as they say, a fate worse than death."

"I knew Wiedemann was up to no good, Nazi sonofabitch . . ."

She shook her head impatiently. "Not that. I can take care of myself."

He paused just outside the door, voice a whisper. "What, then?"

Her mouth drew together in a hard line. "Shooting the bastard. I would have lost my license."

They were almost at the foot of the stairs when Stephanie looked up, mouth a bitter, biting smile. The crowd had dwindled to twenty or thirty diehards, including Jasper, who stood in a corner sipping a drink.

"Ah, Miss Gouchard, our friend from the French consulate. Since you are obviously a champion of the Weimar epoch and its artistic and cultural license—everything from 'degenerate' art to cabaret shows and 'free love,' I should imagine—Fritzie has proposed moving the party to a more suitable locale . . . in your honor, of course."

Wiedemann opened his mouth to say something and she preempted him, waving a bejeweled hand in the air, voice like ground glass.

"Our own little consulate is far too old-fashioned for a girl of your sensibilities, my dear. And Fritzie—shh, everyone, don't tell the Fuehrer!—Fritzie rather enjoys his nightclubs too, don't you, dear? Benda's Fantasy Palace is too far—all the way to San Bruno. Fortunately, I understand there is a suitable locale nearby on Broadway. It's called Finocchio's!"

The princess whipped the tired and mostly drunk crowd into a whoop, while Wiedemann looked like he wanted to crawl under a Panzer. Miranda's mouth pulled into a tight smile. The princess was maneuvering Wiedemann out of bounds and trying to humiliate them both in the bargain.

"How marvelous! *Merci,* Madame Princess. Surely you recognize that in San Francisco, even *entartete Kunst* may have its charms. I thank you for what will be a memorable evening."

She glanced up at Wiedemann. He avoided her eyes, barked at Hübner.

"Call for my Mercedes."

The tired, out-of-key orchestra fell mercifully mute as the leftover Teutonic knights and eighteenth-century royalty scrambled for the new destination. Rick headed toward the door, reporter's notebook flipped open, maintaining his cover by asking for names and occupations for the Atascadero *Beacon Light Herald.* The Civil War soldier she'd noticed earlier was leaning against the wall, eyes on the crowd.

Miranda approached Jasper. "I am sorry I disturbed you, Doctor. I hope you forgive me—and that you will join us at Finocchio's."

He nodded and drained the wineglass, setting it down on a low table.

"Yes, Mademoiselle. I will see you there. But tell me—are you from France? Your accent puzzles me."

"Quebec originally, raised in Chicago. Do you know Chicago, Doctor?"

"Rather well. I visit often. Excellent art galleries."

"You are a man of diverse interests. Tell me, please—who is the real Dr. Jasper? Brilliant research scientist, art aficionado, world traveler?" She gestured toward the alchemical robe. "Perhaps you have learned to convert iron to gold, yes?"

He folded his arms, eyes burning down into hers. "We all wear masks, Mademoiselle Gouchard. Tonight I am Faust. I wonder—I very much wonder—who you are."

She caught her breath and smiled. "Perhaps you will find out at Finocchio's. But I'm afraid I will bore you."

Miranda slipped through the crowd, feeling Jasper's eyes on her back. Guts and instinct, only things she had, and the doctor was too fucking curious. Tried to remember the backstory she'd made for Marion, tried to get the goddamn details straight.

She gave a small, nearly imperceptible nod to Rick. They walked into the foyer separately but waited together at the elevator, riding down with the shipping magnate and his wife, discussing weather in San Francisco and the next German ship due in at the port.

Outside, the wife huddled in mink trotted out by the waiting chauffeur, wind whipping fog through the downtown canyons. The older couple scurried away under cover of night and cloud, Nazi menace in San Francisco dispersing like so many brown rats.

Miranda shivered at the sudden cold, glanced at Rick.

"Not the right weather for a convertible. The car's around the corner."

"I know. I figured I'd ride with you."

She unlocked the door, stretching for her black velvet cape in the back. Shrugged herself into it, Rick helping wrap it around her shoulders. She bent forward, pressing the button that was supposed to lift the top. It didn't move. Miranda sighed.

"At least we'll stay awake. I'll drive."

"Thought you would."

She shoved the car into gear and gunned the motor down Stockton toward O'Farrell. "I could drop you off."

"And miss Nazis at Finocchio's? Besides, you never know when you might need a green shoulder to lean on."

Miranda made a left and hurtled past the consulate, brakes screeching in the mist. Another left on Grant and one more on Geary, passing Union Square, Alma Spreckles's statue shining dimly, lights from the department stores and hotels blinking blue and pink and gold.

Puffs of wet smoke blowing up the street, San Francisco's summertime trick, muffled sound, too apathetic to rain. It caressed her face, leaving droplets against her skin, swaddling cloth for city light posts and call boxes, gathering around fire escapes and cornices, steady *drip-drip-drip,* while dim yellow lights glowed behind apartment windows. The horn by the orange bridge cried out once more, mourning a lost lover, lament answered by a seagull caught high on the wind stream and the bellow of an oil freighter heading through the Golden Gate.

Right on Leavenworth. "I still can't tell you anything."

He shrugged. "I know the rules. Can't keep me from guessing, though."

"You get anything you can use?"

Rick pulled out a pack of Lucky Strikes from a green jacket pocket. "Got a match?"

"Lighter's in my bag."

He opened her purse and fished around for the Ronson, while Miranda made a quick left on California and an immediate right on Hyde, heading for Broadway. He bent forward, lighting the stick below the fog line.

"Want a smoke?"

She shook her head, checking the rearview mirror.

"I'm out of Chesterfields. Hand me the Pep-O-Mints."

He placed the roll of Life Savers in her hand, and she plucked out two, driving one-handed past Jackson.

"We're almost there. Ever been to Finocchio's?"

He exhaled, blowing smoke through his nose. "Yeah. Not with Nazis, though. And to answer your earlier question: nothing I can use now, but maybe a few things I can build on. We're getting a new war news editor at the News— Marty's being promoted. Maybe it's time to grow some balls and run a few exposés about San Francisco money and Hitler."

Miranda smoothly pulled into a parking lot on the side of the semirustic two-story wooden building, FINOCCHIO's lit in yellow neon, a red COCKTAILS sign glowing below.

"You can't write articles in the army." She turned off the ignition.

He looked at her, scratched his head. "If I didn't know better, I'd think you were trying to talk me out of something, Miranda."

"Just making an observation." She chewed the Life Savers and swallowed, picking up her bag. "Hurry up."

Rick grabbed her hand before she could leave the car, holding it between rough fingers.

"I'll make up my mind soon enough, and when I do, it's done. No regrets. You can't change it. You can't change anything. But in the meantime . . . go knock some Nazis dead, sister."

She looked up into his eyes, blue with the reflected beat of yellow neon. Slowly pulled her hand out of his.

Twenty

*

Joe Finocchio's club had been around, in one form or another, for eleven years. The idea was born at Joe's father's place, when a drunk customer performed a Sophie Tucker number and brought down the house. Originally a speakeasy on the 400 block of Stockton, Joe moved to Broadway after a particularly vicious raid in '36.

Joe reopened, bigger, better, his wife Marjorie introducing acts. More numbers, more "girls," productions more expensive, the City's version of Ziegfeld.

"Finocchio's—America's most unusual nightclub" trumpeted the tourist brochures, and audiences packed the tables every night, watery whiskey and mediocre food, but one hell of an illusion. Chief Quinn was told to stand down, money was flowing to the International Settlement, and besides, everything goes and anything goes, that's the Barbary Coast, even men who looked like women, and besides, some had wives and kids to support.

The other ones—boys who liked boys, the middle-aged impresario who played a mean Hedy Lamarr, the red-hot mama who belted like Tucker, the Chinese dancer, smooth skinned, lithe, and graceful—relished the freedom and hid in plain sight. No running from the law, no code names, no codes. Just the performance.

Rumor was that Joe signed a deal with Quinn: The performers wouldn't "mingle" with the customers, though traded cocktail napkins and matchbook messages were as common as red fingernail polish. Dullea, Quinn's new replacement, showed no interest in killing a cash cow. San Francisco milked its inside-out attraction, destination for the curious and the sophisticated, haven for men and women who lived on the edge, outcast and unwanted . . . except on stage.

Like Chinatown, Finocchio's was a ghetto. And like Chinatown, the outsiders paid to get in.

*

The man in the tuxedo hadn't had time to scrub the rouge off his cheeks. He looked from Miranda to Rick nervously.

"You're with the—the German consulate party, right? Costume party and all that. Well, that's OK at Finocchio's . . . anything goes, as long as you stay off the stage. We're trying to find tables for all of you . . ."

Miranda shoved a twenty-dollar bill in his hand. "We'd like to sit with the man in the purple robe. Tall, thin, about fifty, chemical symbols all over. Is he here yet?"

The host raised plucked eyebrows, licked his lips. "I—I don't believe so, Miss. I'll do what I can." He snapped his fingers for a waiter, handed them two programs. "Clive, show these two to number five."

A young man with blond hair and a curl to his lip led them through the red-carpeted room. Freddie Renault, the tall, elegant emcee, was on stage and dressed in a sparkling ball gown, telling jokes and getting ready to introduce the next number. The waiter found a table on the left, about three rows back from the front. Miranda chose the chair facing the audience. She felt someone staring at her and looked up to find Stephanie and Wiedemann in the fourth row center, the princess wearing a nasty smile. The blond waiter bowed.

"Your drinks?"

"Scotch and soda for me. How about you, Mir—Marion?"

"Bourbon, neat."

The waiter bowed once again and walked quickly toward the bar at the back. Miranda motioned with her head to the seat across from her.

"Sit as far away from me as possible."

"You want me to go?"

"No—someone else would move in. Just leave the closest chair empty."

She craned her neck past a large palm frond. About ten of the party had already arrived, seated in scattered locations. Behind and to Stephanie's right was the masked and bearded man dressed as a Union soldier, head facing front and eyes focused on the stage. Wiedemann looked red faced and bored. He caught her eye and smiled, leaned over to whisper something to Stephanie, and stood up.

"Shit. Wiedemann's coming over. Do me a favor, Rick? Wait in the lobby for Jasper. When he comes in, make sure the twenty I gave to the maître d' pays off."

Rick yawned and nodded, pressed his mask back in place, and sauntered toward the entrance, passing the consul and nodding to him. Wiedemann pulled out the chair next to Miranda, breath still stinking of Scotch.

"You like this place, *liebchen*?"

"It's OK."

"When can I see you again?"

She needed a Chesterfield. Miranda waved her hand in the air, attracting Stephanie's attention and that of the cigarette girl.

"Just telephone the consulate, *chéri*. I am sure we can arrange something."

The cigarette girl wandered over, dressed in short pants and a striped blue-and-yellow halter, while the orchestra launched into a spirited rendition of "South of the Border," the big finale number. Freddie gracefully exited stage right, carefully carrying the train of the sparkling gown. The stage was suddenly filled with señoritas in red and orange low-cut costumes, a giant papier-mâché cactus, and male dancers in sombreros.

Wiedemann knitted his heavy brows. "Who is this man in green? I do not know him."

She handed a dollar to the cigarette girl and took two packets of Chesterfields.

"A reporter for an Atascadero paper—one that approves of you and your Reich. Don't worry, Fritz, he's harmless. You'll get good press out of it. Now I've got a question for you—who is the man dressed in the American Civil War uniform? He seems a brute."

Wiedemann laughed, caught her hand in his and held it tight, keeping her from lighting the cigarette.

"An associate of Stephanie's, she says. I am not so sure."

Wiedemann relaxed his grip, grinned, and pulled out his precious inscribed lighter. Lit the cigarette, eyes drifting down to her breasts. She looked over his shoulder at Stephanie.

The princess was glum and gimlet-eyed, fury pouring off of her like sweat. A few tables behind her and to the right, a clean-shaven, handsome man in his sixties was waving his arms in animated discussion, his companion retreating to the dark side of the table.

Miranda squinted against the stage lighting, still staring at the two men. One of them seemed familiar . . .

Sharp intake of breath, Weidemann too drunk to notice.

The man in the dark corner was Edmund Whittaker, looking fearful and anxious, shrinking back from the costumes of the Nazis surrounding him.

She glanced away quickly, shifting the domino mask firmly in place.

"I think you'd better return to your Stephanie, Fritz. She is already quite angry with me."

He bent over her hand, lips bruising her skin and leaving a wet stain. "I will see you again soon, *liebchen*. We will work together. Stephanie does not own me."

He stood up, clicked his heels together on the second try, and lurched toward the center table and the princess.

The blond waiter returned with the drinks, looking quizzically at Rick's empty chair. Miranda swirled the bourbon in the highball glass, listening to the singer warble on about mañana.

Mañana might be too fucking late. No guarantees from the French consulate on how long they'd maintain her cover—James warned her. But the hints were tantalizing, Jasper's "advice" to Wiedemann on art, his violent reaction to an "expert" label, his dangerous interest in her background. And she wondered just who the hell this "associate" of Stephanie's was . . . Miranda twisted her neck to look over the audience again. The Union soldier was standing up, heading for the bar.

Marion Gouchard needed to last long enough to find out more, find something definite . . . then disappear.

She breathed in the Chesterfield, ice cubes in the highball glass refracting the light, garish pinks and oranges from the stage.

"Good evening, Miss Gouchard. Your friend Mr. Payne tells me you wished me to sit with you."

Jasper stood in evening clothes and a white glove on his left hand, shorn of his role as Faust. Rick stifled a yawn and took the far seat, deftly removing the Scotch and soda from Jasper's place setting.

Miranda smiled up at him. "Good evening, Doctor. Thank you for the honor."

He took the seat, nodded. Looked around.

"I must apologize for my churlish behavior earlier. Attending Fritz's social functions makes me nervous. I imagine I must be on several government lists by now, suspected of the most dire espionage activity because of my work."

Miranda ground the cigarette out in the glass ashtray, while Rick swallowed a shot of Scotch.

"But surely, Dr. Jasper—no one would suspect you of such things. You would not be allowed to continue your chemistry research."

The blond waiter returned on Jasper's signal.

"Thank you, Clive. My usual, please."

The doctor turned to face Miranda. "Don't be naïve, Miss Gouchard. Under such circumstances, they would want me to continue the work in order to trace the leaks and apprehend the spies. No, I am afraid my friendly association with Fritz has made me a marked—and decidedly ill-tempered—man. But tell me— what do you do for the consulate?"

"Many things, Doctor, most of them in public relations. I was a—a liaison with the Soviets, for example, before the Molotov Pact."

He raised his eyebrows. "You worked with the Russians? That leaves us something in common. I have many friends in the consulate here and in New York."

Miranda swirled the bourbon and sipped it. "I'm afraid my work was rather confidential. But the Soviets, too, are art collectors, Doctor. Not on the same scale, of course. Perhaps they will learn from the Germans."

Jasper's lips stretched into a smile. "I see you think like I do. Politics, my dear Miss Gouchard, are not important. One country invading another is but the infinitesimal path of a single electron, a brief flicker of light, but art— to those who appreciate it—art is immortal."

She nodded, carefully choosing her words. "Though there are those who think that the current lightning storm will last a little longer, Doctor. Concentrated power. And if power gets into the wrong hands . . ."

Jasper waved a hand dismissively. "Hitler will continue to scream and Goebbels to burn books. But even they understand the value of what they condemn. Art lives, Miss Gouchard. Art lives and thrives, no matter who is currently invading whom."

The drink arrived, Jasper murmuring "Thank you, Clive," before sipping the tall glass of red wine. "They carry excellent vintages here."

Rick drained his glass, wiped his face with a napkin.

"You're a wine connoisseur, Dr. Jasper?"

The doctor shrugged. "I admire beauty in all things, Mr. Payne. A painting, a car, a glass of wine. There is almost unfathomable beauty in the universe, in the smallest particle of matter, the neatness and order. Chemistry, like art, is the study of beauty—the beauty of life itself."

"It seems like the chemistry business these days is more interested in death."

Jasper leaned back in his chair, more relaxed, and raised his face to the stage.

"Yes, Mr. Payne, I agree. It is manifestly unfortunate that our world is more interested in the beauty of death than the beauty of life—and make no mistake, death enjoys a beauty, an allure all her own. But this is the reality of the times in which we find ourselves. Tonight, however, let us concentrate on a different world . . . the world of illusion."

The orange and red lights from the stage lit his skin, making it less saturnine, catching a gleam from his teeth. Miranda sat back and stared at him.

No wife, no kids, no mistress, no apparent personal life. No personal response to her, other than anger, appraisement, and a barely veiled, barely controlled whiff of fear and curiosity, motivated by intellectual analysis and rather astute paranoia.

Yet here he was, a Finocchio's regular, pulse rate quickened, eyes moist, palms sweaty, staring at the tall brunette belting out the Mexican number.

Jasper was queer.

*

Miranda chattered on about the Picasso show, even brought up Kirchner, the artist the sandy-haired dealer mentioned at the exhibit. Jasper ignored her, eyes focused on the dancers and the singers, body tense with enjoyment.

She glanced at Edmund a couple of times. He looked increasingly agitated, almost trapped, the older man with him more drunk and oblivious. Once she found him staring at her as if he recognized her. She turned back quickly to the stage, head buried in the drink menu.

The show finished at twelve-thirty, after several curtain calls for Carroll Davis, who gave them Ethel Merman and closed with Kate Smith's "God Bless America."

The dregs from the consulate party congregated in the lobby afterward, yawning, drunk, lining up to phone chauffeurs or taxicabs. Stephanie nodded to Miranda, supposed inspiration for the event, disappointed in the tepid response from her flock, no rabid disapproval, no expressions of outrage, no prostrate humiliation.

So much for "degenerate" San Francisco.

Fritz struggled to stay awake, overgrown child in an outlandish costume. Hübner reappeared at his elbow, ready to guide the consul and the princess home, while Jasper fidgeted, nervous and energized. He bowed to Miranda, said good-bye to Fritz, and left quietly.

She limped to the Packard, feet raw from the old shoes, muscles worn and tired. Dress was too heavy, beads wearing her down.

Rick asked if he could drive. She nodded, too tired to move. Closed her eyes, dozed against his shoulder, and listened to the sounds of the city at night, horns and music, yellow light from a few all-night cafés stabbing the darkness. A thick patch of fog on Pine Street woke her before they reached Mason.

"Can you drop off the car at my office tomorrow?"

"Not until lunch. That OK?"

"Yeah. Thanks, Rick. I can't believe how long this day has been."

"Long for me, too."

She held a fist up to her mouth and yawned. Rick let the car roll gently down the hill, hitting the brakes and pulling in across the street from the Drake-Hopkins Apartments.

"Need help?"

She shook her head. "I'm fine. Don't know why I'm so tired. It's not even two-thirty."

He grinned at her, mouth a little sad around the edges. "See you tomorrow, Miranda."

She yawned again, put a gloved hand on his arm. "Thanks. For everything."

He nodded, eased off the brake, coasted down to Sutter and turned right.

Miranda watched him go and then looked up at the apartment house, every light dark except one.

*

She pulled the mask and wig off as soon as she walked through the door, scalp sweaty and itching. Unrolled the stockings from her legs, rubbing the skin. Stayed awake long enough to take off the dress properly, hung it up and left it in her closet.

Twisted the radio dial. Glenn Miller.

Let's build a stairway to the stars . . .

She woke up with a headache, heart thumping, phone ringing. Light from the window looked about six-thirty or seven. Her hand crawled out and picked up the receiver.

"Hello?"

Familiar voice, somber, couldn't place it fast enough.

"Miss Corbie—it's Mark Fisher. Could you come down to 506 Broadway as soon as possible?"

She sat up in bed, holding her breath. Finocchio's.

"What the—what happened? Someone hurt?"

He hesitated, lowered his voice. "We found your card in his pocket and I figured you should maybe ID the guy. Driver's license says Edmund Whittaker. I'm sorry, Miranda . . . he's been killed."

Miranda dropped the phone receiver to her lap, eyes unfocused, staring at the blue forget-me-nots nodding on the wall.

Act Three

*

Price

He that dies pays all debts.
—William Shakespeare, *The Tempest,* Act III, scene 2

Twenty-one

✳

She rubbed her eyes, fighting off the panic of the bad dream. Another client, another friend.

Dead, dead, gone.

Miranda reached for the pack of cigarettes on her nightstand, lighting one with a shaking hand. Yesterday morning, Lois Hart. Today, Edmund.

Lois and Edmund, friends, soul mates, carnival masks in place for eternity. Together forever, what death has joined together let no man put asunder . . .

She gulped the cigarette, feeling the smoke hit her lungs. Reached for the telephone.

"MArket 3741."

Static on the line.

A female voice answered. "Your name?"

"Ugly Duckling. I need to speak with James MacLeod."

Click and silence. Four beats, then five. The voice came back on, neutral in tone.

"Mr. MacLeod can't speak with you."

"Goddamn it, it's urgent—"

"Madame, there's no reason to use profanity—"

"I've got every fucking reason to use profanity, sister, so find me MacLeod and—"

Click. Whir, clackety, click, click.

Miranda ran a hand over her forehead, remembering what James had said the day before. He was heading back to Washington.

She was on her own.

*

506 Broadway, alleyway.

Broken cement, nightshade and dandelions, mallow weed growing stalks between the cracks. Dented garbage cans and peeling paint. Fruit crates, faded label, "American Girl California Celery," a damp mop and rusty tin bucket, broken glass and empty wine bottles. Sweet putrescent smell, old perfume, gin, and rotten fruit.

White chalk around a figure slumped against a wall.

Edmund.

He was crumpled in the corner, long arms embracing his ankles, hat shoved too far down on his head. Thin puddle of glistening red around his trouser cuffs, seeping into his socks, streaks and drops like red rain on a windshield.

Miranda took a breath, stabbing pain in her gut.

And she was going to help him. Help him like she'd helped Betty Chow.

Fisher stood by her elbow while another cop used a pencil to move Edmund's head and prop it against the wall. Someone with gloves took off his Borsalino and bagged it.

Fisher's voice was gentle. "That him?"

She watched the white lab coat boys work on the body, the photographer taking photos.

Snap. Pop, pop, snap.

"Used to be. Garrote?"

Fisher shrugged. "Looks like it. Could be a copycat."

Poor goddamn Edmund. Couldn't even get his own fucking murder.

The inspector touched her arm. "I'm sorry. Friend of yours, huh?"

She looked around the alley, acrid smell of old dishwater and steak fat, beer and wine and sour whiskey, ground slick with potato peels and coffee grounds, last week's newspaper melted into the pavement.

Her voice was short. "We served together."

He scanned her face, speaking slowly.

"We can head to the office in a couple of minutes. Got a lot of questions, Miranda . . . between you, me, and the wall, orders are to bring you in and keep you there. I figured the least I could do is let you ID the poor bastard first." He shook his head, voice sad. "You'd better call that lawyer of yours."

The inspector moved aside, directing the crime scene, yelling at a couple of uniforms to chase bystanders out of the alley entrance. Miranda stood and watched, remembering Edmund's averted face, more comfortable in the dark, palpable scent of fear clinging to the carefully pressed clothes.

Pop-snap.

Open bottle of rye and they were as tight as a goddamn snare drum, muffled laughter and a yellow slice of light under the closed door. Miranda and Edmund, drinking until dawn, suppressed giggles over the wrinkled socialite from Kansas City, mink coat with fleas, and the fat Elk from Seattle who wanted to play doctor. Whispers that rattled the cage, words that bit Dianne . . .

Pop-snap.

Summer night at Dianne's and his eyes when she came to him, shaking, in shock, room 103. Edmund's hands rubbing her shoulder, repeated motion, comforting, not alone, not alone . . .

Pop-snap.

Last night, final night, when she told him of Spain and the man she'd killed, the callused hands ripping her shirt, bruising skin, hard fist against her cheek and mouth, thrust upward between her legs. Fingers crawling, stretching, separate from the rest of her body, desperate to reach the tiny gun, fight the pain, fight the pain, a different body, not your own, life only in hand and fore-finger, not in legs and breasts and most of all between her legs, not her voice screaming, not her body. Not her. Just the sound of the gun going off, quiet *pop* and a red summer rain . . .

Ghosts of the past, ghosts of the present, they flitted about the alleyway behind Finocchio's, mourning a dirge, gray and insubstantial, voices like the rumble of the streetcar down Columbus and the foghorn by the pier. Memory and friendship, disappeared and transmuted with age, nearly forgotten and never forgotten, buried too early and resurrected too late.

Miranda stood in the alley with her head bowed, silent amid the whir and click and grunts and shouts of the cops and medical examiners.

She was listening to the ghosts.

✳

The buttermilk donut was old and stale, but Miranda broke off a piece and ate it without thought. Meyer was looking at her, eyes worried.

"My dear Inspector—you must realize that you—and by you, of course, I mean your half-witted superiors—have not a single shred of evidence with which to charge my client? You've questioned her for two hours, and—while we appreciate the fact that you allowed her to identify the deceased at the crime scene—we must, sir, protest."

Fisher sighed, drumming his fingers, looking tired and hungry. Remains of a donut with chocolate sprinkles sat haphazardly on a loose pile of files.

"Look, Mr. Bialik—I'm just the poor schmo from homicide who's supposed to be handling the case. Miranda—Miss Corbie—was a person of interest in yesterday's murder, and she's a person of interest in today's. Both victims were known to her, both were her clients. Both had an appointment with her hours before they were murdered, and both were killed by strangulation. That's a hell of a lot of coincidence. Mir—I mean, Miss Corbie—hasn't told us much more than what we already know, and the D.A. is getting awfully fidgety."

Meyer gestured with the ebony walking stick. "What does he expect? Miss Corbie's relationship with her clients and the work she is contracted to perform is privileged information."

Fisher ran thick, muscular fingers through his hair. "Not with two homicides."

"Inspector Fisher—"

"Wait a minute, Meyer." She raised her eyes to the stalwart cop sitting across from her. Slumped, worn shoulders, brown eyes hard and fair and almost pleading with her to cooperate.

"I trust you, Inspector. Not the D.A. or the chief of police. If I come across, what kind of guarantee have I got? O'Meara is spinning his Communist fairy tales and the new police chief is weak-minded enough to listen . . . so I ask you again: What's my protection?"

Fisher leaned back, arm on the desk, and countered, "What's your protection if you don't?"

"You're looking at him. Meyer can raise a stink that'll wipe Hitler off the front page. No, David . . . let's start again. I won't work with O'Meara or anybody connected to this conspiracy crap. I've read better plots in the pulps. But I'll work with you—if *you'll* work with *me*. If I get a chance to dig some information on my own, and half a chance to nail the bastard that killed Edmund."

"Miranda, I strongly advise—"

"I know, I know, Meyer. Let's play it my way." She kept her eyes on Fisher, who was drumming the desk again, brow wrinkled.

Her attorney looked from the cop to his client, sighed, the starch wilting on his crisp ruffled shirt.

"Your way, my dear, will lead to an early heart attack for your legal representative."

Fisher bit his lip, fingers now silent on the desk.

"You're overestimating the press in this town, Miranda. No offense to your esteemed counsel, but the papers would hang you out to dry like Hester Prynne. Your background leaves you vulnerable. No, I think you're overplaying your hand."

He thumped his right hand flat on the scarred wooden desk.

"Brady wants you held as an accessory or on an obstruction of justice charge. And all you've given me as an alibi is some *Dime Detective* story about a confidential case for the government. No details, no names, no answers as to where you were last night. First thing you said when I called you this morning was, 'What happened? Someone hurt?' Sounds like the words of someone who'd been at the nightclub."

One Mississippi, two Mississippi.

Miranda opened her purse and shook out a Chesterfield, lighting it with the Ronson on the second try. She avoided Meyer's face, glanced up at the clock on the wall. Blew a stream of smoke over Fisher's left shoulder. Met his eyes.

"If you've got it all figured out, Inspector, go ahead and book me. And good luck finding your fucking killer."

Three Mississippi, four Mississippi . . .

Fisher started drumming the desk with his fingers again. Meyer dabbed his forehead with a starched linen handkerchief. Miranda smoked, eyes glinting green. Second hand on the clock moved to 10:38 with an audible click.

The inspector heaved a sigh and slapped his hand on the desk again, making the chipped glass ashtray jump.

"All right. Let's concede the point that cooperation could be mutually beneficial. But if we do this—and it's still a big 'if'—it's my goddamn head on a platter. Where's *my* protection?"

"You're looking at her. Look—I told you the case I'm on has nothing to do specifically with either Lois Hart or Edmund. But the timing is too close—I don't like coincidence, either. Up till now I've let the Hart murder slide, figuring you'd catch a low-level crook after the jade. I've got some ideas—I braced a pickpocket at the Picasso show the night I met Mrs. Hart—but I've been too busy on this hush-hush assignment to work the angles. Now I don't have a choice."

She leaned forward, voice low, and crushed the cigarette out in the glass ashtray. "Edmund said someone followed them to my office the night of Lois's murder. Then last night he's killed, and maybe with the same murder weapon, and maybe by the same shadow. Yeah, I was at Finocchio's—but not as Miranda Corbie. Someone is stalking my clients and stalking me, and is too goddamn good to leave a trace, good enough, maybe, to see through a disguise. I'm the only person who can tell us whether or not the murders are related to what I'm working on. I'll find the killer. I'm your protection, David."

Green-brown met chocolate brown, pupils dancing a tango. Fisher let out a long, wheezy breath.

"Goddamn it . . . all right, all right. We'll try it. But damn it, Miranda, don't leave town! Any word of this gets out means I'm back on the street breaking up crap games. Mr. Bialik, you can do me a favor and have a habeas ready to go—I'll need backup for why I didn't hold Miss Corbie."

Meyer gave him a delighted smile. "Always happy to help an honest police officer, Inspector. Don't forget—Miranda still has friends here. The rank and file have not forgotten her service to Mr. Duggan."

Fisher raised his eyebrows. "That's so. Miranda, what do you need?"

"Forensic records, any interviews or background information. I heard you raked the Hart chauffeur three times."

"How the hell—"

"Edmund told me."

Fisher ran his hand through his hair again, voice weary. "I'll send the reports by messenger. Didn't look like the same murder weapon, but, as you say, too many coincidences. When will you check in?"

She responded promptly. "Every day, if I can. I've still got to work the other assignment."

The short, well-built cop looked up at her, silent. He reached for a pack of Old Golds on his desk and lit one with a Universal Café matchbook stuck in the cellophane. His voice was quiet.

"It's my job, Miranda."

She pushed herself up from the chair and looked down at him.

"Mine too, Inspector."

Meyer left her with remonstrances, ebony cane tapping on the cement. She tried to assuage his worry, his fat stomach shivering under the ruffled shirt and silver brocade vest. He'd been extra protective since May and the Pandora

Blake case, treating her more like a niece than a client . . . or at least what she figured a niece might be treated like.

Miranda calmed him down with promises of phone calls or telegrams, and escaped in a DeSoto cab, driver a red-haired boy in his twenties.

It was 11:17 by the time she got to the office.

She twisted the radio dial, letting the tubes warm up. Clenched her hands together to keep them from shaking.

Glenn Miller in the fucking mood again, trombone up and swinging, but all she could hear was George Gershwin and a honky tonk piano and 1928.

Miranda opened the safe, grabbing a small stack of bills from the money James had given her. Took out the Spanish pistol, tracing the lines of the leather holster with her finger.

Someday he'll come along, the man I love . . .

Twenty-one and the world was free, college graduate, searching, always searching, Gin Rickeys at Heinold's First and Last Chance Saloon, ham and eggs and a slide down to the basement at Coffee Dan's . . .

She set the pistol on the desk and shoved the money in the top drawer. Sank into the black leather chair.

Sophie Tucker and the scratchy Victrola, Ruby Adams at the speakeasy piano. Mournful, wistful, hopeful.

She reached for the phone receiver. "EXbrook 6700."

The phone rang five times before a gravel voice picked it up with a growl. "*San Francisco News.*"

"Rick Sanders, please."

"Look, lady—I'm in the middle of somethin'. Can he call ya? I'll let Marty know you're lookin' for Sanders."

"Yeah. Miranda Corbie. I'm in my office."

His voice slowed down and climbed higher. "The broad P.I.? I'll let Marty know."

He hung up with a clang and Miranda frowned. Goddamn it, where was he? She didn't want to think about the scene from yesterday. Didn't want to think about yesterday at all.

She hit the switch hook until another operator came on the line.

"AShberry 6000, please."

Female voice, clipped and fresh, smelling of saddle shoes and sorority scarves. "Right away, ma'am."

Buzz-click, and a middle-aged woman in the middle of a yawn. "University of California. How may I direct your call?"

"Chemistry department, please."

Two more clicks, and she was connected. Nasal tenor, redheaded Wilbur, department secretary. She made her voice a little deeper.

"Good morning. I'm trying to reach Dr. Jasper—my son Clark has a class with him today."

"Certainly, ma'am—Dr. Jasper teaches Tuesdays and Thursdays, but he's not feeling well. You can come by or telephone him during office hours next Thursday. Unless there is something I can help you with?"

She let the question dangle. "Thank you—I'll do that."

Miranda pulled out the Big Chief pad from the middle drawer, made a note. Whether from the shock of the crime or for another, unknown reason, Jasper was off campus today—no business as usual. She lit a Chesterfield with the One-Touch, looking at the brief list she'd made under the professor's name. She could stake out his home later and shadow him, try to get some answers.

The black receiver jangled.

"Miranda Corbie."

"It's Marty, Miss Corbie. How you doing?"

Marty Fine, another news hawk, fought in the trenches with Rick. Older, a little more seasoned, looked like a wizened prospector from Arizona. Now he'd been promoted and Rick hadn't. She felt a sudden worry, sharp sting of regret, remembering she hasn't even asked Rick if it bothered him.

"I'm OK, Marty, thanks. Congratulations on the promotion. Sanders around?"

Marty swallowed, voice a little deeper. "Rick's gone, Miranda."

Twenty-two

*

She repeated the words, not understanding them. "Rick's gone. What do you mean 'gone'?"

Apologetic voice, useful for bereaved widows and victims of violent crime. "He quit this morning, Miranda. Just up and quit. Didn't tell us why, didn't say where he was going, though I figure he was going somewhere because he said something about packing up an old kit bag. Haven't heard that since the last war, but hell . . . maybe he just wanted to go fishin'. Maybe he got an offer from the *Call-Bulletin* or the *Chron,* I don't know. We treated Sanders good here, and he didn't seem angry or anything, but Jesus, he lit out this morning and never looked back. Asked us to cut a check for what he was owed, and that was that. I'm—I'm sorry, Miranda. Maybe try him at his apartment, huh?"

Sophie Tucker and the scratchy Victrola, Ruby Adams at the speakeasy piano, searching, always searching . . .

She spoke slowly, syllable by syllable. "Sure, Marty. Thanks. Be seeing you."

"Yeah. Take care, Miranda."

She hit the switch hook until it clanged in protest and an operator's tired voice finally came on the line.

"Hotel Empire, please."

"Hold the line, please. MArket 3400, now ringing."

The clerk picked it up on the third ring, and Miranda spoke quickly before he could announce himself.

"Rick Sanders, please. He's month-to-month."

Affronted and frosty. "One moment, ma'am."

Rustle and a click and the clerk came back, happy to deliver bad news.

"I'm sorry, Madame, but Mr. Sanders terminated his rental early this morning and left no forwarding add—"

She threw the phone receiver at the cradle and the heavy telephone spilled over on the desk, crashing with a loud clatter and *ring-ring-ring* of the bell.

Goddamn it.

To the window, to the safe, back to the desk. He wouldn't, couldn't, just leave, no word, not letting her know where he was going.

She ran a hand over her forehead, fingers trembling. Fell back into the seat, no comfort in the black leather.

He'd told her why.

Miranda gulped the rest of the stick until the end glowed bright red. Dropped it in the ashtray, letting it burn.

She hit the hook again and dialed the answering service.

"This is Miranda Corbie, EXbrook 3333. Any messages from a Rick or Richard Sanders?"

Static while she waited, foot tapping the floor.

"Yes, Miss Corbie. You have six messages and two of them are from Rick Sanders, one to your home number and one for EXbrook 3333, but don't worry, they're the same."

"Read it, please."

"'Car at parking station on 5th and Minna. Packages for you at Monadnock.'"

"Thanks." Miranda hit the hook again, dialed the mailroom.

"Miranda Corbie, number four twenty-one. I should have packages downstairs. Bring them up immediately."

She grabbed a bill from her purse and walked to the window, tremor still coursing through her legs and arms. Watched the florists down below by Lotta's Fountain, pushing dahlias and carnations, tall man in a brown fedora tipping his hat to a woman in pink . . .

He'd always been there. She remembered how he'd met her at Lotta's and tried not to look shocked and sick and angry when she told him she worked at Dianne's. How he'd used the bullshit Irish lilt and a soft voice, calmed her down. Steadied her.

They'd talked about Johnny, the Stork, the deli on 53rd Street. Good times, New York times. He explained how he'd left the sob sister column, hopped on a train to San Francisco, and barged his way into the *News*. She didn't know then, didn't know now, how much of the story was true, and she didn't care. He made her feel something, anything, even if it was irritation at the crinkle in his goddamn eyes or the phony, lilting accent.

She hadn't felt anything for a long time.

He'd even pointed out the Monadnock across the street, told her about Burnett looking for an assistant.

"You'd be the bait, Randy, but hell—it's a damn sight better than where you are now. At least you'd be doing the world a favor by busting up cheaters and frauds—and who knows? Maybe you'll like the gumshoe work."

She left Dianne's the next day, spider spitting when she dared to walk out of the web, soft, mewing noises, vindictive, venomous.

Simple walk through a door at 41 Grant.

Hardest thing she ever did.

Miranda closed her eyes, music swirling in memory, pale gold lights and black-and-white ashtrays, tall gin rickey and a glass of bourbon for Johnny, Scotch in Rick's highball, another Friday night at the Stork. Rick, upside-down grin and wrinkles around his eyes, not quite as tall, not quite as handsome, not quite as good a reporter, blue eyes on her, on the dress she bought at Macy's, swallowing the Scotch, swallowing the envy . . .

Goddamn it.

Knock on the door made her jump. Young man with carefully combed hair and dog eyes holding a small brown box and a larger, legal-folder-size package. She shoved a dollar bill in his hand and shut the door before he had time to say thanks.

Grabbed a scissors from the front drawer, slicing the paper tape along the edges of the small box. Pried open the flaps, took out brown wrapping paper. Inside, a greeting card and another small, wrapped box.

The card was addressed to "Miranda," Rick's handwriting. She ripped the envelope with the letter opener. Red roses on a white and yellow background, "But friendship is the breathing rose, with sweets in every fold" printed in a flowery script. Typed piece of paper inside.

> *Dear Miranda,*
>   *I tried to call you but then found out about the murder at Finocchio's. You're one of the names they're dropping as a person of interest, riding hard on the Hart case. Cops'll probably give you a tough time.*

I'm sorry, for your friend and for you. Sorry to have to write this.

The car is at a parking station on 5th and Minna, paid up for today.

I told you yesterday I had to leave. I know you understand why. I'm thirty-five years old, and it's time I decided what to do with my life . . . what to do, who to do it with.

I'm going away. Maybe I'll join the army—better to get in now than wait till I'm drafted. Maybe I'll make OCS.

For now, you can contact me through general delivery, San Francisco. I'll write you when I'm settled somewhere.

Enclosed is something to remember me by. Please wear it and think of me.

I've packed up all the information on your mother in a separate parcel. I hope it helps you find her.

I'm not John, Miranda—never was and never could be. But he was my friend, and you're my friend, and I figured, hell, we don't get many chances at real happiness. I'm proud of you, proud for you, and want you to find happiness, too—more than anything. If that means Gonzales, you have my blessing.

Be seeing you, kid. Keep your chin up.

Rick

Miranda stared at the paper, eyes cloudy, office swimming, swirling, while she blinked back the moisture, wiped her cheek with the back of her hand. She plucked the small box from the bottom of the package, ripping off the wrapping paper.

Familiar scent, brown-and-gold design. She opened the presentation case.

A bottle of Vol de Nuit, made in Paris.

She cradled it in her hands, rocking back and forth in the chair.

Mission Street church again, bells summoning her back.

Son, observe the time and fly from evil . . .

Wiped her eyes and face with a handkerchief she found in her purse. Grabbed the card and the Vol de Nuit and the other unopened package and opened the safe.

Starting to run out of room, Spanish pistol, government money, and now perfume from Rick. She peered into the back and dragged out Gonzales's dusty fedora, looking it over with a sardonic smile.

Seemed like fifty fucking years ago.

She tossed the hat on the file cabinet, carefully placed the perfume with the card on one shelf, the thinner, flat package of information on her mother on the second.

Catherine Corbie would have to wait, but she'd waited almost thirty years already. Two clients, two murders, one of a friend. A job for the government mixing spies and art, Nazis and Mexico, chemistry and killers.

She'd be alone . . . but Miranda was used to that.

*

A few fries, wilted lettuce, ketchup in a swirl of red on the buffalo China plate. Miranda shoved the remains of the Tascone hamburger aside and read the list again. Under *Wiedemann/princess* she'd written *Jasper, Cranach, spy network, Pioneer Fund.*

She frowned. Nothing specific, nothing definitive, nothing James had hired her for. Cranachs were probably the best lead.

If Jasper was selling secrets, he was selling them to and through Stephanie, the real power behind the swastika at 26 O'Farrell. Wiedemann's coy responses about art expertise seemed more calculated to securing valuable paintings for himself, not formulas for the Third Reich.

She frowned again, tamping the fountain pen on the desk. Jasper was tough, assignment already killed her predecessor. Was he a spy and a murderer, or merely a spy? Or was he just a goddamn opportunist obsessed by art and willing to break the law to acquire it? Was he the head of a ring or acting solo? Too many questions, try again.

This time she scrawled _Dealer_ at the top of the page, quickly adding *Wardon/ Weardon?, Degenerate art, Picasso exhibit, Mexico/Switzerland.* Flipped quickly to the earlier section of the tablet . . . Anthony Weardon, Berkeley, or Hugo Wardon, San Francisco.

She dragged the phone directory toward her, opening the pages to *W.* Ran a finger down the tiny print.

Hal Warden, Benjamin Wardon . . . bingo.

H. Wardon, Zenobia Apartments, 947 Bush Street, PRospect 9823.

Just two blocks from her own apartment, the Zenobia was strictly short term, shabbily genteel. Made sense if Wardon traveled a lot, or owned a gallery in another city. He'd mentioned it to Jasper, described it in self-deprecating terms . . . what was it? "My little shop"?

Miranda lit a cigarette and picked up the phone.

Three rings, four, five . . . no answer.

She frowned, hung up. Turned back to the phone book.

"SUtter 5900, please."

Pick up on the second ring. "Raymond and Raymond, may I help you?"

Sleek, well fed, self-satisfied. She smiled grimly to herself and poured on the flattery.

"I'm positive you can, Mr. Raymond—in fact, you may be the only one who can."

He rose to the bait, preening. "Well, I thank you for your confidence, Madame. I am not one of the Mr. Raymonds, though I shall endeavor to be of assistance. Do you have an art question?"

Miranda raised her eyebrows and grinned, keeping her hand over the mouthpiece to take a hit on the Chesterfield.

"Sir, I surely do. I attended the opening of the Picasso exhibit in San Francisco the other night—we drove up from our winery near Monterey—and I met the most delightful man. He told me he would appraise my father's collection . . . it's been sitting in a dusty old attic for I don't know how many years. My problem is that I've lost his card, and I don't believe his gallery is in the City—in fact, I'm not sure where it is. I called Raymond and Raymond because I know your firm knows everybody and everything." She punctuated the last two words breathlessly, rolling her eyes.

Mr. Sleek was torn between irritation at being asked for a competitor's information, and greed and curiosity over the mythical attic collection. He decided to play it safe.

"What is the gentleman's name, Madame? I will be happy to search my directory for you."

"Mr. Hugo Wardon. That's W-a-r-d-o-n. And I shall remember your kindness and that of Raymond and Raymond when it comes time to dispose of Daddy's collection!"

He made gracious noises, set the phone down. Miranda exhaled, shook her head. No time for dialogue by Clifford Odets or Saroyan, whatever got the fucking job done . . .

Clatter while he picked up the phone and cleared his throat.

"Mr. Hugo Wardon is an agent of the Count Lestang Gallery in Mexico City, Madame. If that is too far to travel, we'd be happy to appraise your paintings here at the gal—"

Phone dropped in the cradle, clanging loudly. No time for niceties, either.

She wrote hurriedly, scratching out *Weardon,* circling *Wardon* and *Mexico,* adding *Count Lestang* to the list.

Miranda stared down at the name, brow wrinkled in memory. Count Lestang, Count Lestang. Odd title, odder name, and yet familiar. If Wardon was Jasper's Mexican connection, maybe Lestang was involved, maybe not, whatever the involvement was, smuggling art or secrets or both. Still didn't explain the professor's anger, though. She remembered the way Jasper's fist closed over his arm, knuckles and face white with strain.

Miranda ground the cigarette out in the tray, eyes still on the list.

Gonzales. Goddamn it, Gonzales.

She remembered now, the brief mention of Picasso and how he'd tried to impress her and overshadow Rick, throwing out that his family owned a Picasso, purchased in Mexico City.

And she'd asked what gallery.

Count Le-fucking-stang.

She bit her lip. Reached for the phone, dialed the number herself.

Three rings, four. He answered on the sixth, out of breath.

"Gonzales."

"Miranda Corbie. I'm sorry to bother you at work—"

Surprise, warmth, like the summer sun over the Gulf of Mexico.

"You are never a bother, Miranda. I'm glad you phoned, I've been worried about you. I have tried to speak with the district attorney, but I'm afraid it's too late. Inspector Fisher mentioned you in our meeting . . . I understand he is taking the brunt of it from Brady. I'm sorry, Miranda . . . sorry to see you dragged through this witch hunt."

She shook another cigarette out of the package. "I'm used to it. Listen, you mentioned a Count Lestang Gallery the other night—place in Mexico City where you picked up a Picasso. Can you get me any information on the business?"

Slight pause, a little stiff. "May I ask why, Miranda?"

"Sure, you can ask. Doesn't mean I can tell you. Let's just say it's important to a case I'm working on—a confidential case."

"Something to do with the murders?"

"Don't push me, Gonzales. Can you get me the information or not?"

He finally answered with a low chuckle.

"Same old Miranda. I will see what I can discover for you, but this much I can tell you now. The gallery is owned by the Count Lestang, a rather fancy gentleman who lives much of the time in Europe. He is middle-aged—about forty-five—wears a mustache. He cultivates the better families in Mexico as clients. My own has done business with him for the last several years."

Soft voice, smooth and caressing, strength underneath it. Like his body next to hers, skin on skin, strong hands but gentle. Goddamn it . . .

"Does he have a partner—or an assistant of some kind?"

Gonzales gave a verbal shrug. "I believe there is another gentleman there—blond hair, goatee beard. I noticed him when I was in Mexico last month. I do not remember his name."

"Is he a co-owner of the gallery, or does he just do work for Lestang?"

"That I do not know, Miranda. Our family has dealt with the count solely. The blond gentleman did mention that he was taking care of business while the count was in France."

Miranda crushed the cigarette out. "Thanks. Will you call me with anything else you find?"

"I shall. Will tomorrow be soon enough?"

"Yeah. Thanks, Gonzales."

"Miranda . . . when may I see you again?"

She looked at the fedora perched on the dusty file cabinet. Felt weary, suddenly, and rubbed her neck with her left hand.

"I've got your hat. You can pick it up at my office."

Two beats of disappointment. He'd figured on a social call. "Of course. Perhaps we may set a time tomorrow, when I phone. Take care, Miranda."

"Be seeing you, Gonzales."

She took a deep breath, hand still resting on the heavy black receiver.

Twenty-three

*

Nondescript killer in a wide-brimmed fedora, trained well enough to disappear.

Maybe the man who nearly sliced Lois Hart's neck in two and hacked at Edmund until he bled to death against an alley wall. Maybe the man that slit the throat of her State Department predecessor.

Miranda breathed in the cold summer air, exhaust from the cars and trucks maneuvering Market, the fresh coffee downstairs at Tascone's. Stretched her legs, sore from sitting too long. White Fronts clanged by, afternoon run to the ferries and the Fair, blending with Frank Sinatra and Harry James and trumpet wails from the Tascone jukebox, up and out.

All, or nothing at all . . .

Goddamn it. Her thoughts needed order, some clarity and purpose, before shadowing Jasper tonight. Find the link, the goddamn link . . .

She fell back in the chair with a sigh and read the words again. Underneath _shadow/Killer_ she'd written *coupe? fedora, strangulation/throat, same person? Fingers?* and *experience*. Not much to go on.

Miranda reached for a Butter Rum Life Saver and popped it into her mouth. Blotted the Esterbrook fountain pen. Was Edmund killed because of the Hart woman? And what about Jasper—two deaths on the day she starts investigating the doctor. Were they—could they—be connected?

She started to write again, back to the beginning.

Jasper
Wardon/Lestang
Mexico/Switzerland
Nazis
Pioneer Fund
Degenerate Art/Old Masters? Buy/Sell?
spy comment/Russia comment/Soviet consulate
Heinsicker—owed a favor?
Smuggle information w/art?
Queer

She tapped the pen against her lip. Wrote <u>*Lois Hart*</u>, quickly following it with *Shadow/killer, Edmund, Chauffeur, Senator? Husband? Raymond? Jade, Fingers.*

So far, so good. Lois and Edmund, obvious connection. Shadow followed Lois, Edmund noticed him, another connection. Edmund remembered things . . . photographic memory, he'd said, and she'd made a goddamn joke.

She frowned. Edmund. Edmund was the nexus.

In a hurry, she wroteout <u>*Edmund*</u>, chased it with *Lois Hart, Shadow, Photographic memory.* Something else, something else . . .

He'd thrown it away and she hadn't paid attention, in a hurry to get to the party, but she remembered something, some offhand remark, Edmund's sad smile, cheeks flushed red.

Something about the Picasso exhibit, he was nervous, wanted to get away . . .

Fuck.

Her eyes opened, and she set the pen down, gazing into space, seeing Edmund's embarrassed face at the door.

"Just ended a relationship," he'd said. "It's so awkward when you run into old lovers, especially at social functions."

Goddamn it. He'd seen someone at the Picasso exhibit, someone he'd had an affair with.

Could it have been . . . Jasper?

Miranda's pulse was racing. She opened the drawer, took out a Chesterfield, lit the stick with trembling fingers.

Edmund knew art, one reason why Lois wanted him to go with her. She remembered how he'd laughed, called it information "picked up along the way." Picked up from where? Old lovers? Picked up from Jasper?

She breathed out a long stream of smoke, willing herself to calm down. Jasper was queer, Edmund was queer. They were both at the exhibit. But there were a lot of queers in San Francisco. She'd need proof.

He saw someone he recognized—someone with whom he'd recently broken up—maybe, just maybe, that meant blackmail. Not by Edmund, not the knight, the perfect gentleman. But by the one person who knew his history and would stoop to use it, who'd make him toe the line or sell him out, or sell him out anyway, if the price was right. Someone who could have called, for example, Mr. Hart, the Lion of the Peninsula, and told him his wife's shaming him with a nancy boy, or maybe a note to the senator, girlfriend's slip is showing.

Dianne Laroche.

Miranda sat back in the chair, deep inhale. Dianne Laroche, the woman she never wanted to see again, never wanted to hear, sweet southern voice, poisoned syrup, mint juleps on the veranda, velvet curtains sodden with blood and tears.

Fucking Dianne Laroche.

Knock on the door. Miranda's hand strayed to the drawer with the Spanish pistol.

"Come in."

Young redhead from downstairs peered around the corner, eyes like saucers.

"Got another package for you, Miss Corbie. Delivered just a couple minutes ago by a policeman—he said his name was Gillespie, and he sent his regards. I figured you'd need it right away."

She took a dollar out of her purse and handed it to the kid, who was gazing at the office looking for bullet holes. She stood by the door until it was firmly shut.

Ripped open the brown envelope.

Medical report on Mrs. Hart, preliminary on Edmund. Interviews with the chauffeur, husband, and son.

Three sessions with the chauffeur, five pages, three pages, and three pages again. One session each with Hart and son, two pages apiece.

She stared at the papers thoughtfully. Seven million dollars can buy you a lot of protection. Maybe even a couple of murders.

She picked up the Esterbrook, wrote *Old lover? Blackmail? Dianne?* under Edmund's heading.

Dianne's Escort Service and Tea Room, "catering to a select clientele." 41

Grant Avenue, mister, no light in the window, come for tea and stay for dessert, cabdriver winks and drives on. Dianne's, where all tastes were catered to, all ages considered, all habits indulged. Just phone EXbrook 9557.

No, no phone. She'd have to go in person, meet the spider in the web for tea, shake the strands and wait for the dance. Only way to tell. Dianne lived a lie, couldn't tell the difference anymore even if she wanted to, which she didn't, lies never leave you, never grow old.

One last drag on the Chesterfield. She faced Dianne for Betty Chow, and she'd do it again for Edmund.

Comrades-in-arms, prisoners on Devil's Island.

Good soldiers. Good soldiers, all.

✳

The phone rang, loud bell blending with a Municipal on Market. Miranda hesitated, then picked it up.

"Miranda Corbie."

"I got some crazy message from Rick, saying he's leaving and wanted to say good-bye—what the hell is going on, Randy?"

Bente Gallagher. Thank God she still had Bente.

"He left to join the army."

Bente started to sputter, words fluent and sandwiched together.

"That bastard! We're the—we're the three musketeers, goddamn it! What about you? What about your mother? What the hell—Miranda—you didn't sleep with the poor bastard, did you? I mean, I figured it'll happen sooner or later, but timing is everything, and—"

"Bente! Rick left, OK? He's got his own life. I've got enough problems keeping the goddamn D.A. from throwing me in jail."

Her friend was quiet for a few seconds. "Gonzales. I bet it was Gonzales. He couldn't stand seeing you and—"

"Can the crap or I'm hanging up." Miranda's jaw was sore and she realized she was grinding her teeth.

The storm subsided. "OK, OK. Tell me more when you feel like it. It's not like I don't care about the guy, you know? OK. So . . . what's going on?"

"The D.A. thinks I'm a Red."

"Yeah, right, and I'm Loretta fucking Young. Not every goddamn FDR supporter is a Communist, but you wouldn't know it from the way these pricks operate. What's it mean?"

"It means we've got to lie low for a while. I don't know what O'Meara's up to, or how far he'll push his vendetta, but they might try to go after you. You're a known associate."

"And your best friend," Bente added promptly. "Practically the only one you got, now that Sanders is gone."

Miranda unraveled two Butter Rum Life Savers. "I'll call you from pay phones. Hopefully the drunk at the Oceanic will take a message. And you can do something to help. You know about Edmund—"

"Goddamn shame."

"Yeah. He was—he was a good man. I've got a lead, maybe not even a lead, but at least a marker. I need to know who Edmund's recent lovers were, say, in the last year or two. It could really help. Think you could find out for me?"

"Maybe. Probably. I've got a lot of friends. The queers and the sapphists tend to live low-rent, too, unless they're rich enough to pass as eccentric. We're all in the same goddamn boat, sinking together, trying to keep one foot out of the hoosegow. Yeah, I'll ask around, Randy, see what I can find out."

Miranda could picture her friend, green eyes narrowed, full breasts heaving, red hair wiry and wild, a Viking goddess with an Irish temper and love of drink.

Her voice was warm. "Thanks. We'll catch up as soon the case is over—and as soon as I'm out of hot water with the D.A. Got a lot to tell you."

"Don't worry. He'll come back to you, Miranda. He always does."

Miranda hung up the phone, passed a trembling hand over her forehead.

She rounded the corner and knocked on the outside door to Allen's office. Shriek of protest from the desk chair and heavy footfalls before the door opened suddenly and the Pinkerton's broad face was grinning at her.

"Hiya, sweetheart. Come on in. Catching up on my paperwork. I was just gonna come by and check up on you."

She perched on the chair in front of his desk, reaching for a couple of lemon drops in a cut-glass dish.

"Thanks. I can only stay for a minute. Thought I'd give you an update and pick your brain on a couple of things."

His grin stretched and widened. "Those couple of things wouldn't be the Finocchio murder and the Hart woman, would they? I read the papers, sweetheart. You're not the golden girl anymore."

Miranda bit down on one of the candies and cracked it between her teeth. "Never was. I'm an ex-escort. I used to work for the most famous stripper in the world, regularly associate with undesirables—Communists and Chinese and Italian nightclub owners and queers, and incidentally even a disreputable Pinkerton op. O'Meara's got Brady's ear, so he's putting the screws on . . . and the news rags eat it up like cake."

The detective scratched his stomach under the brown vest and studied her thoughtfully.

"O'Meara's still sore over the Pandora Blake murder. You made him look like a fool."

"That's not difficult."

Allen shook his head and sighed. "Watch yourself, Miri. You're a good shamus but still green. Don't let 'em give you the bounce. What happened—your lawyer throw a habeas at 'em?"

"Edmund was an old friend and a new client—used to work for Dianne Laroche, and you won't see that in the rags. Fisher hemmed and hawed at first, but he's put his neck on the line for me. He's letting me work the homicides on the QT, even sent me the forensic reports. Don't know how much time I've got, though . . . and I sure as hell can't afford to let him down."

"What about the hush-hush for the feds? Don't bother to deny it, I can read all the signs. And your mother . . . you dropped that bomb yesterday and damned if you didn't shock the hell out of your old pal Allen."

Miranda plucked out a Chesterfield, lighting it with a Rusty Nail matchbook on the Pinkerton's desk. Inhaled, eyes meeting his.

"Hush-hush is still on. May even be connected to the murders . . . at least that's the line I fed Fisher to help convince him. And my mother's situation will have to wait. Rick was able to pull some information together before he left."

Allen shook out a cigarette from the crumpled pack of Old Golds on the desk and placed it between his lips, mumbling around it while he struck a match.

"Sanders's a good egg. He finally take a vacation?"

Miranda looked down at her cigarette critically. "Quit the *News*. Might join the army."

Allen's eyebrows climbed toward the top of his bald, shiny scalp. "Jesus, Mary, and Joseph—that's a goddamn sudden decision, not that any of us'll have any choice soon enough, but Jesus . . . so sudden. He was a good reporter. What happened?"

One last exhale, stream of smoke out the side of her mouth. Miranda bent forward and crushed out the cigarette in a chipped Scotch terrier ashtray.

"You'd have to ask him. Listen, I'm on a tail tonight, and I've gotta get going. Haven't had a chance to read the autopsy report on Hart or the prelim on the Finocchio case yet, but I know we're dealing with a good shadow. Edmund spotted him the night of the Hart murder . . . some thirtyish joe wearing a wide-brimmed fedora. Edmund had a photographic memory—no kidding—could be a factor in the killing. What I want to know from you is whether or not you've got any birds who like to go for the throat—garrote, knife, strangulation—someone just out of the can, maybe, with a nose for jewelry and a well-connected soak."

Allen nodded his head. "I can check the files for you. I can't remember a combination like that, though. Sounds like a smart, well-trained, well-disciplined crook. We got sex maniacs coming out our ears and run-of-the-mill stupid bank robbers and typical crazy gangster bastards flowing in from back east and out from under the rocks Prohibition built for 'em. I'll check. What makes you think he pawned the jade?"

Miranda popped two more lemon drops in her mouth and stood up. "It's out there somewhere, either with a fence or a collector or whoever hired him to steal it. Killer's too smart to keep it for himself."

Allen frowned. "Maybe. You're talking as if there's just one of these creeps, Miri. Chances are still pretty damn good you're dealing with two separate murders. Be careful."

She turned around, hand on the door.

"I'll be in touch tomorrow. Thanks, Allen. For everything."

Miranda pushed the elevator button and checked her watch. Lit another Chesterfield.

Time for tea at 41 Grant Avenue.

Twenty-four

*

Deep breath.

Her fist hit the door, loud rap.

Franklin opened it, raised his eyebrows.

"Miss Corbie. Business, I assume?"

"Worst kind. Not that Dianne indulges in anything else."

The immaculately dressed majordomo nodded, his black skin smooth and young looking except for fine wrinkles around the eyes.

Howard graduate, summa cum laude, playing antebellum house slave on Dianne's Southern Gothic stage. Franklin was Cecil B. DeMille and the Wizard of Oz rolled into one, dedicated to making the illusion possible, illusion of youth and beauty for Dianne, illusion of arousal for the clients.

There were no illusions for the escorts.

He'd anchored Miranda, helped her more than once, most recently when Duggan trapped and arrested her. He was the only source of quiet kindness at 41 Grant Avenue, and not for the first time did Miranda wonder why he stayed.

"Excuse me for a moment. I'll see if she is available."

Miranda nodded and lit a Chesterfield, smoke from the stick and burnt match helping to dispel the aroma of decaying magnolias and spilled burgundy.

She inhaled deeply, looking around.

Same goddamn crypt.

Red velvet curtains with faded gold sash, black-and-white marble table in the foyer, one crack through the middle. Silver candelabra, darkened with age, candles slightly bent. Hunting print on the wall, little men in red suits chasing a minuscule fox, and in a place of prominence but too high to examine closely, a thirty-five-year-old oil of Dianne, all coiled ringlets and powdered décolletage, waist cinched tighter than her goddamn bank account.

Dianne Laroche. As she was, or pretended to be. Dianne created her illusions young and lived in them ever since, slightly tattered but still in place, smile still girlish, Cupid lips still curving upward in a red velvet bow.

Franklin stepped quietly into the room, shutting the door behind him.

"She's in the sitting room, taking tea. She'll see you now."

Miranda stubbed the cigarette out on the marble. "Thanks, Franklin. How've you been?"

His voice was measured, considered, as if really answering the question.

"I'm well, thank you, Miss Corbie. I didn't expect to see you again."

"I wouldn't have bet on it, either."

"One thing—"

She turned around, surprised at the sudden emotion.

"If you are here about Edmund, as I expect—the papers are full of it today—please be careful. Miss Laroche has not been well. She was quite upset."

Miranda raised an eyebrow. "I'll keep it in mind."

She opened the door and stepped into the corridor, brocades and heavy wallpaper giving off the musty perfume of Cuban tobacco and San Francisco mold. Dianne always preferred her "gentlemen callers" to smoke fragrant cigars. They masked the smell of other, less pleasant odors at 41 Grant.

Portraits of pretty women in neck-plunging gowns lined the wall, lace and velvet, next to dandies in tight trousers and sideburns, dogs at their feet and horses in the distance. A few bucolic frolics of Greek shepherds and maidens mixed in, Greek robes transparent, nipples pressed tight against fabric, mouths open in eager anticipation.

Et in Arcadia ego, Dianne's Arcadia, crisp sound of folding money and rustle of bank receipts, idyll of a lost girl from Tupelo, never to be found again.

Miranda paused in front of the door. Took a breath and twisted the china knob, eyes adjusting to the red-tinted shadows.

Faded chinoiserie squatted on a low mahogany table. The small woman with dyed black curls, scalp line a thin, jagged white, delicately held the teapot by the handle, pouring water over dry leaves.

Dianne Laroche. Face and eyes and mouth of a Gibson girl but too many wrinkles around the pen and ink, lines blurring and caving in, past catching up and outrunning her.

She grimaced at Miranda and waved a hand in the air. Nails were hardened with wine-colored polish, fingers wrapped in gold.

Miranda moved forward, eyes taking in the room, matching it to memory.

Burgundy curtains and horsehair chaise, rubbed brocades and English landscapes, curios in an ebony cabinet. Acrid tang of bitter-black tea and red wine, Dianne's particular aroma, commixed with Aucoin's Southern Lilac and the rich, fulsome smell of apricot brandy in a cut-glass decanter, family heir-loom from Mississippi and the ole plantation, while the tapestry peeled off the walls amid swinging, clinging Spanish moss, gentle strum of a banjo drowning out the screams . . .

"Please sit down, my dear. After Franklin told me what happened to poor Edmund—and of your connection to the murder—at least, your *printed* connection—I expected you to come. You always do, when one of them dies."

Southern belle costume still intact, powder and rouge spackling cheeks and chin and forehead, magenta lipstick only a little smeared and rubbed into the cracks of her lips. Dianne reclined against the horsehair, studying her, smile revealing small teeth like little knives, bloody at the tips.

Miranda's fingers twitched and she closed them in a fist. No cigarette. Not even a goddamn Life Saver, not at Dianne's.

"I prefer to stand."

Dianne opened her eyes wide, reproachful, hurt. Large, dark eyes, so easy to get lost in, easy to forget yourself, forget the johns in the upstairs rooms, forget the probing hands and eager lips, shriveled organ, stretched and plumped by illusion, fed by fantasy.

Día de los Muertos, día de los Muertos, always the Day of the Dead at Dianne's Escort Service and Tea Room.

The lightly cadenced voice throbbed with emotion. "Why you insist on your own discomfort—"

"Let's cut the crap, shall we? You understand perfectly. We're not friends, Dianne, and I'm not your dear child or your protégée or even your greatest dis-appointment, as I believe you described me the last time we met. This is business. And, as you say . . . you knew I'd come."

Steam was still swirling from the china cup. Dianne picked up a nearly empty glass of wine from the mahogany table, raising it to her lips.

"I should have known you wouldn't have the manners or decency to phone first."

Miranda moved a step closer to the couch. Tried to keep her face impassive. She said: "When did you last use Edmund for a job?"

Plucked eyebrows rose high into her forehead, face smooth and lined at the same time, like a prematurely old child.

"My, my. Not even tea and conversation? Surely you can spare some time for the woman who picked you up from the gutter, shedding tear after tear for your poor, beloved Johnny, the stupid fool—"

"Shut up."

She tried to hide her quick intakes of breath, keep her voice low. Dianne's eyes crawled over her again, head cocked to one side, mouth curved upward in a limp bow.

"Still cold at night, Miranda? Still sexless? No making love with your dead lover, dear girl, I never could understand why you so morbidly cling to dust and bone . . ."

Another step forward, face white, fingers straying to the gold cigarette case before she clenched them tight again. Her eyes were fixed on Dianne's face.

"Answer my goddamn question. The bulls haven't chased you down yet because I haven't told them the connection—out of respect for Edmund. When did he last work for you?"

Another gulp of wine, chased by a sip of tea from the china cup, scent of lilacs and burgundy rising with the pale wraith of steam. Dianne sighed and waved her hand again, curls shaking, eyes narrowed, old and young and forever full of malice, running up and down Miranda's body.

"All the work—all the effort—and you still dress like a dime-store mannequin. Tragic, really—such wasted potential—"

"Answer my fucking question, Dianne."

The older woman raised her head in a regal pose, child's mouth pinched in a wrinkled pout.

"You are beginning to bore me. Why should I give you any information? The papers seem to think you had something to do with it. I shan't save you, Miranda . . . I tried that once, and look how you've repaid me—"

Miranda's voice cut like a razor, brown eyes glinting green.

"Better think about saving yourself. Mann Act, Dianne. That's just for openers."

Jet-black curls and red lips trembled, hand holding the china cup shook, making the tiny spoon rattle.

"You wouldn't dare."

Her eyes met Dianne's. "I would. Now talk."

Dianne reached for the bottle of burgundy hidden by her feet and poured liberally into the glass. One sip of wine, one sip of tea, one foot in the bank, one in the fucking asylum, small feet and teeth like a baby's, eyes even larger, artificial curls bouncing in fear and loathing, breath straining against the stiff corset under the layers of blue velvet and cotton. Her voice dropped half an octave and most of the southern spice.

"Edmund left me last year. He came back once or twice for a special client, even flew down to Mexico with him, the lucky bastard. Bet he never told you that, no, not the connections, the life he was able to lead through me—"

"Name, Dianne—give me the name."

Outrage and disaffection, stench of wine stronger now, mixing with the must and mold from the heavy drapes and Oriental rugs, faded into sepia. Dianne's décolletage heaved under the costume, wrinkles in her neck pleated like a worn paper fan.

"I never divulge the names of my clients! Not to you, not to anyone—you think you can barge in here and threaten me—"

One more step forward, eyes on Dianne's contorted heart-shaped face, aging child vaudevillian, never outgrew the act.

"Were you blackmailing the client, Dianne? Or just Edmund?"

The older woman pushed herself up from the couch, rings sparkling in the low, imitation gaslight. She gestured dramatically toward the door, painted finger stretched and shaking.

"Get out! It's your fault he's dead—just like Betty Chow. They see you in the paper and think they can just abandon me, find love and marriage like some fairy-tale ending, and what happens to them? What happens? Both dead—killed brutally. Your fault, you ungrateful bitch, your fault . . ."

Miranda turned back from the doorway. Dianne was fatter underneath the worn velvet, unsteady on her small, slipper-wrapped feet, face flushed red under the layers of makeup. Her Cupid's bow of a mouth trembled, voice a jagged rasp. Words like bullets, scattershot, shotgun style.

"You've been dead for years, but you're not just content to kill yourself. Sooner or later, Miranda Corbie, everyone you care for will be dead and gone.

Everyone. You'll be alone, so alone . . . and you'll have killed them all. Just like your precious Johnny."

Dianne bit the last syllable, gasping for air before sinking into the horsehair couch. She stretched out a hand again for the wine bottle, small animal sounds coming from her throat, bile and burgundy.

Miranda stood rooted in place, roar in the ears. *Bam-bam-bam*, artillery fire, scorched earth and dead orchards, dry parched soil and the smell of Rioja mixed with blood, laughter over the roar of cannon and bomb, birdsong in olive groves, fingers and hands and his mouth on her body, in her body.

She gasped suddenly, eyes open again, blinking. Unclenched her fists, holding her hands together, and looked down at the older woman. Her voice was almost gentle.

"I've spent a long time hating you, Dianne. Hating you and fearing you, thinking you're a black widow in a sticky web, something small and venomous with power over others. Even power over me."

Miranda shook her head.

"I was wrong. You don't have any power. Not even over yourself. I don't hate you, Dianne. I feel sorry for you."

The dyed curls trembled and the Cupid's bow drew open in shock, bent fingers with swollen knuckles picking at the blue velvet bodice, clawing the wineglass, large dark eyes stinging with tears and fury.

"You—you dare—"

"And by the way—don't send any more johns my way. The last one got his teeth knocked out."

Miranda strode through the door, shutting it softly on her way out.

She met Franklin in the foyer, his normally placid face anxious.

"I see what you mean about Dianne. What happened?"

He shook his head. "International Settlement. It's cut deeply into business, and you know Miss Laroche isn't . . . well, she's not young anymore. She was quite upset about Edmund."

Miranda raised her eyebrows. "I never knew Dianne to be upset over anything except Dianne. Look, Franklin—I never asked why you stay with her, and it's none of my business. But I know you care about her. "

He nodded, eyes troubled. "She's—she's been ill since February. I don't know how much longer she'll be able to keep—to maintain—the business."

She looked at him appraisingly.

"I figure you're running things by now, anyway. At least I hope you are, because I know it'll be cleaner—no room 103. I need your help, Franklin. The name of her client—the one who took Edmund to Mexico. Dianne wouldn't give it to me."

Franklin's face flushed, and his voice was low. "I'll try to find out for you."

"Thanks. I thought Dianne might have tried to blackmail one of Edmund's lovers—or Edmund himself. She's got some teeth left, but after seeing her I don't think they're sharp enough for that. Right now I'm walking a tightrope with the bulls . . . but I'll do what I can to protect you."

She put a hand on Franklin's blue uniform sleeve and met his eyes.

"If things get bad, call Joe Merello at the Club Moderne. He used to be sweet on her."

Franklin nodded. "I'd forgotten."

Miranda shuddered, lingering odor of wine and decay. "Let's hope Joe hasn't."

She stepped outside onto Grant Avenue, blinking at the afternoon glare from overhead summer fog, the hats and new frocks enticingly displayed in the I. Magnin windows.

Checked her watch: 4:26.

Time to shadow Jasper.

Twenty-five

*

Miranda slipped her foot out of the sturdy brown walking shoes and flexed her toes, stifling a yawn. A spot between her shoulder blades twitched, and she rubbed her back against the broad seat of the Packard, tweed jacket almost as itchy as the ugly but practical brown lace-up pumps. She'd dressed this morning in mourning clothes, preparing to say good-bye to a dead friend and hello to a night's worth of shadows.

Another gulp of tepid coffee, bitter and sour, eyes struggling to stay open against the terminal gray fog surrounding lower Nob Hill. A half-eaten cheese-and-dill-pickle sandwich sat on crumpled wax paper beside her.

Cold, tasteless dinner, corner market on Polk and California, fat proprietor too busy listening to *Amos 'n' Andy* to make a goddamn proper sandwich.

But what the hell . . . it matched the fucking coffee.

She peered out the window of the Packard, car lid up. Nobody noticed anything about a convertible except for the fact that it was a convertible, so if Jasper happened to glance her way, he wouldn't connect Marion Gouchard and a red dress and red shiny convertible to a lonely woman in frumpy brown tweed and a dusty red car.

She sighed. Looked around the building again.

1541 California and the California Court Apartments, cozy little flats for bachelors and couples, mid-Victorian in style, coveted placement on lower Nob Hill with just a short drive up to where the real money lived. Not too far from the Interurban or Key System trains, maybe thirty-five or forty minutes to Berkeley.

Easy in, easy out. Except the bastard wasn't coming out.

The yawn escaped this time and she checked her watch: 6:35. Glanced over the typewritten papers lying next to the sandwich. Maybe reading them for the fourteenth time would yield something new. She shifted position to get a better light from the lamppost ahead of the car, plucking a Chesterfield from the open pack on the dashboard and placing it between her lips.

The M.E. figured Lois was killed by a professional—quick and relatively clean, no signs of a struggle, no movement of the body. Somebody with medical knowledge or practiced with a piano wire or both. Made sense, with robbery of the jade and other jewelry as a primary motive.

Edmund, on the other hand . . .

Edmund was hurried and sloppy. Her gut twisted when she read the words again, remembering his smile the last time she saw him.

"You can tell me all about it tomorrow," she'd said.

Edmund had been hit on the head, fought against the killer, and dragged into the alley. They weren't sure where the murder took place, but from the fibers on his clothes they figured backstage at Finocchio's. His throat was seesawed open, raw and savage, red and white flesh open and exposed for the world to see, propped up against a wall like a message.

She closed her eyes, trying to forget this morning.

Same murderer? Or two different killers with throat fixations?

The Chesterfield tasted better than the sandwich and coffee, and she gulped it down, warmth hitting her lungs like a shield against the cold. She rolled the window down a little, watching a middle-aged woman with a bag of groceries waddle past the apartment. Miranda's eyes squinted, making the familiar rounds of the yellow-and-white door at Apartment 2, the black 1939 Buick parked across the street.

No Jasper.

She twisted the knob on the radio and waited a few seconds.

Goodman clarinet and suddenly Martha Tilton warbling "This Can't Be Love."

She sighed again, closing her eyes.

All the goddamn waiting. Worst part of tailing someone. She remembered Burnett's red, gap-toothed smile, derisive laughter, explaining it to her like she was five years old.

"You gotta wait, Corbie. And waitin' 's the hardest goddamn thing about being a dick. An' everyone knows dames hate to wait."

Burnett. Seemed like another lifetime ago.

Success had come, in small doses, solving Burnett's murder, bait-cum-private eye, then the Incubator Baby case that legitimized her, license finally her own. License to live, not as a room number at 41 Grant, not as a Red Cross nurse, hurriedly trained, woman-soldier with a gun and Spanish dirt under her fingernails. No idealistic teacher of English or Mills College girl, swirling bathtub gin and jiggling dates with Stanford boys, no twelve-year-old in a thin dress, hiding in a corner, listening to the thumping sounds and soft sobs, frightened and trying hard to not be seen, no, for the first time in her thirty-two years, a license to live and a license to be Miranda Corbie.

Whoever the hell Miranda Corbie was, all of the above or none, reinvented, reimagined . . . like the city that birthed her.

My heart does not stand still, just hear it beat . . .

And nobody to talk to, no memories to share, no warm nights and cold mornings, bare feet on stone floors, giggles and hot pots and cheap cuts of meat, no perfume behind the left ear, no favorite earrings, no song. No sorrow, no sighs . . .

Miranda stared through the windshield, watching the neon flicker on California Street, watching the evening grow darker, fog wrapping around San Francisco like a shroud. Her brown-green eyes grew enormous, glinting in the uneven light.

She whispered it, voice against the void, memory slippery and desperate and almost out of grasp, litany and prayer and catechism, until the light came back on in her eyes and the neon faded, the smell of carnations and roses, orange-blossom sweet . . .

"I love you, John Robert Hayes."

*

7:12 P.M. The door at number 2 opened and Jasper walked quickly toward the Buick, looking down the street in both directions. Miranda turned on the car ignition before Jasper opened his car door.

He pulled out into traffic, heading northeast toward the Mark Hopkins, and she followed him, threading her way past trucks from Bethlehem Steel and the United Fruit Company.

They passed the Mark and the Fairmont and Jasper sailed down the hill toward Market. She almost lost him when he made a right turn toward the Bay Bridge, cursing the stalled Municipal holding up traffic, but quickly shifted and managed to move around the streetcar. The nondescript two-door Buick was hard to track, but she thought she saw it ascending the ramp to the Bridge. She followed quickly, keeping four or five car lengths behind.

Traffic was slow, commuters coming to roost in Berkeley. Jasper maintained an easy speed until he reached Yerba Buena, then shifted into a higher gear and put on his blinker.

Miranda nodded to herself, face grimly lit by the bright white lights on the Bridge towers.

Jasper was headed to Treasure Island—and the World's Fair.

✳

Dancing lights, green and blue, orange and violet, music of the calliope calling her like a lost lover, siren song of the Gayway, step right up, folks, you won't believe your eyes . . .

Smell of popcorn and day-old hot dogs, grease from where they fried the donuts, and oh, the scent of Threlkeld's making a new batch of scones, cotton candy in small, sticky fists, mother looks down at the little girl softly, eyes shining.

And the young man in army uniform joshed the sailor in whites, while the blonde looked on, smile of power playing on her lips, band playing "Frenesi" as they fought over a dance. Older men, single, in patched dungarees and faded cotton shirts, placed bets on the Monkey Speedway, too thirsty to sweat until they won enough for a pint, Spanish dancers and Flamenco guitar, while the Boy Scout troop leader drags the kids to the Foreign Pavilions, educational trip, education.

The Gayway, the Fair, Treasure Island.

She missed every goddamn acre.

Jasper bought a hot dog and a Coca-Cola near the Ferris wheel, strolled down the main strip past the Python and Ripley's, the Incubator Babies and Sally.

Miranda wondered why the hell he was slumming. Jasper seemed all work, except for Finocchio's. He might pick up a sailor or two by the parking lot, but hell . . . he could do that along the Embarcadero for a lot less trouble.

Miranda flicked the Ronson and lit a stick, flame flickering in the Bay wind, sun spot of yellow-orange against the dark rear of Madame Zena's fortune-telling tent.

Fuck, maybe she should pay a buck to Zena.

A couple of cops passed her, no second look, not in the frumpy clothes and broad hat, no kilowatt smile, no Club Moderne walk. Sally's lit up like Radio City, line still forming to get in, girls on third or fourth shift, playing gin rummy in the back until it was time to strip and ride the donkey.

Miranda breathed in the smell of sawdust and wood shavings, grinned at the barkers and Ken Silverman, still hawking the Diving Bell, girlfriend Nina at his side. Ken's dream was to explore under the sea, and the closest he'd gotten was a twenty-foot plunge with planted carp and goldfish, water dark and filmy from discarded popcorn, cigarettes, and the occasional penny. Nina hung on his elbow, looking up at him like he was an Aquadonis, while Ken convinced another bucketful of sailors to prove they were seaworthy.

Jasper slowed down at the edge of the midway, spending two bits at Como's shooting range and winning a Kewpie doll. Odd choice for the professor. Miranda hung back in the shadows by the Chinese Village and Fong Fong, still the best and only place for a chop suey sundae. Her stomach growled. She lit another Chesterfield, kept her face in the dark.

A D-route Elephant Train was pulling up along Heather Road, and Jasper picked up the Kewpie and walked quickly to fall in line. Miranda stepped back, waiting for more riders, then moved ahead while there was still room.

The professor was standing up near the front of the vehicle and she had to pass him. Kept her head averted as she fell into a seat in the rear, facing his back. The excitable woman in glasses and a five-year-old hat was making oohs and ahhs at the lit fountains and the bright, sparkling mica of Vacationland, numbers clicking on the giant cash register, marching band playing in the Open Air Theater.

Jasper stared straight ahead, made no sign of getting off the car.

She expected him to push his way through the small crowds at the Foreign Pavilions, no Germany here, not anymore, but Switzerland and Mexico were still represented. The only move he made was to take a seat vacated by an elderly couple who got off at the Federal Building.

The train slowly rounded the corner past the California area, and Jasper straightened, his body tense.

Of course.

Next stop—Palace of Fine and Decorative Arts.

*

Miranda hadn't been inside the Fine Arts palace since last year's fair, and the scope and layout had changed considerably. No Botticelli's Venus, no Raphael, much smaller European galleries with paintings from American collections and by minor artists. Emphasis was on modernists, particularly American and South American, the "Art in Action" program—where eager art lovers could watch Diego Rivera brush crumbs out of his mustache—dominating the cavernous space.

Miranda wandered forward, looking up and around briefly, pretending to study a map of the exhibits. No Rivera on display today, just a disconsolate young woman in a smock painting blocks of color on a canvas in the middle "Art in Action" station. An architecture exhibit faced the entrance, more about contemporary engineering, and Jasper paused in front of it before checking the Kewpie doll and making small talk with the young woman behind the counter.

He was obviously familiar with the layout and strode toward the back right side of the building, against the wall. Miranda nodded at a uniformed guard standing outside the European and American Nineteenth-Century gallery and accepted a one-sheet map, glancing down at it.

Jasper was headed for Drawings by Old Masters, funny area for a lover of "degenerate art," plenty of which was on display in the American and European Contemporary galleries. She ambled forward, stopping to make noises over the miniature rooms by Mrs. James Ward Thorne with a gaggle of middle-aged women in large print dresses and noting the three artists on display at "Art in Action." The depressed-looking woman at the center dropped a tube of blue down her brown smock, sighed, and switched to orange.

Miranda walked through the largest of the contemporary galleries and spotted Jasper tucked into room 18, far right corner of the building, standing in front of a Rembrandt in the Old Masters section. A door on his left opened into an area closed off to the public, abutting the storage space for the art sales room in back of "Art in Action."

She waited around the corner in room 26 of the contemporary gallery, one eye on the professor. Painting in front of her was by John Sloan, called *Sixth Avenue Elevated at Third Street*.

Dark blue-violet night sky, roar of the El driving past women in cloche hats and short skirts, smell of Prohibition gin on their lips, lights from the train, the

Italian café on the corner, women laughing, on their way to a party at a speak or a night out with the egg, duck soup.

Goddamn it, not New York.

She needed a Chesterfield, needed to know what Jasper wanted. Maybe he just liked Rembrandt. Maybe he wanted to buy something from the woman artist in the brown-blue smock. Maybe he just collected fucking Kewpie dolls.

She moved backward toward the opening between rooms, careful to keep her face averted from the professor's line of sight. A tall man in a dark blue suit and matching hat was the only other person in Jasper's room, reading the plaques on the wall and holding a catalog, mouth moving while he read, eyes too close together. Jasper glanced his way, no sign of recognition.

The doorway in the corner opened, letting out a short, stocky man about forty in a workman's one-piece jumpsuit. He brushed dust off the speckled gray uniform and paused, looked around. Made a grunting noise and walked purposefully toward the professor. Miranda walked quickly to the other side of the room, keeping her back to Jasper and the workman.

They clustered in front of the off-limits doorway, voices low. Thought she heard "Mexico" and a raking laugh by Jasper. The other man's voice was deeper, more guttural, an easier carry across the room. He said something about "Chicago tomorrow" and "San Francisco." Another laugh by Jasper, with a garbled sentence . . . something about "birth" and "track." The stocky one was nodding, smile grim, responded with "you're well out of it."

Pause in the conversation. All she could hear was her heart.

She dared a quick glance over her shoulder, and the two were moving closer to the private door, the stocky worker's arm on Jasper's back, heads down and voices unintelligible. She glided to the left, keeping her face in profile if they turned around, desperate to hear more.

The man in the uniform fumbled with a key in his pocket and unlocked the private door, twisted his neck around to call out "Cummings!" Security officer from the Contemporary gallery came at a brisk trot.

"You needed something, Mr. Cheney?"

Jasper's friend smiled, teeth showing, easy tone. "Just mindin' my p's and q's and wanted to let you know I'm taking Professor Jasper to my office for a chat. He'll get a look at what's in storage."

The guard, lanky and tall, with pasty white skin and freckles, laughed like a hiccup. "Sure thing, Mr. Cheney. I know the professor. You two fellas go right in."

Jasper nodded cordially at the guard, while Cheney smiled again, lips compressed, and opened the door. Once it shut firmly behind them, the guard removed his cap, scratched his ear contemplatively, and wandered back to room 26.

Miranda bit her lip, slid sideways to the private door.

No markings, no noise behind it.

She raised her hand, about to try the knob, when she felt somebody quickly move behind her. A deep voice breathed in her ear.

"I wouldn't do that, Miss Corbie."

Miranda spun around and faced him. Eyes were still too close together, blue and sharp with wrinkles at the corners. He smiled as if it came easily to him. Arrogant—and attractive.

Her jaw was clenched tight, and she kept her voice low. "Who the fuck are you?"

The deep voice spoke as easily as the smile, and he nodded his head toward the opposite corner.

"There's a da Vinci study over here. Come on and take a look."

He moved away from the office door where Jasper and his stocky friend had disappeared, keeping his back to Miranda and seemingly unconcerned about it. She followed, opening her handbag, gold cigarette case in easy reach.

The tall man in blue gestured toward the drawing of a horse and rider, eyes checking the room.

He murmured: "Ugly Duckling, huh? Some joke from MacLeod."

She frowned, looking him up and down. About thirty-six or -seven, six feet even, trim 175 to 180. Brown hair, blue eyes, navy blue fedora with a wide brim and cream band and a few specks of lint. He'd managed to seem like an open-mouthed gawker with reading comprehension problems a few minutes ago, and now his eyes gleamed, keen and aware, muscles tense and posture alert.

Her voice was cautious. "I asked you a question."

Eyebrows raised, he looked down at her, lips amused. "So you did. Call me Scott."

She glanced at her watch, running out of patience.

"OK—Scott. Now explain to me who the fuck you are and why the fuck you interfered with me back there and, incidentally, how the fuck you know who I am."

Another survey of the room. Two young women in bookish clothes had wandered in from the Contemporary gallery, chattering about a landscape by Rivera.

"Keep your voice down. It's obvious I'm here to look out for you. You walk in now and you'll queer the racket."

She stared at him. "I'm supposed to work alone."

"Yeah, well . . . let's say your friend James was worried and sent me out to make sure you don't screw up. Good thing, too, or you'd barge in and they'd cheese it all."

Her eyes narrowed as she took in the wrinkled clothes, the wide-brimmed fedora casting a shadow over the top of his face, the infuriating tone of condescension.

"I don't need a nursemaid, especially one who thinks he's Melvin Purvis. Dust."

Scott tried to grab her elbow and she took a step forward, shaking it off hard. He backed away, palms up and facing her.

"OK, OK, look, I'm here to help, not to hinder. We don't have much time, so listen up. Go to Jasper's car and follow him from there. We think he's getting ready to travel, catch a rattler somewhere . . . probably spooked by that murder last night at Finocchio's. Friend of yours, wasn't he?"

Miranda's brow wrinkled, her hand still inside her purse. "Why don't you tell me?"

He laughed, shook his head. "James warned me you'd be a tough nut. Look, sister, believe me or don't believe me. I'm doing my job, same as you. We've got this spot staked already. Go careful and stick to Jasper like a barnacle. Grab yourself a ticket and get on that train. That's what we need—the goods on him personally. Oh, and by the way . . . officially speaking, you didn't see me here tonight."

She looked at him thoughtfully. "Mind if I phone James?"

He shrugged, brushed off some dust from his lapels. "Go ahead, sister. No skin off my teeth. Like I said, just doing my job. I've gotta drift now, and you should, too."

She nodded.

He looked down at her, another brief smile. "Wait a few minutes before you leave."

He turned away from the da Vinci, brushed by her arm, voice very low: "I can see why Jimmy cares so much."

Miranda counted to three and pivoted, catching a glimpse of his blue-clad back turning the corner into room 36 on his way back to the entrance.

She needed a goddamn cigarette.

✳

The Bay air bit through her tweed like shards of ice, salt spray almost solid, fog not much of a shield. Horns lowed mournfully off Point Lobos and the bridge, container ship answering like a stray calf, violet and orange lights from the Elephant Towers bathing the parking lot in a lurid, limited glow.

Miranda crouched low in the Packard and shivered, breathing smoke through the open window and waiting for Jasper.

She'd already looked through his windows for any brochures left on the seat, but the good professor kept his car as clean as his Bunsen burners. No train ticket.

Still, it didn't mean this Scott character was off track.

She frowned. "Chicago" and "San Francisco" both came up in Jasper and Cheney's conversation. And the word she thought was "birth" could have been "berth" . . . a berth for Jasper on the famous—and expensive—streamliner.

It made sense. Almost too much sense. And she didn't fucking like it.

Noise, four cars over. Crunch of gravel under heavy feet, guttural laugh.

Cheney. And Jasper was beside him.

She quickly rubbed the cigarette out in the ashtray, lowered the hat on her face. Rolled the window down and tried to fade into the rainbow-lit shadows.

"You can let Fritz know he'll have to wait a little longer—he was at the god-damn nightclub, too, so he should understand—and thank God he was, or the dicks might be telling everybody to stay put. As it is, you're out in time. Lucky for you the SP's been so hopped up over accidents or you'd be taking the *Forty-Niner* and not the *City of San Francisco*—but then you always were a lucky sonofabitch."

The professor's voice was ruminative. "In some ways, yes. Though our success has not been due to luck, Cheney, but to chemistry. Remember that. Wardon tends to forget it, too. As for Fritz, he has his hands full with Stephanie . . . waiting for his promised Jan Steen is not uppermost on his mind, which, frankly, is already taxed to the uppermost with all the skullduggery of late. Chicago happens to be convenient right now . . . Heinsicker thinks I'm too ill to teach, too upset over—over the murder."

Cheney hawked up phlegm and spit on the pavement, while Jasper paused, resuming his lecture with an acid tone. "Your habits are most disgusting. I'm relieved I was able to book the streamliner. I'd almost rather stay and take my chances than travel halfway across the country in a cattle car."

Cheney shook his head and laughed, irritation and admiration equally mixed. "I don't know what I dislike about you the most, Jasper—that you're a fairy or too stubborn for your own good. Clark will contact you at the Drake on Friday evening. That should give you plenty of time to get settled. The bastard's expecting another Renoir, and he can afford it, so don't forget to jack up the price. Wardon's looking for his cut, too, you know."

Jasper sighed heavily, reaching into his coat pocket for the car keys. "Did I tell you he approached me at the Picasso show? Even mentioned the Kirchner, of all things. I'm wary of Wardon and I don't like his cheek. Lestang is never here, and frankly I'd rather deal with the Count, even if he has trouble getting back from the Continent. The Renoir, remember, was not my idea—too much, too soon, too untested. If we could just get Miguel out from under Wardon's thumb—he exploits the poor lad's ignorance and I could teach him so much . . ."

Cheney laid a large, hairy hand on Jasper's sleeve. "People. Keep your voice down."

Jasper bit his lip and nodded, climbing into the car, while a party of four, two young couples, wove their way through the lot, searching for their cars and laughing. More fairgoers were trickling back from the Gayway, headed into the City for the main act. Jasper turned on the ignition, while Cheney raised his hand in a low-key salute and bent forward to the window, talking to Jasper in words too low to overhear.

The professor nodded again and began to back out. Cheney turned toward the Gayway, walking in a hurry.

Miranda shivered again, fingers clenched hard on the wheel, eyes on the black Buick and the black swirling waters surrounding Treasure Island.

Twenty-six

*

She followed Jasper home and waited in the car for about twenty minutes and two Chesterfields. Not too much foot traffic, too well-bred a part of town. The lamplight finally blinked off in number 2 and she yawned, hungry for sleep, rolled down the window and lightly patted her cheek to stay awake. Next stop was Market Street and the Ferry Building.

About twelve people were fighting to stay awake in the Southern Pacific waiting room. One man in a rumpled gray suit and dingy mismatched socks had already shoved his fedora over his face and was snoring against the tall, wooden back of his seat, while a middle-aged woman seated kitty-corner peered at him through round glasses, fascinated. A lone janitor in a Southern Pacific uniform halfheartedly ran a push broom over the floor, while strains of Benny Goodman and Mildred Bailey filtered from a jukebox in the mostly empty café, bouncing against the marble columns.

And while I'm waiting here this heart of mine is singing . . . .

Goddamn music, love, love, love, you made me love you just the fucking way you look tonight, so let's fall in love, why shouldn't we fall in love, just come back to me, goddamn it, come back . . .

Miranda approached the thin, elderly man behind the ticket booth, face buried in the latest issue of *Railroad Magazine.*

"Next train to Chicago?"

Count to five while the old man pulled away from the pulp paper and raised bleary blue eyes to hers, rolling around a plug in his cheek. He turned his head slightly and she heard the *wang* of wet tobacco hitting a spittoon.

"Depends, lady. Got the *Overland Limited* goin' out at eight thirty-five to-morrow morning. She leaves Oakland Pier at nine fifteen, if'n you don't want to take the ferry, some folks don't. Cost you sixteen fifty-five for a standard lower berth. Then there's the *Challenger* if the *Limited*'s too much, she's got what they're callin' economy meals, cost you thirty-five cents for dinner. Ferry to Oakland's at eight A.M. I've got maybe two or three reclining-chair cars left—"

"What about the *City of San Francisco*?"

He raised his bushy gray eyebrows, giving her an up-and-down look, voice a slow drawl. "That's our de-luxe streamliner, lady, and she usually goes out on the 2nd, 8th, 14th, 20th, and 26th of the month." He raised an arthritic finger to the sepia-toned SP calendar on the side of the booth.

"This here says today's the 27th."

"But I heard—"

"I know, I know." He shook his head. "You heard about the accident in Cheyenne, lady, was in the papers a couple of days ago, and you're right. Made the *City* late . . . she didn't get in till today and she's goin' out tomorrow—two days late." He leaned forward slightly, wet whisper with the odor of tobacco behind it. "They don't like anybody to know. Brass hats been mighty sensitive since last year."

She let out a sigh of relief, opened her purse. "Can I buy a ticket?"

His tongue shoved the tobacco around for a couple of seconds while he took her in again.

"Funny thing, you ain't been the only one askin' about the streamliner. Had a fella in earlier who talked his way on board. The *City* does go out tomorrow afternoon at three forty-five . . . but she's a diesel streamliner and she's usually booked in advance, late or not. You could wait till Saturday and take the *Forty-Niner*, it's almost as pretty, just no special club car and not quite as fast . . ."

Miranda shook her head emphatically, put on her best mystery woman look, and leaned in close.

"Look, I'll give *you* the skinny. I'm a private eye, see—trying to track down a scientist. The G-men want to talk to him and they asked me to help. You know how people are in trains . . . chatty, more easy. Figure his guard'll be down if I follow him to Chicago. Now—you'll keep my secret, won't you? I need to get on his train and in a nearby compartment. I think he's booked a separate room on the streamliner. You think you could check for me, Pops? It would mean a lot to your country. Might even be a decoration or medal in it for you."

The old man's yellow teeth bared in a smile of delight, while he rubbed the tobacco off with his tongue and shot another wad in the spittoon.

"Must be somethin' new they're tryin,' fe-male detectives and all. Never heard o' nothin' like it in my day. We had Pinkerton and that was it. Just a minute, young lady, let me get my book."

He reached under the counter and pulled out a large, thick album. Shoved a pair of pince-nez glasses on his nose and looked up with a shy smile.

"Don't use 'em when I'm readin' for pleasure. Now, then . . . *City of San Francisco*. No duplex, no doubles, no open berth, no roomettes. Fella I told you 'bout—came in couple of hours ago—got the last one. Say . . ." He leaned forward eagerly, teeth still coated in bits of tobacco. "You think maybe he's the fella you're after?"

The old man thought for a moment, then shook his head in disappointment before she could answer. "Never mind, girlie, my imagination's runnin' riot. That was a younger fella, no scientist like you're talking about. Well, then . . . I've got a single seat in coach left and a smaller-type drawing room suite I'm supposed to hold for Southern Pacific families." He shook his head regretfully. "Not much to choose from, girlie."

Eyes large, brown and pleading. "Pops—can you look him up for me? He'd take a drawing room—your best compartment. Name of Jasper, Dr. Huntington Jasper."

"Just a minute." He ran a gnarled finger over first one page and then another, chewed and spit again. Wiped his lips with a soiled handkerchief beside the ticket book.

"I ain't supposed to give out this information, young lady, but seein' as how you're workin' with Hoover, I suppose it's all right. There's a party named Jasper that took one of our largest compartments. That one's usually reserved for top SP men travelin' back and forth . . . says here Jasper just paid for it today. Didn't do it through me or else I'd've remembered. He's in the Fisherman's Wharf car, room G, just one behind the club."

Miranda bit her lip. "I really need my own room. For privacy."

He sat back and closed the book, a frown stretching his weathered face.

"I don't hold with immoral activity, girlie, not even for Uncle Sam."

She grinned. "Believe me, Pops, neither do I. I'm all business. Wish I could tell you more, but that's as much of the lay as I can risk."

She opened her purse and plucked a five-dollar bill from her wallet, sliding it under the glass window. "Consider that some early reward money from the government."

He melted again, made a harrumphing noise while he opened a smudged can of chewing tobacco and stuck another wad in the side of his cheek. Didn't touch the money.

"Well . . . seein' as how these Nazis seem to be everywhere—Huns never learnt their lesson in '18, did they? Even on our best train, *City of San Francisco,* we've got problems, you remember that accident that killed all those people last year? Nazi sabotage, so the SP men say, and believe you me, if'n it had been the conductor drivin' too fast that day, he'd be hung out to dry. You think . . . you think maybe this Jasper fella was in on it?"

His face was pressed against the glass with a pleadingly hopeful look, mouth parted and open, teeth even more yellow. She narrowed her eyes and looked from side to side before whispering: "I can't say. They don't tell me everything, you know. But between you, me, and the *City of San Francisco* . . ." She made a gesture across her throat and threw him a meaningful glance. The old man nearly swallowed his tobacco.

"Let me see what I can do, Miss."

He rummaged in a drawer and opened the green book again, making a humming noise as he ran his finger down the page once more.

"I've got a double bedroom reserved here that ain't been picked up yet and it's for two people. I think they'd be more comfortable in that drawing room compartment." He picked up his pen and winked at her.

"That'll be fifty-eight eighty, Miss, including the ferry to the Oakland Pier, which leaves here at three forty-five P.M. tomorrow, June 28th. The *City of San Francisco* arrives in Chicago on Sunday, June 30th at nine-thirty A.M. Breakfast is forty cents and up, lunch is seventy-five cents and up, and dinner's a dollar and up. You've got a club-lounge car, a lounge-observation car, and of course the coffee shop and dining cars, plus radio. There's a secretary for telegraphs and a stewardess-nurse aboard in case you run into any trouble. Guess you're used to that, though, ain't you girlie?"

His watery blue eyes twinkled at her as he surreptitiously pocketed the five-dollar bill.

She smiled at him and took the ticket he pushed forward. "Thanks. What's your name, Pops?"

"Hal. Railroad Hal, they call me."

"Well, Hal . . . wish me luck. 'Cause yeah . . . trouble's my business."

She gave him a wink and shoved the ticket in her purse before gathering her jacket together against the cold and walking quickly out of the waiting room.

*

She sat up in bed suddenly, catching her breath, breast heaving against the yellow silk nightgown. No phone call reporting a dead client or dead friend this morning, just bad dreams.

8:04 A.M. Seven and a half hours.

Longest stretch she'd had in weeks.

Miranda yawned, threw her legs over the side of the bed, drank some water, made a face. Dialed the long-distance operator. Asked for the number James had given her.

"State Department." Gruff male voice with a slight roll to the *r*'s.

"James MacLeod, please."

The voice got sharper. "Who is this?"

"Ugly Duckling."

"Just a minute."

She tapped her foot, resisting the packet of Chesterfields on the nightstand. The voice came back on, still unpleasant.

"He's not here."

"It's important."

"I'm sure it is, Miss. But he's not here, all right? Try some other time."

"Look, whoever the hell you are, it's crucial I get a message to MacLeod—"

Click.

She swore and hit the switch hook a few times. The operator came on.

"Can you connect me to that number again please?"

More clicks and a whir. "The number is busy, Madame. Would you like me to ring you once I connect?"

Miranda hung up the phone with force. "Goddamn stupid State Department sonofabitch . . ."

She made a pot of coffee. Phoned Berry-U-Drive and told them where to pick up the car. Left telegrams for Bente and Meyer, with instructions to Meyer to phone David Fisher and tell him she was out of town on government business.

She shook her head. Honest, decent cop and his goddamn neck on the line.

And Jasper might stay in Chicago for one day or a fucking week . . . she flung open the closet door.

She'd need the right clothes.

No glamour, no hint of Marion Gouchard.

A comfortable dress and face-concealing feminine fedora for the first day of the trip. Green frock with pink flowers, puffy shoulders like Snow White. She completed the look with a high-waisted brown jacket and the same sensible, itchy shoes she wore yesterday.

Thirty minutes later Miranda was finished, packing extra underwear, stockings, a nightgown and robe, three skirts and blouses, three jackets and two dresses. She added a small case of makeup and face creams, double-checked her purse for Chesterfields, Life Savers, and bullets for the Baby Browning.

She dialed the answering service, found a message from Allen.

"Yes, Miss Corbie. 'From Allen,' it says. Message reads, 'No mugs for throats, but something of interest. Call me.'"

She thanked the eager operator and rang back the Pinkerton. No answer.

Miranda sighed, stomach growling for food.

The waitress spilled coffee on the counter in front of Miranda, smiled wide, teeth jagged and chipped, wiping up the brown puddle with a dirty rag.

Miranda stared across the street at Waverly, remembering the Rice Bowl Party. Crinkly blue eyes and dirty tie and bullshit accent everywhere she looked . . .

The coffee burnt her tongue and coated her throat, black and bitter enough to drive away thoughts of Rick.

She pulled out the memo pad. Wrote *Cheney (Fair), Miguel? Mexico? Wardon (Lestang?) Steel (Chicago), Renoir, Weidemann.* In large, capital letters at the top of the page she penciled *SCOTT.*

The waitress threw the plate down with a thump, eggs steaming. Miranda dug into the sausage first, still writing.

> *Who is Cheney and what is his position?*
> *Why run after Edmund's murder?*
> *Is Jasper complicit?*
> *Scott: Why do they need me if they already know about Cheney and smuggled art? Sacrificial sheep?*

Miranda frowned at the last sentence, put the book back in her purse. Ate the eggs and sausage methodically, automatically, filling her stomach like an empty tank of gas.

On her way out of the restaurant, she spotted No-Legs Norris on the sidewalk in front of Sam Wo, and crossed the street.

"Hey, Ned."

"How are you, Miranda?"

"All right. Missus OK?"

"Sure. First time she's glad her old man's got no legs . . . knows I won't be called up again." He grinned, the leather brownness of his skin folding up like a suitcase.

"Ned—if you hear anything about the jade—"

He nodded briskly. "I know where to find you."

She shoved a ten-dollar bill in his aluminum cup. "I'm on the road for a little while. Be back in a few days."

"Righto. Be careful, Miranda."

She nodded, a glance up Waverly Alley and down Washington Street, remembering Spofford Alley and the Yick Lung pawnshop. The sun was starting to break through the clouds.

"You too, Ned. Be seein' you."

✳

Roy was on duty at the Drake-Hopkins, and she tucked a fin in his pocket and told him not to let anyone upstairs.

His Adam's apple bobbed alarmingly. "No one, Miss Corbie. Don't you worry."

She smiled at him, helping him lift the valise and cosmetic case into the Luxor taxi.

They drove down Mason, driver taciturn, about fifty. Market Street trains ripped and roared, natives nimble enough not to get caught in the tracks. They passed the Monadnock, and Miranda thought with a pang of Gladys, who'd be worried.

Lotta's Fountain gleamed in the sun, costumed in flower stalls, her footlights the neon of pool halls and sailor bars, fog her only curtain. A warm breeze carried the sound of the tambourine, miners stomping stiff, dirty boots on the rough, clay-baked ground.

At the end of Market rose the Ferry Building, tall and friendly, white against the impossibly blue sky. No Washington's Monument this, no decorated scraper, all chrome and gleaming arches. Alive and watchful, awake at night to the mournful lows of cargo ships and crab boats, awake in the morning to the coffee factories and dockworkers, the ferry passengers and dreamers who gazed across the water, heeding the call of the calliope or the promise of gold in the east. The Ferry Building clock had stopped once and once only, while the earth destroyed the City around her, but she held on, a beacon of life, the only lighthouse that really mattered, while the fires and the tremors raged on.

The Ferry Building meant San Francisco.

The Ferry Building meant home.

Miranda was scared. No city to give her strength, no car drive away. No long trip for her since '37, and here she was, taking a streamliner to Chicago, chasing a potential Nazi spy, chasing a dream.

Miranda looked up at the Ferry Building, hand on her hat, eyes watering in the bright light, a glancing ray catching the phoenix perched on the Tower of the Sun.

Tight city, bright city, the city that knew how, that knew her, the city that gave her birth, that nursed her and raised her, taught her how to live again.

A momentary shiver made her shoulders tremble, from the chilled winds swirling in under the Golden Gate or the errant threat of white fog gathering behind the Headlands. Miranda glanced up at the Ferry Building clock one more time, shielding her eyes, stepping hurriedly across the street.

Her City. San Francisco.

She wondered if she'd be back.

Act Four

✳

Frame

Let every eye negotiate for itself,
And trust no agent; for beauty is a witch
Against whose charms faith melteth into blood.
—William Shakespeare, *Much Ado About Nothing*, Act II, scene 1

Twenty-seven

*

The streamliner rested on the Oakland mole tracks, poised to make the run
to Chicago in just thirty-nine and three-quarter hours, bright yellow snake
stretching over desert, plain, and salt flat, climbing hard through mountain
passes and curling across redwood trestles, before the low of cattle from the
Chicago meat markets competed with the whistle and she finally pulled into
Union Station, tired, spent, still the fastest ride on rails.

Pride of Southern Pacific but jointly owned by Union Pacific and Chicago
and North Western, the *City of San Francisco* boasted both speed and the most
luxurious accommodations of any train in America. In-room radio, telephone
service to the sumptuous dining cars or to any connection in the country, once
they pulled into a station. Stewardess-nurse, barber shop and hair salon, shower
and club car, observation deck, and most of all . . . privacy.

Top of the line were the drawing room bedrooms, suites with in-room tele-
phones and more space than a Manhattan apartment. Each train car sported
the name of a San Francisco district or landmark, from Market Street to Mission Dolores. Miranda noted Jasper's—the Fisherman's Wharf—as she walked
down the platform toward her own.

No sign of the professor himself.

"Get your gen-u-ine replica of the *City of San Francisco,* folks, only twenty-
five cents and makes a wonderful souvenir . . ."

Hawkers selling miniature trains and SP personnel with toothy smiles lined
the sides of the platform, the latter pressing menus and brochures into passenger

hands, eager to dispel the aura of bad luck that still clung to the streamliner after last year's tragic derailment.

Miranda remembered the newspaper coverage last year, dwarfing even Eddy Duchin Variety Week at the Fair.

August 12, 1939, 24 people dead, 121 injured, gleaming metal train cars twisted like a game of kick the can, broken child's toy hurled across Nevada desert. Nine-hundred-foot drag before five cars tumble in the Humboldt River, another three thrown down an embankment, brakes screeching like the men and women trapped, Southern Pacific's special streamliner now just crumpled tinfoil, bodies sheared and crushed, blood on polished aluminum. Cries of the still-living answered by grasshoppers and coyotes, watching from the dry, hot foothills, ears pricked and noses moist.

Hearst's papers screamed sabotage, along with the SP-led investigation, no excessive speed, no fault of the railroad, no, some group of men with tools and a grudge had tampered with the track, covered up the crime with a tumbleweed, engineer Ed Hecox promising to catch up on the schedule and push the train to ninety, not a factor, and by the way . . . investigation was still ongoing. SP detectives searched for convincing explanations and even more convincing scapegoats, while more union-friendly rags complained bitterly about a cover-up.

"Do the double bedrooms have phones?"

Young black man, carrying both Miranda's suitcase and cosmetic case, striding ahead through the crowds of women in furs and men in beaver fedoras, the young couple who'd saved up for their honeymoon and the old lady out for one last family trip. He didn't turn around to answer her.

"No, ma'am, no telephone in any room except them drawing room compartments. You can ask for one to be sent in if you need it, or line up and use the one in the observation car when we stop. You got a radio, though. What car did you say you are at?"

She studied the ticket in her hand. "Bedroom A, Twin Peaks."

He nodded, dodging a small boy in short pants holding a baseball. "Nice room in front, real quiet. Here's the car."

He paused in front of the steps, waiting for a blond woman who was standing in the door and berating another porter, a sixty-year-old Negro with a slow southern drawl.

"Don't drop it again, you stupid fool. Harvey—Harvey! Call another porter, would you? This nigger's too old and stupid—he dropped my trunk twice on the way. I swear I don't know what Southern Pacific is coming to, hiring these apes . . ."

The old man's hands were shaking, thick, leathery skin hardened with calluses. His shoulders slumped and he stumbled backward while the woman's heavy trunk dropped and banged on the cement, rolled but didn't open.

"Har-vey!"

Miranda took a step forward and put a hand out to steady the older man. The younger porter carrying her baggage was flushing red beneath dark skin. Harvey, two more porters, and a white Southern Pacific official in uniform came scurrying forward, Harvey emerging from the direction of the club car and already smelling like gin.

The Southern Pacific official looked from the blonde in new May Company clothes and too many rhinestones to the potbellied Harvey to the old porter and young porter and finally back to Miranda.

Her hand was still on the porter's back.

The official was a thin man with wire glasses and a Southern Pacific hat too large for a bony skull. He cleared his throat.

"Isaiah, did you drop this lady's luggage?"

The older porter's breathing was shallow and he wobbled backward, muttering something unintelligible. Miranda looked up sharply.

"This man is ill. Call one of your nurses."

The SP man stared at her as if she'd asked him for money.

"We don't use our nurses for the porters."

"I'll say, I don't want no nurse touching me who's touched one of them—"

Miranda turned toward the blonde. "You're lucky Harvey touches you, lady, and that's because he's a drunk. Pick up your fucking baggage and drift."

Her mouth opened and shut like Charlie McCarthy's, while red flushed her skin and Harvey raised his eyebrows, thick lips twisting up at the corners. The Southern Pacific official stood stunned, unsure of what to do.

Miranda spoke to the younger man still holding her cases. "Drop mine and hoist theirs. I'll wait."

The young man carefully lowered Miranda's two pieces of luggage and easily picked up the heavy trunk, while the blonde retreated into the shadows of the car, shooting baleful looks at Miranda. Harvey bent forward and passed the old man a dollar bill, almost falling off the steps, then corrected himself with dignity and followed his wife into what Miranda hoped was not a room near her.

More passengers had lined up behind them, most with porters.

The SP official made some tut-tut noises and said: "Can he sit down on that bench? I'll call the doctor."

The official disappeared, glad to be out of the scene, and Miranda helped the old porter to a wooden bench. He was still unsteady, still making noises she couldn't understand. A middle-aged man in flannel pants slid over to make room.

"What's wrong with him?"

She shook her head. "I don't know."

The younger porter jumped down from the train and picked up her luggage. Walked slowly toward where she stood over the older man. Isaiah was holding his head in his leathery hands.

"You ready, Miss?"

She nodded and thrust a five-dollar bill into Isaiah's palm. She whispered: "Hold on. They're getting a doctor."

The old man whispered something she couldn't hear. The *City of San Francisco* shrieked a whistle, and she followed the younger porter to the platform, looking back once she climbed the last step. A doctor in a white coat was running from the station.

The young porter stood stoically outside room A, an en suite double bedroom on the right side of the car, just in front of the drawing room compartments. His mouth was tight.

"Here you are, Miss. Room A, Twin Peaks car."

"Thanks." She handed him another five.

He looked down at the money, jaw working.

"Miss, I'm on this train. Substituting for Joe in the shoeshine service. You need anything . . . you let me know."

"Thanks. What's your name?"

"George."

"Mine's Miranda."

She held out a hand and he stared at it, hesitated, then grasped it in his own and shook it.

"If you find out how Isaiah is, I'd like to know."

He lifted his face to hers, a genuine smile raising his cheekbones impossibly high. "I'll make it my business to find out. And thank you, Miss."

The door shut noiselessly behind him. She looked around the small room.

She was on the *City of San Francisco*.

The small room was airy, big double windows—"fog-proof," boasted the SP brochure—providing plenty of natural light. Flush against the short wall was a small vanity sink, complete with built-in lights for the mirror above and 110- and 32-volt outlets for a curling iron or electric razor. A lounge chair sat comfortably next to the sofa-cum–folding bed, positioned by a Formica table with a small console radio on top, ready for cards or conversation before getting folded up and stowed under the bed when Miranda wanted to go to sleep. Color scheme was a bright Nantes blue and apricot, with the sink and mirror a complementary French green.

She pushed open a folding door directly across from the sink. The commode was tucked in a crevice smaller than most closets, a cellophane bundle of Southern Pacific tissue perched cheerfully on a glass-and-chrome shelf above. Miranda smiled wryly, thankful she'd never been claustrophobic.

With a grunt, she hoisted the luggage on the blue sofa, the vibrating hum of the engines traveling up her legs.

A whistle blew and the train started to move, *bump-bumpety-bump* rhythm section beginning its marathon session, wooden ties adding a higher note, iron tracks beating steady, and Miranda remembered the Jimmie Rodgers song she heard the hobos sing in '32, Salinas lettuce pickers, strawberries, grapes, oranges, whatever fruit, whatever vegetable, eyelashes thick with dirt, skin like dry leather.

Every time I see that lonesome railroad train . . .

She took a breath.

Time to look for Jasper.

*

6:07 P.M. The streamliner pulled out of the Sacramento depot, California's state capital bustling with politicos and their brethren, lobbyists, aggrieved citizens, and the omnipresent lawyers, younger versions sharply dressed in crisp-brim fedoras and double-breasted suits, or, in the William Jennings Bryan tradition, elder statesmen with wavy gray hair and a black cravat, starched white shirt and watch fob, everyone with a mouth open and hand out.

She watched as an older couple in formal wear climbed the steps, helped up by George, the same porter who'd carried her luggage.

Miranda sighed. Third walk through the train. Try again.

She stopped for a drink and smoke at the club car, Embarcadero, where an older couple had already launched a bridge game, then on past the open-berth sections, most curtains drawn, except for a large man with white and gray stubble who scratched himself and grinned as she squeezed through the aisle, and finally double-backed to the Fisherman's Wharf, the car where Jasper held his suite.

No one in sight. She lingered in front of the door to room G, no noise within, and very carefully tried the knob.

Locked, but possibly . . . pickable.

She kept walking, pulling open the heavy doors in between cars, roar and scream of the engine, warm air blasting from the rails below. Passed her room in Twin Peaks, smiled at a tall young man in a brown fedora, eager-eyed and wide grin, with a young woman holding his arm, mouth lipsticked and impish. He reminded her of Rick, and she hurriedly plowed ahead.

Four more cars, open section, double bedrooms or roomettes, some with families or couples but mostly single business travelers, arranging deals back in the City or planning a call ahead to Chicago as soon as they reached the next station. Finally, the observation car Nob Hill, with three double bedrooms and a drawing room compartment tucked in the front and thirty-odd seats for scenic viewing lining the sides. A small buffet and bar filled the inner corner, wood and chrome, streamlined but with a nod to '49er days. A tall, thin man with a white glove on his left hand sat in the nearest chair on the left, legs extended, drinking gin or vodka.

Jasper.

Miranda twisted her head toward the right, strode quickly to the far end of the car and one of the few empty seats on the same side as Jasper. A middle-aged woman with dyed red hair and too-orange nail polish sat next to her, reading last month's *Vogue,* while a boy about twelve in short pants and ruffled white shirt with chocolate stains was kicking his legs up and down in the seat on her left. The mother—a washed-out debutante in her mid-twenties—finally pulled him out of the chair and dragged him and his little sister screaming from the car.

Miranda picked up a newspaper, pretended to read it. Jasper was wearing a gray suit, dark blue tie, no hat. No book or magazine either, just a glazed, almost troubled look while he sipped the clear alcohol.

The young couple she'd passed earlier walked in, spotted the two empty seats on her left and sat down, still grinning like newlyweds.

The tall young man was holding the hand of his girl, speaking in an undertone while she laughed. He looked Miranda's way and caught her eye, smiling broadly.

"Hello, fellow passenger. This train's all right, isn't she? Just passed Sac Town, and now we're cookin' with gas . . . be in Reno before ten-thirty tonight. Whaddya think of that?"

Miranda grinned. "I think it's plenty fast. You two on your honeymoon?"

He raised his eyebrows skyward in mock horror while the young woman laughed and dug her elbow into his side, leaning around him to address Miranda.

"I'm embarrassed that you guessed so easily. Tom and I are heading to Virginia . . . he's got a job for a newspaper there. We're from Portland. My name's Marie."

"Marie O'Day," her husband added. "I married her for her gams."

"Tom!" She dug her elbow in again, while he laughed and held her mock fists in his.

Miranda glanced to her right again. Jasper showed no sign of interest in anything but his drink. She faced Tom and asked politely: "You're a news hawk?"

"He was one of the best reporters in Portland." Marie spoke proudly. "Maybe too good."

Tom's face grew serious. "Marie . . ."

"Well, it's true! If Mr. Easton had any courage or ethics at all, he'd have run that piece you wrote on Jim Elkins and Rayden Emlou."

O'Day leaned toward Miranda, face flushed, lopsided, embarrassed smile. "You know how it is. She said yes and so now I'm a hero."

"Tom . . ."

"Elkins and Emlou are the resident hoods, I take it?"

He nodded. "Poised for a big takeover of the city—all kinds of vice and getting worse by the day. And the police weren't too keen on my information."

Marie's generous mouth stretched thin. "They're getting paid off by Elkins and Emlou. That's why we're moving to Virginia. Who knows how long we'll stay, though . . . Tom has itchy feet."

The tall, lanky young man shoved his fedora off his forehead and Miranda winced. Too goddamn much like Rick.

"Now, Marie . . . I told you that someday we're going to see every state in this great country of ours—from sea to shining sea—and until then . . ."

"Service Two is ready in the dining car. Please make your way to the dining car. All the way at the front of the train, Madame."

A slight, balding white man in a waiter's uniform stood at the front of the car, alternately ringing a well-bred dinner chime and nervously tugging his collar, steering hungry passengers down the narrow passageway, and repeating the information to a deaf old lady sitting across from Jasper.

"Service Two is read—"

"I believe everyone has heard the announcement. And some of us have already partaken of your excellent Service One." The professor looked up from his reverie, mild irritation crossing his face.

The waiter raised untrimmed eyebrows, series of three wrinkles forming in the pasty white skin of his forehead. "Sorry, sir."

Miranda quickly turned to the young couple, speaking softly. "Have you eaten dinner yet?"

Marie shook her head and laughed. "We've been much too excited to eat. But come to think of it, I am a little hungry."

"Then let's go, honey." Tom stood up and held out his hands to help her up.

Jasper's eyes were closed again, legs outstretched. Miranda bit her lip. The car was empty except for the professor.

"Do you mind if I join you?"

"We'd like nothing better! And what kind of manners you think we have, I'm sure I don't know . . . sitting here and boring you with our life story. Why, we don't even know your name!"

Miranda glanced again at Jasper before turning back to Marie with a big smile.

"Miranda. And we'd best get to the dining car before they run out of mashed potatoes!"

Tom and Marie both laughed, and Miranda followed closely behind them, keeping her face averted from Jasper's view.

✳

Miranda barely tasted the dinner. Baked Red Snapper au Gratin, consommé, browned new potatoes, fresh garden peas, and a Brown Betty with vanilla sauce for dessert. She ate perfunctorily, eyes on the door in case Jasper should come in, absentmindedly deflecting questions from Tom and Marie, who chattered continuously about Virginia, Portland, train travel, and visiting the Lincoln Memorial just like Jimmy Stewart did in *Mr. Smith Goes to Washington*.

She avoided direct answers, changed the subject frequently, sticking to well-worn anecdotes about movie stars and the Depression, the war abroad and how long England could hold out against the Nazis.

Too much talk about England and Miranda changed the subject again, hands shaking, craving a cigarette, and glancing yet again at the doorway. The young reporter's eyes sparkled. He leaned over the fruit pie he shared with Marie and lowered his voice to a whisper.

"Who are you looking for?"

She gave a nearly imperceptible jump. She stared at the young couple, eager, honest, excited to start a life together.

Goddamn it.

Miranda spoke in a low monotone. "Your fiancée is right. You're too good a reporter. Can you keep a secret?"

Marie's eyes were as big as the saucer of tea biscuits. Tom nodded, serious. "You can count on it."

Miranda opened a pack of Chesterfields. Asked, "Mind if I smoke?" before lighting it with her Ronson Majorette, Tom and Marie shaking their heads no. She leaned forward over the half-eaten Brown Betty.

"I'm a private detective from San Francisco. Name's Miranda Corbie."

"A real lady detective?" Marie stared at her, fascinated.

Tom's voice was low. "I knew it. You're here for someone, aren't you? You've been watching that door for the last twenty minutes. Crooks? The saboteurs from last year? Or are you just chasing a wayward husband?"

She cracked a smile and exhaled, sending a stream of smoke skyward.

"I can't tell you. And I should be going."

Miranda stood up and pushed her chair in, bending forward over the table, voice barely above a whisper.

"I told you this much so you'd understand and stay away. My work is dangerous."

Marie impulsively put her hand over Miranda's, outstretched on the table. "We're in drawing room suite D in the Twin Peaks car. Let us know if we can help."

Miranda smiled, patted the girl's hand. "Just have a good trip—and a wonderful life."

She nodded, striding out of the dining car as the young couple stared after her, Tom holding Marie's hand under the table.

*

Miranda paused in front of drawing room G, final door of Fisherman's Wharf. The monitor—a woman with a pleasant smile and smart little hat in SP colors—had just disappeared through the connecting doors, loud whoosh of air and steel making a high-pitched whine as she pushed into the next compartment.

No sound from Jasper's room.

Miranda waited, counting seconds in between the passing track lights, watching them slide out from under Jasper's doorway and illuminate the darkened passage, *clackety-clack, clackety-clack,* throb and hum of the engine underneath her feet.

No interrupting shadows, no noise from within.

She took a breath, looked both ways down the corridor, and extracted two pieces of bent wire from her wallet.

Thank God for paper clips.

Stick it in carefully, she remembered Burnett grinning. Shouldn't be too hard for a girl of your experience, and he laughed and slapped her on the back.

Fucking Burnett. Not just bait for out-of-town Elks and the goddamn Chamber of Commerce, he taught her how to pick locks and snap grainy photos and set traps at run-down hotels in Livermore. Why, isn't this a photograph of you, Mr. Pearson? Redheads can be awfully expensive . . .

She frowned, tried to control her breathing. Wiggled the bent pin back and forth until she felt a small click in the mechanism.

A laugh from the club car almost made her drop the other piece of wire, and she swore, palms sweaty and fingertips uncertain. Drove it in. Left turn . . . no. Right turn . . .

Yes.

The lock gave two clicks and a final *clack*. She quickly removed the wires, dropping them in her jacket pocket. Looked again down the corridor and through the connecting door.

Voices coming from the front. Probably on the way from the club car.

Miranda opened the compartment door and squeezed inside, shutting it behind her quietly while the boisterous voices—male and female—carried down the corridor, finally drowned out by the car pass-through door and the roar of the train.

She was in Jasper's room.

Twenty-eight

*

One Mississippi, two Mississippi . . .

She hugged herself, gulping for air, stomach knotted.

The bottom bed wasn't pulled out yet and he'd kept the couch empty as if expecting company.

Miranda straightened up and moved to stand against the thick folding wall between this compartment and the next, eyes quickly scanning the room. Heavy black phone with silver decoration on a light green Formica table, armchair in Nantes blue with its back to the large window. Window shades up, track signals and electric poles splashing bars of colored light across her face.

Squeal of the train whistle, and her hand darted to the gold cigarette case before she dropped it in her pocket, legs trembling.

No fucking time to be scared, look at the luggage . . .

Two large suitcases sat in the upper berth, one casually open and half unpacked, with a few suits folded and two jackets hanging on wooden hangers. On the floor, propped against the table and chair, a large cardboard box, rectangular in shape and not too thick.

Painting shaped.

She glanced at her watch and swore, wishing for a pocket knife. Flung open the lighted vanity compartment on the wall.

Tooth powder, shaving brush, hair oil . . . straight razor.

Miranda carefully opened the blade, touching it gingerly with her index finger, and then ran it along the taped edge of the cardboard box.

Gave it a pull and heard the paper tape rip.

Another run with the razor—not too much violence to the box. Jasper would notice it, of course, and what he did afterward—and whom he called—Cheney? Wardon? Miguel?—would be crucial.

She folded the razor, heartbeat pounding in her ears, replaced it on the drawer behind the mirror. Gave the package another tug, enough to partially unhinge a side and give her a view of the box interior.

Clumsy wooden blocks, protecting corners. Dull glint of gold and carved wood.

She grunted, pulling back the cardboard more fully. She peered closer, taking in as much of the painting as she could.

Lush green landscape, trees, dark patina of age, fading into a lighter sky. Mercury with helmet and winged feet holding a weapon, putti hovering against the trees . . .

Miranda's brow wrinkled. The iconography was familiar, probably French, early eighteenth century, but the individual painting even more so. Mercury slaying Argus . . . somewhere, sometime, she'd seen it before.

The train screamed again as it rounded a curve and started climbing, *clack-clack-clack,* light and shadow locked in a duel on Miranda's face.

She turned too late at the brief *click,* drowned out by the shriek of the train.

Jasper stood in front of her . . . a Mauser C96 in his gloved fist.

*

One Mississippi, two Mississippi . . .

Miranda lifted her face slowly, defiantly, to Jasper's.

"Last time I saw one of those was in Madrid. They usually come with jack-boots."

The tall, lanky man, shoulders still stooped, curled his thin lips in a smile, gestured with the gun. "Sit down, Miss Corbie. Oh, yes, I know who you are. My friends at the French consulate assured me they'd never heard of a 'Marion Gouchard,' and it didn't take long for my other friends to find out to whom that rather unconvincing accent belonged. Still, I applaud your nerve. Go on . . . sit."

She stepped backward and sidewise, sinking into the chair, hoping he wouldn't notice the tremors in her legs.

"You're obviously a man with many friends."

Jasper moved forward toward the table and lowered the gun a few degrees.

"Quite. And you're a woman with more courage than sense. A detective, are you? Your stupidity takes my breath away. I teach the chains that connect us to this earth, I study the most intimate particles of matter, the fundamental building blocks of life itself, and you really thought you could march into the observation car and observe me—unobserved? Go back to being a whore, Miss Corbie—I'm sure you're much better at it."

Her fingers closed around the gold cigarette case in her pocket, stomach tight.

You're a good soldier, Miranda Corbie, a good soldier . . .

She gave an elaborate shrug of her shoulders. "And maybe you should quit slumming as a two-bit spy and go back to Berkeley. Tell me—what chemical secrets are you trading for the smuggled paintings? Or are the Nazis strictly cash-and-carry?"

Jasper's eyes widened. He lowered himself on the couch across from her, head barely clearing the bottom of the upper berth. He passed a hand— trembling, Miranda noticed with surprise—across his forehead.

"I see. At least, I begin to see. I have been puzzled over your intrusion into my life, Miss Corbie, but now I take it you are here on behalf of your govern-ment . . . exactly the sort of idiotic idea I would expect from Roosevelt's Washington."

He braced himself on one arm, lines on his face weary and deep. Miranda's eyes darted toward the lowered point of the Mauser.

"You pose a problem for me. But as you are not here representing a compet-ing interest, perhaps we may reach a détente."

"I don't make deals. Not with murderers."

Jasper's eyebrows lifted in surprise until mirth twisted his features, and he chuckled. "You really are quite entertaining, in a penny matinee sort of way. You think I'm guilty of murder? Whom did I 'do in,' pray tell?"

She bent forward and he raised the point of the Mauser, voice a harder edge. "Come, Miss Corbie. Enlighten me."

Door was bolted. Phone call to the service staff within reach but too slow.

No sign of anyone in the next compartment.

The gold cigarette case was slippery from the sweat on her palm.

"Mind if I smoke?"

He reached into his jacket pocket and threw a pack of Dunhills across the table. "Be my guest."

Goddamn it.

She withdrew her hands and plucked out the Southern Pacific matchbook from the cellophane wrapper, lighting the cigarette with a shaking hand. Jasper's mouth was still curled up at the ends.

"I'm waiting."

She blew out a long stream of smoke, met his eyes.

"Edmund Whittaker."

The tall man flinched at the name and blinked, thick eyebrows matted.

Miranda bent forward, pressing, voice sharp. "And my predecessor—the agent who was trailing you."

Jasper took a long, shuddering breath, licking dry lips, suddenly older, eyes dark and fathomless and focused inward. He sat up straight in the bunk, the nose of the Mauser lowered toward the floor.

"I've killed no one. Harmed no one. I—I—at one time, I cared for Edmund."

"You were lovers?"

"Yes—"

"Did he know you were a smuggler?"

"Collector," Jasper corrected automatically. He looked up at her, gun still pointed downward.

"If I thought I could trust you—"

Miranda studied her cigarette. "I'm not official, Dr. Jasper. I don't wear a badge, I'm not sanctioned by Hoover. I've got my own reasons for what I'm doing, and they're mostly selfish reasons."

She tapped ash in the crystal tray, bands of light and shadow still flickering across the table and her face.

"They want to know if you're selling out and how. I want to know who killed Edmund."

He raised his face to hers, eyes cautious. The Mauser was still in his hands, held loosely and pointing at her feet.

"I would like to know as well. Perhaps, Miss Corbie . . . you are not as unintelligent as I suspected."

"You're frightened."

Jasper transferred the pistol to his right hand, pried off his glove, and wiped his forehead with the back of his scarred left hand. Transferred the gun again, scar glistening against taut skin.

"I'm a sane man. My position entails risks."

"Your position smuggling art or secrets, Doctor? Or both?"

He stood up, Mauser still pointed in her direction, and walked toward the connecting wall, facing her, voice low and halting.

"Five years ago, they came to me—your employers. Would I become friendly with the National Socialists and, later on, the Soviets? Would I perhaps pass certain scientific information that was, in a word, inaccurate? I was bored at Berkeley, and war—the elements of war, the weapons of war—have always fascinated me. And then, too, the Germans are a cultured people, it was not difficult to get close to them."

Face of a grown-up boy, charming smile, words of belief and testimony, you should be a detective, Miss Corbie, I'll help with the fucking license, Miss Corbie, and one of these days I'll come knocking on your door and ask for a goddamn favor and you might die, but it's all for your favorite Uncle, Miss Corbie . . .

Goddamn it. James had lied to her. Though maybe in his world he'd just prevaricated, evaded and avoided, lying by omission alone. Maybe that's what passes for truth in his business. Need to fucking know, and MacLeod had figured she wasn't needy enough.

The words came slowly. "You've been working for our own government all along, then . . . since '37."

"Yes, Miss Corbie, I have been successfully communicating the wrong information to the Nazis for a long time now. Your taskmasters didn't tell you the whole story—they never do. You and I—we're expendable. You more so, perhaps, because as a well-known research chemist I have value. I'm counting on that now."

She looked up at him and nodded. "Go on."

"I became friends with the former consul, von Killinger, and after him, Fritz. I soon found that the friendliness offered certain rewards . . . paintings, art. I'd never been able to afford a Picasso or Braque, and here the Nazis were selling them for a pittance, all in the name of 'degenerate art.'"

Miranda twisted the cigarette out in the ashtray. "So you started to . . . 'collect.' And the government got suspicious."

He heaved a sigh, back against the wall. "Exactly. What if I turned? What if I slipped useful information instead of bad? What the fools don't understand is that it's in my best interest to prolong the war, so of course I have passed nothing of lasting importance. But that didn't prevent them from assigning some young man to follow me—your predecessor. He was murdered three months ago in Chicago. I was there on a . . . to meet a contact."

"And you don't have any idea who killed him?"

The professor shook himself impatiently and began to pace in the small space in front of her, transferring the gun from his right hand to the left and back again.

"I wish I did. He was found on the shore of Lake Michigan outside the Drake Hotel, where I was staying. I knew someone was following me, I'd caught a glimpse of him in front of my house and on the train—this very train, in fact. Then I saw his photograph in the paper. Grant Tompkins, his name was. Left two young children."

Jasper braced his arm on the edge of the upper berth, shoulders sagged, Mauser hung loose and slightly swinging.

"I'm talking to you now because I'm worried. Tompkins seemed more like bad luck, a random killing, especially with Chicago being what it is. But of late, I've . . . I've felt someone, Miss Corbie. Someone tracking me. That woman with the jade—"

"Lois Hart."

"Yes—she was murdered after the Picasso exhibit. I was there that night, and I felt . . . something, someone. I'm afraid whoever it is may be trying to kill me. I thought perhaps I'd outgrown my use to the government—"

"They wouldn't murder you, Jasper."

He stared down at her, eyes amused for a moment, like a professor correcting a student.

"Wouldn't they, Miss Corbie? But no, your presence here proves that our spymasters are as bumbling and foolish as they've always been."

He looked through the dark window, black smudges of hills and trees and dotted ranch lights smearing past the glass. He spoke slowly.

"You see—Edmund's death has shaken me badly. We—we had been lovers. It was over with him last year."

It's so awkward when you run into old lovers, especially at social functions . . .

"I knew Edmund, too, Jasper. And you think his murder has something to do with you—that you were the actual target?"

The professor ran trembling fingers through lank hair. "I don't know what to think. But I don't like coincidence. And if the police connect me to Edmund—"

She asked it casually. "Mind if I smoke one of my own? The case is in my pocket."

He looked up alertly, raising the gun. "No tricks, Miss Corbie. We must come to an agreement. An understanding."

She nodded, took out the gold cigarette case and opened it, careful to shield the view of the Baby Browning from Jasper. Plucked out a Chesterfield, left the case open a crack and slid it carefully back in her jacket pocket.

"What about Mexico?"

Shot in the dark.

He pivoted toward her, voice high, sharp and staccato.

"What do you know about Mexico?"

"Your base is there, isn't it? The focal point and personnel for the smuggling operation."

"Collecting." The word was automatic. He stared at her for a few seconds, moistening his lips again.

"You—you know more than I thought. How much more remains to be seen. Perhaps . . . perhaps we can make a deal, Miss Corbie. Perhaps your employer would provide some protection for me, in payment for services rendered. And for your continued health and safety, of course."

Sweat was dripping down his long neck and the Mauser trembled, scar on his hand ice-white against flushed skin.

"We can try, Jasper. Help me fill in the blanks first. Tell me why you think someone would want to kill you—why you need protection."

"What is there to know?" The words came in a rush, almost a babble. "I began by trading. My European associate has been able to secure paintings and objets d'art from some of the richest collections in Poland—that *Mercury and Argus* you've uncovered, for example. Underneath it is another original, again from Poland—*Time Exposes Beauty*. A lesson for you, perhaps. Each seventeenth- or eighteenth-century painting was worth two or three modern pieces, thanks to the 'degenerate art' devaluation—"

"So you stole artwork from Poland while she was being raped by the Nazis and Reds—"

Jasper held up a long, thick-knuckled finger in admonition. "Not steal. Collect."

Miranda took a long drag on the Chesterfield, exhaling out the side of her mouth.

"I don't see a difference, Doctor."

He stood taller, fear momentarily forgotten, Mauser still cradled in his hands.

"Tell me, Miss Corbie—what would the Jews and the Poles do with their precious art? Scrape off the oil for heat or food in a concentration camp? They have no country anymore, no culture. Between the Soviets and the Germans, there is no Poland and there will very soon be no Jews. I make shrewd deals—and yes, sometimes I do pay—because the Germans have degraded Poland and foolishly undermined the value of modern art and overpriced the kitsch that so appeals to Hitler. Am I to blame because I make a bargain? Is that not something the Jews themselves would appreciate?"

Miranda tapped ash into the glass.

"You sound like your Nazi friends, Jasper. From what I read, the Jews aren't in a position to appreciate anything but survival. So who is trying to kill you—and why? The Reds? Competition?"

He licked his lips again, eyes focused on the window, fear etching itself on his skin.

"I'm worried, terribly worried. Holland is being dismantled as we speak. All the Rembrandts, De Hooch, the Hals . . . in hiding, transferred from one location to the other, or dragged through God knows what kind of filth in a misguided attempt to secure them from the Nazis."

He flicked a glance at her. "It won't work, Miss Corbie. The conquerors will conquer and the Dutch will starve. Selling them to sympathetic collectors is the only option left, both for the owners and the art. And don't you see what's next? France—France, with all her glories, with all the collectors, so many of them Jews, all the galleries . . . France will make Poland and Holland look like a pauper's field. France, Miss Corbie, France."

Miranda inhaled once more before crushing out the cigarette with a vicious twist.

"You're playing a dangerous game. Someone's going to get wise, if they aren't already—someone who wants a cut, or who wants a painting you've . . . 'collected.' Maybe it's time you came home to stay. Get out while you can."

"I have one more delivery to make in Chicago. Then—then I would like to retire to Mexico permanently, where this is both Right and Left and a continual sense of the disorder that makes my business possible. I have friends there already, as you know. Dr. Huntington Jasper will disappear, a sad victim of Chicago violence, perhaps, and I shall sit out the war in Mexico City, continuing to save as much art as I can. The government—your superiors—can help keep me safe."

He looked up at her expectantly. "That is my proposal, Miss Corbie. I suggest you accept it."

Miranda's fingers closed around the gold cigarette case in her pocket. "I'll have to contact them in Reno."

Jasper glanced at his watch and stood up, raising the point of the Mauser. "Eight-thirteen. We're a little over two hours away. Ample time for you to tell me exactly what you know about Mexico."

The fear and exhaustion seemed to have dissipated from his body. The pistol was steady, aimed at her chest. Miranda clenched her stomach, lips curled in a sardonic smile.

"You just said you 'save' art, Jasper. 'Collecting,' 'saving' . . . pretty words for stealing and smuggling."

He looked out the window, pupils lit rhythmically by the lights along the track, voice soft and resonant.

"What is art, after all? A unique combination of shapes and lines, drawn by a genius, a mind possessed . . . I understand art as I understand how life exists, how the interplay of positive and negative energy creates all matter in the name of God himself. Does it not belong best to the man who truly appreciates it, a man who understands its significance? Think of what we have lost, from Alexandria's library to Louis's silver, melted down to make war for the French. No, Miss Corbie, I am Elgin reborn, and I will save the art . . . save the so-called *entartete Kunst* from burning in Hitler's bonfires. Save it from the Jews and the Germans, the Reds and the Slavs. Save it for all time."

"And keep it for yourself, Jasper. For yourself. Funny thing—I always thought art was more than the expression of one man. I thought it belonged to a nation."

Jasper's eyes refocused. He nodded thoughtfully, as if she'd posed a question in a seminar.

"And if the nation belongs to Hitler?"

Her fingers curled around the Baby Browning, still in her pocket. A soft knock sounded at the door.

"Porter, sir."

Jasper turned toward Miranda with the Mauser held high. "In there." He gestured toward the tiny bathroom with the nozzle of the gun. "Not a sound. I'll get rid of him."

The professor shoved a hand against her back, pushing her into the small space and shutting the door. Miranda flattened against the wall in the dark, Baby Browning in her palm. Her thumb slid the safety catch back.

Jasper's voice sounded muffled. "Just a minute, Porter."

One Mississippi, two Mississippi . . .

Rattle of the door opening, Jasper's voice, high-pitched. The train was climbing through a tunnel, engines shrill and straining, clack and clatter of the tracks . . .

Pop.

Miranda gave a sharp intake of breath.

Goddamn it, she knew that sound.

A silencer, smaller caliber, probably .32.

Thud.

That would be Dr. Huntington Jasper, slumped on the floor.

Dead.

Elgin fucking reborn.

She pressed back against the wall, the small Browning slipping against sweaty palms, breath shallow, too fast, too goddamn fast . . .

Johnny and Spain, Rick and Gonzales, Bente and Gladys and all the fucking Glenn Miller tunes and the Stork Club and Fireside Chats, the piece of paper, sacred, holy, Sally and the girls, Allen and his lemon drops, Meyer's starched shirts and ebony cane, and, goddamn it, no, Miranda Corbie was not going to die, not on the *City of San Francisco,* namesake to her town, her home.

Her mother.

She wasn't going to die.

Not now, not here.

Not today.

Slow exhale. The killer was moving around the cabin. Ripping sound of cardboard covering the paintings. More thuds and a bump, this time of luggage lowered and carefully searched.

In and out, breathe in and out, no noise, no movement.

Itchy wool, sweat dripping down her back and under her bra, and goddamn it, she wanted to scream.

Vanity mirror opening, across from her door and five feet away. Too bad she hadn't kept the straight razor. Extra weapon. She'd have to aim for the head.

You're a good soldier, Randy, a good soldier . . .

Rattle again, outside door open, shut again.

She waited.

Counted one hundred Mississippis and listened to the train level off, start to descend in the darkness, climb down from the mountaintop, hallelujah, trust in God and keep your fucking powder dry . . .

Nothing.

No noise, no breath, no sound except the train, steady and sure, winding down through the Sierra Nevada toward Reno, passing ghost towns and gold towns, the infamous Donner Lake, six thousand and more feet up . . .

The Baby Browning clenched in her hand, pointing at the darkness. What if Jasper wasn't dead?

Miranda took a deep, shuddering breath, closed her eyes for a moment, opening them to the blackness of the small, confined toilet room.

Had to try.

She reached out her left hand to turn the knob . . . slowly, agony of waiting.

Crack. Sliver of light dazzling, eyes comforted in the dark, blinded by light.

Didn't see him, didn't hear him.

She fell back into the black, razors slicing her head, mother's voice crooning in her ear . . .

Sleep, baby dear . . . sleep without fear . . .
Mother is with you forever.

Twenty-nine

*

The first thing she felt was the rumble of the engine through the floor, her body shaking like an overweight woman in a reduction belt. The second thing she felt was pain.

Back of the head, side of the face.

Whole goddamn body.

Pain was good. Meant she was alive.

Her eyes opened, blurred vision.

Train compartment.

Miranda tried to stand up, too wobbly, and she landed back on her ass, legs apart in an ungainly pose, as a fleeting image of Dianne Laroche winked in front of her, Dianne telling her how to stand, how to sit, how to cross her legs . . .

"You look like you just came back from war and lost. You're not a soldier, Miranda, you're a woman, remember? And in my house, you'll act like a lady . . ."

Dianne . . . Dianne and Edmund.

Edmund.

She opened her eyes wide, pulled herself up with her left hand and the help of the Formica table.

Memory.

Her right hand felt too heavy. Miranda stared at her fist as if it were detached. No Baby Browning.

Her fingers were clutching a Colt 1903 .32 ACP semiautomatic with a silencer still neatly fastened to the end of the barrel.

The train whistle shrieked and she jumped, dropping the gun with a clatter, pain at the back of her head making her wince, spasm in her hand and arm. Her eyes drifted downward, back to the table.

Propped up on the floor beside it, eyes still open and glazed.

Huntington Jasper.

A red splotch spread in uneven, jagged lines around the pulping hole in his skull.

He'd been shot dead.

And she was being framed for it.

She bent forward, palms on knees, fighting the bile in her throat. Coughed, tried to breathe, in and out, in and out.

Her eyes flicked over the compartment as the train ran over a trestle, roaring down the night, bars of light and shadow in a macabre dance, all twisted corners, odd angles, an old silent movie, Dr. Caligari and his somnambulist.

Head was aching, vision still unclear, pulse shaking her already shaky eyesight.

Thump-bob, thump-bob, thump-bob . . .

Goddamn it, she had to get off the *City of San Francisco*.

She felt her pockets. Gloves were in her handbag, back in her compartment. She moved as quickly as she could to the bathroom, stumbling once but catching herself on the wall. Opened the cellophane-wrapped, flat package of toilet tissue, shoving the cellophane in her pocket and wrapped the tissue in her palm.

Not much, but it would have to do.

More breath, in and out, in and out, fighting the pain in her head. Looked around again, eyes falling back to Jasper.

She glanced at her watch. 9:03. She'd been out for over thirty minutes. The train was less than an hour and a half from Reno.

She sat gingerly on the Nantes blue armchair, trying to think, tissue starting to get damp from her palm. The killer hadn't alerted the train officials already— why? Not an airtight frame, and . . .

Miranda twisted her neck suddenly to the right, a spasm of pain making her regret the haste.

No. No paintings. He'd taken them and he knew she'd be able to identify them, maybe stir up enough murkiness to hold him for questioning. He was banking on her being out until the real porter knocked on the door or until someone else wondered what happened to Dr. Huntington Jasper . . . or until he could make an anonymous call from the Reno train station.

Her eyes darted to the door of the compartment.

The killer was still on the train.

Waiting for her.

Miranda swallowed hard, wishing for a cigarette to stop the shakes, no time to light up, no time. She bent down, almost blacking out again, and picked up the Colt with the tissue in her hand.

One sheet gone.

She pulled out another and wiped the prints off as best she could, then stooped down next to Jasper's body, fighting the knives at the back of her head.

He already smelled dead, blood coagulated, drying at the edges, bits of skull and brain splattered around what was left of his forehead and the side of his head.

One shot. A clean, professional kill.

She positioned the pistol in his scarred left hand, his fingers still pliable enough to make an impression. Sat back on her heels and studied the layout.

The killer was right-handed and maybe didn't realize Jasper wasn't. Bullet hole was off center, on Jasper's left . . . near where he'd hold a gun to his own head, if he was aiming for the front and not the side.

Goddamn long shot, but at least a plausible-enough suicide until the Reno bulls finished their hand of lowball and decided to earn a paycheck.

Third sheet of tissue.

Her hands moved to Jasper's jacket, which was gaping open from how he was slumped upright against the couch and table. She gingerly removed a wallet from his inside coat pocket and carefully examined the interior.

About four hundred dollars in fifties and twenties, a driver's license, a University of California identification card. Clean, neat, and precise, just like the professor. Under the driver's license, a newer-looking business card, off-white with raised letters in black:

THE DRAKE HOTEL—LAKE SHORE DRIVE, CHICAGO—"THE ARISTOCRAT OF HOTELS"

Edges still sharp. Jasper hadn't had it for long.

Miranda turned the card over. Blue ink, precise, careful writing: "Clark. 511. 12:30. 30th."

Miranda carefully slid the card into her own jacket's outer pocket and realized the killer had taken her Baby Browning, but not the trick cigarette case.

She pulled herself up with the edge of the table, wobbling. Crumpled the used tissue and dropped it in her other pocket.

Checked her watch again: 9:28. About an hour left.

The killer had lowered Jasper's luggage onto the bottom berth, scattering carefully pressed shirts and trousers. She ran an eye over the contents. He'd already looted anything important.

She straightened up, head a dull, throbbing ache, and using the last three tissues from the bathroom, methodically wiped down the doorknobs, the table, and the mirrored wall vanity, suddenly remembering the straight razor.

She opened the mirror again and dropped the razor in her pocket with the tissues. Needed another weapon, anyway.

Noise from the corridor and the room next door, celebration, high-pitched laughter.

Passengers getting ready for Reno . . . and the signal for her to go.

She waited, breathing hard, until she couldn't hear the voices outside. Just the train, smooth and fast, rolling down over rugged landscape on the way to dice games and slot machines, drop a pair of Cs at the Bank Club, women bitter over the lines around their eyes lining up for a saddle lesson by one of the dude ranch dudes, take their minds off the divorce from Henry . . . all fucking in a fucking day's work, and she'd helped plenty of them find freedom and a fat alimony check thanks to Nevada divorce laws and the Biggest Little City in the World.

She hoped like hell it was big enough to hide in.

Miranda counted to three and opened the door a crack. No noise, no footsteps, so she squeezed through quickly, patting her pockets to make sure she still had her cigarette case.

She missed the Baby Browning.

Her left hand shook with a spasm, and she shoved it in her jacket pocket, walking as quickly as she could toward the rear of the car.

A portly man in a dark brown derby was walking toward her, probably on the way to the club car for another drink. He grinned, squinting at her, wobbling a little, but managed to hold the door open while she squeezed past.

Open-section sleeping car, loudest part of the train. Harried mothers with hair in curlers were hushing fidgety boys with kazoos, husbands snoring. Single salesmen swigged from flasks, jawing with their buddies and comparing territories, while elderly ladies yanked the curtains together, worried someone would get a peek at their nightclothes.

Miranda hurried through, stumbling once, wondering if the killer was hiding behind one of the pea green curtains.

Portsmouth Square was next, well-bred duplex bedrooms for honeymooners and vacationing bankers, set up and quiet, just large enough for them to hold their own parties. Giggles erupted from number 5, probably a few girls someone smuggled aboard.

One more car, Chinatown, louder and more crowded, sporting roomettes with not-so-thick drapes instead of doors, couples within either together or à la carte on separate bunks, enjoying more privacy than the seats in the front, but not by much, keep your voice down, Clark, didn't you read the sign? "Quiet is requested for the benefit of those who have retired." . . . They'll hear you all the way down the train . . .

She braced herself against the side wall, throbbing pain behind the eyes, vision still as wobbly as a two-year-old. Bright lights, red and green like Christmas. Only a few dozen feet from the Twin Peaks car—and her own room. She passed a hand over her forehead. Wished the fucking pain would go away.

He'd be watching her car and her room—not Jasper's, couldn't afford to be near Jasper. He was sitting pretty, ready to make a call to the bulls in Reno, report a homicide, suspicious character, wanted for questioning in San Francisco . . .

Goddamn it.

Her hand trembled again, and she pulled open the cigarette case and stuck a Chesterfield between her lips. What to fucking do . . .

She thought of Rick suddenly, his laugh, that goddamn half-Irish bullshit accent. How he pushed his fedora off his forehead, how his eyes got bluer when he was on a story.

No Rick. But maybe—just maybe—Tom and Marie O'Day could help her.

*

Marie opened the door to room D, Twin Peaks, generous mouth slightly agape, eyes as wide as saucers. She was dressed in a red silk robe with embroidered fish, the kind they sold in Chinatown.

"Miss—Miss Corbie?"

Tom appeared over her shoulder wearing a T-shirt and blue flannel pajama bottoms. His voice was clipped.

"Get her in here, Marie—she's in shock."

Marie pulled her inside the large compartment, looking up and down the corridor. Guided her to the armchair by the window. The bed was already made up with brown and green wool blankets, and Marie patted her hand. The cigarette was still dangling from Miranda's mouth.

She looked up at the couple, anxiously peering down at her.

"Got a light?"

Tom picked up an SP matchbook from the table next to the bed, lit the Chesterfield. Miranda gulped it down, shoulders shuddering.

"I'm sorry to involve you, but I need your help."

Tom spoke to Marie: "I left my clothes in the bathroom."

Turned back to Miranda, forehead creased and mouth turned downward. "You look like hell—white as a damn ghost. And that"—he pointed to the right sleeve of her dress—"looks like blood."

Miranda raised her arm, examining the sleeve with a frown. A small red stain spread outward from the pink flowers, purple and almost black against the green fabric.

"That's because it is. The man I was following has been killed—and I'm being framed for it."

Marie let out a gasp. Tom nodded, jaw tight.

"You need to get off the train. I'll change." He clambered his tall frame into the small toilet room. "Excuse me while I dress."

Miranda took one last puff on the cigarette, squeezed out the end with her fingers and dropped it into her pocket.

"The killer hit me over the head—I was out for half an hour. We don't have much time."

Marie stood up, drawing the robe tighter. "What do you need?"

Goddamn it. These were fine people, young, in love, made for each other . . .

She ran a hand over her forehead, winced. Still clammy.

"I'm sorry, Marie. I need to make my way back to San Francisco without being stopped. I need a change of clothes and a bag for this dress. It's evidence on my side—no splatter, just a soaked-in bloodstain from examining the wound."

Marie nodded. "I'm a good three inches shorter than you, but as soon as Tom gets out, he'll lift down the trunk and you're welcome to whatever I have."

"Tom is going to do what?" The tall, lanky young man emerged from behind Marie, where he'd hurriedly thrown on clothes over his pajamas, cinching his belt. "Oh, get down the trunk. Of course."

"Wait." Miranda held out a hand, palm down, to stop him. "You haven't asked me details and I can't give you any. This is dangerous. The killer is still on the train."

Tom bent down, peering into her face. "She's got a concussion, Marie. Find my flask—it's gin, not whiskey, but it'll help."

He lowered the trunk from the upper rack to the bed while Marie opened a drawer underneath the vanity mirror.

"Portland's dangerous, too, Miss Corbie. Danger is everywhere in this crazy, lopsided world. So save your breath and tell us what you need and what we should do."

Marie extended the silver flask to Miranda with a smile. She took it gratefully, feeling the heat of the alcohol course through her neck and back, giving strength to her arms and legs. She wiped her mouth on her sleeve, handed the flask back to Marie.

"I've got to disappear in Reno. Can't let the bulls find any trace of me, including my luggage. Collect it and deposit it at the Reno train station under the name 'Marion Gouchard.' Here's the key to my room. It's at the front of this car, bedroom A. I'll need my handbag before I leave."

She pulled the key out of her left pocket and set it down on the ledge of the bed. Tom picked it up quickly and shoved it into his trousers.

Marie lifted up a pretty brown dress with cream dots. "Will this do?"

Miranda bit her lip, closing her eyes briefly. Head hurt like hell.

"Got a better idea. Tom, can you find the porter named George? He's the shoeshine this trip. Slip him two fins." She pulled out the wallet from her pocket. "Lucky I brought this and my cigarette case with me. The killer stole my gun." She peeled out four twenties. "I'll add to that when I can."

Tom shook his head. "Uh-uh, nothing doing, Miss Corbie. Marie and I, we figure whoever you were chasing was a bad hombre. Whoever killed him is the same, or maybe even worse. I told you the first time—we're glad to help."

She smiled slightly. "Take the money, Tom. Consider it part of a wedding present."

He grumbled under his breath, his shirt still askew from dressing hastily. But he folded the cash, crammed it into his pocket.

"What do I say to George when I find him?"

"Tell him the lady who tried to help Isaiah needs some help—a porter suit and cap, the smallest they've got."

"Is that it?"

"Thank him for me and tell him I'll send him more thanks as soon as I can."

Tom nodded, shoving his fedora on his head and giving Marie a quick kiss on the cheek. "I'm on the way for your handbag and the uniform."

They watched him squeeze through the small door. Marie shut it carefully behind him, letting out a deep breath. She turned to eye Miranda critically, gaze traveling up and down.

"If you're going to pass as a man, Miss Corbie . . . we've got some work to do."

Thirty

*

Miranda plucked at the tight cloth bandage around her breasts, studying herself in the long, narrow mirror fastened on the inside of the bathroom door. She frowned.

"Still too much of a bump, but I figure the uniform will be big enough to hide it. I can pick up another bandage at a Reno drugstore."

Marie stepped back, voice doubtful. "I don't know, Miss Corbie, your shape is awful . . . womanly."

Miranda's mouth twisted in half a grin. "Thanks. I'll slouch a lot. Does Tom have a T-shirt I can use?"

"Sure. He always wears them, even in the summer."

The young woman turned to the suitcase on the bed, rummaging through white socks and thermal underwear before finding a V-neck T-shirt.

"Here you go, Miss Corbie."

"Please—call me Miranda. Formalities seem a little strange when I'm wearing your husband's clothes."

Marie laughed, seemed grateful for the release of nerves. The T-shirt was thick cotton. Miranda pulled it down over the tight wrapping, hunching her shoulders forward in a slouch and studying the effect.

"It'll do. Thank God you thought of the train first-aid kit, though if you run into that Southern Pacific nurse again, you'd better limp."

Marie's wide mouth curved into a smile. "I don't mind. I did a bit of acting in my high school."

A loud thump on the door made both women jump. Miranda darted into the bathroom.

Marie squared her shoulders and opened the door a crack. Tom pushed his way in with his foot, carrying a Southern Pacific laundry bag in both arms, fedora low over his eyes. Marie slammed the door shut quickly, pressing her back against it with her hand on her heart.

"Sorry, honey, couldn't knock and didn't want to talk. Where's Miss Corbie?"

Miranda pushed the handle and opened the bathroom door enough to be heard. Spoke softly. "I'm in here. You find George?"

Tom lowered the bundle of clothes on the bed, along with Miranda's handbag and a pair of men's work boots.

"I don't know what you ever did for George, Miss Corbie, but he caught on right away, no questions. He's the one who thought of the shoes, I didn't. He even looked at me sideways and said if a party ever wanted to leave the car a little early so as not to have their exit noticed, that party should go to the observation car about ten minutes beforehand and wait for a signal. He said we're due into Reno early, about ten-fifteen."

Marie was holding up the clothes, frowning. "The legs are still too long. I can hem them real fast."

Miranda glanced at her watch: 9:47. "Can you hem them in ten minutes, Marie?"

Scuffling, a couple of cases opening, and a playful thwack of hand on flesh and mild protestations from Marie followed Miranda's question, while Tom's voice rose above it to respond. "She's the best damn little seamstress in Portland—though that's not why I married her."

More whispers from Marie, and Miranda smiled, remembering this was their honeymoon. Goddamn it, if something happened to Tom or Marie . . .

"Got a robe I could wear? It's a little cramped in here."

"Of course, Miss—Miranda. Tom, give her yours, it's thick enough."

His long arm reached out in front of the bathroom door, holding a brown flannel robe. Miranda grabbed it, wrapping it around herself before stepping into the main room. Tom was stroking Marie's hair with one hand, his other hand holding her waist while she frantically ran a thread through the cuffs of the thick uniform. Tom looked up at Miranda and moved aside.

"Got the whole outfit right here. Shirt, pants, vest, jacket, suspenders, cap, even the tie. It'll be slow going in the shoes—the smallest size George could find was a seven. He shook his head over the idea of a porter's uniform, said it wouldn't work, and by hook or by crook, came up with this."

Miranda looked down at the worn assortment of dark blue clothes, fingering the raised "SP" on one of the silver buttons.

"I hope he won't lose his job."

"George'll be all right. But your train compartment looks like a tornado's been through it. I had a hell of time finding your handbag, and I had to toss everything in your cases without paying much attention."

Miranda nodded grimly. "Thanks. I appreciate you taking it down to the station. I didn't want to lose it all—some of those dresses are expensive."

He straightened up tall, grinning. "That's the spirit. You'll be wearing them again in no time—to the christening of our first baby."

She grinned back. "I'll go ahead and put everything else on while Marie's finishing up."

He handed her the rest of the clothes. "No need to get back in the outhouse again . . . I'll keep my back turned."

"Thanks."

The train was slowing down as it approached Reno, more lights flooding the compartment, more noise in the hall. Miranda hurriedly threw off the robe, buttoning the man's shirt all the way up. The collar was too large and sagged enough to show her neck.

"Finished." Marie slammed the needle and thread on the small table next to the bed. "Here're the trousers. Tom, stay where you are."

He raised his eyebrows, grinning impishly. "Don't worry, honey. I'm not going anywhere."

Miranda clambered into the pants. The legs hung unevenly, but they wouldn't trip her. Marie stepped closer to help with the suspenders.

"Tom's right, you're a good seamstress."

The young woman waved a hand in the air. "Don't listen to him."

Her husband started to crane his neck around. "Hey!"

"Face the wall, Mr. O'Day." Marie winked at Miranda.

She bit her lip as Marie helped tighten the suspender straps.

"Thanks. Works much better than a belt. Got a hair band?"

"Just a minute." Marie opened the vanity mirror while Tom started to whistle "Please Don't Talk About Me When I'm Gone."

"All right, Tom, enough, you can turn around. Miranda's decent."

Miranda finished tying the worn, scuffed work boots and straightened up. Her thick auburn hair hit the shoulders of the man's suit, a navy necktie hanging loosely from the too-big white shirt collar. She arched an eyebrow.

"Me?"

The young man laughed and shook his head. "It'll work. At least well enough for you to get off the train and to somewhere else."

She hoped to hell he was right. Marie handed her two hair bands and a brush. Miranda hurriedly made pigtails and folded them up into the Southern Pacific cap. Then she knotted the tie quickly, pulled the cap over her eyes, and hitched up the pants. They all stared at her image in the narrow mirror.

"Marie, put your brown dress and her dress and things in the laundry bag. Better shove the handbag in there, too. Miranda, you've got about five minutes to get to the observation car."

She slouched into the heavy jacket and turned to face them. The SP work boots were about a size too big, but not so large that she couldn't walk—and walk fast.

"Thanks. Remember to send me an address when you land in Virginia. Now, until you hear otherwise—forget me. Don't watch me leave. Clear out my trunks as soon as I go, before everyone else is off the train for a leg stretch and the Reno passengers are coming on board. I don't think we'll have to worry about my room being cased—the killer already went through it. If anything, he may try to hop early and place a phone call. I hope to beat him to it."

Marie reached out to grab Miranda's arm. "You will be careful." Statement, not a question.

Tom shook his head, small grin. "There's no arguing with her."

Miranda's eyes darted from the tall, almost gangly young man with the big hat and infectious grin to the small but fiery curly-haired woman beside him. They stood together, not an inch apart.

She smiled and said it gently. "Thanks. See you at the christening."

She heaved the laundry bag up from the bed and onto her shoulder, head still aching, the extra weight making her even more wobbly. Took a deep breath, pulled the hat brim low and shadowed her face. Tom waited until a group of voices passed, heading toward the club car, and then held the door half open while Miranda slipped out into the corridor, blue and green lights from the track and neon lights from the city starting to stream through the windows.

She was alone again.

But Miranda was used to that.

＊

Four compartments between her and the observation car, one open section then double bedrooms and roomettes, most with passengers continuing on through Chicago, blasé and blotto, a few lining the windows to see what the Reno fuss was all about.

No one spoke to her, though a few of the women looked at her oddly. She did her best to stride and not sashay, to keep her back bent and her chest flat, and smiled ironically to herself at what Dianne Laroche would say to her now.

George gave her a quick glance, avoided a double-take, avoided making eye contact. Made a quick motion with his head for her to follow him back through the car—now filling up with matrons who wanted to dump a penny in the bathroom slot machine at the station—and stood waiting, hands in his pockets, in the small passageway between the observation car and Telegraph Hill, the roomette sleeper in front of it. The diesel engines were no longer roaring; the train, she noticed with surprise, was nearly at a standstill.

George raised his arm and trained his eyes on his pocket watch, voice low and hesitant. Gestured to the gangway door on Miranda's right.

"This here will be open in less than two minutes. Before the passengers step off."

Miranda nodded. A traveling salesman in a flashy green fedora pried himself off up from one of the comfortable seats in the observation car, leaving behind an empty highball glass on the table next to him. He was weaving toward the passageway, Miranda an awkward beacon in the SP uniform.

George's eyes flickered. "Bathroom."

She hesitated for a split second, then entered the small room.

Mirrors on the wall, a stainless steel ashtray in front of two red armchairs. Blue floor, off-white porcelain sink. No one at the urinal, no one on the toilet. She leaned against the mirrored wall in relief. Outside, the drunk was arguing with George.

". . . fella below me is snorin' to beat the band, and I didn't pay good money to sleep in the goddamn observation car! Where's that SP fella? He was here a minute ago . . . maybe he can kick this rube back to Modesto where he drove in from . . ."

She heard George make vague, soothing noises. Glanced at her watch.

Time.

Deep breath and she exited the bathroom, pulling up her pants. George was unlocking the door. The salesman stared at her, blinked a few times, and she shoved past him. The porter leaned in close to her ear.

"Real SP man coming in about one minute."

She nodded, stepped down the stairway.

"Hey—hey you—"

George intercepted the salesman and her too-large boots touched the station platform, while the porter stood with his back to the open doorway.

She risked a quick look behind, but George was still engaged with the salesman.

Miranda lengthened her stride, the crisp, dry air cold and clean. She headed for the station double doors.

She'd made it to Reno.

*

The depot building was about fifteen years old and surprisingly small for the Biggest Little City in the World.

Mostly middle-aged women in various stages of elation or depression lined the high-backed, shining wood seats, waiting for the divorcée special, while men in sweat-stained hatbands eyed them with appraisal, wondering if there were odds to be made and money to be had.

Young woman in black, red around the eyes and nose, face to the window, hungry for the next rattler to nowhere . . . No missus, not anymore, just freedom, lady, freedom, ringing down from a Nevada gavel.

The woman in black blew her nose, held on to the back of the bank of seats to support herself as she walked unsteadily back to a chair.

Freedom could be expensive.

And then there were the young matrons from places like Des Moines and Elgin, the ones who saw *The Women* fifteen times at Loew's and wept for Norma Shearer, comforted by the idea that she'd wait for him, that she'd get him back, that all she had to do was paint her nails jungle red. Blame it all on Joan Crawford, men will be men, that is to say boys, and women . . . well, Hollywood says we endure.

Never mind about your black eye and the torn, soiled panties in his overcoat pocket, the late-night grunt and brief slap of flesh on flesh, his breath smelling of stale beer. Never mind the empty nights and cold bed, the excuses to the children, daughter with eyes too old for her face, son with the bruises from fighting too much, never mind the realization that the wrapped bottle of perfume and his new, pressed suit weren't for you.

Never mind and nevermore, don't stop to think, don't let yourself feel, don't try to remember. Above all, don't ask yourself if you want him back.

Or you'll wind up in Reno.

Miranda walked as quickly as she could, trying to avoid people's eyes, SP uniform a beacon for passengers with questions or complaints. She deftly lifted and pocketed a timetable before heading out the double doors on Center Street, bright green and pink and gold neon from Commercial Row glittering against the cold night, high desert stars dull and dim, candles at a fireworks show.

Her breath blew smoke and she huddled in the too-large coat. Couldn't light a goddamn Chesterfield, not till she was safely away from the station.

She trudged down Commercial toward Virginia Street, home of the famous sign. Gambling dives big and small clustered around the arch like an altar, paying respects on bended knee to the Biggest Little City in the World, town motto and sacred oath.

Outside of New York, Reno was a good place to disappear, to vanish, nobody asking questions, nobody noticing anything but the slots and the dames and the odds at Santa Anita.

A beat cop was lounging against the door to the Inferno, a smaller casino dwarfed by the giant lighted signs of the Frontier and Harold's Club, and Miranda strode a little faster, past the Ship and Bottle, headed for the Bank Club.

Her head still ached but she felt surprisingly clear minded . . . as if pieces were starting to fall into place.

The killer had ransacked her room. He'd been looking for something, either information or an incriminating piece of evidence he could plant, or probably both. Her luggage would only tell him the brand of night cream she wore. The evidence—a pair of silk stockings, some underwear—he'd take back to Jasper's room during the Reno stop, expecting to find her still out cold. He'd shrug and style the scene anyway, story of a former whore and private eye who hooked the john for money and then lammed it out of town—after shooting him dead.

Then he'd run straight to a Reno dive where he could place a call or send a telegraph, and cops would stop the train at Ogden. Meanwhile, the killer would hide in Reno and prepare for his next move.

Just like her.

The Bank Club loomed in front of Miranda, smoke pouring from within, din and clatter of metal and cards, sharp-eyed men in visors and vests dealing poker, blackjack, and chuck-a-luck. Girls in too-tight dresses stood with hands on hips, fingernails dirty, waiting under the Golden Annex Hotel sign, while prospective customers ignored them for the casino next door. Other women, less discreet or more desperate, rendezvoused in the deep alley between the Bank Club and the Palace. From inside the casino, someone was playing an old record of Paul Whiteman and Ramona Davies, Cole Porter musical, gangsters and debutantes, Depression-era attempt to make sense out of the insensible.

But now, God knows . . .

And Miranda Corbie was in drag in Reno.

She shrugged the bag off her shoulders and strode into the Bank Club.

"Anything Goes" . . .

Thirty-one

*

Cigarette and cigar smoke poured through the door as Miranda squeezed her way past the crowd of men in straw hats and suspenders, floppy caps and fedoras, murmurs of hope and sudden cacophony of disappointment rippling through the thick crowd. Perspiration perfumed the air, twirls of the ceiling fans too apathetic to dispel the damp odor of sweat.

Small, compactly built men in white shirts and suspenders and green-shaded hats stood behind long tables, offering twenty-one and poker, craps, hazard, keno and the wheel, eyes on the crowd and the chips, hands fast and sure and practiced.

Women lined the bar, mixed with a few society dames taking the six-week cure and looking for a quick high in low places.

Jim McKay and Bill Graham, owners of the Bank Club, made sure the company whores weren't quite as worn out as their sisters who worked the eight-hour, rotating-door shifts at the Stockade, commonly known as the fuck factory, located near the Truckee River. Open twenty-four hours a day, the Stockade was a fortress not only in name. Miranda remembered meeting an escort at Dianne's who'd escaped after a week. She'd described a giant, horseshoe-shaped building as large as an entire city block, one where the girls worked in a prison room, one bed, one window, one never-closed door.

The girl—Claire, she suddenly remembered—looked thirty-five at twenty-two, and the bitterness in her voice when she spoke of the place lingered in Miranda's memory long after the girl had passed through Dianne's and moved on.

Licensed to sell, with the Biggest Little City and the state of Nevada taking a sizable cut on the three-dollar, thirty-minute fee, the Stockade whores lasted maybe a year before they got too sick, too pregnant, or too carved up to be legal. Only option left was Douglas Alley, next door to the Bank Club, where they took a chance on getting picked up for selling without a license, and the johns ran the risk of syphilis.

Fuck factory. Grinding out sex for a never-ending supply of customers, men from California and Oregon and Arizona, men who traveled by train and bus and car to put money down and pull the slots, men who'd come to Reno, Nevada, to satisfy whatever itch they wanted scratched.

The supply of whores was never ending, too, Divorce Capital of the World attracting women with lost hopes and last chances, six-week cure-all taking a wrong turn toward the river, hotel bill overdue, no money from home, no home at all, with the would-be divorcée pressed into service at the Stockade or one of the other, smaller operations. Short bald man with a gold tooth and a gleam in his eye, I'll get the paperwork put through for you on credit, girlie, can't run back to no old man, now, gotta support yerself somehow, just a couple weeks an' you'll get that bus ticket back to Omaha . . .

Miranda pushed her way to the bar between a fat man in a felt fedora and one of the prostitutes. She needed some goddamn time to think.

The whore—a henna-haired woman who still retained some freshness in her face—scooted closer.

"Got a light?"

She thrust out a Lucky Strike under Miranda's nose. Miranda turned her head away, spoke gruffly.

"Go chase another one, sister. I'm here on business."

The redhead withdrew her arm, sniffed, got up off the barstool. Said, "So am I—brother. Boys ain't legal in Reno, even for the SP."

She flounced off toward the keno table, and the stool was immediately filled by a sharply dressed, blue-eyed man with a gun holster and hard muscle under his suit. Miranda instinctively inched away from him. He smelled like blood.

The bartender smiled, fear at the corners, spoke to her new neighbor. "Usual, Elmer?"

The young man nodded. "Just cleaned the fish out of the alley. Goddamn whores. Jim and Bill want the Bank Club nice and legal, only whores in here got a license to fuck."

The bartender laughed, wattle of flesh under his chin quivering. He poured a straight-up shot of rye and a glass of beer, set them in front of Elmer.

"Nobody wants to end up on your bad side, Elmer."

Elmer flared. "Whaddya mean, bad side? I ain't got a bad side, Joe. You get that from my old lady or something? Fucking bitch and her alimony payments . . . don't let me hear you talk about no bad side, all right?"

Joe backed away. "Sure, Elmer, sure . . . didn't mean nothing by it, nothing at all." He suddenly seemed to realize Miranda had been standing for five minutes with no order and turned to her with a frozen smile. "What'll it be, mister?"

"Bourbon, straight up."

Joe poured from a bottle of Old Crow, shoved it toward Miranda. The liquor felt good, warmed her arms and legs. She suddenly realized she was hungry.

"Hey—the *San Francisco* was late this week. What the hell happened?"

Elmer was facing her from the barstool. She didn't turn around. "Accident."

He made a derisive noise. "Yeah—like last year. You people never caught them sab-o-tours, did you?"

She tossed the rest of the bourbon down her throat, dug out fifty cents from the wallet in her pocket. Slowly pivoted the bar stool toward Elmer, keeping her head down.

"No."

She got up to go and he suddenly thrust out an arm, holding her down. "You know what I think? I think it was SP's fault and your goddamn conductor. That's what I think. Whaddya say to that?"

Miranda shrugged off his arm. Her fist closed around the folded straight-edge razor in her left pocket. Made her voice as deep as she could.

"I say you're drunk—but maybe you're right."

He looked surprised for a second, then threw his head back and laughed. "All right, go throw before the next one comes through. You ain't so bad for a railroad bum."

Miranda nodded, picked up the laundry bag, and blended into the crowd around the roulette wheel.

Time to change clothes. The uniform was drawing too much attention, too many questions. The *City of San Francisco* would be gone by now, and she needed to plan her next move.

Maybe it was safer to be a man in Reno, Nevada . . . but not, apparently, if you worked for Southern Pacific.

✳

Miranda hurried across the street toward the Elite Café. Red booths lined the long, narrow space, some filled with women, some with men, some with couples. She lugged the laundry bag, arms aching, nodding to one of the waitresses and heading toward the back and what she hoped was a bathroom with a stall.

She pushed through the door. A portly man was standing at the urinal, baring his teeth in the mirror and trying to clean out a piece of spinach with his tongue. A small slot machine stood next to the sink. She bent down to look under the jade green partition, which hung crookedly. Nobody home.

She sidled into the stall and stood in front of the toilet, waiting for the fat man—still sucking his teeth and wringing out an occasional drop—to leave.

One Mississippi, two Mississippi . . .

Heavy footsteps and the outside door squealed shut.

Her head still hurt, couldn't move fast. Untie the laundry bag first.

Marie's dress and Miranda's underclothes were at the top, handbag at the bottom. She plucked out the clothes, laying them on the toilet, and threw off the hat and the jacket.

Still no takers for the men's toilet at the Elite Café . . . goddamn it, she needed her luck to hold.

Unknot the tie, unfasten the suspenders, pull the shirt off, don't bother to unbutton. Pants stay on in case someone comes in and checks under the door . . .

She started to unwrap the cloth bandage from around her breasts when the outside door flung open, and another man approached the urinal. This one was all business, didn't bother to check under the stall or wash his hands when he finished. She exhaled when she heard the door bang shut.

Fastened the bra, pulled the camisole over her head. Breasts felt bruised from the wrap. Marie's dress would be too short, but that didn't matter in Reno. What mattered was not getting caught dressed as a man, a crime in San Francisco and probably a crime in Reno, too.

You can fuck until the cows come home, just don't do it in drag, anything goes, mister, but not that, not here, why we got community standards an' all . . .

Another lump was still visible in the laundry bag, and she pulled out her coat, thoughtfully sandwiched in by Tom and Marie. She smiled to herself, slipped the dress on first and then the coat. Undid the pigtails, shaking her hair until she got dizzy again.

Goddamn concussion.

Still no men with too much beer or coffee in their bellies crowding her out of the bathroom in the café Elite.

One Mississippi, two Mississippi . . .

She shoved the uniform pieces back in the bag, first removing her wallet, cigarette case, lighter, and SP schedule from the jacket pocket, then lifted her boots up on the toilet seat and had them both unlaced when the door opened again.

Two men this time, in conversation. She held the pants up with one hand. Left the boots on.

"D'ja see the face on that whore in the alley? Elmer knows how to make 'em pay, all right . . . they say he's takin' it out on 'em on account of his old lady's makin' him pay alimony."

The other one bent down to look under the stall. "Yeah. Jim an' Bill're gonna have trouble on their hands, one of these days . . . once Elmer kills one of them broads. Mark my words."

Sound of the water faucet. "Eh, they'll buy off the jury, just like they did during Prohibition. Nobody gives a shit, Lou . . . got too many goddamn whores here as it is."

A loud thump on the rickety door of the toilet room made Miranda jump, hold her breath.

"Hey—you in there? I need the can."

She lowered her voice. "Few minutes."

The other one laughed. "Guess you do give a shit, Lou. Leave the poor sonofabitch alone with his hangover . . . sounds like he's been crying."

"I'm gonna cry if I don't get to a fucking can . . ."

"C'mon, we'll go back to the Bank and see if they got a doctor for the broad . . ."

Lou left grumbling, the other man still chuckling. Miranda exhaled, sank down on the toilet seat.

Too fucking close . . .

She bent down to the bag again, pulled out her own shoes. The plain Jane lace-ups looked like Cinderella slippers compared to the boots. She hurriedly stepped out of the boots and dropped the trousers, dress falling to a few inches below her knee. Squeezed into the lace-ups, lifting first one foot, then the other, on top of the toilet to tie them.

Bent down and shoved the trousers in the bag, retied it. Picked it up with her left hand, handbag in her right.

Now she had to leave.

She closed her eyes, counted three Mississippis.

Still no sign of a customer.

Cracked open the door. Took a breath.

Ran for it.

The din of conversation and clinking dishes enveloped her in the hallway, and she quickly pushed open the ladies' room door on the left. Lee Wiley's slow, plaintive voice filtered from the restaurant juke.

Fools rush in, so here I am . . .

Miranda twisted the sink faucet, filled her hands with water, splashing it on her face. Washed her hands and dried them on the broken machine, cloth filthy from previous visitors to the Elite Café.

Opened the cigarette case, hands cleaner but shaking. Her stomach growled, and she plucked out a Chesterfield, lighting it on the first try.

She raised her eyes to her own reflection.

*

Miranda slid into an empty booth at the back of the restaurant, laundry bag positioned across from her in case anybody felt like sitting down.

A man in a dark gray slouch fedora with a yellow shirt and blue jacket dropped a nickel in the jukebox to hear "In the Mood." He ambled past Miranda and leered, as if the song were an advertisement, intercepted in time by the worn-looking waitress with the dirty blond hair.

"Your bill's due, Leroy."

The leer transformed into a whine. "C'mon, Mary—Hal knows I'm good for it."

She looked at him, hand on her hip, voice flat. "Hal's the one who told me to make sure you paid in cash, Leroy. You don't like it, take it up with him." She tossed a menu in front of Miranda. "Here you go, Miss. Special of the day is bacon, lettuce, and tomato sandwich or a cheese omelet. We're out of the ham steak dinner."

From the looks of the Elite Café, Miranda suspected the lettuce would be wilted and the cheese would be stale. She shut the menu and glanced up at the large, grease-yellowed clock on the wall above the cash register, opposite end of the diner. Leroy was leaning on the counter, grumbling to the cashier. Mary the waitress was still waiting by the booth for her order, watching Leroy.

Twenty minutes to midnight, seats full and discussion animated. Apparently the Stockade wasn't the only business to never close its doors.

"Hamburger and fries with the works, please."

"Tomato, lettuce, pickles, and olives, no onions. That OK?"

"Yeah. And a cherry Coke and apple pie à la mode, if you've got it."

The waitress nodded as she wrote down the order. "Just made yesterday. I ain't seen you in here before, have I?"

Miranda gave her a big smile. "Just got in. I'm here for 'the cure.'"

Mary nodded again, dark blond straggle of hair falling toward her face. "Thought so. Took it myself back in '31, soon as they changed the residency requirement back to six weeks. Been here ever since. Somethin' about the air agrees with my lungs. Hamburger'll be up in a minute."

She stuck the pad back in her apron-uniform and abruptly marched down to the cashier, where Leroy was still trying to wheedle the younger girl at the register. Mary was probably no more than Miranda's age, but she looked ten years older, the dry, desert air agreeing with her lungs but not her skin.

Miranda lit another Chesterfield, ruefully examining her fingernails. Looked like miner's hands, needed a goddamn manicure from the train and the crime scene and the pale brown dust that blew through the cracks in Reno.

She gulped down the cigarette in a long inhale. Nails were the least of her fucking worries.

The *City of San Francisco* was on the way to Ogden, Utah. The killer would think he had her trapped, even after the surprise of finding her gone. Planted physical evidence in the room, history with Jasper, disappearance from the train . . . all pointed to her guilt.

The bulls would lock her up and conveniently forget the inconsistencies, given how much Brady liked O'Meara to whisper in his ear. Oh, so much easier to figure she'd shown her true colors, the "notorious" private eye who'd been tempted by priceless jade and cut a bloody swathe through her client list.

She passed a trembling hand across her forehead. No protection. The sonofabitch hadn't lied about that. Her deal with the government had died with Jasper.

A well-built young man in a cowboy hat and alligator boots dropped another nickel in the juke, walking back to an older woman in a chinchilla wrap wearing a self-satisfied smile. Shep Fields and his Rippling Rhythm . . .

South of the border, down Mexico way . . .

Mexico. Goddamn it, Jasper and Cheney and Wardon and Mexico, Miguel and Count Lestang. Gonzales asking if tomorrow were soon enough for information on Wardon and the gallery, but she hadn't known tomorrow would mean a murder and a frame, gilt-edged and rococo scallops, the whore-cum-detective boxed in and wrapped up tight. Gonzales had probably left her a message already, if she could just get to a phone and if the cops weren't squatting at her answering service.

She frowned, eyes fixed and staring, red embers burning through the white paper.

No, her only chance was to go home. Go back to where they least expected to find her, and find Jasper's murderer herself, trace his contacts in San Francisco and Berkeley and figure out where he was headed with the paintings he'd stolen from the professor.

Find out what was going on in Mexico.

Mary suddenly appeared at the table with a cherry Coke and a large platter, and Miranda jumped.

"Didn't mean to scare you, Miss. You thinking about it? Maybe reconsidering?"

Miranda smiled, crushed out the cigarette. The gold letters in the chipped glass ashtray were faded and flaked, "The Bank Club" still legible.

"Yeah. You ever have regrets?"

The waitress shook her head vehemently. "No, ma'am. I was married to a varmint when I was fifteen years old. And even if I'm one of the only women livin' in Reno who ain't for sale, I'm glad to be where I am—without him."

She pointed to a large painting on the wall to Miranda's right. "He weren't no more than an imitation lover, Miss . . . and there's a lot of them around. Don't you get so's you're soft, remembering the sweet talk. That sweet talk, nine times out of ten, was for other women than you, women he don't hit or swear at, women he don't leave in the middle of the night." She shook her head, starting to move back toward the counter. "Stick to your guns, Miss. You know the real thing when you find it."

Miranda was staring at the painting above her head, eyes wide.

Know the real fucking thing when you find it . . .

She finally realized why the painting in Jasper's compartment looked so familiar.

It was *Mercury Slaying Argus* by Nicolas Bertin . . . the painting in Dr. Heinsicker's office.

Thirty-two

*

"A nother original," Jasper had said, referring to *Time Exposes Beauty*, the painting from Poland she hadn't unwrapped.

Another original.

She should have realized the import of those words, the way he jumped when she mentioned Mexico, his conversation with Cheney and plaintive desire to get Miguel "out from Wardon's thumb," all linked to an order for "another Renoir" . . .

Another Renoir.

Not an original.

Fuck.

Jasper wasn't just stealing and smuggling paintings, he was *forging* them, with the help of a formidable background in chemistry and Wardon and Cheney and the mysterious Count Lestang, his "European associate."

And Miguel . . .

Who could Miguel be but the artist, the young genius Jasper rhapsodized over as he grew jealous of Wardon's control?

"He exploits the boy's innocence," Jasper had said to Cheney. "I could teach him so much . . ."

Goddamn it. She had to get back to San Francisco—fast.

Miranda chewed three bites of the hamburger and drained the Coke. Caught Mary's eye and the blonde ambled over.

"Everything OK, Miss?"

"Yeah, I just remembered I've got an appointment . . . can you wrap up the rest of this with the pie? I'll try the ice cream another time."

Mary tilted her head at Miranda. "Sure thing. You sure you don't wanna eat here? Body can get dyspepsia like that, eatin' on the run."

Miranda opened her wallet and flattened a dollar bill on the table. "I've gotta go. Keep the change."

The waitress raised her eyebrows. She picked up the dollar with practiced hands and loaded her left arm with the still-full platter of food.

"Drugstore down the street's open twenty-four hours if you need it."

Miranda smiled. "Thanks."

Mary reluctantly left for the kitchen, and Miranda dug out the SP pamphlet she'd taken from the station. The fastest way home would be the *Overland Route,* one of the SP trains that made the run from St. Louis, Chicago, or Omaha back to San Francisco. By the time one of the smaller locals rolled in, by way of Shasta or Yreka or Klamath, Jasper's body would be found and the city would be that much harder to break into.

Her finger traced the columns on the page. Already missed the *Overland Limited* and the *Challenger,* and waiting for either one would mean an overnight in Reno and a departure tomorrow night. *Pacific Limited* offered a better shot, departing tomorrow afternoon, and the *Treasure Island Special* didn't run until the 30th. That left the *City of San Francisco,* which wouldn't be back for a few days, and . . .

Yes.

The *Forty-Niner.*

Due in from Omaha and Chicago on the 28th, departing Reno at 1:35 A.M. Now if she could just get a fucking ticket . . .

Miranda slid out from behind the booth as Mary dropped a large paper bag full of wax paper–wrapped food on the tabletop. Miranda lifted the laundry bag with one hand and the paper bag and her purse with the other. She nodded to the waitress, who was staring at her.

"Thanks for everything."

She glanced up at the painting on the wall. "That's a copy of a French picture, by the way—I think it's called *Happy Lovers.*"

Mary raised her plucked eyebrows again. "You a teacher or something, Miss? Nobody ever come in here and told me that before."

Miranda headed for the door. "Be seein' you."

"Don't step on no dead snakes."

Mary started to wipe down the table, every now and then sneaking a glance at the painting on the wall.

✳

The SP ticket agent was no more than thirty, with flaky skin and dandruff on the shoulders of his dark uniform. He yawned.

"'Scuse me, Miss. We got three open sections, one compartment and one double bedroom left . . . the double bedroom occupant leaves the train here, so you'd be clear to 'Frisco."

"I'll take the double. What section of the train?"

"Observation car, Miss, the California Republic. First-class accommodations. That'll be six dollars and thirty cents."

Miranda dug out her wallet and handed him a ten.

"My luggage is in storage here . . . a friend of mine drove it out."

He yawned again, belatedly raising a fist to his mouth. "Sure thing, Miss. We can load it for you once the *Forty-Niner* rolls in. What's the name?"

She hesitated for a split second, visions of Reno police appearing at her elbows. Jail was jail and iron bars were iron bars, but fuck . . . she'd rather take her chances with Brady and O'Meara than spend time in a Nevada cooler.

Her voice was clear, calm, and low. "Marion Gouchard."

The agent scratched his freckled cheek absentmindedly.

"Don't remember that name, and I would've, on account of it soundin' French an' all. When did he bring 'em in? I've only been on duty about half an hour."

She waved a hand vaguely. "Oh, around half past ten. Can you check?"

"Sure thing," he said automatically and stood up, the black leather stool emitting a hiss from escaping air. "Be right back."

Miranda looked around the waiting room. Three women, middle-aged widow or divorcée in black, rhinestones glittering at her wrist, younger woman in drab brown with two small children, boy and a girl, and a secretarial type in glasses and a glare. They sat on the benches, the young mother hushing the children and trying to get them to fall asleep on the seat next to her.

Standing, not sitting, were six male passengers, half of them low-level gamblers with just enough change to limp back to San Francisco. Two grifters leaned close in muted conversation, long, slicked-back hair tucked under black fedoras, bright display handkerchiefs flashing from pin-striped suits. A balding salesman, hair threaded over the top of his skull, propped himself against the depot wall, body limp and exhausted, leather display case cracked at the corners.

No killers in the crowd, not even in a game of craps. Jasper's murderer was either still on the *City of San Francisco* or spending the night in a Reno pleasure house, waiting until morning to make his next move. She'd make hers first.

The SP agent reentered the booth with a cough. She turned around, flashed him a big smile.

"You found them?"

He nodded. "Sure did, Miss Gouchard. Looks like quite a bit of luggage to take to San Francisco . . . you planning another trip?"

Tom O'Day had come through for her. No luggage left at Ogden, no trace of Miranda Corbie.

She plastered the smile. "I'm thinking of staying awhile, then perhaps taking the *Daylight* to Los Angeles. I've heard it's a lovely ride."

He yawned again, gold gleaming from the back of his throat. "That it is, Miss, that it is. Some say it's the most beautiful in the whole country. Here's your ticket—double bedroom D in the buffet observation car California Republic." He glanced at his watch. "Train should be here in about twenty minutes. I'll call the porter once she pulls in."

She gathered the ends of her coat together, tried to make it nonchalant. "Any news from the line? I don't mind telling you I've been a bit nervous since the accident on the *City of San Francisco* last year."

He shook his head. "No, ma'am, you don't have a thing to worry about. Telegraph's been quiet all night. You know, train travel is the safest there is, why, more people are killed and hurt in auto-mo-biles every day than in a train . . ."

She let him go on until he ran out of steam, smiled again, and sat down at one of the row end seats facing the platform.

No news. No murder on the *City of San Francisco,* no death and certainly no murder, or he wouldn't be yawning and there'd be a fat SP rail dick wandering the yard outside.

So far, the only people who knew about Jasper were her, the killer, and the O'Days.

Miranda bit her lip, stomach growling. She lifted out the foil-wrapped hamburger from the bag and ate it methodically, the two children staring at her until their mother reprimanded them. Finished the meal with a handful of fries, stood up, stretched, and threw the apple pie in the trash can.

So much for where the elite meet to eat . . .

She was taking a chance, using the Marion Gouchard alias, since Jasper had deciphered the cover—but that didn't mean the killer had. Besides, it was the first name that came to her and she'd had a fucking concussion.

Miranda shivered, trying to squeeze more warmth out of the coat. Checked the room again. All concerned were unconcerned with her, except for the two kids.

Next move.

She could find out who the buyer was, maybe queer the deal for the killer, if he knew about the Chicago sale and was planning to carry it through. Maybe the mark would even call the cops.

She walked purposefully into the phone booth, shutting the wooden door with a clack that woke up the salesman. He'd been dozing against the wall and now moved to a seat.

She hit the switch hook. "Operator? I need long distance, please."

Bored voice. "Where to?"

"Chicago. Drake Hotel."

She tapped her fingernails on the wooden shelf, idly leafing through the phone book. Prominent ad for the Bank Club. Thought of Elmer and "cleaning the fish" and she slammed the book shut.

"Ma'am? Please deposit seventy-five cents."

Miranda plucked out three quarters from her change purse, dropped them in the slot. The phone was about ten years old, worn and repaired, witness to too many late-night calls and early-morning tears. She hoped it would hold on till she was through.

Click. Click. Click . . .

"Got the Drake Hotel on the line. Go ahead."

She could barely hear a sleepy male voice with a flat midwestern twang. "Drake Hotel. Hello? Hello? This is the Drake Hotel."

She raised her voice, spoke loudly and clearly. "This is a message for Mr. Clark, room number five eleven."

"Drake—what? Oh, oh yes. Thank you. A Mr. Clark, you said?"

"Mr. Clark."

"Hold one moment."

More waiting, more fingernail tapping. Easier to send a wire except her location would be in writing, should a cop get wise and trace the information. Goddamn it, waiting was worse than running, waiting for the news, waiting for the papers, waiting for the headline on page four about the private eye and ex-escort wanted for murder on the *City of San Francisco* . . .

"Ma'am? Mr. Robert Sterling Clark, did you say? He is checking in tomorrow, room five eleven. What is your message?"

She took a breath. "Renoir is a fake."

"What? I'm afraid I can't understand you . . ."

"Renoir. R-E-N-O-I-R. Is a fake. Stop."

Pause on the line, while the clerk woke up. "'Renoir is a fake.' Very good, ma'am. I'll make sure Mr. Clark receives the message."

The all-Pullman *Forty-Niner* pulled in on schedule, solid, heavy dark gray colors matching the smoke pouring from the engines, black and gold stripes on the side an echo of the rush it was named for. Not a diesel, not a streamliner, just a bullet nose to mark it as modern, with powerful mountain engines and the iron heart of the trains that built the West.

Miranda liked it better than the *City of San Francisco*.

The porter hustled all her luggage out of the storage area, most of the other Reno passengers carrying small bags or, in the case of the grifters and the gamblers, nothing at all. She tipped him well, a pudgy little man with drooping eyes and deep dimples. He yawned continually.

The cars, like all Southern Pacific passenger trains, bore evocative names. She passed the Joaquin Miller and the Captain John Sutter, the Gold Rush—an open section—Roaring Camp and Bear Flag until, at last, she climbed aboard the California Republic.

Double bedroom D was just in front of the buffet, a quiet room.

She glanced at her watch: 1:47 A.M.

No sleeping tonight—not with a noose around her neck.

She thanked the porter, who bowed and yawned again on his way out, making Miranda yawn. Wished she had some goddamn bourbon or even coffee, but the buffet was closed until morning.

She arched her back and looked around. No Nantes blue and apricot, more of a drab olive green. Miranda sank heavily onto the bed and stared at her suitcase. She wouldn't be able to take the luggage back to her apartment—best to store it at the depot.

Grinding noise, shrill whistle.

She shook herself awake, lit a Chesterfield. Threw open the blinds and stood and watched as the heavy steel train began to move out of the station.

Yellow and blue, pink and green, neon still glittering in the thin mountain air.

Chance and divorce and luck and money, your fantasies come to life. Sex and sin all legal and licensed, where gangsters sat on council boards and whorehouses ran like factories. Biggest Little City in the World, oasis on a high desert plain, city of possibility, city of escape.

A city where everything and everyone had a price to pay or a price to wear, city of buyers and sellers where nothing came for free.

Miranda shivered.

She was glad to get the hell out of Reno.

*

She ground the Chesterfield out in the ashtray, head aching and muscles tired, visions of a smiling O'Meara and Tehachapi prison snapping her eyelids open.

Sacramento was just five hours away. The *City of San Francisco* was due in Ogden about an hour later.

If the killer had decided to wait—to not drop a nickel in the phone booth and dial the Reno police—the porter was bound to discover the body when they switched trains in Ogden. The latest they'd find Jasper was seven-thirty this morning.

Not much goddamn time, but maybe . . . maybe enough.

Miranda frowned, squinting at the last lines she'd written in the notebook.

> *Who is Cheney and what is his position?*
> *Why run after Edmund's murder?*
> *Is Jasper complicit?*
> *Scott: Why do they need me if they already know about Cheney and smuggled art? Sacrificial sheep?*

First question seemed obvious. Best place to hide a hot painting is in a warehouse of paintings. Cheney worked for the exhibition, and given the time line—Jasper's trip to Switzerland, his sale of the *Mercury and Argus* copy to Heinsicker—what, a year ago, the secretary had said?—they'd used the Fair as a cloak and shield, an easy way to transport and store paintings until

Jasper could get them to his buyers. She nodded, adding *storage* next to Cheney's name.

Selling Heinsicker the phony *Mercury and Argus* was probably a preliminary test of the artist, to see if they could really pull it off, and she could see Jasper's cynical smile when his overbearing department chair thanked him for his generosity. Heinsicker—like most buyers—wouldn't think twice about buying looted artwork, especially if the price was right. He'd been fooled . . . Miguel had passed the final exam.

She tapped the pencil on her notepad impatiently. How had Wardon come across the boy, discovered his talent, and how—most importantly—had he fallen under the dealer's control?

He exploits the lad's innocence and I could teach him so much . . .

Had Jasper been speaking as a would-be mentor—or a lover? She wrote *MIGUEL?* in the margin of the notebook.

Miguel's talent and Jasper's chemistry made it possible for the ring to sell stolen paintings *twice*. Count Lestang and his Nazi cohorts smuggle an original painting—nothing too famous, nothing too noteworthy—out of occupied Europe, particularly a newly conquered and fertile territory like Poland—while Wardon and Jasper unload a copy of it to no-questions-asked buyers.

Concoct a story about a family escaping the Nazis and needing money, little Jacob's ship to America, a bargain and helping refugees in the process, why the painting's been in the family collection for years . . . and fat men with fat bank accounts wipe the spittle on their lips, handkerchief starched, can't see a goddamn provenance with greed in their eyes, Berkeley to Chicago, Los Angeles to New York, glory in good taste and a European collection to rival Frick's, bought at bargain-basement prices from a connoisseur of impeccable reputation.

Some were private collectors, like Sterling Clark in Chicago, some were Nazis and Reds, Jasper's connections, but all of them shoved hands out, wallets open, depending on oil paint and ancient canvas, a dead man's eye and the stroke of a brush, art to own, art to possess, like a country or a woman and for the same fucking reason, so they could prop up their manhood, inflated by power and money and prestige, owning beauty, displaying it, hoarding it, raping it in private, again and again and again . . .

Miranda wiped her forehead, right hand shaking.

If the forged painting was more modern, Jasper's beloved *entartete Kunst*—like the Kirchner Wardon mentioned at the Picasso exhibit—the professor could sell the fake to different discerning buyers, ones who didn't toe the official Nazi party line on art but were scavenging for bargains the Nazis had devalued. Easier to duplicate the modern pieces, too, no thorny issues of fractured lines and hardened oil paint, no yellow veneer of the antique.

Duplicating the old masters—the traditional landscape and portrait paintings in oil like the seventeenth-century French *Mercury Slaying Argus*—would pose much more formidable challenges. Jasper must have developed a process—something cooked up in his lab—to replicate the look and texture of centuries-old oil paint. Hell, even laypeople knew you could swipe an old oil painting with alcohol to make sure it was really old—just like scratching glass with a diamond. Maybe he'd been secretly working on this for years, hoping for opportunity, and Hitler and the United States State Department had finally given it to him.

Jasper's artist could slap up a Frans Hals or a Pieter de Hooch, the original pillaged from Cracow or Amsterdam, and the professor could sell it here or even trade it back to the Nazis for more "degenerate art" and double his revenues. The Germans were always competing with one another anyway—the Reichstag didn't know what the Wehrmacht was buying.

Miranda shook her head. Dug out a Butter Rum Life Saver and popped it in her mouth.

The cycle offered an almost endless supply of art for whatever market presented the most opportunity—and allowed Jasper, connoisseur and collector and would-be "savior," to keep the paintings he most coveted for himself.

She crunched and swallowed the candy. No wonder the poor bastard was nervous.

He'd mentioned "competing interests" . . . maybe not just Nazis or Reds, but interested parties in art, competition for the fresh French carcass that would soon be picked clean.

Fuck.

What if one of his buyers discovered his purchase was a phony?

Huntington Jasper was passing fake information to the Nazis—according to his account, and she believed him—and probably fake paintings. The Reds, the Germans, his buyers in both trades, had more than one reason for wanting him eliminated.

So was he complicit in Edmund's murder?

She frowned again. Didn't make sense. The professor seemed genuinely afraid—deception was catching up to him—and genuinely fond of Edmund.

But what motive—and whose motive?—was there for killing a queer escort? Was it a warning of some kind for Jasper, something engineered by—perhaps— the not-so-dull-witted Fritz?

Goddamn it. She frowned and circled the question.

Why do they need me if they know about Jasper's connection to Cheney?

Yet another murder, the young agent who was originally sent out to check on Jasper. Grant Tompkins left a wife and children, and that bothered the professor, and the murder scared him. James had told her the truth about one thing: He hired her because she was expendable. Scott's presence at the Fair proved they knew about Cheney and therefore knew about the art, but what they didn't know is whether or not Jasper's greed had led him to start coughing up real secrets to the enemy.

The professional agent had been killed in Chicago, but the backstreet P.I. might dig up the truth and turn one more trick, figure out if Jasper was cheating the government or just cheating—or so that bastard James had hoped.

Miranda lit a Chesterfield. Drew a heavy pencil line through the question and next to it wrote *pigeon*.

Scott was probably sent by James to make sure that she didn't blow the espionage trail by going after the smuggling ring.

Well, fuck that—and fuck him.

Jasper, Edmund, Grant Tompkins, and oh, incidentally, Lois Hart—all murdered, and all of them except for Tompkins shared a connection . . . her. Maybe Lois was slain by a different killer, but Edmund had been the socialite's escort that night, and that was one goddamn coincidence too many.

She angrily crushed out the cigarette in the glass ashtray. She'd done her job for James: Jasper hadn't turned, for predictably selfish reasons. Prolonging the world's misery made for a fertile art market, and his little contributions to stringing along the Nazis must have assuaged his already minuscule sense of guilt. James, the lying sonofabitch, already owed her money and a ticket to England.

No, she'd do precisely what Scott had warned her against: go after the smuggling and forgery ring. Seemed to be the best—maybe the only—way to save herself from a murder rap.

The best lead she had was Wardon. Wardon, Jasper's partner in criminality along with Cheney, Wardon, who had teased the professor with a remark about Kirchner at the Picasso show, Wardon, who kept a tight rein on the prodigy Miguel.

Miranda looked out the window. The powerful engine under her feet hummed a percussive, iron lullaby, and she stretched and yawned, and set her pencil down.

3:17 A.M. Maybe she could sleep for a couple of hours before dawn and Sacramento.

She stretched out on her side, head by the window, listening to the moaning of the wooden rails, the howling of the wind.

Miranda didn't dream for the next three hours.

Act Five

*

Art

For I have sworn thee fair, and thought thee bright,
Who art as black as hell, as dark as night.
—William Shakespeare, Sonnet 147

Thirty-three

*

T*hud.*

Miranda woke up with a start, grasping for the cigarette case in her pocket and the Baby Browning that wasn't in it. Laughter and more banging in the corridor outside, someone falling against her door on the way to the buffet behind it.

She exhaled and blinked, nose wrinkling at the smell of scrambled eggs and bacon, waffles and syrup, while her stomach growled, almost as loud as the train starting to pull from the station, whistle loud and piercing.

Wristwatch read 8:31. Must be Berkeley.

Fuck, she'd overslept through Sacramento, dreamless and lulled to sleep by the lullaby of the rails, *chug-chug-chugalug, chug-chug-chugalug,* winding down through hills of gold, droning through the flat agricultural land and fruit orchards, farmers already awake for their midday snack, coaxing lettuce and tomatoes from parched brown soil.

Her head still ached from the concussion, still dizzy from sitting up. She reached for her bag and unwrapped the second-to-last Butter Rum Life Saver.

Couldn't take a chance on the buffet or dining car, not until she'd heard about Jasper.

She crunched the candy, wishing it were bacon flavored, and snapped open the window shade, shielding her eyes.

They'd be in Oakland in just fifteen minutes, and she wasn't prepared, not by a long shot, not prepared to be hauled away in handcuffs or sent to Napa State Insane Asylum, reading Ecclesiastes behind barred doors.

They'd switched trains at Ogden, the *City of San Francisco* changing to Union Pacific cars. That was an hour ago, and if the killer hadn't called in a tip-off, the porter would walk in after increasingly loud knocks and discover one very dead passenger.

Goddamn it . . .

She stood up, fighting the pain in her head and legs. Squeezed the tap on the small water basin, cold drops on her face. Raised her eyes to the mirror.

No Club Moderne night, no kilowatt smile, more like Marjorie Main's younger sister. Preview of Tehachapi, go in a girl and come out something other than a woman. She ran her hands under the water again and cupped her face, lightly slapping her cheeks.

No, not Miranda Corbie.

Like mother, like daughter, she'd run first.

She sank down heavy on the bed and lit a cigarette with a shaking hand. She needed a safe haven, someplace she could come and go without being traced, without being seen.

Miranda squinted at the sunlight starting to break through the clouds, glancing off the Bay, orange and red, like a New Year lantern . . .

Chinatown.

One quick ferry ride and she'd disappear, just like the opium and hooch from bootlegging days . . . and Lois Hart's precious jade. Chung Hing Hotel, no questions asked, girls of all races and all prices, where Doyle and the other beat cops plied their lunch money.

She'd check the newspapers, fill her belly . . . then pay a visit to Mr. Hugo Wardon.

*

Check-in at the Chung Hing consisted of a passed fin and an illegible scrawl in a dusty registration book. The thin man with thin hair and a dirty collar showed her upstairs, one flight, to a room that stank of fermented rice and stale beer. She nodded, wrinkling her nose, handing him another five to forget they'd met.

The cot was clean enough, at least on the surface, no bedbugs visible. Her stomach growled, reminding her how hungry she was, and she lit a Chesterfield to cut the pain.

You're a good soldier, Randy, a good soldier . . .

She crushed out the cigarette on the scarred wooden floor and shook herself loose, stood up and stretched, trying to get some vitality in her limbs. Goddamn it, Miranda, stay awake, stay alert . . .

Back downstairs, quiet except for a businessman making a social call to number 17. The man in the dirty collar took no notice of her when she pushed open the glass door and reentered Chinatown.

She passed Washington and Clay, staying behind crowds, keeping her head down. Hoped she wouldn't spot No-Legs, couldn't afford anyone putting the finger on her, too goddamn tired to know if she was being tailed.

The smell of eggs and bacon wafted from the Chop Stick Café, and Miranda found a counter stool facing away from the door. Ordered a cup of coffee, hotcakes, bacon, and eggs. The man in the wrinkled gray suit next to her left, leaving behind a paper. She stretched out a hand for it, heart in her throat.

Chronicle. Nothing on page one, page two, page three . . .

Page seven. BERKELEY PROFESSOR APPARENT SUICIDE ON STREAMLINER. "The *City of San Francisco* streamliner has endured another tragedy, this time the death of a local chemistry professor from the University of California . . ."

She scanned it quickly, searching for her name, any reference to homicide.

"Authorities have made no official announcement and the investigation remains ongoing. Anyone with any information should immediately contact Southern Pacific."

Miranda exhaled, long and slow. SP must have buried the story, too much bad publicity after the wreck the year before, and they'd put pressure on the Ogden police to make the suicide official. One man killing himself was a page-eight story and a two- or three-day sensation—a chemistry professor murdered on the streamliner was another million or more dollars kissed good-bye.

She read the article again, slowly. Wondered why the killer hadn't turned it into the newspaper circus she'd expected . . . and why he hadn't tried harder to implicate her.

The waitress nodded and smiled, gray hair tightly pulled back, shoving a glass jar of homemade Chinese pepper sauce toward Miranda along with a Buffalo China platter of eggs and hotcakes.

For the next fifteen minutes, all she thought about was food.

*

No phone booth at the Chop Stick, so she hustled two blocks down Grant toward the Republic Pharmacy, renewed energy in her legs from the eggs and bacon, threat of ankle irons and dirty gray prison smocks receding. The saboteurs of 1939 had done her a fucking favor.

She wasn't in the clear, not yet, but business was on her side at last, Southern Pacific eager to clamp down on any hint of danger to their passengers. A thorough investigation would mean going through the passenger manifests and realizing that Miranda Corbie never left the train. She could count on the porter George to keep her secret, but there were other porters, other passengers. Better for SP to hush it up, better for her. Homicide demanded a suspect, and fast—as long as SP promoted the suicide theory, she'd be safe.

Just a whiff of murder and the bastards would hang her out to dry.

Miranda pushed open the door into the Republic and grabbed a fistful of Life Saver rolls, Pep-O-Mint and Butter Rum, throwing cash and a smile at the chubby man behind the counter and extracting a roll of dimes. A small, rickety phone booth was tucked in a rear alcove, where dusty jars of traditional herbs sat next to Bayer aspirin.

Switch hook was sticky. Found a long-distance operator, three rings.

"James MacLeod, please. Ugly Duckling reporting."

Pause, almost imperceptible gulp. "Hold one moment."

One moment rolled over into two minutes, Miranda increasingly impatient, feeding coins to the operator. A fat woman in an orange dress with last year's hat and a midwestern twang waddled through the door, exclaiming loudly over how everything in Chinatown was "one hundred percent genuine heathen," and how no one back in Indianapolis would believe the things she'd seen.

Voice on the line. Apologetic.

"Sorry to keep you waiting. Mr. MacLeod is unavailable. He did leave a message in case you called in, however. 'Forget hunt, ticket and money are yours. Too many hounds.'"

Miranda stared through the cracked glass of the phone booth, the fat woman's orange fractured into a garish kaleidoscope.

"Thanks. Here's one for him: 'Try telling the fucking truth.'"

She slammed the phone on the wall, breathing hard, then hit the switch hook a few more times and asked for her answering service.

"Teleservice Answering Company. Number please."

"EXbrook 3333. Miranda Corbie."

"One moment, please."

She was running out of goddamn dimes. The orange woman finally left the store, toting a bag of Clark Bars and a package of Dr. Scholl's foot powder.

"Message from Allen. Left June 28th. No last name given. Message states: 'Unsolved garrote case in Baltimore. Be careful and call me.'"

Miranda frowned. Baltimore was a country away, not much of a lead.

"Second message. Left June 28th. From Mark. No last name given."

She spoke quickly into the receiver. "Yes, go on."

"'Hugo Wardon partner of Count Lestang. Lestang abroad. Hope this helps you. Be careful, Miranda.'"

"Thanks, that's—"

"Third message. Left June 28th. From Rick Sanders. Message reads: 'Am in San Diego for training. Joined the navy. Miss you. Don't do anything stupid.'"

She held on to the phone, "Edna Loves Eddie" and "Tom + Ann" and "Bob and Betty Together 4ever" plus some Chinese characters probably announcing the same news swirling against the wall, splattered graffiti.

The voice droned in her ear. "Miss Corbie? Miss Corbie, did you receive the message?"

Her voice was short, clipped. "Yeah. I received it. Good-bye."

She hung up the phone with force, unaccountably angry.

Miranda held her head up, neck stiff and sore, skin crawling from no sleep and no shower and a four-hundred-mile round-trip. She smiled perfunctorily at the man behind the counter again, who was too busy reading a *Photoplay* to notice.

She leaned into the door and walked into the Chinatown sun.

Hugo Wardon was next.

The Zenobia was a typical San Francisco apartment building built just a few years after the quake and fire, low rent but not broadcasting it. A building where the tenants knew enough to mind their own assorted businesses and the landlord looked the other way, where the cops rarely got a call, and if they did, it was all a misunderstanding, sir, Waldo here just lost his temper a little, didn't mean nothin' a'tall . . .

The leeward side of outwardly respectable and a perfect base for Hugo Wardon.

She ventured across the street, almost sideswiped by a speeding yellow roadster, young girl in a scarf and holding on to her hat, laughing, red mouth and lips and white teeth, young man with eager, knowing eyes and fast hands, hair slicked back with oil, paying more attention to the girl than to the road. The car radio was blaring loud swing music.

Miranda caught her breath, holding on to her stomach, while they speeded past on Bush. She glared after them, tried to recompose herself.

"Some people ought to have their license revoked."

Deep male voice, familiar. She spun around.

Scott.

The blue eyes crinkled at the corners in a way that reminded her of Rick. Dressed in browns this time, pin-striped suit excessively wrinkled, more lint on his shoulders.

She met his eyes, spoke with a deliberate tone. "I didn't expect to see you again."

He laughed out loud, reaching for her elbow to pull her toward the side of the apartment stairway, and Miranda shook him off, teeth gritted.

"Look—Scott, or whatever your name is. It's over. I don't work for you or James or anyone else but me anymore, so why don't you crawl back into your government hole and leave me the fuck alone."

He looked down at her, still smiling. The bastard exuded charisma.

"Tell you the truth, Miss Corbie, I didn't expect to see you again, either. But seein' as how we're both here—and probably both after the same thing, and that's who offed the good professor—yes, news travels fast these days, even in the government—why don't we pay Mr. Wardon a joint visit? Jimmy won't mind you tagging along."

Her fists clenched, voice low and throaty and full of warning.

"Oh, but I do mind you 'tagging along,' sonny. And this is still my case, so back off."

He tilted his head and smiled at her. "Now, now, Miranda. You won't object if I call you Miranda, I hope? It's hardly wise to stand here and argue. We both have a job to do. And I apologize if I seemed disrespectful. I have the highest respect for your . . . talents."

The blue eyes traveled down her body, slower on the way back up to her face. They met hers and he grinned at her.

Goddamn patronizing sonofabitch, ought to punch him in the fucking nose and watch him bleed over the goddamn suit . . .

He raised his eyebrows in feigned innocence.

One Mississippi, two Mississippi, three Mississippi, and Miranda struggled to tamp down the anger, exhaustion finally winning the battle. She turned her back to him abruptly and started to climb the stairs to the door.

"Hey, wait for me . . ."

She pressed the call buttons next to the names with fresher ink, figuring newer tenants at a place like the Zenobia would be more likely to have callers. Scott stood and watched her, still grinning. The fifth button finally answered, buzzing them both in.

Foyer was small, dark, and damp, a large tree outside blockading the sun. Wardon had been number 11, up the flight of stairs. The agent headed straight up without pausing. Miranda lengthened her stride to catch up with him, and they made the second-floor landing at the same time. The burgundy-and-tan carpet was threadbare, a few dark stains of what looked like motor oil spotting the threshold.

Scott was raising his fist to knock when Miranda yanked his arm down. She nodded her head toward the still-full milk bottles on the floor, her voice a hiss.

"Wait a minute. Either he hasn't been home for two days or something's wrong."

His eyes flickered. "You know, you're not a bad shamus. But we still need to knock, whatever the score."

Her mouth formed a thin line of entrenchment, and she nodded curtly. "Just be prepared."

Scott's lips curved up. "I'm a Boy Scout, honey. I'm always prepared."

He raised his fist to the thin door, rapping the wood loudly.

No answer.

He tried again, this time attracting the attention of the tenant in number 9, who cracked the door to peer out and listen, pretending to be invisible. Miranda cleared her throat.

"Mr. Wardon? Are you there?"

She nodded to Scott, who knocked again. Miranda moistened her lips, fought the urge for a cigarette, instead unraveling the Life Saver roll in her jacket pocket and popping two in her mouth.

"We'd better find the manager."

He shrugged his shoulders. She'd caught the manager's number and name while pressing buttons and headed back downstairs to number 3. The occupant in number 9 abruptly shut the door as they passed.

This time Scott waited for Miranda, and she slid in front of him, knocking on the manager's door.

A man about fifty, in a three-day-old beard and plaid pajamas, answered the door, rubbing the sleep from his eyes.

"Mr. Butterick?"

"Yeah—the heat's goin' on in number seven, I already called—"

Scott's deep voice interrupted him. "We're not here for number seven. We're looking for a tenant, a Mr. Hugo Wardon."

Butterick opened his eyes and looked from one to the other, frowning. "So look already, Christ, it's still a free country, at least for now." He was about to slam the door shut when Miranda stuck her leg over the threshold.

"Wait a minute. He hasn't picked up his milk in two days. And unless you want to get hauled to Kearny Street for questioning on his disappearance, Mr. Butterick, I think you should put on some pants and open the apartment."

Butterick looked at them again, eyes traveling from Miranda to Scott and back. He rubbed his chin, made a face. Sighed.

"You ain't cops, but you act like 'em, so you're probably dicks of some sort and I like my life nice and peaceful. It's true, I ain't seen Wardon for a week, but that don't mean nothin'—I don't see him regular, anyway, guy disappears for weeks on end and keeps hours like a goddamn—excuse the language, ma'am—like a bat. Hold on for a minute and I'll throw on some trousers and get the key."

Scott stepped closer to prevent Butterick from closing the door, and the apartment manager grimaced.

"Yeah, keep the door open, you will anyway, I know better than to argue with a dick, even if she's a lady."

He smiled ruefully at Miranda and meandered toward a bedroom, path strewn with empty beer bottles and some dirty laundry. Scott cocked an eyebrow at Miranda. She ignored him, eyes focused on Butterick.

One Mississippi, two Mississippi . . .

The manager returned, wearing long johns, shirt stained brown and yellow, and a pair of patched blue jeans held up by suspenders. He held up a key and dangled it.

"C'mon, coppers, let's go see."

They stepped back and he carefully closed the door behind him, trudging up the single flight and breathing hard. He nodded at the milk bottles when they reached number 11.

"Yeah, that ain't like him. Neat as a pin, not like most of the ones we get."

His nose wrinkled as he fit the key in the door. "That milk's startin' to stink already."

Scott and Miranda looked at one another. The agent said: "Just open the door, Mr. Butterick, and . . . step back."

Butterick pushed the door open and blanched. Warm air was sucked into the corridor by the vacuum of the opening, and the smell was stronger, mixed with shit and urine.

Scott plucked out his display handkerchief from his jacket pocket, and Miranda held a Kleenex to her nose. She glanced at Butterick, who was trying not to throw up.

"Call Inspector David Fisher at the Hall of Justice—do it now. Nobody else, just Inspector Fisher. And hurry."

Scott had already marched into the small apartment. She followed, coming to a stop in the living room area.

Boxes of unframed paintings stood upright in stacks, next to heavy antique chairs and a couple of Chinese vases. More paintings hung on walls, old master and modern, gilt-edged frames still sporting numbers, museum or collection. One work in particular drew her eye, a luminous eighteenth century oil of a young woman, partially disrobed, with a letter on her lap.

As if in another tableau, an artistic arrangement by Duchamp or Dalí, a stiffened finger stretched out to touch the canvas.

Hugo Wardon, his throat sawed neatly in half, the blood coagulated, dried and covered in flies. The dealer lay on the floor in his living room, reaching for his last painting.

Thirty-four

*

Scott looked up at her. "I'm not supposed to be here. What do you give the cops—five, ten minutes?"

Wardon's eyes—what was left of them—were focused on the painting of the girl with the letter, as if he'd willed himself, as he lay dying, to touch the paint, hold it one final time.

Her face shone down at him from the crooked position of the frame, leaning against a half-open box of other prints and paintings stacked upright on the floor, eyes pensive, lips pursed, arms wrapped around her breasts as if she were cold and trying to cover up.

Miranda turned her head away for a moment. Spoke to Scott without looking at him.

"More like five. Fade if you want, but the manager can still ID you. And if you don't spill it—I will."

The agent stood up from where he'd been crouched by Wardon's body, a frown on his face. "I'd rather take my chances with the bulls than my boss. Sing all you want, canary—I'm checking the joint over for three minutes and I'll be out by four. If you're smart, you'll join me for lunch. That is, if you can hold it down after this. Crab salad at Fishermen's Grotto—my treat."

She raised her eyes to his. Ignored the invitation.

"The bulls will find you."

"Not behind State Department walls." He grinned at her, nose still wrinkled. "Peace pipe, Miranda?"

She shrugged. "You don't stay, I don't stay. I don't get left holding the god-damn bag."

He was bent over Wardon's body and picked up something from the floor with a pocket handkerchief. "Whatever you want, lady. Look at this."

Miranda's eyes were focused on the stacks of paper and envelopes, match-books and ashtrays of cigarette butts on Wardon's coffee table. Small black-and-white snapshots lay underneath a pile of receipts and a matchbook, and she moved them around with a finger.

Sudden intake of breath.

In front of her was a photograph of a smiling, immaculately suited Edmund Whittaker.

She looked up at Scott, who was still bent over Wardon. The agent was hold-ing out an employee ID card from Treasure Island.

"It was wedged under Wardon's shoulder."

Cheney's florid, smiling face was smiling up at her from the green card.

Her eyes met Scott's.

"You know where he lives?"

The agent nodded, slipping the card in his pocket. "My car's outside. And our five minutes are almost up. You coming?"

She twisted her neck, trying to memorize the arrangement of the paintings in the room, eyes traveling back to the girl with the letter.

Miranda paused on the ground-floor landing, breathless from rushing down the stairs.

"I don't have the fucking government to hide behind, and I worked too hard to lose my license over some hotshot G-man who's listened to *Gang Busters* one too many times. I'm leaving a message for the cops before we see Cheney."

He shrugged, started to push open the main double doors.

"However you get your kicks, honey. Just don't be more than a minute, or you'll lose your ride."

Her voice was short, fingers clamped together in fists at her sides.

"You'll wait."

A gust of fresh Bay air, carrying the cleansing smell of eucalyptus and salt, blew in through the open door as the agent strode outside. Miranda quickly ran to number 3.

Mr. Butterick's door was still open about a foot, and he was on the phone with what sounded like a friend, voice higher-pitched and almost hysterical.

"Yeah, I might need one quick, Harry, you know they always point their goddamn finger at the super . . ."

Miranda cleared her throat and he looked up at her, hand over the phone, eyes scared.

"I called the cops, lady, like you said."

"Good. When Inspector Fisher gets here, give him this."

She opened her purse and pulled out a business card from an inside pocket, grabbed the pencil she always carried, and scrawled a note on the back.

"It's very important. Don't lose it, and don't forget."

The manager held out a shaking hand for the card, glancing down at the phone he was still holding.

"Ain't you staying, lady? Somebody's gotta stay with—with—"

"Yeah, I know. Get up there, Mr. Butterick, before the busybody in number nine gets overly curious."

He shook his head, clutching the phone like a life preserver. "Uh-uh. I got rights. I'm gettin' a mouthpiece. I'm not goin' back up there."

She turned to leave. "Suit yourself. Maybe you're tired of living here for free, putting off maintenance complaints for months and ignoring a knock on the door. Maybe the owner of the building won't mind a little bad publicity for his super."

She headed out the door, whisper behind her back.

"I gotta go. Call you later and get Zeike lined up for me, all right?"

By the time she was at the front doors, Butterick was trudging up the stairs with alacrity, breathing hard, face red, mumbling to himself.

Scott was double parked outside, ignoring the honks and glares of a delivery truck and a gray sedan trying to move around him.

Miranda climbed in, looked around.

1938 blue Ford coupe, on the fast side. Maps for California and Nevada jammed in the side door. Cigarette butts in the ashtray, couple of stray match-books on the floorboard. Not much in the way of personality.

"This your car?"

"Yeah. Why, don't you like it?"

"It's OK."

Legs trembling, body starting to shake. Goddamn it, no time to break down, not now, now with Cheney ahead of them. She dug out a Chesterfield and lit it with a Bank Club matchbook. Deep inhale, rolled the window down.

"You smoke?"

"Yeah."

"You know where you're going?"

He glanced at her briefly at a red light on Mason, grinned.

"Yeah. Told you we had Cheney doped."

"So where are we going?"

"Blumset Apartments, 1040 Sutter."

Miranda wrinkled her brow. "That's what—five blocks away? Convenient."

He swung the car right, nodding. "Neat little system they got. Looks like they turned on each other, though. Happens with crooks."

She gulped the stick again, trying to quell the shaking. Studied Scott.

Brown pinstripes, medium-brim brown fedora, dirty and badly folded pale yellow display handkerchief. Expensive watch, almost out of place, on his left wrist. Face neither handsome nor ugly but somehow attractive, strong jawline, athletic build. His eyes were continually on the rearview mirror, body tensed and alert, almost jittery.

"Sound like you speak from experience."

"I do."

"State Department stepping on Hoover's toes these days?"

He laughed, as they cruised past Jones toward Leavenworth. "I didn't always work for Uncle Sam."

"Cop or private dick?"

The coupe rolled to a stop in front of the Blumset, a large apartment build-ing squatting at the foot of one of Sutter's low hills. Scott pulled the car into a parking spot at the corner of Larkin.

"Save the interview for the crab salad. We're here."

She reached into the ashtray and pulled it out. Camel butts.

She crushed out the Chesterfield, spoke slowly.

"I like to know who I'm forced to work with. And by the way—since Jasper is dead, why should you people care who killed him? I thought your interest began and ended with whether or not he was double-crossing you and spilling real secrets to the Nazis."

Scott's hand was on the door handle. He turned his head back to meet her eyes.

"We care, honey, because we want to make sure the Nazis and the Reds know they weren't being duped. The game's not over just because one player is dead. They've been depending on a certain flow of information, and if that information stops, well . . . I'm sure Jimmy explained it to you—lives hanging in the balance and all that. It's true, no bullshit. We gotta chase this down and find out who killed Jasper and why. Gotta protect the program."

She nodded. "So you can line up another pigeon to take his place."

"War's coming, Miranda."

"Yeah." She looked up at the agent.

"You're not local, I've already got that doped. So what's your last name?"

His eyebrows furrowed. "We don't have time—"

"Give me your goddamn last name. Call it professional courtesy."

He stared at her for a few seconds, face flushed, then laughed.

"Petrie. Ian Scott Petrie. Hell of a lot easier to just call me Scott. Let's go, toots—you can learn more at lunch. Though I gotta say your Dungeness doesn't hold a candle to blue crab."

Goddamn, arrogant sonofabitch . . .

Miranda opened the door of the Ford and stepped out onto the curb. Her legs and ankles ached. She closed her eyes, fighting a dizzy spell.

Shit, fucking exhaustion, not now, not now, they were so close . . .

Scott was already walking toward the entrance doors. She held her hat on with one hand, running toward him.

He glanced over at her. "Cheney's in number twenty-four."

Together they walked into the decorated foyer, old and dusty but still clinging to a self-image of respectability. Most of the names on the mailbox outside had been scrawled in blue ink a few years ago. Not much turnaround, not like the Zenobia.

The Blumset had an elevator, the old-fashioned kind, cage and wires and a prayer to take you up five floors. An old man in a faded red uniform was sleeping on a wooden stool in a corner, spittoon on the floor at his feet. A few flies buzzed around it, reminding Miranda of how they'd found Wardon.

"We need apartment twenty-four."

The old man opened white-blue eyes with a start, focused first on her, then on Scott, then back to her again.

"That be the fourth floor. Get in, young folks, get in. Gertie won't drop you."

The old man pushed some buttons and levers, and the elevator shuddered with a loud groan.

"She don't like to get woke up from a nap. Hell, neither do I!"

He laughed, red mouth lined with a just a few teeth, yellow and worn from tobacco juice.

Miranda smiled at the old man as the elevator slowly rose, clanging metallic noises accompanying every few feet of movement.

"Thanks, Pops."

"It's my job, girlie. Always glad to help a young couple get to where they need to go."

Miranda glanced at Scott, frowning, while he grinned at her. The crate finally arrived, settling in at the fourth floor like an old lady with a hot-water bottle. The operator pushed the doors open with an effort.

"Fourth floor. Apartment twenty-four is down to your left, then turn left again."

She pressed a dollar into his withered hand. "Thanks."

He raised his eyebrows, nearly toothless grin. "Anytime, girlie, anytime."

Scott was already making strides down the dim hallway, faded lithographs of sentimental scenes and English villages dotting the walls, a few torn pieces of furniture filling empty space. Most of the apartments seemed on the small side, suitable for singles or couples with indifferent taste and lack of means.

The light grew stronger when they made the second turn left. Sun shone through a dirty eight-paned window at the end of the hall.

The agent glanced at Miranda as they stood elbow to elbow in front of number 24. He raised his fist to knock.

"Mr. Cheney? Mr. Cheney?"

He tried three more times. Either the neighbors weren't home or nobody cared, no snoops, no cracked-open doors.

Scott turned toward her. "Manager?"

She shook her head. "No time. I left a message for the cops to meet us here. Did you try the door?"

He looked down at her, lips twisted upward in a smirk. "You really think it's going to be open?"

He reached a hand out to the tarnished brass knob and gave it a twist and a pull.

The door swung wide.

They stepped across the threshold.

Clothes on the floor, boxes packed, all the signs of a quick and hasty exit.

They walked into the main living area, sun motes streaming gently on a few books and boxes of china and other kitchen items sitting haphazardly on the floor. The room was eerily soundless except for honking cars outside on Sutter. A five- or six-year-old radio sat crookedly against the corner, pile of newspapers and letters spread out on a coffee table.

They moved into the small bedroom, mattress stripped clean of sheets and blankets, more papers on the nightstand, and then into the kitchen, where china lay in unpacked boxes. Bathroom and closets, every door in the apartment, methodically opening and shutting.

No blood, no sign of foul play.

No paintings.

And, Miranda thought, forehead wrinkling, as she fought the exhaustion overwhelming her . . . no suspect.

Cheney was gone.

Thirty-five

*

The next three hours blurred by, haze of cigarette smoke and two rolls of Life Savers, Meyer's hand on her shoulder, gently paternal, lines on David Fisher's face and fresh gray hair around his temples.

Uniforms showed up, followed by the inspector. The super of the Blumset, a thin, querulous woman somewhere between forty and sixty, made her presence—and displeasure—known.

No, Mr. Dirk Cheney was a good tenant, always paid on time, no loud parties, no "unsuitable company" at odd hours, no complaints except for those policemen's boots all over the rug, who is going to pay for the cleaning, she'd like to know, and what about all that funny powder?

Scott flashed a badge, speaking in low undertones to Inspector Fisher, grin and a handshake. The cop's troubled eyes returned to Miranda, brow wrinkled, mouth holding on to mystery.

Her legs trembled as she leaned against the wall, looking around the apartment.

Not much dust, not like Wardon, so Cheney had waited awhile before the disappearing act.

She'd poked in one of the piles of old mail on the kitchen table before the bulls arrived, unearthing a brochure for the *City of San Francisco* and a tourist sheet on hotels in Mexico City. That combined with a torn ticket from Friday's train, dropped in haste by the fugitive and scoured from the floor of the bedroom by a zealous cop, cemented the story. Fisher called Southern Pacific, confirmed a room had been reserved for a Mr. Cheney on the *City of San*

Francisco, confirmed that they had no record of him ever leaving the train at Ogden.

Open and shut, just like a fucking coffin.

Only funny thing was the missing art. Maybe he was out of room in the car he drove—a '37 DeSoto—maybe he had it stashed under a different name in storage somewhere in the city, to be reclaimed when Jasper and Wardon were forgotten and all the heat turned off.

She passed James's number to the inspector, hoped like hell the State Department bastard would at least confirm she'd been working for him. They owed her that much, and the case, as described, was over. Couldn't tell Fisher about Nazi secrets and Fritz's parties, and *entartete Kunst* and the millions Cheney was figuring on making, by himself, partners eliminated.

Couldn't mention Miguel, the one player whom Cheney couldn't do without. She sighed, shoulders slumped, wall propping her upright.

Dull yellows, angry grays, orange lights, and purple shadows, spinning, spinning, and the girl with the letter, eyes wide and empty, imploring, asking for help . . .

Sharp, sudden pain in her skull where she'd fallen on the train, and Miranda closed her eyes, voices underwater and screaming her name.

✳

Blue forget-me-nots on pale pink wallpaper.

She sat up in bed, wincing. Meyer was dozing in a chair he'd taken from the dining room. Bente was looking out the window, smoking a Lucky Strike.

Sudden pang. Goddamn it, she missed Rick.

"How long have I been out?" Her voice sounded strange, thick and chewy.

Meyer woke up with a start and Bente turned quickly, generous mouth in a broad smile.

"Glad you've rejoined the living. I'm getting tired of your couch."

"It's still better than the *Oceanic*."

The redhead threw her head back and laughed, big and throaty. "It's about eleven A.M., Monday, July 1st. Charles de Gaulle has been officially recognized by Churchill as the only decent French politician left, while the rest of the bastards swill like pigs in Vichy water. The island of Jersey surrendered to the fucking Krauts, and U-boats have been sinking ships everywhere. At least the Poles finally got a bomber squadron with the RAF—H. V. Kaltenborn just trotted that one out."

Meyer shook his head. "Dear Miranda. Perhaps, Miss Gallagher, it would be best not to overwhelm our darling girl with such news just yet."

Bente raised her eyebrows. "War's her bread and butter, chum. You should know her better than that by now."

Her attorney stood up with difficulty, relying on his ebony cane for support, and smiled tolerantly at them both.

"The doctor said she should rest and avoid excitement. Exhaustion and concussion are not easily dismissed."

Miranda sat up farther, gathering the white brocade bedspread around her chest. "Was Nielsen here?"

Meyer nodded. "You lost consciousness at the crime scene, my dear. We've been very worried. His number was listed in your address book, so we contacted him—Miss Gallagher said it would be all right."

Bente sat next to her on the bed with a sudden plop. "You're not as young as you used to be, Randy. Getting bashed on the head and going without water and sleep for days on end . . . had to call the quack, didn't have a choice." She gestured with her head toward Meyer. "At least your mouthpiece found a silver lining . . . the coppers couldn't question you while you were unconscious."

Miranda sat silent, looking from one to the other. She noticed a glass of water on her bedside table, suddenly realized how thirsty she was, and drained it. She wiped her mouth with the back of her hand, looked up at her attorney.

"Did they find Cheney?"

He shook his head. "I'm still in the dark, Miranda."

They were both looking at her expectedly, as if she were a goddamn magician about to saw herself in half. She swallowed, throat still dry.

"The full story is off-limits. I'll tell you and Fisher what I can at the same time—no use in repeating myself. Let me get dressed and we'll go."

Meyer opened his mouth and shut it again. A sigh filled his body and he emptied it slowly, light wheezing sound.

"I would prefer not to hear any surprises, my dear. There is attorney-client privilege, you know."

"Yeah, I know. Go wait in the living room, Meyer . . . and thanks."

Her attorney waddled slowly out of the room, shaking his head, leaning on the cane. Bente's eyes followed him, her voice uncharacteristically soft.

"Your mouthpiece's been worried about you, toots—stayed up all night, and he's no spring chicken. Try not to worry him so much, huh? Or me. Or

Sanders, for that matter. I thought he was gonna go AWOL, the crazy bastard . . ."

"Goddamn it, who phoned Rick?" Miranda's voice was muffled as she pulled a sweater over her head. "I don't want him involved."

Bente plumped down on the bed again, leaning back on one arm. "Too late for that, Randy. Christ, you should just fuck him and get it over with—"

The brown pump missed Bente, landing on the other side of the bed with a thud. Miranda's eyes were wide, her voice shaking.

"Don't you ever say that to me."

The redhead stared at her, green eyes wide and surprised. Then she shrugged, stood up.

"I'm gonna drift. I miss my own dump. Figure you're OK now, especially if you can throw shoes."

The two women looked at one another for a few seconds, until a hesitant smile started to play around Bente's lips. The redhead hugged Miranda, holding her off at arm's length.

"Nielsen may be a quack, but he knows his shit. You be careful. Don't go jumping at work right away. That Gonzales copper looks like a nice piece of vacation, if you forgive me saying so . . ."

Miranda buttoned the brown wool skirt and stepped into the shoes she'd thrown, turning around to glance in the vanity mirror. She sat down on the stool, opening up a tin of Coty face powder.

"He asked me to marry him."

Bente's eyebrows climbed into her hairline. "Jesus Christ, honey. I was just thinking a summer fling. He's that serious?"

Miranda shrugged, mouth open while she dabbed on the Red Dice lipstick. Her stomach growled. She studied the effect of the makeup, stood up.

"Least I can do is buy you both lunch first. I need a full stomach before facing the bulls."

Bente eyed her thoughtfully. "What you need is—well, never mind. Those goddamn shoes are heavy."

*

They shook hands, and Inspector David Fisher grinned at Miranda, relief making him look younger for a moment. Then his face settled in for questioning, composed copper with careful eyes, humor and humanity held in check.

Three murders and the disappearance of the main suspect, a fourth murder not in his jurisdiction but apparently connected to the first three, D.A. and the mayor breathing down each other's necks, and toss in art smuggling and theft on Treasure Island and government involvement whether anybody wanted it or not. Poor Fisher, good cop, decent cop, and now he was working sanitation, trying not to explode shit all over the City and let any hit the D.A. in the face.

At least Johnson'll get a thrill . . . Miranda caught a glimpse of the bastard in the hallway, giving orders to someone, throwing his chest out. Probably licked his lips at the prospect of the Bureau's boys, had to settle for the god-damn State Department. Lieutenant Walter Johnson, put him in a black uni-form and he'd jackboot his way to Hoover's lap.

Her gut tied itself in knots around the cheeseburger and fries from Cohn's Coffee Club.

Easy to read Fisher's face, flicker of emotion across his cheekbones when he looked at her, worry and regard and just the right amount of suspicion. God-damn it, he was a fair cop, the best one she knew, and her finger traced the knife holes and cigarette burns on his desk, and she sat straight in her chair and kept her fucking mouth shut.

No, Inspector, I can't tell you any more than what I have. An art smuggling ring based in Mexico with connections abroad. I was working for the State Department, which I hope Mr. MacLeod verified. No, I can't detail the specific assignment, it's confidential, as I'm sure Mr. MacLeod told you. Yes, it looks like Cheney eliminated his partners. No, I don't know why he would leave valuable paintings in Wardon's apartment. Maybe he was in a hurry. No, I don't know why he would want to kill them, unless it was the profit motive.

She sipped the coffee, black as a bad dream, and chain-smoked a pack of Chesterfields, watching the thick black hands of the clock tick down, glass face cloudy with age and smoke and flies, the sharp, raspy voices of cops and ac-cused punctuated by an occasional sob and more occasional laugh, questions barked and relentless and never ending.

Yes, I understand that Edmund Whittaker was known to both of the other victims. I assume they were lovers. No, I don't know why Cheney would kill him. No, I don't know why or how he would kill Lois Hart or where the jade might be. I'm guessing opportunistic theft. Yes, I know I wasn't supposed to leave the state. Yes, I found Jasper on the train, but I couldn't call it in because of my assignment. Yes, I will remain in the City for further questions.

Gonzales poked his head in the door and handed a sheet of paper to Fisher, looking stiff and uncomfortable and pretending he was there by accident. She glanced at him quickly, then puffed the Chesterfield and blew a stream of smoke in the other direction. He looked older and tired, but fuck, she did too. He let his gaze linger a little too long, left the room in a hurry.

Meyer interjected queries and objections, verifying that the bulls had a statement from Scott Petrie regarding the discovery of Wardon's body and Cheney's disappearance, verifying that the Ogden police and Southern Pacific had declared Jasper a suicide, a verdict now in question, verifying that James had confirmed Miranda's employment but had given no information beyond it.

Miranda smoked, asked for water, chewed some Pep-O-Mints, and watched the shadows move across the wall.

Fisher finally sighed and laid down his fountain pen, scratching his head.

"OK, Miss Corbie. Your story—such as it is—has been confirmed. Confidentially, the whole thing stinks, and we've been told to take our noses elsewhere." He leaned forward, desk chair squeaking, eyes tired and bleary and fixed on hers.

"The layout is this: Wardon, Jasper, and Cheney were smuggling stolen art from Europe, with the help of some schmuck named Lestang. Wardon apparently shipped Cheney the art and he stored it at the Fair until Jasper or Wardon could sell it. Edmund Whittaker was involved, too, as the, er, lover of Wardon, and as an associate. Maybe the fact that he was an architect has something to do with it, I don't know—maybe he helped sell paintings to clients. He also may have been the one to kill Mrs. Hart—in fact, he's the only connection between her and the art ring."

She crushed the stick on the desk before dropping the butt in the chipped glass ashtray.

"Edmund wasn't guilty of any crime."

"Homosexuality is illegal."

Brief flicker upward, mouth like iron. "He was a moral man, Inspector. And we both know morality has nothing to do with the law."

Fisher shifted uncomfortably in his chair. "He's dead, whatever he was guilty of. Somebody murdered the Hart woman and stole the necklace, and it looks like that was Edmund—before Cheney got greedy and eliminated him. Cheney's employment record shows he was working the Fair the night Mrs. Hart was killed, so he's got an alibi, and the D.A. and your boys in the government want this all neat and tidy, remember?"

Her fingers clenched around the Chesterfield.

"I don't give a good goddamn what they want—Edmund was an innocent victim, not a murderer."

Fisher gazed at her, jaw chewing on itself.

"Look, Miranda. This is the story that's been handed to me and I'm trying to jibe it with what I know to be true. Maybe Whittaker was in on the theft of Lois Hart's jade and iced the dame, maybe not, but somehow they—and by they, I'm not exactly sure who the hell I mean—got involved with the necklace and then the whole goddamn operation fell apart. First Mrs. Hart, then Whittaker, then Jasper and Wardon—Wardon was killed before Jasper according to the M.E.—all of them except Jasper with a garrote. Jasper looks like a suicide but that's probably a setup. Cheney's the last one left, and he took a powder, obviously, plus we've got all the evidence linking him to the train. Lestang isn't even in the goddamn country and we don't have the authority to call him in for questioning."

The inspector slumped forward in his chair, shaking his head.

"It's a goddamn mess, and that's a fact. But like I said in the beginning, I can't do anything about it."

Meyer spoke gently. "Thieves do fall out, Inspector."

Fisher looked up, irritated. "Yeah. So where does the government come in? And what about Fritz Wiedemann? The goddamn Nazi consul general was at Finocchio's the night of Whittaker's murder—so was Jasper." His hand thudded, suddenly and forcefully, on the desk, making the papers jump. "I can't get a goddamn straight answer out of anybody."

Fisher's eyes held on to hers, and she sat and smoked and stared back, unflinching. He leaned forward, voice raspy from exhaustion but still razor sharp.

"They stitched it together, and if you keep it in the dark and don't look at it for very long, it'll hang. But shit, Miranda . . . do me a favor. You get a better angle, give me the story sometime, OK? My goddamn file reads like James Joyce." His shoulders suddenly relaxed and he waved his hand in the air. "Go on, beat it. And get some rest, for God's sake."

She stood up, looking down at the tired cop. There had been no mention of secrets, of spies, of forgery. She paused on her way to the door.

"Edmund wasn't involved, Inspector. I'll prove it to you—and the fucking State Department."

Fisher scratched his head, eyes red and weary.

"I hope you do, Miranda. I hope you do."

Thirty-six

*

M eyer looked five years older by the time she pushed him inside a taxi and told him to go home. She watched the Yellow Cab dart through the traffic on Clay and Kearny, frowning.

She hailed a DeSoto around the corner on Commercial, made the driver wait while she picked up her luggage at the Southern Pacific depot. The attendant at the depot gave her a funny look when she showed him the ticket, and she waved her license in his face. He was still staring at her suspiciously when she pushed through the doors, porter behind.

The hack driver, a mustachioed man in his forties, prattled on about the Seals and the ponies at Tanforan. Then he started in on FDR and the look she gave him in the rearview mirror made him shut his mouth and drive straight to Mason Street.

Roy helped her unload the luggage and she trudged up the hill. Bought a bologna and cheese sandwich at the Cottage Market on the corner of Bush and Mason, chitchat with the toothy grocer, new Campell's soup display.

Careful walk, step by step, back down Mason, not tasting the bites of sandwich. Thinking of Edmund.

Smuggled gin in a flask at Dianne's, a whisper and a laugh at the opera behind a fan, the businessman who pretended to be escorting Miranda but who was really there for Edmund . . .

Late night and sad stories, tears on cheeks, his sister who disowned him, still married and living at the old house in Bakersfield, only family left, parents died when he was fifteen, and she hadn't seen him in eleven years, vowed never to see him again . . .

Edmund with his smile, his flair, his gentility. How he could remember birthdays, even if you'd rather forget, how he could remember everything in a room and everything he ever saw . . .

Miranda's eyes opened wide.

Edmund.

Memory.

✳

She raced up the stairs, Roy calling something after her, probably about her luggage. Reached the landing, out of breath.

A burly man with a bald head turned around and grinned at her, blue suit crumpled and tie stained with mustard.

Allen.

"I've been worried about you, kid . . . there're easier ways of getting out of interrogations."

She grinned back at the Pinkerton. "C'mon, let me put this food up and I'll buy you a drink at the Rusty Nail. That'll prove I'm in the pink."

Allen snorted while she turned the key in the lock. "That'll just prove your stomach's still cast iron, sweetheart. But better your stomach than your head, I always say."

He looked around the apartment while Miranda shoved the remains of the sandwich and Coca-Cola in the refrigerator.

"Pretty rooms. You ever get my message?"

"Yeah. That's what I want to talk to you about."

The bald detective fell in beside her as they stepped across the threshold and Miranda relocked the door.

"I thought this whole business was done—that's what the papers say, anyway. Mrs. Hart was murdered by a gang of thieves and then they turned on each other."

"You should know better than to trust the papers."

The Pinkerton scratched under his vest sheepishly. "And we should both know better than to drink at the Rusty Nail. But—like they say—what doesn't kill you will cure you."

The heavyset, pudgy detective took her by the elbow. He and Miranda hurried down the steps together, footsteps keeping pace.

✳

Mostly sailors and fishermen and workmen in the Rusty Nail, a few girlfriends and the occasional wife, listening to juke music and cooing over the stars above the Bay Bridge, oohs and ahhs at the colored lights on Treasure Island. Ships in at Piers 9 and 7, work and a paycheck and the glory in muscles that paid for the kids' shoes, salt air and sharp wind carving old faces on young bodies, bite of the bourbon keeping the dark away, loneliness forgotten, lumps and arguments and bruises to pride dead and temporarily buried.

Miranda gulped her shot, looking around at the faded wood paneling, the thick nautical rope, the old buoys and lanterns covered in rust.

"You got me drunk last time we were here. I remember that much."

"You needed it, kid. Hell, that was just in February or March, wasn't it? You've been through a lot in the last few months."

She stared at the thick brown liquid. "So has the whole goddamn world. What time is it? I forgot my watch."

He glanced at his, underside of the wrist. "Five forty-five. You got somewhere to go?"

She nodded regretfully. "Yeah. Office. Gotta make some calls."

The burly detective sat back in the booth, shaking his bald head. "Miri, Miri. What the hell am I going to do with you? You just woke up from a concussion and exhaustion—yeah, your lawyer told me when I called—and you get right back on the goddamn horse. Kid, you're a fine shamus—more guts than most men—but you gotta learn to pace yourself, use your head. And not just as something to land on."

Miranda laughed, drained the bourbon. "All right, Father Time. Teach me the Pinkerton Way. In the meantime, I've got some calls to make."

The detective lit an Old Gold, inhaled and puffed and met her eyes.

"I'm serious. You're young, but not that young. You push yourself too hard. Take a few days off."

"I'm OK, Allen."

He stared at her, the stubborn line of jaw, the glint of green in her eyes. He sighed, smoke billowing from his nose and mouth.

"Yeah, yeah. I'm thankful you sat down long enough for a drink. And thanks for the story, or what there is of it you can tell me. The papers made it sound like you're a combination of Mata Hari and Lizzie Borden, then all of a sudden you're in the clear again. I'm glad it's over." He took another puff on the Old Gold.

"You ever find out anything about your mother?"

Miranda's eyes flickered. She picked up the shot glass and fiddled with it.

"Yeah. A little. Thanks to Rick."

Allen's eyebrows raised. "Sanders still away? I was surprised not to see him with you."

"He joined the navy."

The detective's eyebrows climbed even higher. Long pause, while he puffed on the cigarette again, sipped the whiskey. Watched Miranda turning the bourbon shot glass around and around, lines around her mouth and eyes. His voice was gentle.

"So . . . before you go. My message wasn't much, but I did look up garrote cases for you. Nothing lately, but there was a rash of robberies with the same M.O. about three years ago in Baltimore. Pinkerton office out there handled it. One of the ops spent months—nearly a whole year—on the case. He testified against a vagrant they picked up but couldn't make it stick. That particular op isn't with Pinkerton anymore—I take it from the report that there were some political repercussions to the case not sticking—there always are—or I would've wired to get his name for you. I was thinking that since they never really nailed the guy, maybe you could look for Baltimore connections." He shrugged. "Wasn't much, but you never know what could turn out to be important."

Miranda nodded thoughtfully. "Thanks, Allen."

She slid out of the booth and stood up. Held out her hand. He took it in his.

"Thanks for everything."

He let go of her fingers, stuck one in his own ear and made a face. "Goddamn itchy ear canals." Looked up. "Be seein' you, Miri."

"Be seein' you, Allen."

The bald detective exhaled another cloud of smoke, watching Miranda twist her way through the dark, narrow bar and into the soft neon of Battery Street.

✳

Gladys dropped the *Harper's Bazaar* she was leafing through and rushed from around the counter, enveloping her friend in a hug.

"Sugar, I've been so worried—the papers said you were in trouble, hinting around at all kinds of things, calling you 'notorious' and all . . . I wasn't sure if you were even coming back! I'm glad I worked the evening shift tonight, so I could see you for myself."

She held Miranda at arm's length, looked her up and down. The blond curls, piled on her forehead, wiggled as she shook her head.

"We-ell . . . you don't look so bad, but then you don't look so good, either, Miri. You need more rest. Maybe some time with that nice Inspector Gonzales?"

Broad wink, wide smile, and she hurried back around the counter to wait on a dyspeptic businessman holding his stomach and frowning at the delay.

Miranda smiled, watching Gladys for a few minutes. Less than a week and it felt like a month. She looked up at the high ceiling of the venerable Monadnock, the constant traffic from the railroad offices, a few footsteps making their way to the Pinkerton offices.

It was good to be back.

She climbed in the automatic elevator, stomach still full from the bologna sandwich lunch, bourbon dulling her appetite, though the smells of beefsteak and fried chicken and spaghetti from Tascone's caught her nose and made her think about dinner. She checked the wall clock above the elevator bank: 5:10.

Time enough for food later. Edmund came first.

Edmund and his memory, a photographic memory. Handy for an architect, not so much for a man who had to hide his bed partners. He said he never forgot anything.

So awkward when you run into ex-lovers, especially at social functions . . .

She'd thought he'd been referring to Jasper, but that was before finding his photo on Wardon's table. So who was the client—the client he traveled to Mexico with, the client Dianne wouldn't divulge? Jasper or Wardon or someone else?

She flicked on the light in her office, smell of old paper and stale cigarettes. Relocked the door, tossed her purse in a wooden chair, and sank into the oversized seat behind her desk. Pulled out the Big Chief tablet.

Miranda studied the coarse lined paper, chewing her bottom lip. Grabbed a pack of Chesterfields from the top drawer, shook one out and lit it.

Dialed the phone number.

Franklin answered after four rings.

"It's Miranda. Were you able to get the name of that client for Edmund Whittaker? The one who took him to Mexico?"

She picked up the pencil on the desk and started drawing circles on the tablet, around and around and around. Nodded her head slowly, exhaled a cloud of smoke.

"All right. Thank you, Franklin."

She dropped the phone in the cradle gently, staring into space.

A Mr. H. Wardon had taken Edmund to Mexico City about four months earlier.

She nodded, heart beating fast, and scribbled *forgery* next to Edmund's name. Underlined it three times, and sat back against the leather, eyes closed, inhaling the stick.

Edmund had been a lover to both Jasper and Wardon. Not so unusual. He liked art, moved in the same circles. Maybe he met one or the other through Dianne's, Jasper, for example, and then Wardon moved in.

Wardon and his glasses and goatee, the unctuous, silky force of his voice, the casual anti-Semitism, the predatory pseudo–sales technique, now revealed as a secret message for Jasper and an effective way to needle him. Wardon was competitive, for art, for Miguel. And Jasper was jealous. Maybe Wardon had moved in on Jasper before, taking Edmund away, to his bed and to Mexico to meet Miguel . . .

She frowned, crushing out the cigarette with a twist. Goddamn it, all conjecture, make-believe, a fucking detective story. Maybe Jasper had a motive to kill Wardon, but who had the motive to kill both of them? Cheney? He was the security man, good job at the Fair, kept it safe and hidden—why risk it all for a larger cut?

Miranda stood up and shoved open the windowsill. Her head still hurt, body still numb and tired and sore from hitting the floor of the goddamn *City of San Francisco*. She needed the cold, moist air, the smell of the City.

Her City.

You'll always come to a bad end, my girl, it's in your blood, wind up in the gutter like your mother . . .

And Hatchett nodded sagely, sipping gin in the teacup, and Miranda clutched the short muslin dress closer, waiting for night and the San Francisco fog to cover her tracks to Purcell's or Spider Kelly's or even the Hippodrome, once or twice, the ladies in big hats and corseted waists, breasts pushed up from clouds of lace, feeding her steak and potatoes, then a penny to go away when one of the men in bowler hats and mustaches walked up, eyes on fire and teeth reflecting light.

The neon blinked across the street, yellow and pink, blue and green.

Someone dropped a nickel in the Tascone Wurlitzer, Ray Eberle singing about imagination.

Imagination. The cops imagined that Edmund was guilty, but he was innocent—that much she knew. Innocent of it all. Whether he traveled south with Wardon or met Miguel or even Lestang, he didn't know about the forgeries. And Jasper, the costumed Faust, chemistry professor and spy and professional smuggler—Jasper was innocent of Edmund's murder. She knew that, too.

But Wardon . . .

Wardon, the ambitious art smuggler and forger, the dealer who'd taunted Jasper openly at the Picasso exhibit, the man who'd managed to get control of their priceless Miguel—had Wardon been frightened by a chance remark, an innocuous question? Edmund and his perfect memory, recalling, for example, a painting from Jasper's apartment . . . one he saw again, in Wardon's?

Did you buy that Kirchner back from Jasper, Hugo? I never thought he'd part with it . . .

And then—maybe—Wardon panicked, figured he'd better keep Edmund's mouth shut.

Imagination is crazy . . .

And then there was the mark.

Robert Sterling Clark was a rich man, known in certain circles as a Nazi sympathizer, heir to the Singer fortune and money behind the failed plan to oust FDR in '33. The papers dumbed it down, calling the Business Plot a cocktail putsch, but the threat—according to Bente—had been real. The McCormack-Dickstein Committee agreed, though the people involved were too powerful to be indicted, and Clark was one of those people.

Maybe that's why James had told her the Pioneer Fund was out of the picture, nothing to follow.

She picked up the phone. "Long-distance operator, please. Yes, Chicago. The Drake Hotel."

Miranda tapped her pen on the desk, faint tinkle of a piano drifting from the pool hall across the street and blending with Miller's brass. Neon blinked on and off, on and off.

"Yes? Hello?" Her voice was smooth, silky. "Yes, I'm terribly sorry, but my associate left his cigarette case in Mr. Robert Sterling Clark's room . . . yes, he was there yesterday, on the 30th. On a business call, naturally, the sale of some artwork . . . What? Are you sure? That's odd. Our records show that—well, never mind. I'm sure there's been a mistake somewhere, and the Drake's not at all to blame. What? Oh, I'm sorry, I should have mentioned it earlier. The Lestang gallery. Yes. Well, thank you—I'm sure we'll clear it all up."

She hung up the phone.

According to the Drake manager, no one had visited Mr. Robert Sterling Clark on June 30th.

✳

Miranda opened the safe and withdrew five C-notes and the Spanish pistol. Felt a pang when she realized, again, her Baby Browning was gone.

A cabbie outside leaned on his horn and her thoughts drowned in the rumble of a White Front hurtling toward the Ferry Building.

Maybe Wardon was a murderer, maybe not, but something about Wardon and that painting, the one that unaccountably reminded Miranda of her mother, the woman with plaintive eyes clutching a robe, trying to cover herself, his outstretched hand pointing, reaching, grasping toward the canvas. Wardon was trying to tell them something.

And Cheney . . .

Cheney knew about the Clark sale, he'd mentioned it to Jasper. If Cheney had killed Jasper and Wardon to increase profits for himself somehow, why wouldn't he follow through with a surefire deal? Why not go to Chicago and try to sell it? He couldn't know she'd found the card and warned off Clark.

She closed her eyes, picturing the stalwart, swarthy Cheney, the guttural laugh and hearty manner.

Not a timid man, but a cautious one. And not a killer.

Goddamn it.

Her green eyes flickered and she sighed, deep and long and tired.

It wasn't fucking over.

Whatever James and his bosses decided, whatever bullshit they fed the police and the public.

Edmund was innocent.

And Cheney . . . Cheney was missing. Probably dead.

She lit a cigarette with shaking hands.

Goddamn it, they were right, Allen and Bente and Gladys, she needed a rest, a break of some kind. Her brain was still sore, still tender, the insides of her gut like mush from too much booze, too many cigarettes and not enough goddamn sleep.

She moved to the window, early evening breeze blowing in the curtains. Her eyes roamed the brown stone of the de Young Building, lighting on the dull gold of Lotta's Fountain.

A young man stood waiting, black pressed dress pants and vest, sharp fedora, white carnation in his black satin lapel. He was holding an orchid, looking back and forth from Market to Kearny, as the orange and yellow streaks from the summer sun mixed with gray and black shadows, cool fog blowing in from Marin, wrapped around hot neon, flower vendors packing up for the night, piano from the pool hall fast and raucous, hustlers darting up the alleys toward Montgomery and south to Mission and beyond. Rumble of cars and shrill laughter from Tascone's, "In the Mood" playing on the juke. She could almost touch the coming night with her fingertips.

Allen had figured Rick would be with her, and she'd figured that too, couldn't get rid of the sonofabitch. "Hey, Randy, got a story? How 'bout dinner at John's Grill?" Half-Irish bullshit brogue, how he'd dressed up like Robin Hood at the Nazi embassy, how he'd shown up on a Napa road when she thought she'd have to blow her brains out.

How he'd looked at her when she told him she was working at Dianne's, and how she'd quit the next day.

Rick, Richard Sanders, news hawk, Johnny's friend . . . and her friend.

She missed him.

Miranda shook herself, sudden chill. The young man was gone.

She shut the window with a clatter.

Fog was rolling in early tonight, orange bridge haunted by gray-white ghosts, ghosts of the City, past, present and future. They floated across San Francisco, damp and heavy, comforting and quiet, stilling arguments in barrooms and the fires in sailors' eyes, crab fisherman with leathered skin suddenly kissing his wife over the steaming pot, faded socialite sipping a martini at the Top of the Mark, eyes wet with lost youth and misspent chances, mournful bellow of a foghorn lonely and plaintive on the moon-darkened Bay.

The words of a Billie Holiday song played over and over again in her head, blending with the foghorns and car horns, the laughter and the tinkling piano.

Ghost of yesterday . . .

Her stomach growled and she nodded to herself.

The ghosts would help her. Help her find a murderer.

*

Miranda was walking up Grant toward Washington when she heard her name. She turned around quickly in the busy street, a few of the sidewalk vendors still selling exotic teas and coconut sticks to tourists looking for dancing girls and the keno room in a "gen-u-ine Chinese nightclub."

"Miranda—over here."

She looked toward her left and saw Ned, sitting as upright as a man with no legs could. He was wearing a new pair of leather work gloves and resting on the plywood platform with wheels he called his office.

She peeled off a ten-dollar bill and dropped it in his cup. Spoke softly, out the side of her mouth. "Careful."

The man who'd lost his legs in the War nodded, face lined, skin thick and brown.

"Figured as much. Just take what the papers say and read through the lines. When I saw you, I figured you was workin' again."

She gave him half a smile. "Hungry. I'm on my way to the Twin Dragons for a Singapore Sling and some fried rice. What've you got?"

He shook his head. "I don't rightly know, Miranda, but I don't like it. You know Fingers Molloy, right? The pocket?"

She could feel her stomach tighten at the name. Fingers had been at the Picasso exhibit the night Lois Hart was killed—she'd braced him. He'd also been a key element in her tracing the jade—she'd passed him a C-note for the tip-off on Kwok and the pawnshop.

"What about him?"

No-Legs Norris shook his head. "He's missing, Miranda. Nobody's seen him for two days."

Thirty-seven

*

You're sure he's not chasing horses at Santa Anita? You know Fingers—dips are like that. They blow town on a whim, always looking for better pickings. Jesus Christ, Ned, maybe he's on a bender . . ."

The leather-skinned man shook his head decisively. "No, Miranda. Fingers been acting funny since the Hart murder. He's been spending more money and stayin' quiet. I been keepin' an eye on his hotel—figurin' I'd get something from you out of it all—and I ain't seen him come or go for two days. If he was travelin' south, he'd a' bragged about takin' a vacation. You know Fingers."

She swallowed, mouth bitter. "Yeah. I know Fingers. All right. What's his address?"

He looked up at her and squinted. "You want I should go with you?"

She gave him half a smile. "I'll be OK. I'll say I'm his parole officer."

"Hotel Felix. Don't know how long he's been there. 1242 Market, cross street Hyde."

A young couple strolled by, chattering about Treasure Island and Chinatown, girl clutching the boy's arm tight, laughing with a plump, pink mouth and cheeks and young, unworried eyes. Miranda's eyes followed them to the corner of Washington. She pried herself from the brick wall.

The twenty-dollar bill dropped on Ned's platform, and he pocketed the money like a magician's trick. He looked up at her, eyes squinting at the yellow and red lights, face half in shadow, red lanterns in Waverly Alley painting his cheeks a deep purple.

"You going now?"

She nodded. "Thanks."

He bent his head. "Let me know when you find out what's wrong with Fingers."

Miranda dug out a Chesterfield from the half-empty pack in her purse. Ned tossed up a matchbook.

"Be seein' you, Miranda."

She caught the matches and lit the cigarette, deep inhale, blew out the smoke through the side of her mouth. Dropped the matchbook back in Ned's palm. Her voice was weary.

"Be seein' you, Ned."

✳

The Hotel Felix was a tall, thin, run-down rent-by-the-week place with droopy brown masonry and no ornament to boast of, sandwiched between better-known and better-looking rooming houses in the Civic Center district. No smell of cabbage like the Hotel Potter, where Pandora Blake had roomed, and the dingy, threadbare carpet and half-dead plant in the lobby spoke of pretensions to self-respect some twenty years before. They'd long since dried up and died, along with the plant, as lifeless as the gray dust that lined the cracked and dirty terra-cotta pot.

Miranda crushed her cigarette out in the dented aluminum ashtray tucked in between the springless couch and the rocking chair. She pushed the button marked MANAGER again.

Footsteps stomped upstairs in response, and she took another look around while she waited.

Three blank slots and faded ink on a couple of numbers, no names she recognized. Fingers was in number 7, top floor of the four-story building. The blue ink was fresh, no fly specks on the worn cardboard, SEAN G. MOLLOY written in a careful, semiliterate, and painstaking hand. He'd hadn't lived there for very long.

The galumphing grew louder, and she looked up to see a fat, florid face in a bleach-stained blue work shirt peer down at her through the banister.

"Yeah? I already buzzed you in, lady—what's your business?"

He was somewhere between forty and fifty, no hat, T-shirt showing at his collar, grease stains on the shirt and dungarees. Probably did maintenance for the cheap bastards that owned the building. She mustered a prim smile.

"I'm here to see Mr. Molloy."

The manager-cum-maintenance man jerked his thumb in an upstairs motion. "Fourth floor, lady. You ain't got call to bother me for that—I'm busy."

He turned around to head back up the landing. Miranda made her voice smooth as she started up the stairs.

"I'm sure you are, Mr.—Kerokian, was it? The problem is that Mr. Molloy seems to have—well—gone missing. He didn't, er, make a certain report on time."

The large man stopped in his tracks, hoisted his pants up by the worn brown belt, turned around with matted eyebrows lowered, and gave Miranda the up-and-down.

"So he's a jailbird. Ever'body knows that. Told us when he moved in, 'bout two months ago. What's it got to do with me? An' who the hell are you? His parole officer?"

Her eyes fixed on his. "Yes, Mr. Kerokian—I am. And I'd appreciate your assistance for a moment, while I ascertain whether or not Mr. Molloy has left town—an act that is a violation of his parole. I'd also like to remind you that you could be held as an accessory after the fact, so I strongly suggest that you forget about the radiator right now and, if necessary, let me in his apartment."

By this time she was toe to toe with Kerokian, nose wrinkling at the stink of cheap cigarettes and cheaper beer. He flushed, piggy eyes dropping to the floor, and hitched his thumbs in his belt.

"All right, lady, don't get your knickers in a twist. Seven o'clock's a funny time for a parole officer to visit, but I'll take you upstairs. Molloy's probably in there, sleepin' one off."

He turned around abruptly, started to climb the stairs, breath labored. "Watch the third step—it's warped."

She said nothing, kept his pace easily and stayed a comfortable distance behind. The landings became more dilapidated as they climbed higher up the building, mended carpet giving way to worn carpet and finally no carpet at all. Someone on the third floor was listening to a tinny radio, shrill sounds of the organ on *Amos 'n' Andy* vibrating through the thin walls. Kerokian glowered, an ad for Campell's Cream of Mushroom soup drowning out the sound of his heavy breaths.

Why not try Campell's Cream of Mushroom soup tomorrow? Drink soup and life can be beautiful, all clean and happy and grand, here in the happy fucking Hotel Felix . . .

They arrived at number 7. Lucky number 7, Miranda thought, and shivered slightly, remembering Fingers and the way his eyes had shifted toward the door at the Picasso exhibit.

Kerokian jerked his thumb toward the door. "What're you waitin' for? Go ahead and knock."

She raised her fist. Three raps, loud and firm.

No answer.

The manager yawned, hairy fist in his mouth. He strode up to the door, kicked it with a boot and banged it several times with his fist, the wood shaking under the strain. He yelled "Molloy!" loud enough to make numbers 8 and 6 open their doors a few inches.

No answer.

Miranda stepped forward, eyes narrowed as she faced the large man, trying not to breathe in the stench of sweat and motor oil and day-old beer.

"Open the door, Mr. Kerokian."

He scratched the heavy five o'clock shadow on his cheek, voice slow and suspicious.

"What's your name, lady? You got some identification?"

Miranda was tired. She sighed, took out her wallet, and handed him a fin.

Her voice was dry. "My name, Mr. Kerokian, is trouble. Open the fucking door, take your fucking money, and get the hell back downstairs."

His jaw dropped, mouth open and gaping, then he grabbed the five with a large paw, fished around in his pocket, and unlocked the door. Made a move toward the landing and halted for a moment, triumph in his thick voice.

"I knew you weren't no goddamn parole officer."

She watched as he galumphed down the hall, heavy boots thudding in the distance.

*

Fingers's apartment was a one-room utility, hot plate and sink, small bathroom off to the right. He'd furnished it with second- and thirdhand pieces, simple and functional and surprisingly meticulous. Maybe not so surprising, she thought. Precision was necessary for a successful dip, and Fingers had been successful.

The bed was made, not slept in for a few days, judging from the dust on the covers. She moved to the armoire, a scarred bit of good furniture from before the quake, and threw open the double doors.

Five suits hung carefully with two leather belts, and on the shelves to the right, a few pairs of socks with underwear and faded striped pajamas. Three hats, two derbies and a fedora, lined the rest.

Whatever else he'd been, Fingers was neat—and showed no signs of leaving town.

The bottom of the armoire was filled with four pairs of shoes—more shoes than hats, since dips needed to be quiet on the approach, and for that they needed good shoes.

Miranda squatted down in front of the armoire. Not much in the way of hiding places in the apartment, and if Fingers was holding on to something, he might tuck it in his footwear or a hatband.

She pulled the shoes forward toward the edge, one by one, her fingers exploring the interiors. Nothing in the brown Florsheims, black soft-soled dress shoes, or tan Roblees. Last pair, the one at the very back, another pair of Florsheim stout brogues, dark brown.

Her fingertips touched something cold and smooth.

She withdrew her hand, picked up the Florsheim, and stood up quickly, knees creaking. Cursed under her breath and moved toward the floor lamp near the one small window.

Miranda held the shoe up vertically and probed the toe with two fingers, reaching something sticky. Round, smooth balls, about half an inch in diameter, were strung like pearls, and she gently tried to pry them out. They came loose with the third tug, and she nearly dropped the shoe and sent them flying across the room.

Her legs were trembling by now, as she looked at her hands and sank slowly on the mattress.

She was holding a jade necklace.

*

Miranda stood by the window and smoked. The jade looked enough like Mrs. Hart's to be Mrs. Hart's. Cold, implacable, a brilliant green.

Miranda clicked the beads together, *click-clack, click-clack,* only sound in the small, stuffy apartment except for her breathing. She'd searched the rest of the shoes, the hatbands, and the pockets of Fingers's clothes. She'd discovered a jade bracelet in a fedora hatband and a pair of earrings in some socks.

Click-clack, click-clack, click-clack . . .

Not much paperwork, no trail in ink for Fingers. Camels and Lucky Strikes in the almost full milk-glass ashtray, no lipstick on the stubs. Maps of San

Francisco and Oakland in his nightstand drawer and a Catholic Bible. No postcards, no letters, no photos. He'd hoarded matchbooks, penny saved was a penny dipped, and there was a small pile on a scarred coffee table in front of the two-seat couch.

She poked a finger through the pile, found one for Finnegan's and the Koffee Kup and Pig n' Whistle, Topsy's out by the beach. There was one from Los Angeles—a donut shop—and a new book on top from United Airlines.

Click-clack, click-clack, click-clack . . .

She picked it up and held it to the light. The small print under the logo read: "Hubbard Field—closest air transport to Reno, Nevada. All flights daily."

Her fingers closed around the matchbook, and she drew down on the Chesterfield, expelling the smoke through her nose and mouth, watching it cloud the already cloudy room.

Miranda thought of Baltimore and Pinkerton and the State Department, the price of art and the price of fakes and the price of information, a whole fucking world at war, with no one to look over your shoulder. Jade and art, movable feasts, stable assets when currency becomes obsolete. She thought of means and opportunity and the motive in front of them all, the motive behind everything.

Greed.

Behind the first stone thrown, behind the first sin sinned, behind the blown-up bodies and bleeding children, behind the jackboots and the yellow stars, refugees trudging down dusty French roads, bombs falling like rain on Warsaw and Guernica, drops red, so very red . . .

A woman with money. Mrs. Lois Hart, millionaire's wife, politician's mistress, hophead's mother. Lois and her improbable friendship with Edmund, her insistence on paying off and paying quietly, her attachment to a priceless jade parure, gift of her husband.

Lois Hart, whose whispered word could buy her mink but not a pretty death. And then Lois fell and the dance continued, marathon and never ending, and they danced until they all fell down, after the jade, the art, the secrets.

Before Lois, Grant Tompkins. A man with a wife and children, the man who held her job. Grant Tompkins, the State Department agent who opened the door to possibility, and Lois Hart, who made it all come true.

First Grant and Lois—then Edmund—then Jasper and Wardon and Cheney. Dominoes and ducks, all in a row.

And now, Fingers.

Miranda pinched the end of the stick, watching it until the embers were extinguished, and dropped the stub in the pack.

Fingers had gone the way of Cheney, she was sure. In the Bay, over the highway by Devil's Slide, somewhere they wouldn't be found by humankind, only by the buzzards or the fish and always the insects, picked and eaten until their bones were as clean as their newly scrubbed souls.

She picked up the jade from where she'd laid it on the bed, wrapped in a handkerchief, and placed it carefully in her purse. Looked around the small apartment once more, face lined and weary, chest and limbs heavy and tired.

Miranda took a breath. Her voice was quiet and bitter.

"Hell is empty and all the devils are here."

*

She dreamed of ghosts that night.

Ghosts of yesterday—her mother, desperate to protect her, *I'd rock my own sweet child to rest,* until she was ripped from her mother's arms and tossed in a prison, lines on Hatchett's face made by knife tips, lines on her father's forming rivulets of Scotch, flowing, always flowing.

Mills College days, a year or so to be happy, to think happiness was a bottle of bootleg gin and oblivion and a quick, unfeeling encounter in the rumble seat of a sedan, forget your past, forget your future, forget who you are and who you might become, dance, girl, dance the Charleston, life's a bowl of fucking cherries and we don't need blackbirds, bye-bye . . .

Dust bowl refugees and children with ancient eyes, stomachs swollen from not enough food, and she learned and her own eyes opened.

Then she met John Hayes, and his smile blinded her and his eyes shot out beams of light, and she was helpless, held captive, enveloped in arms once again, arms that wouldn't leave her, couldn't leave her, someone to watch over her . . .

But the ghost became a ghost, bombed and bloody and broken, hull of a man, no soul left, no soul on earth, no earth. Just an empty shell, a functional place to breathe and eat and defecate, not hell on earth because earth was hell, no hope, no love, no Johnny, and death swallowed them all.

Miranda spun around and around and around . . .

More ghosts. Rick, with his smile, eyes desperate, how she wished he didn't love her so much. Gonzales and his body, the smell of his skin, and she thought about giving herself over, as she'd done in the dark days, the days of black on the calendar when she'd fallen, fallen, fallen, and reached the bottom and found Dianne.

Rick held out a hand and she started to climb, her nails broken and bloody and full of earth. She passed Sally and laughed, watching the girls twirl lariats at the Fair, and in another room Burnett was drinking tea with Dianne, until he fell over, too many bullets in his chest.

Miranda pointed a finger, mouth open, "*J'accuse! J'accuse! J'accuse!*" And James walked in, charming James, James wouldn't lie to her, wouldn't use her, he admired her for more than her breasts and thighs and what was between them, and he gave her a gilt-edged proclamation and a bow and a wink. Said he'd be back.

The ghosts flocked around her . . . Betty Chow and Phyllis Winters and Martini and the blood on the bathroom walls, and Dr. Gosney and the patient in number 114 and Joe Merello and Edwina Breckinridge and Annie Learner and Pandora Blake and Mickey Cohen and Allen and Gladys. Bente rose above them all, orchestrating a strike with Eddie Takahashi in the front, holding a sign. She tried to talk to him, but he could only smile and nod and thank her for saving his sister.

And then other ghosts floated in and Ozzie Mandelbaum performed a high dive at the Aquacade while Meyer tried to pull her away from Duggan, who was holding out handcuffs. And in a long line, solemn procession, a gray parade formed at the Tower of the Sun, light streaming through them, first Grant Tompkins, hat in his hands, face downcast, then Lois Hart wearing her jade, and Huntington Jasper and Hugo Wardon, each carrying the same painting. Cheney ran after them, laughing and hearty, and Fingers trailed, furtive and shy.

At the rear of the procession was Death, not so tall and not dressed in a robe, wearing a three-piece suit and wide-brimmed fedora. A certificate was pinned to his chest and his face was featureless, entirely blank, and he held her Baby Browning in his right hand and a piece of piano wire in his left.

He slowly turned to face her.

Miranda screamed and sat upright, sweating. The clock on the nightstand read 3:15 A.M.

She blinked a few times, still trembling, and reached a hand to turn on the light.

She didn't sleep for the rest of the night.

*

Miranda spent the morning on the phone. Left another message for James, no response, no sign the State Department knew who she was.

She ate another bite of buttered toast and moved on.

Called Meyer to get the name of a reliable jeweler, someone who could appraise. Phoned Chinatown jewelers, too, I'd like an appointment for an appraisal, yes, jade, thank you very much. Kwok she'd have to visit in person, she'd make the rounds for lunch.

Miranda made notes and smoked half a pack, fuck the Life Savers. Called Southern Pacific and asked for Railroad Hal, called United Airlines and called Fisher, reported Fingers missing. Thought about calling Rick but pulled her hand away from the phone at the last second. Tried to reach Allen, left a message instead. Spent ten minutes waiting for the operator to put a call through to Baltimore but finally found someone at Pinkerton who said he'd get back to her.

Fuck. No confirmation, she'd have to go on her gut.

You're a good soldier, Randy, a good soldier . . .

By mid-afternoon she was ready, hot shower and Elizabeth Arden for her neck and legs, dressed in a red-and-white summer frock with wide hat and Red Dice lipstick.

Roy looked up with a hesitant smile.

"You goin' out, Miss Corbie?"

"Yeah—be back later."

"Have a good day, Miss Corbie."

"You too, Roy."

She was halfway up the hill toward Bush, panting a little, when she heard her name. She looked up, holding her hat down with one hand in a sudden gust of wind.

Scott.

*

The agent was standing on the corner of Bush looking down the hill at her, and she could see his smile half a block away. She grinned back at him, walking slowly up the hill, still holding the hat against accidents.

Brown eyes crinkled at her and he smelled like bay rum. Goddamn it, he reminded her so much of Rick . . .

No cocksure tone today, no arrogance. His voice was polite, almost deferential, with more than a hint of flirtation.

"Miss Corbie. I heard you were better. Thought I'd pay you a visit before I get sent back home . . . should be any day now. This is for you."

He held out a small package of See's candy, neatly wrapped in yellow and blue stripes, face blushing, athletic body seeming smaller and more hesitant. She took the candy with raised eyebrows, looked up and gave him smile.

"Thank you. But please—call me Miranda. We're far past the formalities, don't you think?"

He grinned and nodded his head, falling into step beside her as they proceeded past the Cottage Market and down Bush toward California and Chinatown.

"So . . . Miranda. It was, uh, quite an experience working with you. I never worked with a female op before."

She paused to light a stick. He extended a gold-plated Ronson and she held his hand briefly to steady the flame while she inhaled. Her eyes flickered upward.

"Not many of us around—not even at Pinkerton. So is this a social call, Scott?"

"You could call it that. My car's around the corner at the garage. I thought maybe you'd like to go to lunch somewhere—on me. Crab salad, like I promised? Look, I know Jimmy owes you, but I figure the government in general does, too."

She shook her head regretfully, blowing smoke out the side of her mouth. "I'm sorry. I'm actually chasing a lead. It's funny you showing up—I was going to call you later this afternoon, after I confirm a few things. I may need some help."

The agent grabbed her arm and drew her toward a slanted angle of shade under the Hotel Grant awning. His voice was low, urgent, concerned.

"You draw a bead on Cheney?"

She made a motion with her head for them to keep walking, and when they moved farther away from the hotel she said: "No. Not exactly. But I've got to tell Old Man Hart that the jade set I found for his wife—the one she died for—was a phony."

Scott whistled under his breath. "Christ, Miranda, that's a kettle of fish. If what the Hart dame had was fake, where's the real stuff?"

Miranda paused at the corner of Powell and Grant, dropped the stick and ground it under her navy blue pump. She raised her face to his.

Scott Petrie was a good-looking man, the arrogance he normally wore like aftershave making him seem more so. Eyes too close together were his only real flaw and she could feel him standing next to her, strong and tense and alert, almost too alert, like a quivering watchdog. "That's what I was going to call you about," she said slowly. "I've got a lead at a pawnshop. Yick Lung. I could use a little muscle, and the friend I normally count on is out of town. You doing anything tonight?"

"Nothing more important," he said promptly. "Where and when?"

She glanced at her wristwatch. "It's one-thirty now. Let's say seven tonight at Yick Lung. Washington and Spofford Alley."

The agent smiled and drew his arm through Miranda's. "It's a date."

She removed her arm, eyes on his. "It's an appointment. And bring your gun."

Thirty-eight

*

Miranda's stomach growled at the smell of rice drifting through the open casements. No food, no cigarette, no time.

She crouched on the rough and unvarnished wooden floor, no red-and-white summer frock. She'd prepared, wearing wool trousers and a cotton shirt, thick auburn hair up and covered in a bandanna.

Not exactly Club Moderne material.

Different kind of trap.

The July sun smiled over the City, still high over Playland at the Beach, but shadows kept falling in Chinatown, over the men in scuffed pants throwing dice against the green door, wide-mouth lion looking over the game, or the grandmothers raking in dollar bills, playing mah-jongg in underground rooms.

She checked the Spanish pistol again. Temples throbbed in time to her heart, and she drank in the dank air, almost tasting the rice and bok choy.

Footsteps.

Miranda tensed, stood up. Held the pistol in her right hand, waiting. Not heavy, light and fast.

A young boy about ten or eleven rounded the corner. He met her eyes and nodded.

The signal.

She nodded and he ran, swiftly and softly, back up through the warren. Now if she could just manage to remember her goddamn way out . . .

The peeling walls gave off an acrid stink, tempering the smell of rice and cooking vegetables and cigarette smoke and cinnabar incense, mingling in the middle, where she was, from the gambling room below and whatever was up-stairs. She walked quickly, the sound of her footsteps making a soft echo.

What the hell was it . . . right, then left. Then up, no lights in the dark cor-ridor, warped floorboard squeaked and made her jump and almost fire the fucking gun.

Left again. Light broke through in small pieces around a heavy door, sun-dappled pattern on the ancient wooden floor.

Miranda grunted, tucked the gun back in the holster, and shoved the door open. Ran quickly around the corner to Spofford Alley, breathing hard, dodg-ing tourist families from Minnesota and Chinese laundrymen.

Turned the tarnished brass doorknob slowly and pushed open the small, narrow door.

The room was as dark and cluttered as it had been just a week before. An-cient silks, moth-eaten furs, jade and alabaster and granite carvings, teakwood chests and imitation Ming vases, along with the standard pawn assortment of musical instruments and cameras.

She blinked, felt dizzy. Nothing had changed since June 25th. Not the furni-ture, not the shadows, not the smells. Not even what she was seeing.

A man in a Chinese smock stood with his back toward her, one hand around Kwok's fat throat. The pawnshop owner's face was red and contorted, eyes start-ing to bulge.

Miranda pulled out the Spanish pistol, slipping off the safety. Her voice was loud and firm and real.

"Let him go, Scott."

*

The agent froze, straightening his strong back. His left hand dropped from Kwok's throat, and the fat man stumbled backward, wheezing and coughing. The agent's right hand still held a long, thin wire attached to a small, broken wooden handle.

He didn't turn around.

"That you, Miranda?"

"Drop the wire."

His voice held a chuckle. "Whatever you say, boss."

The garrote hit the ground with a light thud and faint tinkle. Kwok re-treated behind his cage, his loud, raspy breath the only other sound in the room.

"Raise your hands in the air and turn around."

"Yes, ma'am."

Scott Petrie complied, both arms halfway above his head, and pivoted slowly in the orange-and-red robe. He faced Miranda and grinned.

"OK, lady boss. Sorry for the getup, I know I don't look my best. Didn't you like the candy?"

Miranda studied him, the strong cheekbones, the compact, muscular body, the always-moving eyes that looked back at her knowingly, arrogantly, no apologies.

Benzedrine eyes.

Her voice shook a little as she held the gun out. "I don't like murderers."

His posture relaxed and he took a small step forward. "Oh, come on, Miranda. No dialogue from some Humphrey Bogart picture, please. The men I killed needed killing. It was only a matter of time before Jasper turned on us. I did the government a favor."

Her voice was dry. "Just like you did Grant Tompkins a favor, Petrie?"

For the first time, his face showed surprise and anger. "How the hell—well, never mind. Tompkins was an idiot. Didn't recognize a good thing even if it bit him on the ass."

"And you did."

Another step. His face was charming, convincing. Miranda licked her dry lips.

"Of course I did. I got tired of living on beans and hamburger and working my ass off for people like James MacLeod. I'm a talented young man, Miranda . . . I'm going places. I learn fast, and I've learned well, and I can make twice as much money as Jasper and Wardon did. Tompkins didn't want any part of it— didn't even realize what it all meant."

Miranda lowered the gun a fraction, eyes on his.

"Explain it to me."

Scott smiled, ingratiating grin, eyes crinkling at the corners like Rick's. Another small step. He was almost within reach of the pistol.

His voice was soft, caressing, while his eyes traveled up and down her body. "You know, I could have killed you back on the streamliner, but you looked so damn luscious . . . if I hadn't been in such a hurry, I would have taken you right there. But it's not too late, Miranda. Put down that ridiculous gun and we'll go away together. Mexico is where the base is, and I've already reached out to Lestang. Just tell me where this lying bastard hid the real jade and we'll use it to finance the trip. There's so much money to be made in art . . . the morons we sell to don't know the difference between the real thing and a fake, and all we're doing is giving them what they want. And we'll get what we want . . . won't we?"

One more small step. She could feel the warmth from his body. His voice was thick.

"I can give you what you want, Miranda. What you need. Between the jade and the art ring, we'll finally have all the money we deserve."

Miranda's eyes flickered green. She lowered the gun slowly. Scott grinned.

"That's my girl. I knew you were smart—hell, you had to be, to be here. Telling me to show up at seven and then waiting for me three hours early. I'll buy you your own jade, wait and see, and you'll look a hell of a lot better in it than that Hart broad did." His voice was seductive, soft, knowing. "We'll have a good time, you and I."

His right arm flashed and he reached for his robe pocket, pulling out something small and bright and brown, and the Spanish pistol fired, loud reverberation, rattling the vases and china in the shop.

Scott's eyes grew wide. The red spot on his chest grew wider. He fell backward, dropping the gun and stumbling against a long wooden counter, knocking over some brass cymbals and an ancient abacus. The cymbals rang with a high-pitched whine, around and around the crowded room.

Miranda stood over him, looking down. Kwok crept from behind his cage, still coughing and clutching his chest.

She didn't look up.

"Call the inspector like I said, Kwok. Tell him we'll need an ambulance."

She bent down to pick up her Baby Browning, eyes never leaving Scott's white face.

"I could have killed you, too, Petrie. And I wanted to, for what you did to Edmund. But I changed my mind. The government should take care of its own."

Her stomach was growling and she ate two rolls of Life Savers and smoked half a pack of cigarettes, answering Fisher, avoiding Gonzales, leaning on Meyer. The D.A. was green at the gills, a State Department man shot and apparently a killer, and a nondescript, precise little man from the local office was brought in to smooth things over, make all the pain go away. James MacLeod, they were told, was on his way west.

No, there needn't be any publicity.

Would Edmund's name be cleared?

Averted eyes, rumble in the throat, no answers, and Miranda grew angry, her voice louder, until Meyer whispered something in the nondescript man's ear, and the D.A. promised to issue a statement.

Her eyelids were too heavy, like weights on a fallen abacus, but she lifted them up and said she'd be watching for it.

The men in the room laughed nervously, and Fisher—poor, tired Fisher—resumed his questions.

Yes, she'd needed to confront Petrie because she didn't have any hard evidence, and who the fuck would believe her? The bulls looked at each other. No argument there.

Too many disappearances, for one thing, and Fingers had a United Airlines matchbook from Reno. Fingers wouldn't know an airplane from a tractor. Jasper's killer could have doubled back to San Francisco the same night by flying—the *Californian* takes off at 11:36 P.M., and he'd be back in the City by 1:21 A.M., she'd confirmed with United. Plenty of time to get rid of Cheney and plant evidence in his apartment—the train ticket he'd booked in Cheney's name, the brochure. The SP ticket agent had remembered a man, and the man he remembered looked like Petrie.

He was on his way to plant more evidence at Wardon's place when he ran into her—it was Petrie who conveniently found Cheney's ID in Wardon's apartment. He was hopped up on Benzedrine, no need to sleep or eat, just eliminating people in his way . . .

And then there was the ex-Pinkerton from Baltimore who'd dogged a garrote case, and Petrie likes to brag he learns fast. He'd been an op, though Pinkerton hadn't returned her call yet, so again she was working from her gut. That, and a chance remark about blue crab. Funny how people can't hide where they're from . . . opportunity, means. Motive, gentlemen? Smuggled art. Diamonds at Lois Hart's ears, jade in her pocket. Greed. Makes the fucking world go around . . .

No, Cheney and Fingers are dead. Get the sonofabitch to tell you what he did with them. While you're at it, check the painting Wardon was holding. He probably hid something under the frame, maybe something to incriminate Petrie.

But what about the jade, the phony jade?

She looked at them, wavering like underwater plants, mouths open, eyes confused.

No phony jade, not what Mrs. Hart was killed for. The stuff in Fingers's apartment was phony, sure, dyed green, ask any good jeweler in Chinatown. He and his chubby partner had planned to knock Lois Hart on the head and substitute the necklace, not kill her, and somehow the poor bastard stumbled to Petrie. Don't know about the pudgy one, ask around.

Fingers knew something, had seen something, he'd been quiet and spending money—blackmail, probably. Ask Petrie, the murdering bastard. But the Hart jade was real. That's the joke, don't you see? Laugh a fucking minute . . . Petrie didn't know real from phony, genuine from fraud . . . paintings or jewelry or government agents . . .

They looked at each other and the worn, shaking woman with the auburn hair and feverish green eyes.

Gentlemen, you can resume your questions in the morning. My client is exhausted and you don't want another medical bill on your hands. Meyer's voice, stern, commanding, the kind he used in court.

The waves of blue parted, brass buttons shining. He found a taxi while she concentrated on breathing in, breathing out. Called Bente and they got her upstairs, goddamn elevator broken again.

Somebody took the Baby Browning from her hand and tucked it under her pillow.

Miranda didn't dream at all that night.

✳

James MacLeod faced the window, looking over Market Street. His voice was quiet.

"I knew you could do it. That's the only reason, Miranda. There was no one else."

The smoke sailed high into the ceiling, carried by the warm summer breeze from the window.

"So you lied to me."

"Not exactly. I told you all along you were on your own. That was meant as a warning—a warning not to trust him."

Miranda's hand slapped her desk with a clatter. "Goddamn it, James, you lied. Don't lie about lying. This wasn't about Uncle Sam and chemistry formulas and all the other bullshit you sold me. You knew Jasper was an art smuggler; you suspected Petrie murdered Tompkins but couldn't prove anything. So you set him up and set me up, and six more people died."

He raised a hand to his forehead. "I couldn't have known."

Her voice was bitter, sharp as a razor. "You could have fucking guessed."

Quiet filled the small office, the leaves of the Martell's calendar flipping gently. She watched as the red ember swallowed the thin white paper of the cigarette.

"You'll have to live with it. But don't come knocking at my door again. We're done."

He bowed his head, turned around, and looked at her. His face was lined, weary.

"Understood."

"Has he explained Cheney and Fingers yet?"

"No. He's making it a game. I think some part of him still expects to get out, be rewarded somehow. He's a psychiatric case, of course."

Miranda shook her head. "Hang the bastard. You've got enough evidence, thanks to Wardon's diary. I figure Petrie doped out the play and players from Tompkins, and when Tompkins wouldn't cooperate, he killed him. Then when you sent him out here—just what he'd been hoping for—he kicked it into high gear."

James sank into one of the wooden chairs, fedora in his hand, eyes on the floor.

"We thought he'd make a slip, Miranda. Figured we'd catch him before any more damage was done. Caught us all by surprise, how quick he was."

She leaned back in the black leather, studied the man she'd liked, trusted. The man who'd set her up in business.

"Petrie's not only quick—he's an opportunist. I think he was originally following Jasper the night of the Picasso exhibit, but learned through the grapevine—just as Fingers had—about the jade. So he switched off targets, maybe because he recognized Edmund from Wardon's picture and figured on a connection. Followed Lois and Edmund when they left the show, then tracked Lois here. He must have killed her right after she left my office."

James's voice was heavy. "He is smart and skilled and calculating—the hardest kind of criminal to catch—and we should have known he'd take advantage of the situation. We didn't want Hoover involved, thought we could handle it ourselves . . . with some outside help from you."

She inhaled the Chesterfield, her eyes glinting green. "So what have you gotten out of the bastard?"

"Not much in statements, but the diary is key. That was a lucky hunch you had about the painting."

Her voice was dry. "It wasn't women's intuition, James. It made sense—Wardon was obviously trying to tell us something. "

He nodded, frowning. "And Wardon was no innocent, not even by his own admission. Petrie approached him first and offered to kill Jasper, eliminate another share in the take, a rival for Miguel. After the Hart murder—which, as you say, seemed spontaneous—it was easy to convince Wardon that Edmund was another threat—particularly with Edmund's memory. That's all in the diary. Wardon sanctioned both murders, Jasper and Edmund, not seeing where it would all lead. He thought he could control Petrie. The last entries are full of fear but still clinging to hope."

Miranda ground the cigarette out in the Tower of the Sun ashtray. "Wardon died the way he lived. And he didn't deserve any better. What about Baltimore?"

"We still don't know if Petrie was behind the garrote murders or just learned from covering the case. That was before he joined the department, of course, and his Pinkerton record was full of triumphs, no sign of any trouble. He covered his tracks, tried to eliminate any and all possible witnesses. Except for you. He'd been on your trail since he murdered Lois, even talked himself into Weidemann's party, dressed as a Civil War soldier. He laughed about that, about how clever he was."

The agent's face was grave. "He liked you, Miranda. Luckily."

She looked away, sunlight making rays through the window. "Yeah. Funny thing is, I kind of liked him. He had charm."

"A lot of them do."

Silence again. MacLeod stood up, holding his fedora. She met his eyes.

"So let me know when he spills it."

"He may never tell us."

"Their families need to know. Make him talk."

The government man ran his fingers through his hair. "Easier said than done, Miranda."

"So was catching your fucking killer with no information."

His lips twitched. "Touché." He raised the briefcase to her desk and opened both latches at once.

"You want this now?"

"Yes."

He counted out the money, laying it out neatly in piles on Miranda's desk.

"James?"

"Yes?"

"What about the art? And the people who bought it—like Sterling Clark? You can't arrest Wiedemann, I know, but there's Lestang and Miguel and—"

"Miranda, leave it be. The government has more important things to worry about right now."

She leaned forward. "So you won't do anything about it. Christ, what was I thinking? You won't help save the Jews, why the hell would you save their art? That's where this is coming from, you know—countries like Poland, ground under Hitler's boot. And the Jews are being dispossessed of everything. But yeah, James . . . I guess the government's got too many other things to worry about."

Miranda made a gesture with her hand. "Leave the money and go. You can send the *Cameronia* ticket in the mail."

MacLeod's eyes looked stung for a moment. He straightened a pile of money on the desk and slowly shut the briefcase.

He spoke softly, deliberately. "Most of what was purchased was a fake. The buyers will find out eventually. The ring is eliminated, with the exception of Lestang, who has fled to Europe. There's nothing more we can do."

He held out his hand. Miranda stared at him for three beats before giving him hers.

"Good-bye, James."

Edmund's service was small and tasteful. His sister from Bakersfield showed up, grimly satisfied that God had wrought his vengeance and sin had not gone unpunished. She pinched her mouth and ignored his friends, mostly single men and a handful of society women, a few clients and Miranda.

Better dead than queer.

Miranda watched as the coffin was lowered, flowers and clumps of dirt hitting the wood with a dull clod.

She left a white rose by the side of the Colma hill.

James was true to his word. He kept her updated on progress with Petrie, who delighted in leading them in circles, insinuating that Cheney had been tossed off Point Lobos and Fingers was buried on Twin Peaks. They found nothing to corroborate his stories, which changed weekly.

Miranda slept for three days, ate steak at John's Grill and Tadich with Meyer and Bente and oysters at the Cliff House with Allen, went to see *The Mortal Storm* at the Fox Theatre, Margaret Sullavan and James Stewart about good Germans vs. bad Nazis. At least Hollywood had the balls to fight back.

Cases came in, mostly divorce, bread and butter to a shamus. She could see Burnett and his gold tooth glinting, mouth open, loud laughter.

She bought two new dresses at Magnin and stopped by to visit Joe at the Moderne.

Miranda looked around at the careful lighting, the faux marble and the potted plants, the old men with potbellies giving the cigarette girls the eye, faint sound of Vicente and the roulette wheel spinning behind closed doors while the redhead at the microphone warbled "It Had to Be You."

Funny how it all felt empty. She missed Rick.

He called her and it was good to hear the bullshit brogue for once, and he said he'd be getting leave and asked her if he could come up and see her and she said yes. He asked about her mother, since Germany bombed Britain on July 10. Had there been any word, any word at all?

Miranda stared out the window of her Monadnock office, watching the White Fronts rumble by to the Ferry Building.

No word from her mother, not since the mysterious postcard from Westminster Abbey. Was Catherine Corbie alive? Was she real? What was real and what was phony, after all, Johnny's girl, Johnny's Miranda, and her heart still jumped a little when she heard Rick's voice, and her pulse still quickened when the phone rang and it might be Gonzales . . .

She closed her eyes and saw them in the bright pink neon and felt them in the fog, heard the laughter and soft murmurs, the promised whispers and the unlooked-for, tender sighs.

Ghosts.

Ghosts of yesterday. They had helped her find the murderer, whispering the might-have-beens of Lois and the senator, the memories of Edmund laughing and drinking gin at Dianne's, the could-have-beens of Grant Tompkins, father to a boy and a girl.

But now it was time to put the ghosts away, lock them back in the Memory Box.

All the ghosts.

A spasm of pain crossed her face and she almost felt a caress on the side of her cheek, the nape of her neck, one of the secret places he loved to kiss her, strong arms holding her against the world, protecting her.

Watching over her.

She blew a stream of smoke out the window and watched it dance in the wind of Market Street.

Somewhere in Britain—somewhere—was the woman who first sang to her about ghosts, some Irish lullabye, the woman who tried to protect her but couldn't protect herself. And there was a man in San Diego who loved her, and whom she cared for, and people here—in her City, the City who fathered and mothered her, the City who gave her life—who cared about her.

The ghosts would fade, ghosts of yesterday, always a part of her.

Always watching over her.

She smiled, watching a flower vendor hand a carnation to a young man in a brown derby.

It was time for tomorrow.

Author's Note

*

City of Ghosts is set in 1940, before America entered World War Two. Even at this relatively early period, much of the cultural patrimony of conquered nations like Poland was being looted by the Germans and Soviets.

Many, many paintings—including several described in this book—are still missing—looted and subsequently destroyed, sold, hoarded, or lost. My hope is that *City of Ghosts* will generate greater awareness for the need to continue the search and call attention to the fact that the highest expressions of a culture are often the first casualties of war.

For those searching for more background information, I recommend the following texts:

The Rape of Europa: The Fate of Europe's Treasures in the Third Reich and the Second World War by Lynn H. Nicholas.

The Lost Masters: World War II and the Looting of Europe's Treasurehouses by Peter Hartclerode and Brendan Pittaway

The Lost Museum: The Nazi Conspiracy to Steal the World's Greatest Works of Art by Hector Feliciano.

The Monuments Men: Allied Heroes, Nazi Thieves and the Greatest Treasure Hunt in History by Robert M. Edsel.

The Forger's Spell: A True Story of Vermeer, Nazis, and the Greatest Art Hoax of the Twentieth Century by Edward Dolnick proved invaluable.

Also of great help was the Polish Ministry of Culture Web site on wartime losses: http://kolekcje.mkidn.gov.pl/.

As with all the Miranda Corbie novels, much of what you read in terms of detail—from the mysterious Count Lestang to the Picasso exhibit to the character of Elmer in Reno and the mention of crime in Portland—is actual history, eddies and back alleys not found in large tomes on twentieth-century conflicts, but the flotsam and jetsam of real life that help make Miranda's world as alive and immediate as possible.

For a more in-depth look at some of my sources and inspirations, including photos, video, audio, and ephemera, please visit my Web site at http:// kellistanley.com. I hope you enjoy *City of Ghosts* . . . and from the bottom of my heart, thank you for reading. I look forward to hearing from you.